DENIED DESIRE

"Let go of me!" Sarah insisted, endeavoring to twist free of Adam's bruising grip.

"You are my wife, now and forever, and you will do as I say," Adam persisted.

"Haven't you humiliated me enough for one evening?" Sarah tearfully responded, struggling against him, feeling a familiar weakness descend upon her as she viewed the naked desire in Adam's eyes.

Then, lowering his head, Adam took Sarah's lips with his own. And sooner than she realized, he was pressing his hard, masculine body to her softness as he pulled the straps of her chemise down and began untying the strings of her corset.

"No! Please, not again!" she pleaded.

"It will be different this time, Sarah, lass. You'll see."

Much as she despised Adam, Sarah sensed deep within her that he was right. This time would be different....

HISTORICAL ROMANCE IN THE MAKING!

SAVAGE ECSTASY (824, $3.50)
by Janelle Taylor
It was like lightning striking, the first time the Indian brave Gray Eagle looked into the eyes of the beautiful young settler Alisha. And from the moment he saw her, he knew that he must possess her—and make her his slave!

DEFIANT ECSTASY (931, $3.50)
by Janelle Taylor
When Gray Eagle returned to Fort Pierre's gates with his hundred warriors behind him, Alisha's heart skipped a beat: would Gray Eagle destroy her—or make his destiny her own?

FORBIDDEN ECSTASY (1014, $3.50)
by Janelle Taylor
Gray Eagle had promised Alisha his heart forever—nothing could keep him from her. But when Alisha woke to find her red-skinned lover gone, she felt abandoned and alone. Lost between two worlds, desperate and fearful of betrayal, Alisha hungered for the return of her FORBIDDEN ECSTASY.

RAPTURE'S BOUNTY (1002, $3.50)
by Wanda Owen
It was a rapturous dream come true: two lovers sailing alone in the endless sea. But the peaks of passion sink to the depths of despair when Elise is kidnapped by a ruthless pirate who forces her to succumb—to his every need!

PORTRAIT OF DESIRE (1003, $3.50)
by Cassie Edwards
As Nicholas's brush stroked the lines of Jennifer's full, sensuous mouth and the curves of her soft, feminine shape, he came to feel that he was touching every part of her that he painted. Soon, lips sought lips, heart sought heart, and they came together in a wild storm of passion. . . .

Available wherever paperbacks are sold, or order direct from the Publisher. Send cover price plus 50¢ per copy for mailing and handling to Zebra Books, 475 Park Avenue South, New York, N.Y. 10016. DO NOT SEND CASH.

TEXAS BRIDE

BY
CATHERINE CREEL

ZEBRA BOOKS
KENSINGTON PUBLISHING CORP.

ZEBRA BOOKS

are published by

KENSINGTON PUBLISHING CORP.
475 Park Avenue South
New York, N.Y. 10016

Copyright © 1982 by Catherine Creel

All rights reserved. No part of this book may be reproduced in any form or by any means without the prior written consent of the Publisher, excepting brief quotes used in reviews.

Printed in the United States of America

For my own
"Texas Oilman"

Chapter One

1887: Sarah Bradford quickened her steps along the cobblestoned streets of Philadelphia as the cold, brisk wind of the early March evening whipped against her face, which was only partially protected by the hood of her warmly lined cloak. Reaching the steps of Miss Warren's Rooming House for Single Ladies with a sigh of relief, she wrenched open the heavy front door and swept through to the warm sanctuary inside, closing the door securely against the damp night and strengthening wind.

"Sarah? Is that you?" she heard a high-pitched voice inquire as she shook out the folds of her cloak and placed it on the ornately carved hall tree in the entrance foyer of the boardinghouse.

"Yes, Miss Warren," Sarah replied with a patient sigh as she proceeded to tidy her hair and smooth her skirts. She tucked the wayward strands of black hair back into place and adjusted the bustle of her blue taffeta dress before approaching the small, warmly lit parlor.

"How was the meeting tonight, dear?" Miss Emily Warren asked as Sarah entered and took a seat beside her on the well-worn brocade sofa. Her petite, gray-haired head was bent to her work as she busily embroidered a white pillowcase. She paused momentarily to peer sideways as Sarah sat down.

"The meeting was very successful. We actually had quite a few new members in attendance tonight. A cousin of Mrs. Stanton's was the guest speaker. There was such spirit, such a true sense of purpose and unity tonight! I know it cannot be long until our voices are heard!" she remarked with an enthusiastic light apparent in her glowing eyes.

The older woman next to her smiled at her young friend's excitement. Sarah Bradford was such a pretty little thing, she thought as she silently appraised her. All that coal-black hair and those opal eyes. Though she wasn't much over five feet tall, her figure was trim and well shaped, and her whole manner was thoroughly delightful. Sarah always appeared to be so self-sufficient for one so young, so very independent and resourceful. She was totally refreshing, much more interesting than the other ladies in residence, Miss Warren mused. It was still a mystery to her why such a beautiful young woman such as Sarah would be content to remain unmarried, to teach at that girls' school where she had graduated three years before, to live among other single women.

"Miss Warren," Sarah's rich, mellow voice interrupted her thoughts, "Perhaps you would care to attend our next meeting, as my guest? The Philadelphia Women's Suffragette Association could certainly benefit from your involvement."

"That might be very nice, dear," Emily Warren answered noncommittally. "I'll have to let you know. By the way, another letter arrived for you today. It's on the hall table. I could see that it is from

Texas, so I assume it's another letter from your uncle."

"Why, that's strange," Sarah commented in puzzlement. "I received a letter from him only last week. I suppose he must have something new and exciting to tell me about those oil wells of his!" She immediately thought back to the time, several months ago, when her uncle had first told her about his latest adventure, about his proposed plans that would take him to Texas. She recalled having persuaded him to allow her to meet him for dinner at his hotel, something that had been accomplished after wisely mentioning that Miss Warren would keep him at her establishment half the night if he insisted on calling for his niece there.

She remembered how excited her uncle had been as they had sat talking in the hotel restaurant. He hadn't been able to tell her much about his new oil venture, but she had realized that it would be entirely useless to try and talk him out of it. After refusing his assistance, she had gone outside to hail a carriage to take her home.

She smiled to herself now as she remembered what had happened next. It was a pleasant recollection, one that entered her thoughts now and then. It had remained ingrained in her memory for several reasons, most particularly because it had been the first time she had asserted her independence so daringly.

She had finally been able to summon a carriage, but, just as she stepped forward, a gentleman collided with her, obviously intent on procuring the vehicle for himself. Sarah faced him with a severe frown, saying, "I beg your pardon, sir, but this carriage is already taken!" The man's hand on her arm steadied her as she nearly lost her balance, and she grew silent as she peered up into his face.

"I apologize most sincerely, ma'am," the gentleman said with a soft drawl. Sarah quickly noted that he was both young and reasonably attractive, that his clothing was impeccably tailored. She observed the way his brown eyes sparkled as he met her gaze, the way his dark-brown hair waved close to his head, and the fact that he was only a few inches taller than herself. He was smiling at her in a disarming manner, and she blushed as she realized that he was also silently appraising her in a like manner. She firmly disengaged her arm from his grasp.

"That's quite all right." She turned away to step up into the carriage, but he remained at her side.

"I hope you'll forgive me for being so bold, but would it be possible for the two of us to share the carriage?" the charming young man suggested, smiling at her still. "You see, I've been waiting here in front of the hotel for one to come along for quite some time."

"I'm afraid that wouldn't be possible," Sarah quickly replied, though her pulse suddenly quickened. Why not? she heard a tiny voice at the back of her mind ask. After all, she was an independent young woman, wasn't she? What harm could there be in sharing the carriage with this gallant young gentleman? The driver would be their chaperone. And, she mused, she had never met anyone quite like this man, so it might prove to be very interesting.

"I can assure you that I will behave very properly,"

the young man remarked with a mocking grin. His brown eyes spoke of his admiration for her, and Sarah, blushing again beneath his scrutiny, decided that she would be daring after all.

"Very well," she finally agreed, allowing the gentleman to assist her up into the carriage. She gave the impatiently waiting driver her address, then settled back beside the attractive young stranger as the carriage pulled away from the hotel.

She now recalled that they had spoken of many things, and yet of nothing in particular. He had told her of his many travels about the country, as well as Europe, throughout the brief ride. She, in turn, had spoken of her work as a teacher, and had even told him a bit about her family. She had been disappointed when the carriage pulled up before Miss Warren's. As she stood on the doorstep and watched the young man ride away into the distance, she had suddenly realized with dismay that she didn't even know the man's name, that she had forgotten to introduce herself.

There had been something about him that had set him apart from the other young men she had encountered in Philadelphia, she now reflected. He had obviously been a man of the world, a well-educated gentleman, and he had made her feel somehow special with his flattering attentions. She thought of that brief encounter every once in a while, but she knew it held no real significance. It was simply thinking of Uncle John tonight that had brought it to mind again. She forced her attention back to the present and said, "Uncle John wrote me in his last letter that one of his wells had already come in. He also said that the other two were expected to produce at any time now. Evidently things are going quite well for him down there. He did mention that he was expecting some sort of trouble in the near future, but he did not elaborate upon the details. For some reason, he has been very remiss in writing me since he left here eight months ago. I've received only three letters from him in all this time!"

"Well, Sarah dear, you know very well that your uncle cannot sit still for very long at a time. He's the sort of person who desires great adventure and excitement, I suppose. Why, when I first met him, so many years ago, he was so full of life and mischief, even then!" she informed Sarah with a smile of fond remembrance. John Bradford had been so devilishly handsome!

"I'm sure he was!" Sarah readily agreed with an answering laugh. "Uncle John may very well be nothing more than an idealist, a restless dreamer, but he is certainly never boring! He would have made some fortunate woman a very interesting husband, to be sure, if he had ever seen fit to marry! But then, that wouldn't have suited him at all."

"Well, I must say, he has certainly been good to you. Anyone can see how fond he is of you, dear."

"Yes. I love him, too. He's been the only family I've had for the past fifteen years, ever since the death of my parents. Though I have only seen him a few times a year, he was always kind and generous to me. Why, at the school, all of my classmates were envious. They all wished they had an uncle as handsome and dashing as Uncle John!"

"I know you must miss him," Miss Warren said

with a sympathetic pat upon Sarah's hand.

"Yes, I certainly do. I wish he hadn't traveled so far away this time. Before, he was always back within a few months. He was so enthusiastic about this latest venture. Imagine, going all that way to invest in the new oil industry of Texas. As if there wasn't enough of that right here in Pennsylvania!"

"But that wouldn't have been quite exciting enough for him, now, would it? I'm sure he is enjoying himself, Sarah. Perhaps he'll return in time for your birthday next week."

"I don't think so. Not from what he wrote in his last letter. Things are happening too swiftly right now for him to be able to get away. Oh, I only pray that he's careful to stay out of trouble!" Sarah remarked with a heavy sigh. Then, rising to her feet beside the sofa, she said, "Well, if you'll please excuse me, I'll take the letter up to my room. I still have a stack of papers to correct before classes tomorrow morning. However, I will be certain to tell you if Uncle John does indeed have anything important to say in his latest letter. Good night, Miss Warren."

"Good night, dear. Don't stay up too late," she cautioned Sarah with a motherly air. She bent her small head to her sewing once again as Sarah left the room, her skirts gently swishing as she crossed the rather threadbare carpet.

Perhaps it was merely a letter congratulating her on her twenty-first birthday next week, since she was certain that he couldn't come in person, she thought as she took the letter upstairs to the privacy of her small room. Plopping down upon the softness of her bed, she quickly tore open the envelope and pulled out the letter, frowning slightly as she saw that it consisted of only one small piece of paper. Hastily scanning its brief contents, her face mirrored the news contained in the letter, her features registering shock and dismay.

No, it cannot be! she told herself fervently. She simply could not believe the few scrawled sentences on the paper. There must be some terrible mistake, it must be some sort of cruel jest! She took a deep breath and read the letter once more.

"Dear Miss Bradford," she read, "your uncle, John Franklin Bradford, is dead. He was a good man. He got a decent, Christian burial." It was simply signed, "A friend." She glanced down at the envelope once again, noting that it was indeed from Wildcat City, the Texas oil boomtown her uncle had journeyed to several months ago.

"I refuse to believe this!" she declared aloud, her voice defiant, her eyes blinking rapidly as she fought back the gathering tears. Uncle John could not be dead. But, she thought as she took a firm grip on her emotions, what if it is true? What if he is indeed dead and buried in that faraway land?

The letter didn't even say how he had died, she told herself. It made no mention of his properties, his oil wells, or any other possessions. The whole thing was terribly mysterious and suspicious, she bitterly reflected. There was something terribly wrong, something that didn't quite ring true.

She suddenly realized that she could not, would not, settle for such a brief, impersonal letter written by some anonymous stranger! She couldn't rest thinking that her uncle had died so far away from home and was probably buried in some unmarked grave. She loved him far too much to allow him to pass virtually unnoticed, unmourned.

I must go to Texas, she decided, her mind racing feverishly as she formed a plan. I must journey to Wildcat City and discover for myself why so much has been omitted from this letter. Uncle John's death must be accounted for!

She would give notice at the school the first thing in the morning, informing them of her plans, as well as of the fact that she planned to return within the space of a month, possibly six weeks. She would also inform Miss Warren.

Thinking of Miss Warren, she felt even sadder. That poor, dear woman would be much upset by the news. It was obvious that she still carried a torch for John Bradford, even after all these years as a spinster.

Sighing heavily with a touch of despair, she thought of her uncle. She still couldn't believe that he was gone, that he would never again appear to entertain her with his tales of high adventure, to delight her with his charm and generous personality. She knew she would grieve for quite some time, but that she would need all her wits about her during the next few weeks in order to carry out the important undertaking she had planned.

Dear, beloved Uncle John, she thought as a sudden, overwhelming need to cry washed over her. In some ways, she knew that she was even more like him than she cared to admit. She knew that she had inherited at least a small degree of his sense of adventure, his restlessness. Only, she had never given in to such urgings, she had always quelled them immediately.

Oh Uncle John, she lamented silently as she began to cry in earnest now, why did I have to lose you, too? I'm completely alone now, but I will not give in to hopeless despair. No, Uncle John, I will carry on, she vowed, burying her face in her arms.

Chapter Two

One week later, Sarah carefully stepped down from the train steps, blinking and coughing delicately as a sudden surge of smoke from the engine engulfed her. She had celebrated her twenty-first birthday while traveling on the train, alone in her tiny compartment, feeling sadder than ever that her beloved uncle would not share the passing of time with her ever again.

Raising her fine linen handkerchief to her nose, she briskly walked away from the train and entered the small, ramshackle building that served as the Wildcat City train station.

"Pardon me, sir," she said as she approached the lone man seated behind the rough wooden counter. "Could you please tell me where I may find a hotel?"

The young red-faced clerk whirled about in his chair, raising his astonished eyes to the beautiful, fashionable young woman standing before him. He continued staring, his mouth slightly agape.

"I said, could you please tell me where I may find a hotel?" Sarah repeated with a small degree of exasperation. Really, she thought, the man was being very rude!

"Yes, ma'am," the young man gulped, still

flabbergasted by her appearance. "Down this here street, fourth building on the right."

"Thank you," she responded politely, then gathered up the skirts of her dark-brown woolen traveling suit. Grasping her valise and bag, she resolutely marched out of the station and into the warm sunshine of the March afternoon. Blinking against the bright rays of light, she brought her hand up to shade her eyes as she paused a moment in order to survey the town across the small distance.

She noticed that the main street was rather wide and definitely unpaved. It had obviously been raining recently, as there was thick brown mud everywhere. Several different types of buildings lined the streets, and the boardwalks in front of the structures were crowded with a bustle of activity. There seemed to be people everywhere, and it appeared that the great majority of them were men.

Concentrating her attention now upon the people, she noticed that the men were all different shapes and sizes, but that they all apparently wore the same drab attire. The few women and children she spotted were dressed in a similar fashion.

As she stood there surveying the town and its inhabitants with a quick sweep of her blue eyes, Sarah realized that it was even worse than she had expected! Everything and everyone appeared to be concerned with only the present moment, and not with the future at all. The buildings were certainly evidence of that fact, she reflected, as she viewed them once more with a critical eye. Nothing in the busy town had the look of permanence about it; the buildings themselves looking very rough and primitive, all needing a coat of paint.

Taking a deep breath, she carefully stepped across the muddy street with determination to the boardwalk lining the other side, taking extra care to hold her skirts above the slushy mess. She was forced to dodge several horses and wagons that were being driven precariously down the street, and she finally reached the other side with a sigh of relief. Carefully climbing the wooden steps, she proceeded toward the building the man at the railroad station had indicated was a hotel.

"Well, look at that, will you? If it ain't a right fancy little gal, the fanciest little thing we seen around here yet!" she heard a rough, uncultured voice exclaim as she made her way down the boardwalk, sweeping past the people with a proud lift to her head. She stole a quick glance at the speaker from out of the corner of her eye, noting with disdain his dirty, unkempt appearance and yellow-toothed features. Several other men standing about on the boardwalk were now taking notice of her, and there were similar remarks made about her as she continued to sweep haughtily past them.

"Hey there, honey! How's about coming over here and getting acquainted?" she heard one of the men suggest, and then winced inwardly as another rather lewd suggestion followed.

Scum! she thought to herself in anger, steeling herself to ignore their disgusting manner and comments. It was quite obvious what sort of place this boomtown actually was. It was definitely an uncivilized, disgraceful hovel!

Quickening her steps, she soon left the ribald

group behind and swept inside the hotel, gazing curiously about at the surroundings as she slowly walked across the lobby. The draperies hanging across the streaked windows were faded and dusty; the carpet was tracked and worn by scores of muddy footprints. There were few people inside, and she hesitated before approaching the unpainted, splintered counter. It certainly wasn't her idea of a hotel, but it was in all probability the best Wildcat City had to offer!

"I would like a room for the night, please," she informed the desk clerk, who had his back to her as she placed her valise on the filthy floor beside the counter. The man whirled about in surprise at the sound of a feminine voice. Sarah had time to note his dirty, frazzled blond hair, his untrimmed beard and mustache, his rumpled clothing. She then became aware of the several curious pairs of eyes now riveted upon her as she waited for the man to respond.

"What did you say?" the clerk rudely answered, his eyes widening in further astonishment as he took in her stylish appearance. He boldly appraised her as she stood there before him, his narrowed eyes traveling the length of her person before returning to her beautiful face.

"I said that I wish to have a room for the night," Sarah repeated with a growing edge to her voice. Why in heaven's name did everyone treat her so strangely?

"We ain't got no rooms," he finally told her, then added in a disrespectful tone, "and, even if we did, we don't rent no rooms to 'ladies' who come in here without a man," he said, placing special emphasis on that particular word. His meaning was all too obvious to Sarah.

"How dare you!" she declared indignantly, striving to maintain control over her temper. "I am a decent woman who is merely requesting to rent a room in this establishment! How dare you insult me in such a disgraceful manner!" she raged, her eyes blazing, her whole manner the very picture of outraged dignity. She drew herself even more rigidly erect, lifting her head proudly as she faced him.

"This here's a boomtown, ma'am, and we ain't got no rooms to spare. This here place has been filled up for nigh on to a year now," the clerk informed her, acting a trifle sheepish as Sarah continued to glare at him.

"That's all right, Sam," a deep, rumbling voice suddenly piped up as a large, evil-smelling man moved close to Sarah. "She's with me, ain't you, honey?" he said, his broad, black-bearded face leering down at her as he took a firm grip on her arm.

"I most certainly am not! Let go of me at once!" she demanded angrily, jerking her arm from his grasp. She turned back to the desk clerk once more. "This is a hotel, is it not? I fail to see how you can have no rooms for ladies," she informed him imperiously, her small flat bonnet on top her pompadoured hair shaking as she nodded her head to indicate the premises.

"I'm real sorry, ma'am, but there ain't no rooms available," the clerk reiterated, beginning to grow impatient with this strange woman's failure to comprehend the facts.

"I told you, honey, you can be with me. I got me a

room. You and me can have us a real good time up there. Come on now, missy, I'll take real good care of you!" the large man insisted, moving closer to Sarah once again. Then, before she knew what was happening, his huge hairy arms had swept her up tight against his broad chest, holding her effortlessly as if she were a mere child.

"Put me down! Put me down, you big oaf! Let go of me!" Sarah stormed at him, beating against his arms and chest with her small, clenched fists. She helplessly glanced about the lobby for any sign of assistance, but it appeared that the other men in the lobby interpreted the entire scene as a domestic squabble of some sort, and none of them would dare to interfere between a man and his woman.

"Now, we got to get on upstairs and have that good time I told you about, honey," the grinning giant boomed down at her, still clasping her squirming form tightly.

"Help! Please, someone help me! What sort of a town is this?" Sarah began to scream as she tried in vain to free herself. Her voice held an edge of panic to it now, as she realized that this wild man was evidently going to be able to carry her off with him to his room upstairs, and that no one would stop him. She, who had always felt perfectly capable of taking care of herself, now felt completely defenseless. Squirming and twisting with renewed energy, she didn't see the man who had just entered the hotel and was now bravely tapping her captor upon the shoulder.

"Put her down," he commanded with a calm air. Sarah still couldn't see his face, but she ceased her struggles at the sound of his deep, commanding voice. It had a strange, foreign lilt to it, but she had no time to think about it further.

"What the hell..." the large man growled in surprise, swinging Sarah about in his arms as he turned to face the intruder.

"I told you to let the little lady go," the young stranger repeated. Sarah was facing him now, and she made a quick appraisal as she stared at him.

Her rescuer was young, in his late twenties or so, his sun-browned, handsome face topped by thick, reddish-blond hair. He was clean-shaven, and his green eyes were narrowed dangerously as he faced the other man. He was tall, well over six feet, and lithely muscular, but the man imprisoning Sarah was even larger. Her appraisal was suddenly interrupted as her captor threatened, "This ain't none of your damned business, MacShane! Now, get out of my way or you'll be real sorry!"

"Swenson, it appears to me that the lady isn't all that willing to have you as her escort. So, I suggest you put her down right this instant, or I'll have to get rough with you," the younger man insisted, his eyes glinting as he took a stance of wary readiness.

Sarah remained silent and open-mouthed as the two of them faced each other. Finally, she felt herself being lowered to her feet, and then released completely. The large man pushed her roughly out of the way, and she stumbled to her knees on the hard floor. Regaining her balance, she drew herself upright and straightened her bonnet as she turned to watch the two opponents facing each other.

"Swenson, there's no need for any trouble between

us, but I can't allow you to go about accosting young ladies any time you damn well please, now, can I?" the man called MacShane remarked with a sardonic grin. "I suggest we step outside into the street and settle this matter right now if you've still a mind to," he then suggested with a tight set to his mouth.

Sarah's captor appeared to be considering the suggestion, and she drew in her breath sharply as she realized that someone might actually be killed over such a ridiculous incident. What sort of place was this? she asked herself once again in confusion.

She heaved a grateful sigh of relief as she saw that the man called Swenson was backing down now. He glared once more at Sarah's rescuer, then at her, before turning swiftly about on his booted heel and stalking out of the hotel in anger.

"Thank you, Mr. MacShane," Sarah breathlessly told the tall young man as she hurried to his side. She smiled up at him in gratitude, but her smile faded as she heard his next words.

"And just what do you think you're doing, coming to a hotel all alone in the first place?" he demanded, gazing down at her in stern disapproval. Sarah couldn't help noticing once again that his voice held a slight accent of some sort, but she certainly didn't feel like analyzing it now!

"Why, I . . ." she began to explain, then told herself that he had absolutely no right to demand an explanation from her. After all, he was still a total stranger, even if he had rescued her from that awful man. "That is really none of your business, is it? I've said my thanks to you. Good day to you," she said dismissing him curtly as she grabbed up her valise and clutched her bag once more.

"And where do you think you're going?" Mac-Shane demanded, his voice detaining her. "You don't have a place to stay yet, do you?"

Sarah turned back to him, noting with a touch of irrational anger the maddening grin on his handsome, tanned face.

"No, I do not. It seems that this particular hotel is completely occupied. Do you have any suggestions?" she inquired with a twinge of sarcasm in her voice. She wanted nothing more than to turn her back on the man and march right out of this disgusting excuse for a hotel, but she realized that such an action wouldn't solve the immediate problem of a place to spend the night.

"As a matter of fact, I do know of a place. A friend of mine owns a boardinghouse down the street. Her daughter might be willing to let you share her room for a night or two," he responded, ignoring her sarcasm. He couldn't seem to take his gaze from her. She was the prettiest little thing he had ever before set eyes on! All that shining black hair piled atop her head, that beautiful little face with those striking light-blue eyes. And her figure was well rounded and womanly, though she barely came up to his shoulder. She was certainly feisty and spirited for one so young and petite, he thought to himself in mingled amusement and admiration.

"Very well, thank you," she stiffly thanked him once again. "If you will be so kind as to direct me, I'm quite sure I can locate this boardinghouse. Whom may I say sent me?" she asked him politely, still a bit out of sorts with him for scolding her.

"My name, dear lady, is Adam MacShane. And who might you be?" he answered with a charming smile.

"My name is Sarah Bradford. Now, where is this boardinghouse?"

"It's on the other side of the street, near the edge of town," he responded with a gesture to indicate the direction of the building.

Sarah then turned away from him and started for the doorway. She had only reached the threshold when he was there beside her, taking control of her valise and grasping her elbow in a firm grip with his strong hand.

"I'd best see that you get there without any further trouble," Adam told her with a twinkle in his green eyes. "By the way, where did you come here from?"

"Philadelphia. I came to . . . to see a relative," she told him evasively, not wishing anyone to know just yet her true reason for traveling so far. She hadn't had time to form any plans yet, and she was still too unfamiliar with the place.

"I see. How long are you planning to stay?" he then asked, gazing down at her as he guided her expertly out of the hotel and onto the boardwalk outside. He steered her down the walk, making sure that a path was cleared for her among the people who seemed to be everywhere. Sarah reflected that they must make a rather comical sight; Adam MacShane so tall and muscular, she so petite. She answered him, "I don't really know just yet. Where did you come here from, Mr. MacShane?" she inquired conversationally, wishing to steer the talk away from herself. She glanced about at the town as they walked. She saw that there were several two-storied saloons, several livery stables, various boardinghouses and restaurants, and other businesses that she could not recognize because of the lack of any identifying signs. To her mind's eye, she thought, this was nothing more than a hole in the ground compared with the vast, progressive city of Philadelphia!

"I'm originally from Scotland, Miss Bradford. Here we are," Adam said as he propelled her up the steps of a neat two-storied building near the end of the boardwalk. The sign above the doorway read "Mrs. Patterson's Boardinghouse." Sarah glanced down in dismay at her muddied boots and hem, and she hesitated before crossing the threshold and the bare wooden floors that led into the entrance foyer.

"It's all right," Adam remarked as he caught her glance. "Everyone here is used to the mud. You wait here while I go see if I can find Emma or her daughter," he told her as he left her alone in the front hallway.

Sarah watched him go, noting that he possessed an easy grace of movement for a man so tall and muscular. She couldn't help reflecting that he was certainly one of the most attractive young men she had ever before encountered, though his manner was a bit too overbearing for her taste. She had always resented being ordered about or managed by anyone! She knew that she had been allowed to become much more independent than most young ladies she knew. The few young men she had allowed to call on her back in Philadelphia had all been very easily handled. That certainly could not be said of Adam MacShane, not from what she had already seen! Still, he had been most helpful and she couldn't help but be grateful.

"Sarah," Adam said, returning with a rather large, middle-aged woman with graying brown hair, "this is Emma Patterson. Emma, this is Sarah Bradford." The woman's strong features were kindly and curious, and Sarah readily answered her welcoming smile. It was so very good to meet someone who seemed halfway decent!

"You didn't tell me she was so pretty, Adam!" the older woman commented as she approached Sarah and shook hands with her. "Adam told me you need a place to stay for a spell. Well, he brought you to the right person all right. My daughter, Clementine, will be right glad for some female company. There sure enough ain't many young women in Wildcat City! Certainly none that ain't married. Well now, I guess I better show you up to your room. Clem's upstairs cleaning some of the rooms. She'll be right glad to meet you. I reckon you're in need of some rest," Mrs. Patterson said as she began climbing the stairs.

"Thank you again, Mr. MacShane," Sarah told him as she turned back to face him. "You've been most kind in your assistance."

"Think nothing of it, Miss Bradford. I'm sure I will be seeing you later. Emma and Clem will take good care of you," he replied as he replaced his felt hat on top of his thick, wavy hair. Giving Sarah one last grin, he sauntered out of the boardinghouse.

She stood looking after him for a moment, then suddenly awakened to hear Mrs. Patterson calling to her from upstairs. She quickly followed.

"Sarah, dear, in here!" Mrs. Patterson called once

more. Sarah entered the room at the head of the stairs, gazing quickly about the room with surprised approval. The curtains were yellow gingham, the bare wooden floors were clean and polished, and the few pieces of furniture were also shining. The room was certainly not luxurious, she thought, but it was bright and cheerful.

"Ma? Who's this?" she suddenly heard a voice behind her inquire. She turned to face a tall young woman of about the same age as herself, perhaps a year or two younger. The woman was tall and slender, her dark blond hair simply tied back with a blue ribbon that matched her deep-blue eyes. She was very attractive, and Sarah surmised that she must be Clementine Patterson, the girl whose room she was to share.

"Oh, Clem honey, this here's Sarah Bradford. She's just come all the way from Philadelphia. Sarah, this here's my daughter Clementine," Emma Patterson made the introductions.

"How do you do?" Sarah responded politely.

"Pleased to meet you," Clem said in a friendly voice, though she was apparently sizing up this new, petite young beauty.

"Adam brought her on over here. Said he found her in the hotel, where that no-account Swenson was bothering her. I know you two girls are going to be right good friends. Well now, I'd best get back downstairs and start supper," Mrs. Patterson declared as she left the room with a last encouraging smile directed toward Sarah.

"Adam MacShane?" Clementine suddenly demanded, her smile fading to be replaced by a frown.

"Yes, that's right," she replied calmly.

"How long have you known Adam?" Clem asked, her whole manner altering abruptly following the mention of his name.

"Why, as your mother just told you, I have only just arrived from Philadelphia. Mr. MacShane was good enough to rescue me from a perfectly dreadful man at the hotel, and then to bring me here," Sarah answered her, growing suspicious of the young woman's increasingly hostile attitude. Could it possibly be that the woman was jealous?

Clementine crossed the room to the window, her green calico skirts rustling softly as she walked. Turning back to face Sarah once more, she said, "Since we're going to be rooming together here for a while, we'd best get a few things straight. Adam MacShane and I have been courting for the past six months. There ain't many women around here that are unmarried, especially young ones. So, Miss Bradford, I think you'd best understand something. You're a stranger here, and I don't guess you're meaning to stay here permanently, so don't go causing any trouble. The women here won't like it one bit."

"I see," Sarah remarked with a tight little smile. "I suppose you are inferring that you don't want me chasing after any of the men you and your friends have chosen, is that it? Well, you needn't worry, Miss Patterson. It's quite true that I do not intend to remain here any longer than is necessary. As soon as I have finished with my business, I will be returning to Philadelphia. So, Miss Patterson, there is no need for you to be apprehensive about my presence here," she finished with a touch of amused sarcasm.

"Good," Clem answered, not recognizing the sarcasm. "As long as you understand the way things are." She turned and walked out of the room and down the stairs without a backward glance.

Sarah sank down upon the softness of the feather mattress on the bed, realizing that she might have some difficulty with Clementine Patterson as her roommate. But then, she reflected with a heavy sigh, it appeared that everything was going to be difficult there in Wildcat City.

Chapter Three

The next morning, Sarah awakened to the bright rays of sunshine filtering through the gingham curtains over the window. She turned to see that Clementine had already risen and gone. Quickly climbing out of the tall iron bed, she dressed in the same traveling suit she had worn the day before, then pinned her thick hair into its fashionable pompadour. Drawing on her small leather boots, she opened the door of the bedroom and quietly descended the stairs, looking about for anyone else who might be up at that time. Glancing at the wall clock hanging in the front hallway, she saw that it was barely seven o'clock in the morning, and yet it appeared that everyone else in the boardinghouse had already gone out for the day.

"Sarah, child, come on out to the kitchen and let me rustle you up some breakfast. I decided that you might want to sleep a little late after your trip and all," Emma Patterson spoke as she rounded a corner of the narrow staircase.

"Thank you, that was very thoughtful," Sarah replied warmly, following the older woman back down the short hallway and into the spacious kitchen area.

"Where is Clementine this hour of the morning?" she inquired conversationally as she watched Mrs. Patterson begin her preparations of the meal.

"Oh, Clem's always out and about somewhere by this time. There's always something going on in a town like this one. Course, it ain't much of a real town yet, not with all the people coming and going so much. But it will be, you mark my words. Someday, Wildcat City is going to be a lot more than just a boomtown like it is now. It's going to be a real city," she spoke proudly as she scrambled the eggs with a perfection born of years of practice, then poured them into the hot iron skillet on top of the stove.

"Can you tell me where I may rent a horse and buggy for the day?" Sarah suddenly asked, her beautiful face thoughtful as she sipped her coffee.

"Sure can. Any of the livery stables would rent you one, but I'd recommend Johnson's, right across the street there. He'll see to it that you get whatever you want at a reasonable price. That's something else you'll soon learn about a boomtown. Prices around here can go sky-high at the drop of a hat. And folks ain't got no choice but to pay them, either. By the way, if you don't mind my asking," she said as she stirred the cooking eggs, "just how long are you planning to stay out here?"

"I'm not sure. No longer than is necessary, though, I can assure you," Sarah answered her with an expressive grimace.

After finishing the hearty, delicious breakfast, Sarah left the boardinghouse and hurried across to the livery stable. She arranged with Mr. Johnson to rent a horse and buggy for half a day, then informed him that she would be back to take them in a few minutes' time. From there, she visually searched the buildings lining the muddy street for the particular sign she sought, then headed in that direction. She entered the small office with the word "Sheriff" painted on a weathered sign hanging in the window.

"Pardon me, but are you the sheriff?" she asked the older, paunchy man leaning negligently back in his chair, his dirty boots propped up on his littered, dusty desk. He opened his eyes and literally jumped to his feet as he realized that a beautiful young woman, obviously a lady, had just strolled into his office and was now speaking directly to him.

"Yes, ma'am. What can I do for you?" he responded, his small, squinting eyes taking in her attractive appearance and petite size. What in tarnation was a young lady like her doing in such a hellhole? he wondered silently.

"I've come to ask you a few questions, if you don't mind," Sarah told him, then took a seat in the chair he indicated with a gesture of his hand. She drew the brief letter from her bag and handed it across the space of the desk to the sheriff, then carefully watched his face as he read the terse note notifying her of her uncle's death.

"You Miss Bradford?"

"Yes. John Bradford was my uncle, my legal guardian. I have traveled all the way from Philadelphia in order to discover exactly how he died and why I was not notified in a proper manner by a person who had the decency to identify himself. I wish to find out about my uncle's properties and oil wells, and also about any of his personal belongings."

"Well now, I really don't think I can help you out too much, then. I didn't know your uncle, except in passing. I ain't been out here but a couple of months myself. I sure enough don't know too much about his death. Or about what he might have left you. That's a legal matter you'll have to take up with a lawyer, I reckon," he remarked, his face revealing a certain unwillingness to become involved in something he apparently viewed as none of his business.

"You are the sheriff of this town, are you not? Didn't you bother to investigate my uncle's death? Isn't that what you usually do whenever someone dies?" Sarah insisted coldly.

"Didn't see no need for it in this particular case. His partner just said he died in a drilling accident, didn't give no other details, and I sure enough didn't go and ask for no more. There weren't no need to question a man's honesty."

"His partner?" she asked in confusion.

"Yep. You didn't know about his partner? He and Frank Mead were partners for the past two months I been here, anyway."

"I see. And where may I find this Mr. Mead now?"

"He ain't around here right now. Had to go out of town on business for a spell, didn't say when he'd be back. But, Miss Bradford," he said, leaning closer to her, clasping his grimy hands in front of him on the desk, "I'd like to give you a piece of friendly advice, so to speak. It'd be best if you was to take the next train out of here and go on back up to Philadelphia where you belong. A boomtown like this ain't no place for a proper young lady like you," he commented with a condescending air that Sarah found very irritating.

"I hope that you will not mind if I choose not to take your advice, Sheriff! I intend to remain here as long as it takes to discover the true and complete facts about my uncle's death, and I don't intend to return to Philadelphia until I do!" Sarah snapped, then composed herself enough to ask politely, "Could you please tell me, by any chance, where my uncle's properties are located? You see, I happen to know that I am my uncle's only living relative, and, therefore, his legal heir. It is my duty to see to his things."

"Well now, it won't do you no good to go out there."

"Nevertheless, would you please direct me?" she insisted.

"It ain't safe for no young lady to go gallivanting about the countryside all by herself," he replied, then answered with obvious reluctance, "But I don't guess it'll hurt none to tell you. Your uncle had a cabin due west of town, some five miles out, just off the road. He's supposed to be buried out there somewheres, too. That's where his wells are, right out there with his cabin. But if you're planning on going out there by yourself, you'd best be careful," he cautioned her.

"Thank you," Sarah told him, then rose to her feet abruptly and marched back through the doorway of the small, cramped office. Once outside, she took a deep breath as if to clear both her lungs and her thoughts, and turned her steps once more toward the livery stable.

It was perfectly obvious that she would receive no cooperation from that infuriating excuse for a sheriff! And, she thought to herself, what was this about a partner? Uncle John had never made mention of this Mr. Mead in any of his letters to her. It was all quite puzzling, and it merely served to strengthen her determination to get to the bottom of things.

As she trudged back across the muddy street, carefully holding her skirts up about her ankles, she noted with relief that there were few men present about the town this morning. She surmised that they must be out in the oil fields doing their jobs by this time of the day. Reaching the livery stables once again, she was assisted up into the small, black buggy by the proprietor. Gently flicking the reins, the single horse pulled the buggy out of town and in the direction of her uncle's cabin.

As she drove along, she had ample opportunity to gaze about the countryside. It was developing into a gray and overcast day, and she hoped that there would not be a storm before she was able to return to town. She saw that the landscape was really quite picturesque, covered by waves of green grass and brightly colored wildflowers. The terrain consisted of softly rolling hills, frequently dotted by tall groves of trees.

A handful of people in wagons and on horseback passed her with curious and admiring looks on their faces, but she simply nodded to them and concentrated her attention on her driving and the beautiful countryside. She had always possessed a more than adequate sense of direction, and she knew that she should arrive at her uncle's property in a matter of less than an hour.

Not too far from the town, Sarah's attention was

suddenly drawn to the sight of quite a number of tall wooden towers jutting toward the sky. Having spent the entirety of her young life in Pennsylvania, the oil derricks were certainly not an unfamiliar sight. She hadn't expected to see so many of them in such a small area, and she judged that there must be at least two dozen now in her line of vision. She flicked the reins in order to hasten the horse, wanting to reach her uncle's cabin and examine both it and the wells. She possessed very little knowledge concerning the oil industry, but she was curious to learn more.

She finally pulled up in front of a small cabin that sat nestled in a grove of trees just off the well-traveled road. She jumped down and hurried to approach the small wooden structure, certain that it must be the cabin of which the sheriff had spoken. Carefully picking her way through the dark mud and tall, wet grass, she reached the door and gently eased it open.

The cabin was empty, and Sarah breathed a sigh of relief as she stepped across the threshold into its semidarkness. Quickly striding to pull back the flour-sack curtains on the windows, she allowed the gray light from outside to brighten the cabin's rough interior. She saw that there was very little in the way of furniture, merely a single bed and stove, a lopsided table and two benches, and a chest of drawers that looked as if it had been used for quite a number of years.

Shaking her head as she viewed the covering of dust and dirt everywhere, she went to the chest and began rummaging through its drawers. She knew that this cabin might hold some clue to her uncle's death, something to guide her in her plans. Reaching the last drawer at the bottom, she had almost abandoned hope of finding anything when her small hands discovered a piece of paper wedged tightly in between the back of the drawer and the splintering sides of the chest. Carefully easing the paper forward, she managed to extricate it and then straightened to hold it closer to the light for examination.

It was apparently part of a letter, and she saw that her uncle's name was at the top. So, she thought with a touch of sadness and grief returning, this was indeed Uncle John's cabin. The letter was of no consequence, merely speaking of some sort of equipment her uncle had ordered. More than half of it had been torn away, along with the signature.

Searching the cabin further, she found no other evidence of her uncle's habitation there. All of his personal belongings were nowhere to be found, none of his clothing or papers or other possesssions. Giving the musty-smelling cabin one last glance, Sarah walked back outside into the fresh spring air and turned her gaze toward the three oil derricks she perceived to be less than a quarter of a mile away.

There was no sign of any activity about the wells, no men working, no equipment noisily clanking. But, she thought, her uncle's last letter to her had told her that one of his wells was producing quite successfully, and that the other two were expected to come in soon.

Why had the wells been abandoned? And why had her uncle's so-called partner not remained here to see to it that the wells were worked? So many things appeared suspicious and mysterious to her mind. Was there going to be no way she could discover something about her uncle's death?

Turning about, her gaze was suddenly drawn to a simple wooden cross jutting up from the ground a few yards away from the cabin. Stepping closer, she drew in her breath sharply as she spied the name carved upon the cross, the name of her uncle, John Bradford. As the tears gathered in her eyes, she knelt beside the grave, silently praying that her beloved uncle had at last found peace, and yet vowing at the same time that she would not let him pass unnoticed. No, she would have the answers she so desperately sought, she told herself, beginning to weep.

A half hour later, she returned to the buggy, climbing up and turning the horse about with a tug upon the reins. She wanted to return to the boardinghouse and be alone to think everything over, to contemplate her next course of action. She was confused and bewildered, and wondered, not for the first time, if she had indeed done the right thing in coming to Texas at all. Oh, Uncle John, she thought to herself, if only you could have left me some sort of message, told me what you wanted me to do.

As she neared the edge of town again, she passed another man on horseback. Not even bothering to glance his way, she was surprised when the rider reined his mount about and galloped up beside her buggy.

"Miss Bradford? What on earth are you doing out in that buggy all alone?" Adam MacShane demanded in surprise and obvious disapproval.

"Good day, Mr. MacShane," Sarah responded calmly with cool politeness.

Adam frowned at her, his handsome face looking quite stern. Before she knew what was happening, he had brought her own horse to a halt and was dismounting beside the buggy. "Where have you been? Don't you know that it's dangerous to drive about the countryside all alone? Didn't anyone warn you?" he said, his hands closing upon the sides of the buggy, his hat tipped back upon his forehead.

"You are the second person to inform me of how very dangerous it is to drive about alone, and yet I have had no difficulty until now," Sarah told him with an amused smile.

"That's beside the point. The fact is, something might have happened, and you would have been defenseless. Where did you go?" he demanded once more, staring directly into her light-blue eyes with his green ones.

Sarah felt herself growing angry at him. She was certainly in no mood for any lectures or interrogation from this man who had apparently, and for some unknown reason, appointed himself her protector!

"Mr. MacShane," she said patiently, striving to maintain control over her temper, "I appreciate your concern, but it is really quite unnecessary. I simply went out to see my uncle's property. You see, my uncle was John Bradford." She waited and watched his face for any sign that he knew anything about her uncle.

"I know that," he casually informed her, unable to suppress a grin as he saw that he had surprised her. "I knew your uncle, Miss Bradford. You see, my property borders his on the north. We were neighbors and good acquaintances, though not great friends. I didn't see him often, but I liked the man. I was sorry to hear about his death."

"Then you know how he died?"

"No, that I do not. I only know that his partner was the one who reported his death, some four weeks ago it's been now. I don't know any of the details, nor why Frank Mead hasn't returned to get those wells working again. But then, none of that is any of my business."

"It's quite obvious to me that no one in this town is willing to get involved in anything at all, particularly another man's death! I have not come all the way from Philadelphia to leave without the answers I wish to have, Mr. MacShane. I want to discover how and why my uncle died, and why I was not informed by his partner or by the authorities. I only found out about his death because of a short, anonymous letter someone sent to me. There are too many things I do not understand about this entire matter. I loved my uncle dearly; he was my legal guardian, and I intend to have the truth," Sarah said with a fierce determination lighting up her tear-filled eyes.

"I don't think you'll be able to discover much. Folks around here aren't likely to be too cooperative. This is a boomtown, Miss Bradford. It isn't a polite, social little town. It's made up of rough oil-field workers, prostitutes, greedy promoters, and very few wives and children. It isn't the sort of place for someone like you, if you don't mind my saying so."

"I do mind," Sarah responded coldly, then added, "I will remain here, no matter how often I am warned away. As a matter of fact, I intend to occupy my uncle's cabin, at least until his absent partner returns and I can get some honest answers from him. I am also my uncle's legal heir, and whatever properties or possessions he owned are now lawfully mine. So, you see, I have no intention of leaving here until I have settled things with Mr. Frank Mead."

"Are you out of your mind? You mean to live out in that old shack all alone, without any protection?" Adam exclaimed with a deepening frown.

"I have nothing more to say to you, sir. I am indeed grateful to you for your assistance of yesterday, but that does not in any way give you the right to meddle in my affairs! I am perfectly able to take care of myself! Now, good day to you!" With that, she whipped up the reins and the buggy abruptly jerked away from Adam, causing him to jump back a step in order to maintain his balance.

Of all the obstinate, unreasonable females! he fumed inwardly as he watched the small buggy move down the road. He honestly didn't know himself why he felt so protective toward her. She was certainly no concern of his. It's just that she was such a pretty, ladylike little thing, and he didn't want to see her get hurt in any way. From the first moment he had set eyes upon her in the hotel, he hadn't been able to get her out of his mind. In all of his twenty-eight years, he had never been so strangely affected by any woman!

Muttering a curse, he mounted once more and continued back toward his own property. He couldn't let her do such a fool thing. He knew how she must feel about her uncle's death and the mysterious circumstances surrounding it, but this was still no place for a beautiful young female to be alone in. He'd have to find some way to convince her that she belonged back in Philadelphia, that she was only headed for trouble if she remained in Wildcat City. But then, he admitted to himself as he kicked his mount into a gallop, he didn't really want her to leave at all.

Chapter Four

"I'm sorry, Mrs. Patterson, but I have already decided," Sarah told her firmly. "I have already purchased a few necessary provisions at the general store, and I have rented a horse and wagon for an indefinite period of time. So you see, it's really no use trying to change my mind. Your friend Mr. MacShane tried to do just that, but without any success, of course," she remarked wryly.

"But you just can't go off and live in that old cabin all by yourself! You don't know nothing about the ways of the land or the people out here yet. There'll be no one to know if something happens to you way out there. Besides that, what good do you think it's going to do?"

"As I told you earlier, I only came here to discover the truth about my uncle's death. No one appears to know anything about it, or at least they're not willing to tell me. I intend to discover the truth, and I also intend to claim my inheritance. It isn't only the money, Mrs. Patterson, it's also the principle of the whole thing. My uncle's dreams are all tied up in those oil wells, and I simply cannot allow his dreams to die. I will remain here until his vanishing partner returns and I can settle things with him."

"Well, if you ain't one of the stubbornnest little gals I ever laid eyes on! You sure enough got gumption. You ain't at all what I would have thought you'd be, coming from up north and all," Emma Patterson commented in admiration. "All right then, if that's what you say you got to do, then you sure enough got to do it. I really don't have no call to argue with you about it anyhow. It's just that I've always been downright motherly to all my boarders, male or female." She turned about and disappeared into the kitchen once more.

Sarah smiled faintly before gathering up her skirts and climbing the narrow stairway to the room she had shared with Clementine for the past two nights. She entered the sunny bedroom to see that Clem was seated in front of the large mirror hanging above the oak washstand, occupied with braiding and pinning up her abundant blond hair.

"Is it true? Are you really going to stay out in that old cabin all by yourself?" Clem asked without bothering to turn around.

"You were listening, I suppose. Yes, it's true. You should be very happy to have your room all to yourself once more," Sarah replied with a mocking smile. She began to gather up her things, glad that she would no longer have to share a room with the jealous young woman.

"Just when did you see Adam again?" Clem suddenly shot at her, whirling about in her seat, narrowing her blue eyes as she stared at Sarah accusingly.

"I don't really see that it is any of your business, but I happened to see him on my way back to town yesterday. As I have already informed you, Miss Patterson," she said as she approached the doorway with her belongings, "I have absolutely no intention of stealing your man. I did not travel all this way to find a husband, you see. So you really needn't worry about your Mr. MacShane." With one last mocking smile, she swept gracefully from the room and down the stairs, leaving an angry Clementine behind.

Sarah soon put all thought of the jealous Clem from her mind as she climbed up on to the wagon seat and gently flicked the reins. The provisions she had purchased were neatly stacked in the wagon bed, and she felt her spirits lift as she drove away from the town.

Her plans thus far included making her uncle's cabin habitable again. It should only require a bit of elbow grease and feminine ingenuity to do just that, she reflected, lifting her face a bit in order to absorb a bit more of the sun's warmth. In Philadelphia, she mused, it was considered quite unfashionable for a woman to acquire a tan, but she knew she needn't worry about being fashionable while she was in Texas. The few women she had seen in town had all possessed a healthy color and well-rounded figures. Their attire was rather drab: simple flannel or muslin shirts and gathered cotton skirts with no bustles or trimming. Of course, she had seen a handful of women attired in gaily colored dresses and outlandishly feathered bonnets, but she had resolutely tried to ignore them. She may have been raised in Philadelphia, but she was not so naive as to mistake such women for anything other than saloon or dance-hall girls, the like of which she had read about in various books about the wild, untamed West.

For the remainder of the day, Sarah scrubbed, scoured, swept, hung freshly laundered curtains, and aired out the small, one-room abode. By the time dusk began to fall, the cabin was as clean and comfortable as she could make it for the time being, and she was attempting to prime the water pump located on the side of the cabin. She glanced up quickly when she heard the sound of hoofbeats approaching, and she immediately reached into her skirt pocket for the small pistol that had been a present from her uncle on her nineteenth birthday. He had laughed at the idea of presenting his schoolteacher niece with such a gift, but he had then stated quite seriously that one never could tell when one might need the protection of such a weapon, even in the proper city of Philadelphia.

"Miss Bradford," she heard Adam MacShane say as he neared and drew his horse to a halt. Dismounting with an agile grace, he looped the reins about the limb of a tree and casually strolled toward Sarah, who was still standing at the water pump, relieved that it had not been some stranger approaching.

"Need any help there?" he asked with a disarming grin.

"No, thank you. I'm quite certain I can have it in working order soon," she replied obstinately, feeling an irrational anger toward him surge within her.

"Nonsense," he replied, moving to grasp the pump and vigorously work the handle up and down. Sarah stared at him in surprise, feeling quite tiny beside his muscular height. Soon, water was pouring from the pump freely, and she was inwardly grateful for his interference.

"There, all it needed was a little coaxing. Emma Patterson told me you had come out here this morning," Adam said, changing the subject as he gazed down at her.

"I have been cleaning and airing out the cabin. It was in an abominable state of neglect when I first saw it," she responded, feeling a bit breathless and decidedly ill at ease at his closeness. Why did this man have the ability to make her feel as if she were a mere child? She was, after all, twenty-one years of age, had been independent and left to her own resources for most of her life, and yet he made her feel as giddy as a schoolgirl! Well, she decided, it is absolutely ridiculous for me to feel this way!

"Your uncle's partner may not return for quite some time, Miss Bradford. Do you mean to stay out here until he comes back? Have you thought about what you'll do if he never returns?"

"There is always that possibility, I suppose. In that case, the property should revert to me, entirely. As it is now, I have already arrived at a very important decision. I intend to see to it that those wells are worked once again."

"Oh?" he asked in amused surprise. "And just how do you plan to go about doing that?"

"Why, I shall employ men to work the wells, of course. My uncle wrote me that one of them was producing quite well, and that the other two were expected to come in at any time. So I'll simply find men to work the wells for me. And, if my uncle's partner does decide to return, he should be quite happy to find that his part of the investment, whatever it was, is paying off once again," she finished proudly.

"I see. There are a few problems with your plan, Miss Bradford," Adam patiently explained, his face growing serious now. "First off, you won't be able to find many men willing to work for a woman, especially for a young woman who's just recently arrived in Texas. Secondly, drillers and roughnecks don't come cheap in a boomtown. How do you propose to pay their salaries?"

"I will find someone to help me, Mr. MacShane," Sarah insisted. "As for paying them, well, I have a small amount of money from the wages I have saved. There may not be enough to pay the men right away, but they'll be paid well for their labors as soon as the wells begin producing."

"That won't work at all. No one will work on promises or credit when they can get paid in hard cash at another lease. No, lass, I'm afraid your plan won't work at all. You won't find anyone willing to work your wells."

"I am already quite aware of the fact that you disapprove of my being here, Mr. MacShane! However, as I have told you before, I will remain until the mystery of my uncle's death is solved, and I will also try and fulfill his dreams. Pray don't let my size or my upbringing fool you, sir. I am perfectly capable of handling any situation that may arise. I am very independent and can be quite assertive when the occasion warrants. I haven't been a schoolteacher for the past three years for naught!"

"A schoolteacher? What in thunder do you think

that has to do with living in a wild boomtown, in dealing with rough, uncultured, uneducated men who would as soon rape you as work for you?" he countered grimly.

"How dare you!" she spluttered, whirling away from him in anger and striding back toward the cabin.

"Miss Bradford," his deep voice detained her before she stepped inside, "if, after thinking over all I have said, you still refuse to abandon this ridiculous scheme of yours, well, I suppose you can let me know and I'll see what I can do to help you. Maybe I can see about getting you those workers," Adam grudgingly offered. The stubborn young female obviously didn't know a damn thing about working an oil field or handling the workers!

"Thank you kindly for your offer, but I refuse to accept charity from anyone, especially you!" Sarah snapped, before disappearing inside the cabin and slamming the door behind her.

Adam felt his own anger rising to the surface at her behavior. He fought it down and stalked to his horse, mounted, then turned back toward his own property, which was less than two miles away. Sarah Bradford would soon learn that her little plan was impossible, that she couldn't always do everything on her own! he thought as he stole one last glance at her cabin before leaving it behind. Just to be on the safe side, he'd keep a watch on her place. Independent or not, a beautiful young woman like her just wasn't meant to live in this part of the territory all alone!

That night, Sarah slept with the small pistol beneath her pillow, feeling a measure safer for its presence there. She knew that word of her residence at the cabin had probably not been spread about yet, but she also knew that she could anticipate trouble when word did get around. Her last thoughts before drifting off into a troubled sleep were of Adam MacShane's words to her earlier that evening. She would show him, she vowed to herself with determination, she would show all of the men in and around Wildcat City what a mere woman could do!

The next morning, she quickly dressed in a simple sprigged cotton dress that fit her rounded curves to perfection, then drove to town without waiting to eat any breakfast. She wanted to get an early start on her plan, and she knew that she would need to get into town before the sun had been up long. She wanted to find some men to work the wells on her uncle's property, and she wanted to be quick about it. She had no idea when her uncle's partner would, if ever, return. But then, she didn't want to think too far ahead in the future just yet; she simply wanted to get those wells working. Goodness knows she had no idea whatsoever when she first arrived that she would become involved in the oil boom herself!

Driving carefully down the main street of town, she saw that there were already several men about this morning. She pulled the horse to a halt before Mrs. Patterson's boardinghouse, knowing that it would be safe there. Then she climbed down from the wagon seat and straightened her pert little bonnet before marching up to a group of men standing on the boardwalk in front of one of the saloons.

Sarah took a deep breath, then resolutely approached the small group of men. She glanced toward the open doorway of the saloon as she passed but quickly averted her eyes as she perceived that there was some sort of meeting or gathering taking place inside at that very moment. The men outside the building noticed her approach, and one of them remarked, "Well, this one's a new one, I guess. I ain't seen her around here yet. What's your name, honey?"

Sarah stared at the tall, slender young speaker wearing the huge felt hat. She supposed that this might be a bit more difficult than she had believed.

"Pardon me, gentlemen . . ." she began calmly, then was rudely interrupted by another of the grubby-looking men.

"Gentlemen? Did you hear that?" he exclaimed with a hoot of laughter. The others in the group joined in the raucous amusement. Sarah drew herself up to her full height and directed an icy look at the men before continuing.

"I am looking for men to employ. My name is Sarah . . ." She was once more interrupted by another man's loud guffaw. Suddenly, the entire group had surrounded her, and she gazed at them in indignant astonishment. She gasped loudly as the first speaker scooped her up in his lanky arms and proceeded to carry her inside the saloon, his friends following closely behind, still laughing at some shared jest.

"What do you think you're doing? Put me down at once!" Sarah demanded imperiously, then forgot all about behaving dignified as she began to kick and squirm and beat at the hapless fellow's head. He merely laughed at her futile efforts and remarked to his friends, "I sure enough got to bid on this one!

Damn, if she ain't the most spirited little filly I seen here yet!"

He finally set his struggling, furious burden upon her feet once more. Sarah's opal eyes blazed at him, but he smiled broadly and turned his back on her. It was then that Sarah noticed that she was standing beside a long line of other women, and she gazed in open-mouthed shock as she realized the nature of the scene that was taking place in the smoke-filled saloon at that moment.

There was a loud commotion resounding everywhere, many laughs and shouts from the large number of men who appeared to be seated or standing in every corner of the building. There was obviously some sort of auction taking place, and Sarah glanced quickly at the other women beside her near the foot of the staircase. Sudden realization dawned upon her then.

For heaven's sake, she thought to herself, the men were bidding on the women! And, as for the women, they appeared to be enjoying every minute of the outrageous auction! They were laughing and shouting encouragement at the men. Sarah glanced down at their attire, and she was shocked even more. The women wore very little clothing at all, most of them merely clothed in flimsy wrappers or undergarments. Their hair was loose and falling in disarray about their shoulders, and their faces were caked with makeup. Their stale perfume assailed her sense of smell, and she tried to make her way back through the noisy crowd in order to escape the disgusting scene and breathe fresh air once more. Her eyes were beginning to fill with tears as a result of the smoke drifting endlessly throughout the room, and she began to push frantically and shove to try and get out.

"Hey, Jim! How's about starting the bid now on that little gal down at the end there? I been waiting for someone like her!" the young man who had carried Sarah inside the saloon shouted above the other men's voices. There was an accompanying roar of approval, and Sarah found herself lifted in a man's arms once more and transferred to the head of the line. The other women glared jealously at her, but none paid her much attention beyond that.

"No! Let me go! You've made a terrible mistake, I don't belong here! I'm Sarah Bradford, and I simply came to try and employ workers for my uncle's wells!" she insisted, feeling panic grow within her as she realized that no one was listening to her. She found herself set upon her feet on the third step of the staircase, so that all of the eager bidders could have a clear view of her. She stared back at them with frightened eyes, seeing their leering faces and listening to their lewd comments as she feverishly searched the crowd for assistance. Her eyes widened even further when she perceived that it was none other than the sheriff standing at the foot of the staircase a few feet below her.

"All right, then, how much am I bid for this one?" his voice rang out as he gestured toward Sarah, without once turning about to look at her.

"Sheriff! Sheriff, please, don't you remember me? I'm Sarah Bradford!" she shouted at him, striving to be heard above the noise echoing everywhere. She tried to reach his side but was immediately lifted and placed once more upon the step. She knew that if the humiliating experience continued much longer, she would begin screaming! She gasped as she suddenly realized that the bidding for her had already begun, and she could hardly believe her ears when a shot rang out, stunning the entire assembly into momentary silence.

"Sheriff, I'm afraid someone has made a slight mistake. That young lady up there is not one of the group. She's a friend of mine, and she certainly doesn't belong here," Adam MacShane announced, easing his gun back into its holster at his side. The expression on his face and in his eyes dared anyone to dispute his word.

"What's this about a mistake, MacShane?" the sheriff responded.

"The young lady there on the stairs, she's not with the other women," Adam repeated, his voice firm and authoritative. He was now striding purposefully through the group toward Sarah, and she didn't know if she had ever felt so relieved to see anyone in her entire life!

"Miss Bradford?" the sheriff said in shocked surprise as he finally turned to face her.

"How dare you conduct such a shocking, disgusting affair, Sheriff! This is the most demeaning, degrading example of exploitation I have ever before witnessed! How dare these poor women be subjected to such disgrace!" Sarah fumed at him, her eyes blazing, her whole manner proud and angry as she now stood beside him, her arms sweeping outward to include the entire crowd.

The other women stared at her in surprise before

turning to one another and beginning to laugh loudly in pure, unabashed amusement. The men in the room soon followed suit, and soon the entire saloon was filled with hearty laughter.

"Miss Bradford, you'd better come with me now. This is neither the time nor the place to be making any suffragette speeches," Adam told her as he reached her side and firmly grasped her arm to pull her with him. She resisted for a second, then decided that she really wanted nothing more than to escape from the crowd and the so-called "auction." She went along with Adam, who continued to pull her along with him, none too gently. Once outside, Sarah wrenched her arm from his grasp and rounded on him.

"What sort of a town is this? Is there no decency at all? How could there be so many disreputable characters in one place? That is the second time I have been so rudely accosted by a man! I have never been so humiliated in my life! How can those women allow that to happen to them. How can the sheriff allow it, much less participate in it!" she exclaimed, jerking her dress and bonnet to rights once more.

"Hold on there," Adam commanded, frowning down at her. "You don't even know what you're talking about. Those 'ladies' in there aren't ladies at all. You saw them. Those good women in there are part of this town's main class of females. They're prostitutes, Sarah, prostitutes! It's Monday morning. That's when the sheriff rounds them all up and arrests them. Then he holds this little auction. Whoever pays their fine gets to keep them for the next twenty-four hours. Now do you feel that those 'poor women' are being exploited?" he demanded, his eyes appearing even greener than ever as he studied her reaction.

After a moment's hesitation, she cooly replied, "Yes, I do. It's men who cause those poor, unfortunate women to earn a living the way they do!"

"How do you figure that?"

"You refuse to grant us any rights at all! You keep us dependent, you refuse to listen to us! We are nothing but mere chattel to men! But we shall triumph, Mr. MacShane." She turned away from him and started across the street, completely forgetting her plan to hire workers that morning. She didn't remember until she was about to climb up onto the wagon seat.

Where would she find men willing to work for her now? she asked herself in consternation. After the way those men in the saloon had treated her, it was perfectly obvious that none of them would ever take her seriously. She reluctantly admitted to herself that hiring the workers she would need was going to be as difficult as Adam had predicted. But she would still have to try. There must be some way to get those wells working again. She heard Adam's voice behind her.

"Miss Bradford, I think I have a solution to your problems. I rode over to your cabin just after sunup this morning to discuss it with you, but I found you'd already gone. That's how I happened to find you at the saloon, in case you wondered."

"You mean that you were not planning to attend the auction yourself?" she asked with insulting sarcasm.

Adam's lips tightened briefly, but he chose to

ignore her remark and instead answered, "Would you care to hear my proposition?"

"I don't suppose it will hurt to listen to you. What is this plan of which you speak?" Sarah replied, turning to face the tall man beside her with an expectant air.

"Not here. This isn't the sort of place to discuss business, Miss Bradford. Why don't we go on back out to your cabin and talk about it there, where we can have privacy?" he suggested amiably, his eyes sparkling down at her. She nodded briskly in agreement and allowed him to assist her up onto the wagon, then watched as he tied the reins of his horse to the back of the wagon. He climbed up beside her and took control of the reins, and the two of them rode out of town together in silence.

"Well, what is this plan of yours?" Sarah asked him stiffly once they had arrived back at the cabin. The sun had broken free of the clouds again and was now streaming brightly through the glistening windows. Sarah took a seat on one of the benches at the table and looked up as Adam seated himself across from her.

"Do you have any coffee?" he suddenly asked, the lilting tone of his voice more pronounced than usual. Sarah vaguely recalled that he had said he was originally from Scotland.

"I'll make some, if you don't mind waiting." She quickly prepared the fragrant brew, then took a seat once more in order to wait for the mixture to boil. She didn't trust the handsome young man sitting across from her, and she didn't really know why. Perhaps it was because she had never trusted any man, except for her uncle, of course. She had never really known many men, but then she had never wanted to! She had no desire to become a slave to any man's overbearing wishes.

"Now, about my plan. I suppose I might as well come right out with it. You need someone to work your wells, right?"

"You know that is correct."

"Well then," Adam said, "I need something that you can provide, Miss Bradford. I need a wife."

"A wife?" she stupidly repeated, not at all certain that she had understood him correctly.

"That's right," Adam responded, his green eyes twinkling now with some secret amusement.

"But I have no wish to marry you, Mr. MacShane! And, what is even more important, I have no wish to marry at all!" Sarah protested.

"It's not the sort of marriage you think. It's strictly a business arrangement. I will see to it that your wells are worked, and you will consent to marry me. A marriage of convenience, as they say."

"But you've only known me a few days! You can't possibly know if you want to marry someone in that short amount of time! You must be out of your mind!" she continued to protest, wondering why his proposition was causing her to protest so vehemently. Why on earth should she care if the man wanted to marry her or not?

"Please, just listen to my offer for a moment before you start refusing. As I said, you need my help in working your wells. Well, I need a wife. Not for either love or companionship, mind you, but for business reasons of my own. As I told you earlier, I am originally from Scotland. I've been in this country for nearly ten years now. I still had family in my home country when I left, grandparents, brothers and sisters, and the like. But that's beside the point. The point is, Miss Bradford, my grandfather has died and left nearly everything to me. My older brother was to have been the heir, but he was killed nearly four years ago. So that leaves me to inherit my grandfather's wealth, which is quite sizable, I'm told. But there was a certain condition to the will," he paused at this point, watching her lovely face as she listened intently to his story.

"In order to inherit, I must be wed before the age of thirty. Now, I am twenty-eight. If I can prove that I am already legally married, then I may inherit right away. I don't plan to return to Scotland, though. I intend to see to it that my family in Scotland is amply provided for. Then, with the remainder of the money, I intend to invest right here in Texas. So, you see, it is imperative that I get married as soon as possible."

"But why me? I've told you that I have no wish to marry. Surely you must have some other young lady in mind. Someone you must have known longer than me. Someone whom you care for, and who returns your affection. You needn't tell me that a young man such as yourself doesn't know any other young women!"

"I didn't say that. There happens to be no one I wish to marry, at least not yet. You still seem to be confused about something, Miss Bradford. This marriage between us would be a business arrangement and nothing else. After a period of six months or maybe less, I will have my inheritance and our marriage can be annulled. I would see that the matter was handled discreetly, I can assure you. In return for your agreement to marry me, I will have your wells worked. You will still retain ownership of all your own properties."

"This is all quite insane!" Sarah remarked, rising to her feet abruptly. She walked to the stove in the corner, then turned about to face him again. "What about Clementine Patterson? She told me herself that the two of you were courting. Where does this leave her? Why don't you simply marry her?"

"I never gave her any reason to believe I was planning to marry her. What's between us is all in her own head."

"I don't know what to say to all this. Why should I agree to such an unbelievable, fantastic scheme? I may still be able to find the men to work my wells. Besides all that, I plan to return to Philadelphia as soon as I have the wells producing and discover the truth about my uncle's death," she reminded him, her head spinning. It was perfectly true that she had never really intended to marry, but what would be the harm in accepting his proposition? It would solve her problem, it would solve his, and then she would be free to return to Philadelphia. She might even become a wealthy woman by then. And something else. She would have the protection of a man's name, the sort of privileges only a married woman was allowed in today's society. She would be able to participate in the women's movement even more freely when she returned to Philadelphia. She could simply say that she had been widowed, and no one need ever know the truth.

"I can see by the look on your face that you are indeed considering my proposal. Well, I'll leave you now and let you think over all of this. If you do decide to accept, we can work out all the details later. I'll be back tomorrow morning for your answer." He stood to his full height, gazed intently at her for a moment or two longer, then turned and left the cabin, stooping to avoid hitting his head on the doorway, which was obviously not meant for someone as tall as he.

Sarah watched him go in silence, thinking that he hadn't even stayed to drink the coffee. What was she to do? she lamented silently. Should she forget the whole, impossible scheme? Or should she accept? Either way, she knew that she would get very little sleep that night.

Chapter Five

Adam MacShane leisurely urged his mount along the well-traveled dirt road, the early morning sun, on the few occasions it made an appearance from beyond the clouds, beating down upon his bare head. Heaving a sigh, he replaced the hat upon his thick, reddish-blond hair and once more contemplated the situation.

He'd known about his grandfather's will for several weeks now, just as he'd known about that particular one condition of the will. He still couldn't understand what had prompted him to make such an amazing proposal to Sarah Bradford when he certainly had ample opportunity to approach some other young woman on the subject of marriage some time ago. Could it perhaps be that he was beginning to feel something for Sarah, something that went beyond a mere business interest?

No, he told himself sternly, shifting uncomfortably in his leather saddle. It was nothing more than a business arrangement, a way out of their difficulties, and nothing more. It was simply that she had come along at the right time, that she needed his help as much as he needed hers. He definitely didn't want to consider any other possibility, any other motives.

Finally drawing his horse to a halt, he dismounted before her cabin. He hesitated a few moments before approaching the door. He knocked loudly, then removed his felt hat as the door swung open.

Sarah stared at the tall, dashing young man and took a deep, unconscious breath. She only prayed that she had made the right decision, that everything would go as smoothly as she had planned.

"Come in, Mr. MacShane," she said, then stood aside as he bent his head to enter. "I have some coffee ready for you this morning. You didn't remain to drink any yesterday."

"I forgot all about it," Adam replied without smiling, taking a seat on the wooden bench as Sarah sat across the table from him.

"I didn't sleep much last night, Mr. MacShane. There was too much to consider, too much to seriously contemplate. I still happen to believe that your scheme, your proposal, is both impossible and preposterous, perhaps even a trifle insane. Nevertheless, I have made my decision. I have decided to accept your offer of a marriage between us for business purposes."

"You have?" he responded, a bit incredulous at her answer, and feeling some unexplained exhilaration at the same time.

"I have indeed. However," she said, before pausing and gazing across at him with her beautiful opal eyes, her face calm and her expression deadly serious, "there are a few conditions to my acceptance of this business arrangement. Would you care to hear those conditions?"

"By all means."

"Very well. First of all, I want it clearly understood between us that this marriage is indeed strictly a business arrangement. There will be nothing else, no other rights to either person or properties. That is to say," she elaborated, evidently feeling some discomfort at what she considered to be a delicate subject, "there will be no physical relationship between us. Have I made myself clear?"

"Aye, quite clear, Miss Bradford," Adam replied with a serious expression, although his green eyes were twinkling with irrepressible amusement.

"I want to remain free to return to Philadelphia at any time I wish, no matter what other plans you may have. As soon as certain things have been taken care of here, I plan to do just that, to return to my home. You may then arrange for the annulment without my presence."

"I can't see that there'll be any problem with that when the time comes."

"Good. Also, I wish to remain in residence here in my uncle's cabin. I intend to maintain full and complete freedom of myself, Mr. MacShane, total independence. I refuse to feel any obligation to behave as a docile and obedient wife to you, especially given the unique aspects of this so-called marriage. There, I suppose those are the only conditions I wished to outline at this time. I hope they meet with your approval and acceptance. If not, well, we may as well abandon this scheme here and now."

Adam appeared to be contemplating her words, his eyes fastened on his large, calloused hands, which were clasped together upon the surface of the table. He remained silent for several suspenseful seconds before unclasping his hands and raising his eyes to Sarah's expectant face.

"All right. I guess it's agreed then. Would you object to going into town with me right now and getting married? The justice of the peace can perform the ceremony."

"I suppose there is no reason to wait. I have made my decision, and I may as well see it through immediately. If you will please wait outside for a few minutes, I'll get ready."

"You're sure you want to go through with this?" Adam asked, closely scrutinizing her expression for any signs of last-minute reluctance.

"I am quite sure, Mr. MacShane," she declared, almost defiantly. She ushered him out the door, then hurried to prepare herself for the wedding.

Her wedding, she reflected with ironic amusement. She never thought the time would come, especially not under the present circumstances. Stop it, she commanded herself, you needn't become emotional about this. It isn't as if this were going to be a real wedding. It's merely a formality, the signing of a business contract. She turned about and began to dress with meticulous care. If she was to be married, no matter what the reasons, she intended to look her best!

Finally facing herself in the single, cracked mirror hanging precariously above the chest of drawers, she critically surveyed her image. She knew that the pale-blue dress fashioned out of soft cotton and trimmed with peacock-blue ribbon was very becoming to both her hair and her complexion. The bustle at the back consisted of a single large bow. Her white kid shoes peeped out from under her skirts as she walked, and the white straw bonnet perched atop her thick, shining black curls completed her attire. She smiled at her reflection in satisfaction.

"I am ready now, Mr. MacShane. Shall we go? We can take my wagon."

Adam gazed at her in rapt admiration. She appeared even more beautiful and desirable than ever before. He felt his pulse quicken at her appearance, and he felt a tiny voice at the back of his mind asking him once again if his part in this arrangement was due strictly to business purposes.

"You look very nice, Miss Bradford," he remarked casually, without revealing the inner tumult within as he handed her up onto the wagon seat. He climbed up beside her and expertly guided the horse toward the road that led into town.

"Where is the office of the justice of the peace located?" Sarah inquired conversationally, feeling a small degree of nervousness begin to creep into her being.

"You've probably been there. It's at the Ellison General Store. Fred Ellison is the one who'll be marrying us."

"You mean we're to be married by a merchant in a general store?" she responded in surprise. She could almost laugh aloud at the entire predicament. Marrying a man she hardly knew for business reasons, being married by a store owner, the wedding being performed in a general store! Oh, Uncle John, she suddenly thought, you must be quite amused at all of this, wherever you are!

"Don't worry. It will be legal enough, even if it isn't in a church or fancy office," Adam replied gruffly. Did she think she was too high and mighty to be married in such a manner? He started to say more to her but declined. There would be enough to talk about once they were married. Aye, she was in for a few surprises then.

The wedding itself took no more than five minutes. They were married in the back room of the general store, and the whole procedure was quick and efficient, completely devoid of any sentimentality or emotion. Afterward, a silent Adam escorted his new bride back through the store and outside to the waiting wagon.

Sarah allowed herself to be led along without a word. She kept reminding herself that what had taken place was nothing more than a business contract. And yet she still felt sad for some reason. Perhaps she was more sentimental about such things than she cared to admit, even to herself. She chided herself for her foolishness. What's done is done and you must keep your part of the bargain, she thought.

Adam was having very different thoughts as he handed his new wife onto the wagon. He felt anything but sad about what had just taken place in the tiny back room of the crowded general store. No, on the contrary, he actually felt an unexplained happiness about the whole thing. He kept insisting to himself that it was merely happiness for the inheritance he would now receive, happiness at having found an answer to his own financial problems.

"Well, it's done now. Are you all right?" he suddenly asked Sarah. She merely nodded briskly in return.

As the newly married couple drove out of town in thoughtful silence, they were unaware that they were being avidly observed by a pair of deep blue eyes. Clementine Patterson was just on her way to the general store herself when she saw Adam come outside with Sarah at his side. She watched in open-mouthed astonishment as they drove away. Her astonishment soon gave way to angry suspicion.

What on earth was that Sarah Bradford doing in Adam's company? she wondered to herself. That no-account Yankee woman had lied! She'd been after Adam MacShane after all! Oh, you just wait till I get my hands on you! Clem vowed silently as she hurried toward the store. She wanted to discover more about the reason those two had ridden into town together at such an early hour of the day.

Adam drew the horse and wagon to a halt before Sarah's cabin once more. He jumped down, then walked around to help her down. His strong hands lingered a bit longer than was necessary upon her slender waist. Sarah quickly averted her eyes in confusion as he set her on her feet. Releasing her, he suddenly commanded, "Go inside and get your things."

"What? What in heaven's name are you talking about? I am going nowhere," she answered in puzzlement at his authoritative tone of voice.

"You're coming home with me. As my wife, my home is now yours, whether you think it so or not. It isn't safe for you to remain here alone," Adam insisted with a tight frown, anticipating trouble from his new wife over the first conflict of their married life.

"Not safe? Why, that simply isn't true! I've been living here alone for the past two days without any trouble at all. No one has even approached the cabin," she responded, then grew angry as she realized that he was already breaking a part of their bargain. "You agreed to all of my conditions before we were married! You agreed that I could remain in this cabin!" she stormed at him, her opal eyes blazing.

"For your information, Mrs. MacShane," Adam told her, placing special emphasis upon her new name, "either myself or one of my men has been watching your cabin ever since the first night you came here! If anyone had wanted to accost you, I'm sure our presence was a certain deterrent to them! Now listen, woman, I'm not planning to take away any of your precious freedom! I simply want you in a safe place. You'll have the complete privacy of your own room at my cabin. Besides, when these wells start being worked by the men I plan to hire, it won't do for a beautiful young woman to be around, driving them to mindless distraction all day long!"

"That is utterly absurd! I have no intention of flaunting myself before the men, and you know it! As I said before, you agreed to each and every one of my conditions before we were married. I expect you to keep your part of the business arrangement between us. I consider it ridiculous to stand here arguing with you over such a matter! I'll say good day to you now!" she snapped, then began marching angrily toward the cabin door.

"For better or for worse, remember? You are now my wife, whether you like it or not. I never planned to allow you to stay out here alone any longer. If I had told you that this morning, you would never have agreed to marry me, is that right?"

"You know perfectly well that I would not have agreed!"

"If both my wells and yours are going to get worked, I cannot spare the time or the men to watch this place all night any longer! I didn't expect you to like it, but I did expect you to be reasonable about it. Once you finished ranting and raving at me, of course," he said with an amused grin.

"You lied to me. How dare you mislead me in such a manner! I realize now that you are certainly not the sort of person I believed you to be!" she coldly informed him, refusing to consider the reasoning behind his argument.

"Isn't that what all brides say, that they've married a stranger?" Adam remarked. "Sarah, I've got work to do today and I think we've talked about this long enough. I'm sorry I misled you. Are you going to come along with me now, or do I have to carry you?" he threatened, all humor disappearing from his handsome face now.

Sarah considered hurrying inside the cabin and bolting the door but then decided against it. No matter how he had betrayed her trust, she still needed those wells worked. She realized that she had little choice in the matter at all, and she glared at him in fury as she acquiesced with an ill grace.

"I will go with you. However, I will never forgive

you for lying to me, Mr. MacShane!"

"I think it's about time you started calling me Adam," he replied, just as she disappeared inside the cabin to fetch her things. She reappeared a few minutes later and handed him her baggage. Grasping her firmly about the waist, he lifted her back up onto the wagon seat, where she landed with an uncomfortable jolt.

"My cabin's less than fifteen minutes drive from here. It's much bigger than your uncle's. As I told you, you'll have a room all to yourself," he said in an effort to placate her. She merely drew herself proudly erect and turned her head away.

"I can already see that this is sure going to be one hell of a marriage!" Adam remarked ruefully, slapping the reins on the horse's rump as they pulled away from the cabin.

Chapter Six

Sarah looked up to see that the wooden cabin before her surprised eyes was much larger than she had expected, much larger indeed than the small abode that she had occupied for the past few days. The building was completely shaded by the several tall, gently swaying trees that surrounded it, and it was set well off the road. She glanced a bit farther and noted the half dozen oil derricks located in the distant background, their structures tall and majestic, only partially hidden by the surrounding landscape.

"I wasn't aware you had so many wells of your own," she remarked as she allowed Adam to lift her down, her anger beginning to cool a bit after the silence of the wagon ride.

"I hope to drill several more once I receive that inheritance money. As it is now, I'm barely able to keep my head above water when it comes to available capital for the wells. Come on, I'm sure you're anxious to get inside and look the place over. Besides, I've got a lot of work to do today. I can't take a day off simply because I happened to get married!" Adam commented with a mocking smile.

"Mr. MacShane, I certainly do not intend to

remain in your cabin for any longer than is absolutely necessary. I will ask Mrs. Patterson to reserve accommodations for me as soon as possible," Sarah cooly informed him as she began to march resolutely toward the cabin, her head held high and proud.

"We'll see about that," Adam responded good-naturedly. He hurried to intercept her just as she was about to step inside the building. Lifting her easily in his strong, muscular arms, he said, "This is what I've always heard the new husband is supposed to do, carry the new bride over the threshold."

"Put me down at once!" she snapped in reply, the anger returning to her countenance. "You know perfectly well that our marriage is nothing more than a business arrangement, and old-fashioned sentiment certainly has no place in it!" she reminded him, then found herself inside the cabin and her feet on firm ground once again. She glared at her grinning husband once more before allowing her eyes to sweep the cabin's interior.

The room in which she was standing was large and airy, the wooden floors covered by various woven rugs that were scattered about. Four or five chairs were placed randomly about the room, a few rough wooden tables next to them, and there was a huge stone fireplace located in one corner of the room. The windows were covered by the same flour-sack curtains as those in her uncle's cabin. The cabin was indeed rather sparse and rugged, but it appeared to be fairly clean and comfortable.

"I'll leave you alone now. The room on the right there," he indicated with a brisk nod of his head, "is yours. Feel free to inspect or alter anything about the cabin, Mrs. MacShane. I'm sure you'll find more than enough to occupy your time all day while I'm gone," he told her, grinning once more before turning and striding back outside, shutting the door behind him.

Sarah refused to answer him, focusing her attention on the cabin instead. Strolling across to the small room located to the left of the front doorway, she discovered the kitchen area. There was a black pot-bellied stove in the corner, a large basin, three shelves piled high with an array of provisions, and a rustic table and benches in the center of the room. She couldn't refrain from smiling faintly at the sight of the wildflowers arranged rather haphazardly in a glass jar on the table.

She next inspected the two bedrooms, easily ascertaining which of the two belonged to Adam. Several items of clothing were strewn about the sunny room, the bed was rumpled, the chest of drawers was dusty and overstuffed. It is most obviously the bedroom of a single man, she thought to herself in disdain.

She left his room and walked across the main room to the bedroom that Adam had designated as hers. She was pleasantly surprised as she stepped inside. The iron bed was covered with a worn, but clean, quilt, and the few pieces of furniture had been dusted recently. Instead of the flour-sack curtains that were on the other windows, her single window was covered by brightly colored calico. Upon further inspection, she discovered that someone had recently put up a couple of shelves and a mirror above the washstand. There was ample space in the room for both herself and her things, and she grew very thoughtful as she sank down upon the softness of the bed.

Adam, or someone, had apparently gone to some trouble to make her room comfortable. She was confused, then suddenly realized that Adam must have supposed all along that she would accept his amazing proposal of marriage. Why else would this room have been made so apparently ready for her?

She heaved a sigh and contemplated her new situation. She knew that there would be no rooms available anywhere in the town, even at Mrs. Patterson's. And she positively refused to share a room with that catty Clementine again! She could already envision the young woman's expression when she discovered that her precious Adam was now legally married, and to none other than Sarah Bradford!

Still, it was totally improper for her to remain in Adam's cabin, alone with him, even if they were married. To everyone else, it would seem perfectly natural, but she and Adam knew that their marriage was a farce. But, she firmly resolved, she would have to remain here in his cabin and make the best of things for the moment. She would certainly see to it that Mr. MacShane kept the other conditions of their bargain!

Throughout the day, Sarah cleaned and scrubbed, dusted and mopped, washed and swept. If she had to occupy the cabin for even a brief period of time, she intended for it to be clean! Several times during the day, she was tempted to grab her valise and take the wagon and drive back to her uncle's cabin, but she knew that Adam would merely come after her and force her to return with him. Besides, she consoled herself, she did want him to work her wells as soon as possible, and she knew that it would be more feasible if he didn't have to watch her cabin as well. So she went at her various tasks with firm determination. If she had to stay, she would not remain idle!

When Adam strode into the cabin late that evening, he was surprised to see the changes Sarah had wrought in so short a time. The entire place was clean and organized, and he immediately detected the delicious aroma of food emanating from the direction of the kitchen.

"I can see that you've certainly kept yourself busy today, Mrs. MacShane. It seems as if I won't have to eat my own cooking for a change!" Adam remarked as he entered the kitchen, smiling broadly as he caught sight of Sarah. She was enveloped in a white apron, her black curls pinned securely up and away from her beautiful face, which was becomingly flushed as she stirred something in a large pot upon the stove. She whirled about in surprise at his deep voice.

"You startled me," she said accusingly, then turned back to her culinary labors. "Dinner is nearly ready. If you'll please go outside and wash, I'll put it on the table."

"Aye, I guess I do look a sight at that. I'd be willing to do just about anything for a woman-cooked meal!" he commented in amusement as he did as she suggested. He returned inside shortly and took a seat at the table, watching Sarah as she brought the bowls and platters of food and placed them on the table's newly polished surface.

"I didn't even know you could cook!" he said, inhaling deeply as he eyed the food.

"Of course I can cook! I realize that I am not obligated to cook for you, or to clean your cabin, but I simply could not tolerate it the way it was! Besides, we have to eat, don't we? And I certainly don't intend to be forced to eat your cooking. Why, if you cook the way you keep house, I can just imagine how the food would taste!" she replied defensively, appearing a bit embarrassed now by her activities of the day. She took a seat on the bench across the table from him, feeling decidedly uncomfortable at his presence.

"Oh, I've done all right for myself the past year or so. I have to say, though, the cabin looks quite different now. I guess you women just can't resist cleaning and rearranging when you have the chance!" Adam said as he attacked the fragrant stew and the homemade bread.

"What a ridiculous statement!" Sarah retorted. "I suppose I should expect such male prejudice from you, however. For your information, Mr. MacShane, women are good for a lot more than merely cooking and cleaning!"

"Oh, you don't have to tell me that, Mrs. MacShane," Adam replied with a meaningful little smile as his eyes boldly appraised her.

"That is something else I should expect from someone such as you! You may be assured that I will make absolutely certain that you keep the other conditions to our arrangement. You broke your word so easily this morning!"

"I've already explained my reasons for moving you here, Sarah," Adam informed her, the humor disappearing from his face, his eyes glinting with a strange light, his firm tone indicating that he would brook no further resistance on that particular subject.

Sarah swallowed her angry retort and instead attacked her own plate of food. As soon as they were both finished with the meal, she stood hastily and began clearing the table.

"That was a very delicious meal, Mrs. MacShane."

"Please don't call me by that name," Sarah responded irritably, her face tight and unsmiling as she went on with her task.

"That is your name now, isn't it? We are legally married, aren't we?"

"We are, but I prefer not to be called by that name, if you do not mind. We are forced, for the time being, to occupy the same abode, Mr. MacShane, so I suggest that we try to follow each other's wishes. I will respect your privacy, and you shall respect mine."

"All right. But I have to call you something, you know. I'll just call you Sarah, and you can call me Adam. As long as we're to be business partners and live in the same cabin, for the time being, as you said, we might as well be on a first-name basis. As for privacy, I wouldn't dream of disturbing your privacy," he mockingly agreed.

"Very well," she replied seriously as she finished her tasks and headed for the doorway. "I'll say good-night to you now. By the way," she remembered to ask as she started to leave the room, "are you going to start work on my wells tomorrow?"

"Aye. I told you I'd start on them as soon as I could. We'll go over to your uncle's place in the morning and see if we can at least get that one good well producing again. Then, sometime within the next week or so, I'll see about those other wells. It may be slow going for a while, but it will be all we can handle, working those extra wells plus my own," he explained.

"I want to go with you then, for I wish to learn all I can about the oil industry here. If I am to remain very long at all, I must know precisely what is taking place."

"The oil fields and derrick floors are no place for a woman!" Adam informed her decisively.

"Nevertheless, I will be going with you in the morning. They are my wells now, Mr. MacShane, and I intend to be there when you work them, whether you approve or not. Part of our bargain was that I would maintain complete freedom of both myself and my properties, is that not correct? You have absolutely no right to keep me from going!" she insisted, facing him with the light of battle in her opal eyes.

"I am the one who's in charge of working those wells, and I will not have you getting in the way! It's going to be hard enough for the men to see you around here without your 'person' distracting them as they try to do their work. You will not go, and that is final! Now, good night," Adam ground out as he swept past her and stalked from the room with a long stride. Before he entered his bedroom, Sarah heard him call out, "And I told you to call me Adam!" He angrily closed his bedroom door with more force than was necessary.

Sarah's face registered astonishment at his outburst of temper. He had seemed so even-tempered, even good-natured. But then, she reminded herself, he was capable of practically anything, and he was most definitely not to be trusted. He had broken his word to her once; he might do so again. Besides that, she realized that she hardly knew the man at all.

Well, she still intended to go along with him in the morning, and she would do just that, no matter how much he stormed at her! He was behaving like a possessive husband, she complained silently, and not as a business partner.

Leaving the kitchen, she blew out all of the lamps and entered her own bedroom, shutting the door and drawing the bolt after her. She quickly undressed and donned a white lawn nightgown, then sank down on the bed and began to methodically brush her silky tresses. She was feeling rather drained and exhausted from the events of the day, and she decided to cut short her usual one hundred strokes with the hairbrush. She climbed beneath the cool sheets of the bed, and it didn't take long for her to slip into a blissful sleep, unaware that her new husband and business partner was wide awake in the room directly opposite hers.

Adam cursed his damnable temper once more as he lay upon the bed, his muscular arms crossed beneath his head on the pillow. He had always secretly prided himself on his iron control, and he felt quite perplexed that Sarah was able to affect him so strongly. He didn't know why he had reacted that way to her earlier, but he knew that he was right, that she had no business around the oil derricks or the rough men who worked them. Heaving a restless, dissatisfied sigh, he abruptly turned on his side and pounded the softness of the unresisting pillow as he tried in vain to get comfortable.

Sarah was awakened by the soft rays of early-morning sunlight streaming through her window. She jumped out of bed, quickly performed her morning toilette, and dressed in a simple muslin blouse and matching skirt, thankful that the gathered skirt had only a hint of a bustle. She hurriedly piled up her thick hair and opened the door of her bedroom, feeling very refreshed from her night's rest and ready to meet the events of the new day.

Peering quickly inside Adam's room, she ascertained that he had already dressed and gone out, apparently without bothering with breakfast. She opened the front door of the cabin and stepped outside, breathing deeply of the fresh, fragrant spring air of the Texas countryside. Adam and several other men were visible in the near distance, where they were loading some sort of equipment onto a wagon.

Sarah smiled to herself in satisfaction, pleased that she was indeed in time. She saw that the horse had already been hitched to the wagon, evidently waiting for Adam. She quickly climbed up onto the seat and settled her skirts about her, steeling herself for the confrontation that she knew to be inevitable.

Less than ten minutes later, Adam left his workers and strode toward the cabin, his handsome face registering both surprise and stern disapproval as he discovered Sarah waiting for him on the wagon seat. He strove to maintain control over his temper and said, "I told you that the derrick floor is no place for a woman. Besides that, I don't want you around the men. Now stop this foolishness and stay here."

"I informed you last night that I intend to go along and see how the procedure is carried out, to learn all I can. I give you my solemn word that I will not be in your way, that I will certainly not seek to 'distract' the workers in any way whatsoever," Sarah remarked defiantly, a touch of sarcasm creeping into her voice.

"Sarah, I am normally a patient, rather easygoing man, but I do not like to be crossed, especially in matters such as this one. Now, I have already told you that you cannot go along. It's no place for a woman, damn it!" Adam repeated, his eyes flashing his displeasure at her stubbornness.

"Mr. MacShane," she replied politely, "we agreed that these wells are my responsibility, even though you are to be the one to see that they are worked. Therefore, I wish and need to learn how they are worked. It is that simple. I do not like to be kept in ignorance of something that involves me. I cannot learn if I am not allowed to observe things for myself. Also, you have no right to command me, no right at all. I am still an independent woman, and I remind you that you have no right to treat me as a true wife!"

"Sarah . . ." he began with an ominous frown, only to be interrupted by her.

"Not so loud, dear husband. Your employees are nearly upon us, and you surely do not wish to engage in a dramatic, angry little scene before their curious eyes, do you?" Sarah commented with a triumphant little smirk.

Adam jerked his head about to find that the men had indeed driven in their direction and were well within hearing distance now. He saw that their faces were curious and interested, and also that they were eyeing Sarah with something more than mere curiosity. They all knew that he had been married the day before, and he certainly didn't want them to think that anything was already amiss between himself and his new bride. He realized that he had too much pride. His lips tightened in a grim line as he climbed up beside Sarah and grabbed the reins.

"All right," he spoke through clenched teeth, his voice low, "I don't suppose I can force you to stay here, short of keeping you here myself. I'll talk to you about this later, Sarah." He slapped the reins and guided the horse down the road at a brisk pace, the workers following closely behind in the other wagon.

"Aren't you going to introduce me to the workers?" Sarah asked innocently as they rode along the rutted dirt road.

"No."

"Why not? They are working for me, also, in a sense."

"They'll keep their distance better if you keep yours, that's why. Most of them are all right, I guess, but you never really know. These aren't the same kind of men you're used to back in Philadelphia. These are the same kind of men you saw at the saloon the other day, remember? Anyway, they'll all feel the same way I do, I can tell you right now, that a woman has no place around an oil field."

"Why should they, or you, resent my being there simply because I am a female? That makes no sense at all!" she protested indignantly. "It is because of such an arrogant, nonsensical attitude that there is such a dire need for the suffragette movement! How else will we ever receive the recognition we deserve as fellow human beings?"

"You take that suffragette stuff pretty seriously, don't you?" Adam asked with an amused twinkle in his eye.

"It is not 'stuff' as you call it! I think it's about time you realized that I refuse to be treated as a child, Mr. MacShane! I insist upon taking an active part in my business ventures!"

"You know something, Sarah Bradford MacShane? You're very beautiful when you're angry, very beautiful indeed!" he told her with an unabashed grin.

"And you are quite maddening!" she retorted with spirit. "I do not wish to be treated differently by you. I want you to treat me as you would any other business partner, do you understand? Do not think of me as a woman at all!"

"That will be very difficult, I'm afraid," Adam remarked, endeavoring to keep a straight face as he answered her.

Sarah narrowed her eyes in anger, then turned away from him. She fell silent for the remainder of the ride.

She stole a quick glance back at the men in the wagon one time. There were half a dozen of them, all appearing to be rather young. They were dressed in the rough, grimy clothes that she had already noticed the men in the town wearing. She received an uncomfortable shock as she perceived that they were staring at her with avid interest. She quickly averted her head and faced forward once more.

They finally pulled up beside the derrick that was situated the closest to her uncle's cabin. She stiffly allowed Adam to assist her in climbing down from the wagon, still refusing to meet his gaze. She watched the movements of the men as she remained next to the wagon.

"We'll get that one well producing again. We'll have to replace the sucker rods and all. I guess I'd best explain to you now what we'll be doing since I won't have the time to explain everything in detail to you once we get started," Adam grudgingly offered as he stood beside her.

"We'll simply pull the sucker rods out of the hole, replace the parted rods, and run them back in the hole. It will be a tedious process, though, to say the least. Then we'll get the pump going again and make sure everything's all right."

"That sounds very simple to me," Sarah commented glancing upward at his face now.

"Well, it isn't. You'll soon see that it's a very time-consuming task. You're going to get awfully tired of sitting out here watching us all day, especially once the sun rises high in the sky."

"I told you that I won't get in your way, so you needn't bother about me at all," she replied cooly.

"Have it your way then," he said with a mocking grin before striding away to give the other men a hand with the equipment.

Sarah discovered a huge log lying on the ground and made herself as comfortable as possible upon it, adjusting her bonnet slightly in order to shade her eyes from the glaring sun. She watched as Adam and the other men proceeded with the job he had described.

First of all, one of the men climbed to the top of the wooden derrick with a coil of rope in his hand. He fed the rope over a big spool at the very top of the structure, so that the end of it stretched down to the derrick floor, where another man began to weave it through a pulley. Then another worker climbed to the top of the derrick with the end of the rope, and the entire process was repeated twice more.

The last time the end of the rope dropped to the derrick floor, it was attached to a big drum. Another worker started the steam engine operating, several gears began to turn, and the large drum began to rotate, winding the thick rope onto it. After about six or seven turns, one of the workers tied off the other end of the rope to one of the derrick's legs.

Sarah watched the procedure with interest, noting that Adam not only supervised the other men but did just as much work as they did. The first part of their job had taken nearly three hours in all, and she was beginning to grow very weary of sitting on the rough surface of the log. She stood and strolled a bit closer to the derrick, then took a seat upon the grass, adjusting her skirts modestly about her legs and ankles. She removed her bonnet and fastened her gaze once more on the activity.

The men now took the iron structure, which she perceived to be some sort of large valve, off the top of the well. They used a rope loop to grab the top of the wooden rods, which she knew to be the sucker rods from the way Adam had spoken, and began to raise them out of the hole by once again turning the large drum. After they had pulled the rods out of the hole, encountering only a slight difficulty now and then, they set about the task of replacing the one that was broken. It was a lengthy process, just as Adam warned, and she realized that the men must be getting quite tired by now.

Adam called a halt to the procedure sometime after high noon. The men filtered back to their wagon and began to eat the lunches they had brought along with them. Adam found Sarah waiting for him at the wagon.

"Surely you aren't finished yet?" she inquired as he graciously handed her part of his own lunch. She nibbled at the piece of meat without much appetite.

"No, not even close. We've been working for about six hours now, I'd say, and it's likely to take three or four more. Are you getting tired of watching?" he asked as he took a long drink from the water jug he had brought along.

"I'm fine, thank you," Sarah replied stiffly, not wishing to reveal to him how weary she was becoming, sitting out in the hot sun for so long, trying to get comfortable while sitting on the hard ground.

After the men had quickly downed their lunches, they went back to work once more. It took them some time to replace the broken sucker rod, but it was finally accomplished. The sucker rods were run back in the hole, the ropes were removed, and the structure was replaced on the top of the well. The steam engine was started up once again, and the big iron bar over the top of the well began to rock up and down, just like a rocking-horse, Sarah thought.

At this point, Adam left his men and approached Sarah, where she was now sitting in the wagon, having tired of fighting off the various insects that inhabited the grass in great numbers.

"Well, what did you think of all of it?" he asked with a lazy smile, his face smudged and dirty, his brow glistening with sweat from his day's labors.

"I found it very interesting. I told you that I desired to know all I could about it, and it was quite instructive. I have a few questions I would like to ask, but I will wait until later for that, I suppose. Are we ready to go back to the cabin now?"

"Aye, everything seems to be going pretty well now. We'll start loading things up."

"How soon will it be before I begin realizing a profit from this particular well?" Sarah suddenly asked as she glanced toward the pumping unit that was noisily operating on the derrick floor.

"It won't be long. The oil that's pumped to the surface will be carried through the line to that tank over there," he explained, pointing to a large wooden tank nearly a hundred feet away. "From there, it will be sold as soon as possible. You ought to receive some income within the next week or so, I suppose."

"Good. Then, if my uncle's partner does decide to return, I will have all the accounts in order for his inspection. This is the first step in fulfilling my uncle's dreams," Sarah remarked with a sad little smile, her gaze riveted upon the derrick. It seemed as if she had completely forgotten Adam's presence beside her.

"I suppose we all have our dreams, Sarah. But we can't always count on someone else to fulfill them. I'm not so sure your uncle would have wanted this, your coming all the way out here and getting involved in something you know nothing about, something that could be very dangerous for you," Adam replied seriously, his own gaze fastened on her beautiful, pensive face. He lost himself in his own thoughts before suddenly drawing himself out of his silent reverie and briskly clearing his throat. "We'll go on back now. The others can get the equipment."

He climbed up beside Sarah and took a firm grip on the reins. Sarah remained silent as they began to move away from the derrick, unaware that Adam's thoughts were still wholly occupied with her.

Chapter Seven

"You go on inside. I'm going down to the creek and get a bath before dinner," Adam told Sarah as he helped her down from the wagon.

"Don't you have a bathtub? I was hoping for a bath myself," she replied, wrinkling her nose at her own dusty appearance.

"Well, we always bathe down at the creek, but there is a bathtub in back of the cabin. I'll be glad to bring it inside for you as soon as I get back. Come to think of it, Sarah," he said with an amused grin, "it wouldn't do for you to take a bath at the creek, not with all the men around here. I'd more than have my hands full fighting them away!"

"Thank you," Sarah responded stiffly, ignoring his amusement. "I'll go ahead and begin dinner while you're gone." She walked inside the cabin and removed her bonnet. Entering her bedroom, she studied her reflection in the mirror hanging above the washstand.

Why, I look a fright! she thought to herself in dismay. Her hair was tangled and falling down out of its pins, her clothes were wrinkled and dirty, and, worst of all, she detected a faint line of freckles across the bridge of her proud little nose!

Sighing heavily with displeasure, she marched into the kitchen and began preparing the food for the evening meal. Some time later, she heard Adam returning from the creek, and she turned about at the sound of his voice in the doorway.

"I feel much better already. There's nothing like a cool bath after a hot day's work. Of course, the days aren't nearly as hot as they're going to be before too much longer. I'm afraid you may find our Texas weather a bit difficult to take. You know something, Sarah?" he suddenly remarked, staring at her face as she carried the food to the table. "You're beginning to get some healthy color to your skin, aren't you?"

"I do not consider a sunburn and freckles to be a sign of health!" she retorted with a frown.

Adam suppressed another smile, and the two of them sat down to dinner. Sarah began to ply him with questions about the work he and his men had done that day, and he answered her patiently, in between bites of his food. Throughout the meal, there seemed to exist an easier relationship between them, and they both relaxed a bit as they carried on a lively conversation. After dinner, Adam stood to his feet and announced, "That was another delicious meal, Mrs. Mac . . . I mean, Sarah. Now, I'll go get that tub for you. Far be it for a gentleman to say so, but you do look as if you could do with a bit of cleaning yourself," he ruefully commented with a chuckle as he glanced downward at her.

Sarah bristled beneath his gaze, but she swallowed the angry retort that rose to her lips. She cleared the table as Adam carried the old wooden bathtub into her bedroom, setting it down with a clatter. She began heating water in a large kettle on the stove, then carried a bucket full of cooler water in each hand as she approached her room. Adam insisted on taking the buckets from her, saying, "I'll do that. You just sit down and relax a bit. I'll see to the water on the stove, too."

"Thank you," she replied politely, even mustering a slight smile. She entered her room and sat upon the bed. Removing the pins from her hair, she shook her head and allowed her shining curls to fall in a shower of disarray about her shoulders. Then, twisting its mass into a single long coil, she once more pinned it securely atop her head. She sat on the bed and waited until Adam had filled the tub almost to the rim with the steaming water.

"There, that ought to do it. If there's anything else you need, let me know," he offered, smiling before leaving the room and closing the door after him.

Sarah waited until she could hear him leaving the cabin, then jumped up from the bed and hastily began to undress. She unbuttoned her muslin blouse and slipped it off her shoulders, frowning in distaste as she viewed its soiled condition. Next came her skirt, which she placed with the blouse on the floor next to the tub. Removing her petticoats, corset, chemise, and drawers, she stood completely naked. She slowly began to ease her tired body into the tub of water.

She felt her muscles relaxing with the soothing effect of the water's warmth, and she took up the cake of soap that Adam had left for her. She frowned as she discovered that it was very harsh and lacked any fragrance, but it would have to do. She vigorously soaped herself from her neck to her toes, then leaned back against the edge of the tub to soak a while, her body pink and clean once more.

Adam, meanwhile, had strolled outside to breathe deeply of the cool night air. Actually, he admitted to himself with reluctance, he didn't want to remain in the cabin while Sarah was taking a bath. It was all he could do to control his growing desire for her without having to listen to the noises of her splashing in the tub. Just the mere thought of this nearly drove him to distraction!

He knew that he was already confused about her as it was. He knew that he felt more for her than a casual interest. Face up to it, he commanded himself sharply, you appear to be falling in love with the young lady. You've done nothing but think of her since that first day you rescued her from Swenson's clutches. She had looked so young and tiny and so very beautiful.

He had never truly been in love before, had never even met a woman he had wanted to make his wife and the mother of his children. He only knew that he couldn't get Sarah out of his mind, that she appeared to have crept unbidden into his heart as well.

What a mess! he thought to himself in exasperation. Here he was, falling head over heels in love with his business partner, a young woman he had supposedly married for purely business reasons, a young woman who apparently cared nothing for him in return.

Back in the cabin, Sarah decided that it was time for her to finish her bath and get out of the water. Her skin was beginning to wrinkle because she had been content to soak for so long. She turned her head and reached for the towel she had placed on her bed beside the tub.

Her eyes suddenly widened in shock and fright as she spotted the tiny field mouse that entered her bedroom through a small hole in the outer wall. She stared at it, speechless for a moment, watching as it crept closer to where she sat perfectly immobile in the tub of water. She finally jumped to her feet and emitted a terrified shriek, frightening the poor creature back across the floor and sending it scurrying back through the hole in the wall of the cabin.

Adam, of course, couldn't help but hear her screams, and he flew inside the cabin and burst through her bedroom door, which she had forgotten to bolt, startling her even further. She stared at him in horror as his eyes quickly swept the room for any visible signs of danger, before alighting upon her. She was still standing upright in the tub, water dripping unceremoniously from her naked body, her opal eyes as big as saucers. Adam blinked quite rapidly, unable to believe his eyes as he stared at her in a daze.

He quickly took in the sight of her glistening wet body. Her full, pink-tipped breasts, her small waist, her rounded hips, her slender white legs. His eyes traveled once more to her face, upon which was transfixed a totally outraged expression.

"Get out of here!" she recovered her voice enough to shout. She swiftly made a grab for the towel and attempted to cover her nudity, but the damage had been done. Everything had occurred so quickly, she hardly knew what was happening when Adam muttered a curse and strode toward her, catching her about the waist and lifting her bodily from the tub of water.

"What do you think you're doing? How dare you! Get out of here at once!" she screamed in outrage, pummelling his broad chest with her clenched fists. He ignored her frantic cries, his face suddenly appearing very determined and dangerous to her frightened eyes, his expression unfathomable, his eyes glowing with a strange light.

"Sarah," he murmured softly before bringing his warm lips crashing down upon her own. He held her tightly against the hardness of his muscular body as his lips assaulted hers.

Sarah felt as if she were drowning, and she ceased her efforts to free herself as a totally unfamiliar sensation washed over her. She felt herself surrendering against him, felt her soft lips opening beneath his, felt her own breath quicken and her senses stir. She had never been kissed before, and she found the experience overwhelming, overpowering. Before she realized it, she discovered that she had dropped the towel and stood completely naked in Adam's embrace, his passionate kisses and fiery caresses rendering her momentarily helpless.

His strong, hard hands were now roaming freely over her soft, womanly curves, and she gasped aloud at the wondrous sensations he was creating within her. She thought to herself that she must be quite demented to allow him such freedom with her body, but she couldn't muster the energy nor the will to stop him. She opened her eyes wide as his lips traveled downward from her slender neck to her white shoulders, and lower to her creamy breasts. She suddenly appeared to awaken from some sort of trance and began to squirm and struggle in earnest once more, pushing him away from her with all her might.

"How dare you!" she spluttered, her face burning beneath his intense gaze. "Get out of here! I will never forgive you for taking advantage of me in such a shocking manner! You are thoroughly despicable, Mr. MacShane!" she stormed at him, her eyes blazing as she sought to wrap the towel about her once more. She held it firmly in place with both of her hands, her whole body shaking from the effect of their passionate encounter.

"Took advantage of you? Don't lie to me, Sarah! You wanted it as much as I did! Oh, maybe I took you by surprise at first, but you soon warmed to my attentions, admit it! You must know how I feel about you!" Adam spoke through tightly clenched teeth. He was nearly beyond control now, seeing her standing there before him, still with only a thin towel to cover her gloriously beautiful body. Just how much could a man of flesh and blood endure? he asked himself. He wanted her, he wanted her more than he had ever wanted a woman before.

"That is a lie! You took advantage of me, you forced yourself upon me! You care nothing about me, you care only about your vile lust! Rest assured that I will not give you the opportunity to do this again! I should have known that you meant to break your word on this part of our bargain as well! Men are all the same, they think of only one thing where a woman is concerned. I thought that you might be different from the others, but I was mistaken! You married me under false pretenses, you purposely deceived me!" she lashed out at him, seething with both anger and humiliation, her eyes glazing contemptuously as she faced him.

"For your information, Mrs. MacShane," Adam ground out the words, "you screamed, remember? I came flying in here to rescue you from God only knows what! I had no dishonorable intentions toward you when we struck our marriage bargain! You can either believe that or not; I don't give a damn what you think! If you'll ever allow yourself to emerge from that hard, protective little shell you've built around yourself, you'll discover that men are not all alike, that we're all quite different. Just as women are different!"

"Get out of here!" she demanded once again, refusing to listen to him, enraged at both herself and him. She suddenly raised her hand and dealt him a stinging blow across his sun-browned cheek, startling both of them with her unexpected action. She glared at him in anticipation, feeling a small twinge of fear as she viewed his savage expression.

She had never seen him looking so dangerous before. She vaguely wondered in the back of her mind how she could ever have believed him to be so easygoing and good-natured. Why, he appeared positively brutal now!

"Don't ever do that again, Sarah," he said in a low, even tone, his face impassive now, his eyes suffused with a dull light. His own hand suddenly shot out and grabbed a handful of her shining black curls. He roughly forced her face upward toward his own and proceeded to kiss her with a bruising, controlled passion before sending her toppling backward. He watched as she landed safely in the tub of water, sending the liquid splashing everywhere. He then abruptly turned upon his booted heels and stalked from the room, slamming the door behind him.

"Oh!" Sarah exclaimed, angrier than she had ever been in her entire life. She was sprawled in the tub, still dazed by the astonishing incident. She finally climbed from the luke-warm water, tears starting to her eyes as she gingerly ran a hand across her rounded bottom, still smarting from where she had landed in the hard tub. She grasped the dripping towel and threw it on the floor with a vengeance, then donned the dressing gown that was lying on the other side of the bed. She plopped down upon the bed and stared toward the doorway.

She had never been treated so shamelessly before! She was absolutely mortified that Adam had seen her naked, that he had forced his lustful kisses upon her unwilling lips. She refused to admit that her lips had been anything but unwilling throughout the whole scene. She should have known, she chided herself in fury, she should have known that Adam MacShane was no different from the other wild ruffians she had so far encountered in this savage, uncivilized place! And to think that she was actually married to the disgraceful scoundrel!

But no, she decided calmly as she forced herself to consider the situation in a more rational manner. I will see to it that the problem is remedied, that the annulment is taken care of sooner than the six months Mr. MacShane originally planned. She would wash her hands of their so-called marriage for business purposes, and she would never see him again!

Adam, meanwhile, had stormed back outside and several hundred yards away from the cabin. He finally took a seat on a tree stump and looked upward toward the star-filled night sky.

He was still seething with anger, berating himself that he had lost control once again. He had gone temporarily mad when he had burst into her room and seen her standing there in all her glory, stark-naked as the day she was born, her beautiful curves so aptly revealed to him. His desire had overpowered both his control and his good judgment; he had acted on impulse instead of thought. He could still recall the feel of her warm, soft body against his own hardness, of her parted lips beneath his. He knew that he could never be satisfied to let her go.

For he now realized that his earlier suspicions were true, that he was in love with her. He supposed he had seen it coming since that first day, that things had merely been building since then. He loved her; he had never truly loved before, and he knew that she was the one woman meant for him.

He firmly believed that she had not been immune to any feelings of desire herself. Oh no, he thought to himself with a tight little smile, you may be virginal and inexperienced in the ways of love, dearest Sarah, but you felt it, too. There is a hidden fire lying just beneath the surface of that proper, maidenly exterior.

I will win her, he vowed silently to himself as he glanced back at the cabin, his mouth set in a line of grim determination. I will make her love me as well. I will force her to see that we belong together, to each other. I'll be damned if I'll ever let her go now. She is mine.

He stood to his feet and continued on his way toward the creek. There, he would think things over; he would formulate his plan. No matter what, Sarah, he thought as he stole another glance at the cabin, this marriage will never be annulled!

Chapter Eight

Following a restless night, Sarah rose from her bed the next morning and flung her dressing gown about her shoulders. She crept stealthily across the bare floor toward Adam's room, satisfied when she perceived that he had already gone for the day. She then flew back to her own room and dressed quickly, packed all of her belongings in her valise, and carried it outside.

She hitched the horse to the wagon, grateful that the man at the livery stable had been kind enough to show her how, and climbed up onto the seat, placing the valise beside her. She took a frim grip on the reins, gently flicking them as she glanced about once more to make certain she was leaving unobserved.

Guiding the horse toward the well-traveled dirt road, she stole one last look at the cabin, convinced that she would never see it again. She had made her plans late last night, once she had been able to think rationally again about the entire situation.

She had heard Adam's footsteps as he had come back inside the cabin last night, pausing briefly outside her door. She had lain nearly breathless, breathing a long sigh of relief as she had heard him enter his own room and softly shut the door.

She realized that she could not seek an annulment, not just yet. Not until her wells were worked and producing successfully. She also knew that she could not leave and return to Philadelphia until she had discovered the truth about her uncle's death, something that was apparently not likely to happen until her uncle's mysterious partner chose to return. Until then, she simply could not abandon her efforts to fulfill her uncle's dreams, her own wish to learn precisely how and why he had died, why she had received that terse little note.

Driving at a brisk pace now, she passed several men on horseback. A few of them stared curiously at her, some called friendly greetings, still others yelled something entirely different. She proudly lifted her chin and coldly ignored them all, taking comfort whenever she fingered the small pistol that she had concealed in the pocket of her heavy cotton skirt. She was certainly in no mood for anyone to accost her today!

Arriving in town, she drew the wagon to a halt in front of Mrs. Patterson's house and jumped down to secure the reins to the hitching post. She quickly climbed the front steps and knocked firmly upon the heavy door, which swung open to reveal Mrs. Patterson, her jovial face registering both pleasure and surprise at Sarah's appearance on her doorstep.

"Why, Sarah! It's mighty nice to see you! Come on in here right this minute. I ain't had a chance to congratulate you on your marriage yet. You sure enough took us all by surprise when we heard about you getting hitched to Adam MacShane!"

"Oh, so the news has already been spread about,"

Sarah remarked with a frown of displeasure. "Mrs. Patterson, I really must speak with you at once." She followed the older woman inside the house and into the front parlor, where she took a seat on the well-worn sofa and waited until her hostess seated herself in the wing chair opposite her.

"Now, I'm so glad you stopped by, Sarah!" Mrs. Patterson repeated. "I got to say, though, you look kind of upset about something, if you don't mind my saying so. Don't tell me you and Adam have already gone and had your first little spat?" she asked with a broad wink and an accompanying chuckle.

"No, it isn't like that at all. I'm afraid you would find it difficult to understand. Mr. MacShane and I were indeed married the other day, but, well, that is . . ." She broke off, searching for adequate words. She didn't particularly wish to reveal the entire truth of the situation, but she couldn't see any way around it; she couldn't think of any other believable explanation.

"Oh now, you don't have to go and explain nothing to me! Why, I know how a girl can be plumb swept right off her feet in just a few days! It don't bother no one about you two getting hitched so fast and all. This ain't Philadelphia, you know. Things like that are kind of expected in a town like this. Why, most any unmarried gal out here gets snapped up in a big hurry! It did come as kind of a surprise to me, though, it being Adam you married. I kind of thought he and my Clem were . . . well, you know what I mean. It don't matter none now, though. I guess there's just no telling what's on a man's mind when he's in love," she rattled on companionably, oblivious to the fact that Sarah was becoming restless and a bit impatient.

"Mrs. Patterson," Sarah suddenly interrupted, "I do not wish to appear rude, but I came to inquire if you would perhaps have a room available for me. It's very imperative that I locate other accommodations for myself as soon as possible," she said in a rush, then flushed uncomfortably as she realized what the other woman must be thinking.

"So, you and Adam did have a lover's spat, didn't you?" Emma Patterson responded in a knowing tone of voice. "Sarah, let me give you some good advice. This here won't help things none. You've got to go on back and make up with him. It won't do you no earthly good to run away like this. Why, child, you've just been married! You ain't given things enough time yet. Whatever it is he's done, you just got to give him the chance to make it up to you."

"No, you don't understand!" Sarah exclaimed in growing exasperation, then immediately regretted her outburst. She took another deep breath and continued, "You see, we did not marry for the usual reasons, the reasons you are understandably implying. We married for business purposes, a sort of business arrangement between the two of us. There is absolutely no emotion involved."

"Business arrangement? What on earth are you talking about?" the older woman asked in bewilderment.

"I can see that I shall have to tell you the truth," Sarah replied with a heavy sigh. "Adam and I simply needed each other for financial reasons, and nothing more. He needed a wife in order to inherit a large fortune left to him by his grandfather in Scotland; I needed someone to see to it that my uncle's oil wells were worked. We struck a bargain for those reasons. I agreed to it because it was understood that there was to be absolutely nothing personal about our relationship. In six months' time, or less, Adam was to file for an annulment of our marriage. However," she said, her face tightening, "things have drastically changed. It appears that Mr. MacShane is not the sort of man I believed him to be."

"But you two are legally hitched, ain't you?" Mrs. Patterson asked, still appearing confused.

"Yes, but not for long. As I told you, the marriage was to be annulled as soon as Adam received his inheritance, and as soon as I completed my business here. I was to return to Philadelphia whenever I wished after that, and leave all of the necessary arrangements to him. But Mr. MacShane is not an honorable gentleman. In fact, he is no gentleman at all!" she stated with emphasis.

"Sarah, I know that ain't true!" the other woman disagreed with equal emphasis. "Adam MacShane is one of the finest young men I've ever met. If he did marry you for the reasons you just said, I'm sure he meant to keep his part of the bargain. Why, I was always hoping he and my Clem would make a go of it. I would have been mighty proud to have him as my son-in-law. From what you've just told me I can't for the life of me understand why he didn't just go ahead and ask Clem to marry him if he needed a wife so much. He's known her for nigh on to a year now. Maybe there's more to his asking you to marry him than you think," she suggested at a sudden thought.

"No, there was no other reason," Sarah firmly denied. "But all of that does not matter now. The thing is, I need a place to stay for a while. At least until my uncle's partner returns and I can acquire certain facts. Would you please help me?" she entreated.

"Well," Emma Patterson hesitated, "I don't want to go and get involved in your private affairs with Adam. I don't know what's happened between you two, but I guess it ain't really none of my business. Like I told you, he's a right good man, and I know that what's happened must just be some kind of misunderstanding or something. But I'm sorry to say that I don't have any rooms to let right now. Why, there's more folks pouring into this town every day!"

"I know that, but couldn't you find a room for me somehow?"

"Well, I guess you can share a room with Clem again, if she don't mind. I don't think she'll be too all-fired happy about that, though, seeing as how you married the man she'd set her sights on and all. And I know that's just how she thought of Adam MacShane, that he was going to be her man."

"I'm sorry if your daughter was hurt. However, you can see that it really has nothing to do with me. As I stated, I only married Adam for business purposes, because he didn't feel that he was quite ready to make a total committment to anyone just yet, and because we knew that our marriage was not really a marriage at all. I will remain in Wildcat City until certain matters are resolved, at which time I will return to my home in Philadelphia and have nothing more to do with the man! I would leave now if the situation only permitted," Sarah remarked with a frown as she recalled the humiliation of the night before.

"Well, I don't guess it'll hurt none to ask Clem if you can bunk in with her again. I still wish you'd go on back and see if you can work things out with your husband, Sarah. Business arrangement or not, you're still his wife and you have a duty to him," Mrs. Patterson commented decisively as she rose to her feet. She and Sarah were both surprised when they heard a voice from the direction of the front doorway.

"I knew Adam MacShane didn't marry you because he was in love with you!" Clementine uttered in triumph as she rounded the corner and swept inside the parlor. Her mother warned her with a stern look to remain silent, but Clem ignored her.

"I knew that Adam wouldn't marry you so sudden-like unless there was a good reason for it. I figured that you had tricked him into marriage somehow! Well, it's even better than I thought. Now he'll be free again, and I don't intend to let him slip through my fingers a second time!" she vowed with a determined smirk in Sarah's direction.

"Clementine Patterson, that ain't no way to behave toward a visitor," her mother reprimanded her sharply.

"Stay out of this, Ma! This is between me and her, and I think it'd be best if you just left us alone to have it out between us!"

"There is nothing to 'have out.' You have apparently been eavesdropping on a private conversation between your mother and myself. None of this is any of your concern," Sarah said as she rose to her feet abruptly and turned her most forbidding schoolteacher look upon Clem.

"Oh, but it is my concern! Now, Ma, leave us alone for a while," Clementine repeated, her eyes shooting sparks as she faced Sarah.

"Very well, Mrs. Patterson," Sarah suddenly agreed, smiling toward the older woman in a polite manner, "I will hear what your daughter has to say. I appreciate both your advice and your time."

"I'm only sorry I couldn't have helped you out more, Sarah. I still hope you'll take my advice and go on back to your husband," Emma Patterson responded with a heavy sigh as she took her daughter's suggestion and left the room. She realized that it really would be best if those two young women cleared the air once and for all.

Clementine stiffly walked across the room and sank into the chair her mother had just vacated. Sarah sat back down upon the sofa and primly folded her hands in her lap, waiting for the other woman to speak. She certainly didn't relish the prospect of doing verbal battle with this jealous, immature young woman, but she knew that it would appear cowardly if she refused. And cowardice was something she thoroughly deplored in anyone!

"Here I was, thinking you had gotten Adam to marry you because of some underhanded female trick, and all along it was nothing more than a business deal between you two. I can't for the life of me understand how he got a prissy little thing like you to go along with it, though. Maybe it was because you really did want him for yourself all along!" she accused Sarah, her eyes flashing fire.

"For your information, I had personal reasons of my own for agreeing to this incredible scheme, but they are none of your business! I never had any designs toward 'your Adam,' and I will be only too happy when our marriage is annulled! Then you may try and ensnare him for yourself!" Sarah angrily declared, rising to her feet now, despite her resolution to remain calm and collected. She didn't know why she was allowing this spiteful girl to affect her so strongly!

"Oh, I won't have to trap him the way you did!" Clem countered with a derisive laugh, also rising to her feet and striding to stand directly before Sarah now, towering above her. "He'll be glad to marry a real woman like me, after being married to a cold little snip like you!"

Sarah narrowed her blue eyes dangerously, clenching her teeth in order to control her mounting fury. She inwardly berated herself for allowing this young woman to infuriate her, but she could not seem to help it. She drew herself proudly, rigidly upright and turned and marched toward the front doorway, leaving a maliciously smiling Clementine behind. Before stepping across the threshold, however, she turned and said, "If Adam MacShane is so very attracted to you, Miss Patterson, would you please tell me why he didn't choose to marry you instead of me?" She smiled mockingly and stepped outside, softly closing the door behind her.

Oh, that hateful creature! Sarah fumed to herself as she climbed up on the wagon once more and slapped the reins. Adam MacShane deserved Clementine Patterson; they deserved each other!

Before she realized it, Sarah found herself driving back out toward Adam's cabin. She slowed the horse to a halt in the middle of the road and contemplated returning to town and trying to find accommodations elsewhere. But she realized that it would be just as hopeless as before. There were simply no rooms to be found in the boomtown. She would have to either continue living in Adam's cabin or move back to her uncle's old cabin. And that, she told herself angrily, was something she knew Adam MacShane would never allow! No, she was trapped in the present circumstances, at least until a solution somehow presented itself.

Heaving a dissatisfied sigh, she flicked the reins once more and drove straight back to the cabin. She jumped down, unhitched the horse, then turned him into the corral located at the side of the barn. Marching inside the cabin, she didn't even bother to look around and see if anyone else was about and had noticed her return. She went straight into her bedroom and slammed the door behind her, then threw herself down upon the bed.

Her beautiful face grew pensive as she reflected on the recent events. Clementine Patterson was absolutely the most infuriating young woman she had ever before encountered! She didn't know why she still allowed the mere thought of the girl to upset her so. Just the memory of her spiteful words was enough to make her angry all over again.

And the brief lecture she had received from Clem's mother on the duties of a wife to her husband was equally disturbing. What duty could she possibly owe a man who had lied to her and deceived her, who had married her for totally mercenary reasons and had then virtually attacked her?

Why am I even wasting my time dwelling on what happened? Sarah suddenly asked herself. She climbed up off the bed, straightened her crumpled skirts, and resolutely marched toward the kitchen. She realized that she was hungry, that she hadn't eaten since the night before. She might as well bake some bread. It would serve to fill her afternoon, as well as take her mind off her troubles.

When Adam returned that evening, he was both pleased and surprised to discover that Sarah was cooking dinner. He had expected her to be still fuming over last night. He slipped off his hat, hung it on a peg on the wall, and entered the kitchen, pausing briefly in the doorway in order to scrutinize his wife's figure with admiring eyes.

"I heard you took the wagon out today. Did you find whatever it was you wanted?" He knew good and well that she'd gone into town, and he also knew the reason why. He had expected her to do just that. No, dear Sarah, he thought to himself as he watched her beautiful face, you won't be able to leave me that easily.

"I had personal business in town today, and it is absolutely none of your affair," Sarah replied frostily, averting her eyes from his piercing gaze. "From now on, I would appreciate it if you would keep to yourself when we are together in your cabin, and I will most certainly do the same. I will continue to cook our meals, and to clean, but I am under no obligation to converse with you. In fact, I am under no obligation to do anything here, but I choose to remain occupied. We may be forced to live together for a period of time, but we will not interfere in each other's lives, is that clear?" She was surprised to find herself a bit breathless as she waited for his reply.

Adam's lips tightened in a thin line of anger at her words, but he kept tight control over his temper and answered casually, "If that's the way you want it. But don't tell me you can actually forget all about what happened between us last night. We're not exactly polite strangers any longer!"

"I cannot forget the degrading incident, unfortunately!" she replied irritably as she averted her flushed face once more. "However, I would prefer it if you never mentioned it again. Furthermore, Mr. MacShane, if you ever again try and force your disagreeable attentions on me, I will be forced to resort to violent measures of my own!" she threatened with as much bravado as she could muster. Inwardly, she found that she was a bit fearful as she viewed his narrowed eyes and stern expression.

"You won't forget it, lass, you can't. And neither can I. You must know how I feel about you now. I am sure that you feel something for me in return. I could tell last night; I could sense that there was something between us, something special. Last night wasn't an accident, you know. I believe that we were destined for each other. I don't think it was mere chance that you came here," he declared seriously, green eyes narrowing, gazing intensely into flashing blue ones.

"I am quite aware that you feel something for me," Sarah angrily retorted, her cheeks flushing pink beneath his intense gaze. "What you feel, however, is nothing more than animal lust. And that particular feeling has nothing whatsoever to do with destiny! Now, I would appreciate it if you would promise me that you will never so much as touch me again. Otherwise, I do not see how we can possibly continue with our business relationship."

"I'll make you no promises, lass," Adam replied a bit roughly, quickly crossing the few feet of space between them. He stood closely behind her, glancing down at her bent head as she busied herself with stirring the food in the pot upon the stove.

"No, there'll be no promises from me that I won't ever want you again, that I won't love you."

"What on earth does love have to do with this?" Sarah demanded indignantly, moving cautiously away from him toward the table.

"You'll learn someday, when you're good and ready, I suppose. Until then, there'll be no such promises between us. That's just the way it will have to be. I'll continue to fulfill my part of our agreement, just as you will fulfill your part." With that, he took a seat at the table, his stern and closed expression indicating that he was finished with the present discussion.

Sarah stiffly brought the food to the table and set the platters down with unnecessary force. She knew that it would be totally useless to try and talk to this impossible man any more that night!

After dinner, she entered her bedroom and shut the door, drawing the bolt with a purposeful, and rather defiant, air. She even went so far as to place the single chair in the room directly in front of the doorway.

If Adam MacShane had any intention of forcing himself upon her tonight, she would be forewarned! She withdrew the small pistol from her skirt pocket and placed it beneath her pillow as she prepared for bed. She had decided that such precautions would become a nightly ritual from now on!

Chapter Nine

During the next few days, Adam and Sarah spoke very little to each other beyond the merest civilities. Adam was absent from the cabin from early morning until late evening, during which time Sarah sought to keep herself occupied by either sewing or reading. She was, however, becoming quite bored with her inactivity, and it was with an inward sigh of relief that she heard Adam tell her at dinner one evening, "We're going over to shoot that other well of yours in the morning."

"I was wondering when you would find the time," she replied with more than a hint of sarcasm as she picked at the food on her plate. There had been a decidedly uneasy air between Adam and herself for the past few days, and it was beginning to wear upon her nerves.

"I told you once before that I have more than enough to do with my own wells, and that yours would have to be worked whenever the time permitted," Adam responded quietly. "Besides that, the shooter wasn't able to get around to us until now." He was getting damned sick and tired of Sarah's coolness toward him, and he was becoming impatient with waiting for things to improve. He had tried to give her time, time to realize that she didn't hate him at all, time to realize that she might possibly return his affections. But if something didn't happen to change things soon, well, he'd just have to see that this growing tension between them was broken in a manner of his own choosing!

"The shooter?"

"Yes, he's the man who uses the nitroglycerin to break up any tight formations at the bottom of the well. It's a risky business, but it usually works," Adam patiently explained as he took another bite of the beef stew Sarah had made.

"But that must be terribly dangerous, working with such a highly explosive substance!"

"Of course it's dangerous. There's always the possibility of an accident. The nitro may not have been mixed correctly, the shooter himself may not time things right, anything can happen."

"Well, I am certainly looking forward to seeing how it's done," Sarah remarked, her beautiful face alive with interest.

"You won't be seeing it," Adam responded curtly. "I won't have you in the way when that well is shot! I just told you how dangerous it is. It's definitely no place for you!"

"It most certainly is the place for me!" she countered indignantly. "Those are my wells now, remember? I have a perfect right to see to it that everything goes well whenever they are worked," she told him defiantly, her eyes flashing as she abruptly pushed back the bench, its legs scraping noisily on the bare wooden floor, and drew herself up to her full height.

"Sarah," Adam said with growing anger and impatience at her obstinance, "you will not come along, and that is final!" He rose to his feet, tossed his napkin to the table with a vengeance, then briskly strode from the room, leaving a furious and fuming Sarah behind him.

I will be there, Adam MacShane, and there is nothing you can do to prevent me! Sarah vowed silently as she glared resentfully toward his retreating back. She hastily began clearing the dishes from the table, not caring about the loud clatter she made as she dumped them into the kitchen sink.

The next morning, she blinked rapidly as she awoke to the bright, streaming rays of sunlight in her bedroom. She hurriedly climbed from beneath the covers of the bed and dressed in a white lawn blouse and dark-blue cotton skirt; then she twisted her long dark curls atop her head, securing them with pins. Throwing her bedroom door open, she quickened her steps and left the cabin, stepping outside into the freshness of the early-morning air.

They had already gone! she realized with dismay as she viewed the new wagon tracks leading away from the dusty road in front of the cabin. She quickly ascertained that the wagon she had rented was also missing, as well as all of the horses. Adam had apparently sought to make certain that she would not be able to follow!

Oh, that infuriating, impossible man! she stormed in silence as she gave way to the rising anger within her. Well, she absolutely refused to allow him to dominate her, to treat her as a child, to squelch her independence. She would not give in to his high-handed, overbearing ways!

Gaining control of her temper once more, her thoughts raced as she formed a plan. If there were no other means of transportation, she would simply have to walk! It was only a matter of a couple of miles, and she would gain great pleasure and satisfaction out of watching Adam's face when he caught sight of her!

Taking a deep, determined breath, she whirled about and began marching purposefully down the road. The walk wouldn't bother her, for she had walked everywhere back in Philadelphia. She still had the small pistol safely concealed in the pocket of her heavy cotton skirt in the event that she needed any protection. If she hurried, she would be able to reach the wells within the hour. Adam MacShane would then learn that Sarah Bradford was not the sort of female he had apparently reckoned upon!

Meanwhile, Adam and the other workers were watching as the man they referred to as the "shooter" approached the derrick floor. They watched as he placed his equipment on the ground and proceeded to carefully draw the container of nitroglycerin from its protective shell in a small wooden box generously padded with straw. He then took up a long can, which looked something like a stovepipe, and held it over the well. He opened the container of nitro and slowly filled the can. If he spilled so much as a tiny drop of the highly explosive mixture, there could be a fatal accident. So he took his time. Satisfied with the amount of the mixture he had poured into the can, he then began lowering the can into the well by using a small cable.

There was complete silence among the other men as they watched the shooter do his work. Any sudden movement or noise might cause his hands to shake and spill the nitro, or might even cause him to drop the can. The entire assembly breathed an audible sigh of relief as the can was safely placed at the bottom of the well and the cable hauled back up.

"You still sure you don't want me to go ahead and put another shot of it in there?" the man called to Adam, who was waiting with the others at a safe distance several yards away.

"I still think it will be enough, Cade," Adam answered confidently.

The man called Cade drew out a small bomb to be used as the detonator; the bomb was equipped with a watch mechanism. He set the timer, then lowered the bomb by cable to the bottom of the well. After the well had been properly loaded, he emptied several buckets of water down the well in order to keep the force of the explosion from shooting upward. Finally, he stood and wiped his brow, motioned toward Adam, and said, "That's it, MacShane. It's set to go off in two minutes."

"All right. Everyone, take cover!" Adam shouted. He nodded to Cade, then walked back toward one of the wagons to position himself for the blast. As he knelt down upon the ground, he suddenly jerked his head about as he heard someone approaching behind him.

"How dare you leave without me! I told you that I meant to come along! You had absolutely no right . . ." Sarah stormed at him, too intent upon venting her anger to realize what was taking place elsewhere.

"You little idiot!" Adam interrupted furiously, drawing himself upright in order to pull her down beside him behind the protection of the wagon. Before either of them had time to utter another word, there was a loud explosion. Adam instinctively pushed Sarah to the ground and threw his own body on top of hers, seeking to shield her from the debris that was now flying through the air.

In a matter of seconds, there was complete silence once more. Something had apparently gone wrong, and Adam slowly climbed to his feet, yanking a dazed and speechless Sarah up beside him.

"Stay here," he ground out as he turned away from her and strode quickly toward the derrick floor.

"Anyone hurt?" he called out as he glanced about.

The other men slowly appeared from behind their own cover and surveyed the surrounding destruction with shaking heads. Adam satisfied himself that all of his workers were at least relatively unharmed, then noticed that the shooter was lying unconscious a few yards away from the well. He had evidently not had time to seek sufficient cover for himself.

"Cade's hurt! Get me some water!" Adam instructed as he hurried to the man's side. He was still alive, though his pulse was weak and his breathing labored. There were several lacerations upon his face and hands; his clothing was torn and ragged, and his whole body was covered with a thick blanket of dust and dirt. Adam quickly ascertained that, though there were no outward signs of any serious injury, the man was hurt badly.

"How is he?" one of the workers asked as he brought the water.

"He's still alive, but we'll have to get him to the doctor right away. I think he's got a concussion, possibly some broken bones. Help me get him into the wagon."

"Sure thing, Mr. MacShane." The two of them called for some extra help, and the injured shooter was carefully carried to the wagon and placed in its bed. One of the workers sat in the back with Cade, while another one volunteered to drive the wagon to the doctor's house in town. As the wagon slowly pulled away from the sight, Sarah approached Adam and said, "Oh, Adam, do you think he'll live?"

"I told you to stay put," Adam growled as his eyes coldly appraised her. He had already satisfied himself that she was unharmed.

"I was concerned, if you don't mind!" she snapped in response. She took out her handkerchief, dipped it in a bucket of water, and bathed some of the caked dust from her face. Her clothes were rumpled and creased with dirt, her hair falling in a tangle about her shoulders.

Adam relented enough to assure her. "I think he'll live. It might be a while before he's able to work again, if ever," he said.

"What on earth went wrong?"

"It's hard to say right now. I guess he could have put too much of a charge into that bomb of his, or he could have mixed the nitro too strong, anything like that. We're all lucky we weren't blown to bits." He shook his head, then turned his attention to Sarah once more. "What in the hell are you doing here, anyway? How did you get here?"

"I walked! I wanted to observe the shooting of the well, my well, if I may remind you. You had no right to go off and leave me that way, without a wagon or even so much as a horse!" she fumed, brushing the hair away from her face as she wrung out the handkerchief and scrubbed even harder at her skin.

"I'll tend to you later," Adam said through clenched teeth. He turned and stalked away from her, turning his attention to his workers and the well. "All right, let's get this mess cleaned up and see what we've got," he said, forcing his thoughts away from Sarah. Damn the little fool! She could have been seriously injured, walking right into a blasting area that way. He could wring her little neck! But, he reminded himself, he'd have to tend to her later, just as he had told her. Right now, there was a lot of work to be done.

Sarah took a seat upon a rock and watched the activity as the men set about clearing away the debris and making any repairs that were necessary. She silently wondered whether or not the shooting of the well had been successful but decided against mentioning it to Adam just yet. After all, she had no desire to speak to him any further for the time being!

After working and overseeing the clean-up efforts of the men for nearly three hours, Adam finally put another worker in charge and approached Sarah where she still sat upon the rock. She had tried pinning her thick hair up and had shaken much of the dust from her clothing.

"Come on. I'm taking you home," Adam commanded.

"But it seems to me that you still have work to do here. Please don't leave early on my account," Sarah replied cooly, feeling a twinge of uneasiness as she realized that his gaze was riveted upon her face.

"I said I'm taking you home," he repeated sternly, his strong hand closing upon her arm and forcing her roughly to her feet. As she held back and began to protest at such treatment, he nearly dragged her to one of the wagons, where he then swept her easily off her feet and placed her none too gently upon the hard wooden seat. He climbed up beside her and took hold of the reins, and the wagon moved forward at a moderate pace, back down the road toward his cabin.

"You mean to tell me that you walked all this way? Don't you realize how foolish such an action was, to be out here in the middle of nowhere, alone and unprotected?" he chided her as they rode.

"It was no more foolish than your trying to see to it that I was unable to come at all!" she retorted with spirit. "Those are my wells, and I have every right to see what work is done on them. We've been through all of this before, and you're deliberately being rude and childish about the entire thing!"

"I left you behind at the cabin for your own safety, Sarah! You saw what happened. Now perhaps you can understand why I didn't want you around today. As I said, we were just lucky nothing more serious happened. There have been instances where the shooter has been blown to pieces before the nitro is even to the bottom of the well. As it is, Cade is a good man and this sort of accident is unusual for him. I only hope this wasn't his last job."

"I am sorry about Cade, but you still had no right to treat me in such a manner!" she insisted stubbornly, before lapsing into angry silence beside him.

Arriving at the cabin, she jumped down from the wagon and hurried inside to wash up and change her clothes. Adam stayed behind to unhitch the horse and see to its needs, his handsome face reflecting his displeasure at Sarah's actions.

Sarah heard him enter the cabin just as she had finished donning a freshly laundered, pale-yellow skirt and blouse. Her hair was once more securely fastened atop her head as she opened her bedroom door and prepared to confront Adam again.

She stopped short as she caught sight of the growing stain of blood on his flannel shirt. "You're hurt! Why didn't you say something?"

"It's nothing. Just a scratch," he said in an attempt to dismiss the matter. His face, however, registered the pain he was unable to hide. He turned away from Sarah and hung his hat on the peg behind the door.

"It most certainly is not a mere scratch! Why, you're bleeding very badly now. Why on earth didn't you go into town and have the doctor see to it?" Sarah replied curtly, hurrying to his side in order to examine the source of the oozing blood. She gently pulled back the torn edges of his shirt to reveal a large, ragged gash in his left shoulder.

"This wound definitely needs a doctor's care," she pronounced.

"No. Doc has more important things to do than look at this," Adam argued, inwardly smiling at her concern. Her small head was bent as she proceeded to help him off with his shirt.

"Then come into the kitchen at once and I'll see

what I can do," she commanded, as if she were speaking to one of her pupils instead of this handsomely rugged man who stood a foot taller than herself.

Adam smiled ruefully as he allowed her to lead him into the kitchen. Sarah quickly brought a pan of water and some clean dishcloths to the table, along with a sharp paring knife and some alcohol. Adam gratefully took a seat on the bench, feeling a slight dizziness now.

"I don't know why I didn't notice this earlier," Sarah remarked as she prepared to cleanse the wound.

"You were too angry to notice much of anything, remember?" Adam commented with a teasing grin, then added, "It didn't start bleeding this bad until the ride home."

"I'm afraid this may hurt quite a bit," she cautioned him as she began dabbing at the gaping wound. "Once I'm certain that any splinters are removed, I'll have to clean it with the alcohol and stitch the edges together. Do you still persist in your refusal to see the doctor?"

"I trust you," he replied with another grin that belied the extreme pain he was now experiencing.

"Very well." With that, she set to work. She used her fingers to remove two long slivers of wood she was able to find in the wound, then took up the small knife and proceeded to painstakingly loosen and remove another larger splinter. When that procedure was finished, she swabbed the wound with a generous amount of alcohol, then threaded one of her embroidery needles with black thread and began closing the edges of the wound, all the while totally aware of Adam's great stamina, which kept him from emitting any sound. Finally, she completed her unpleasant task and stood away from him with a heavy sigh.

"There, it's done. I'm afraid your shoulder will be quite sore for a few days. We must watch it carefully for any signs of infection. I still think it would be wiser if you would have the doctor take a look at it."

"There's no need for that now. You did a good job, Sarah, lass," Adam said, his tight features beginning to relax a bit now as he wiped the sweat away from his brow. "By the way, where did you learn your nursing techniques?"

"Don't move. I haven't put the bandage on it yet," she ordered sharply as he started to rise to his feet. "We learned quite a number of practical things at the school." She quickly bandaged the newly closed wound and secured it tightly, striving to ignore Adam's steady gaze that was riveted upon her face as she worked.

"Thank you, lass," he said softly, his expression loving and his green eyes glowing as Sarah finally forced herself to look directly at him.

"You're quite welcome, Mr. MacShane," she responded cooly, then gasped in surprise as Adam's good hand shot out and grasped her wrist.

"Don't call me that any longer! My name is Adam. You are my wife, it is only natural that you address me by my Christian name," he insisted quietly as he stood to his feet before her.

"I am your business partner, not your true wife! And I shall continue to treat you accordingly, Mr.

MacShane!" Sarah responded in defiance, endeavoring to wrench her wrist from his bruising grasp. She uttered a command for him to release her.

Adam muttered a curse and pulled her closer, imprisoning her with his good arm. "Sarah, isn't it about time we ended this foolish little war between us? Don't you realize that you're driving me mad? I love you! I've just come to realize how much. Can't you quit fighting me, quit fighting against my love for you, against your love for me?" he entreated.

Sarah felt a strange quiver in the pit of her stomach, but she refused to examine it. She hesitated for only a moment, then brought her open palm up and slapped him across his right cheek. His grip tightened momentarily, then relaxed. Sarah pulled away and said, "I told you never to touch me again! I'm tired of listening to your lies! Our arrangement is for business reasons, as I have already been forced to remind you on more than one occasion now! If you persist in trying to take advantage of me, I will be forced to dissolve our partnership entirely!" she threatened, a fiery blush spreading across her features as she glared upward at him, her eyes spitting fire.

"Didn't you hear a word I said, woman? I love you! This isn't some kind of trick to get what I want!" Adam roared, his own face suffused with an angry color now.

"Mr. MacShane, I am not quite as gullible as you seem to believe me to be! I am perfectly aware of the despicable depths to which a man will plunge in order to obtain the object of his lust! It is men such as yourself that we women are fighting against! How dare you speak to me of such an honorable thing as love! How dare you seek to take advantage of me again!" she raged at him, her eyes sparkling dangerously, her rounded bosom heaving. Why was she experiencing such violent emotions? she suddenly heard a tiny voice at the back of her mind question. Why was she allowing her temper to cause her to lose her dignified calm?

"You don't know a blasted thing about me or any other man!" Adam countered in a low, intense tone. "You refuse to give any man a chance! You might just be pleasantly surprised if you ever allowed yourself to behave as a woman instead of some sort of avenging angel!"

"Oh! I have had quite enough of you and this ridiculous, humiliating discussion! I can tolerate our arrangement no longer! You are the most obnoxious, deceitful, dishonorable, arrogant man I have ever known!" Sarah pronounced feelingly, before turning upon her heel and flouncing from the room, her skirts swaying as she went. She marched into her room and slammed the door resoundingly after her.

Adam found himself transfixed to the spot, his eyes staring after her. He realized that he was almost angrier than he had ever been in his entire life. He knew that he couldn't tolerate things as they were. He couldn't take her coolness, her icy attitude any longer. He had wanted to remain patient, had striven to be understanding. He had wanted to allow her time, time to realize that his love for her was genuine and not something he was using as a means to take advantage of her. But she steadfastly refused to believe him, and he realized that he would have to throw all caution to the winds and take affirmative action to convince her of his love.

He forced himself to gain control over his temper as he suddenly became aware of his throbbing shoulder. He had forgotten all about his injury.

Well, he told himself, right now certainly isn't the best time to decide what to do about the situation. No, he'd better get out of there and cool off a bit, think about things a bit more when he was able to think more rationally.

He approached the front door of the cabin and prepared to step outside into the bright sunshine and the warm, gentle wind when his footsteps were arrested by a sudden, unexpected noise. It was the sound of the bolt being drawn on Sarah's bedroom door.

It was amazing how much such a simple noise affected him then, he was to think later. It was entirely too much for his already stretched limit of endurance, the last straw for a man whose limit has been reached.

Chapter Ten

Sarah moved away from the door and continued undressing, satisfied that she was some degree safer in the event that Adam was entertaining any thoughts of accosting her further. She unfastened and drew off the last of her petticoats, placing it beside the other clothing she had neatly folded on the bed. Clad only in her chemise, she sank down into the softness of the mattress and began carefully unpinning her thick hair, which had somehow become dreadfully tangled in its pins. Soon it fell in shining masses of black curls about her creamy shoulders.

The disturbing events of the morning had left her feeling a trifle exhausted, and she decided that a brief nap would benefit her greatly. It would also serve to help her shut out all thought of Adam MacShane from her mind! She didn't want to think of that man or his preposterous claims of love! He was thoroughly unreliable and without any sense of decency or honor. But there, she reminded herself sternly, you're thinking of him again!

As she repositioned herself upon the bed for her nap, she thought she heard a noise outside her door. She quickly turned toward the doorway, just in time to hear a splintering crash as Adam forced his way into the room, ripping the bolt away from the door frame with his strength.

Sarah was both startled and frightened by his appearance, for he had obviously gone mad! "What on earth do you think you're doing? How dare you resort to such a thing! Get out of here at once!" she commanded shrilly, her breathing not quite steady as she swiftly bounced off the bed, her face paling as she viewed the deadly intent now apparent in his narrowed green eyes. She sought to cover herself with one of the discarded petticoats, hastily clutching it from the bed and draping it in front of her quivering form.

"I've had enough of this nonsense, Sarah. You are my wife. There'll be no locked doors between us any longer!" Adam spoke through tightened lips, his expression appearing very dangerous to Sarah's widened eyes. He began to slowly move toward her, his walk purposeful and steady as he approached. Sarah fearfully backed away from him, halting abruptly when her back came into contact with the hard surface of the bedpost.

Her mind furiously worked to think of some defense against this unfamiliar Adam. He was a total stranger to her now, his usual good humor and easygoing personality no longer in view. Without stopping to reconsider her actions, she snaked out an arm and reached beneath her pillow, withdrawing the small pistol she had concealed there. She pointed it directly at Adam, who now halted mere inches away from her.

"Don't come any closer! I am perfectly capable of using this if I have to. Now, get out of here at once!"

she ordered him, her tone low and threatening. Her hand suddenly began to shake, and she quickly brought her other hand up in order to help steady the gun. Her cheeks were brightly flushed, her blue eyes sparkling.

Adam carefully considered her as he stood perfectly motionless. His eyes traveled slowly over her, his gaze taking in the sight of her full, creamy breasts, which were barely covered by the thin chemise, her shapely legs almost totally revealed.

"Sarah, put that thing down," he coldly commanded. "It won't do you any good."

"I mean what I say, Adam MacShane! Don't come any closer. I will definitely use this if you force me to do so! Now, turn around and leave my room," Sarah repeated boldly, not feeling half as brave as she hoped she sounded.

"You'll put that gun down if you know what's good for you," Adam quietly countered, his frustrated desire and lingering fury mounting as he sought to reason with her.

"I hate you! I'll never forgive you if you force me to pull the trigger!" Sarah responded, her voice rising. She fought down the rising waves of panic that threatened to engulf her.

Without warning, Adam lunged forward and attempted to wrest the gun from her grasp. The two of them struggled violently for a moment, then Sarah screamed as the loud report of the gun shattered the stillness of the air, the bullet whizzing harmlessly past Adam's right ear.

Sarah caught her breath as she gazed at him in shock, his large hand still closed painfully upon her arm. He stood still and silent, his green eyes gazing deeply into her blue ones, as if he sought to somehow peer inside her very mind. Sarah found herself growing faint as she stood watching his face for any sign of what he intended to do next. Finally, his hand moved upward to her hair, grabbing a handful of its luxuriant thickness and unmercifully forcing her head backward and her face upward toward his own.

"No!" Sarah protested breathlessly as his lips came crashing down upon hers. She struggled against him, but her back was pinned against the bedpost, its hardness bruising her skin whenever she moved. Adam's other arm crept about her waist and roughly pulled her close against him. It seemed that his shoulder would cause him severe pain at such movement, but he didn't seem to notice. His lips were hard and demanding, and Sarah pushed ineffectually against him, experiencing a growing weakness that made it increasingly difficult for her to remain standing.

Adam's large hand released her hair and crept to the top of her delicate chemise. Before Sarah could move to prevent him, he had grasped hold of the neckline and savagely ripped the thin garment away from her body, rendering her completely naked before him.

"No! Let go of me!" she shrieked in panic, gasping aloud as her bare flesh came into contact with the hardness of his masculine body, which she could now feel even through the clothing he still wore. Adam ignored her cries and imprisoned both of her hands with one of his own, pinning them behind her back.

"Sarah, lass," he whispered softly as he gazed deeply into her widened eyes, his own glowing strangely. It seemed that the violence and fury he had displayed in the beginning were now being joined by something else as he lowered his head once more and took her lips again.

Sarah was too overcome by the disturbing, delightful sensations she was now experiencing to think clearly. She caught her breath sharply as Adam's warm lips traveled slowly from her face to her neck, then lower. He kissed her softly upon one of her full breasts, making her squirm and gasp anew as he proceeded to draw the erect nipple into his mouth. He lightly teased the nipple with his tongue, then moved to do the same to her other breast while she closed her eyes tightly in mingled rapture and confusion.

Her eyes swept open again as Adam removed his lips and began lowering her to the bed. She seemed to awaken from her momentary trance and began to fight him once more. Adam dodged her flailing fists and legs and placed his own powerful body on top of hers on the bed, effectively imprisoning her once again as he recaptured her hands and forced them above her head on the pillow.

"Let go of me! You're nothing more than an animal!" Sarah lashed out at him, her eyes flashing fire as she tried to twist away from him.

"You are mine," Adam stated in a deep voice, before taking her lips with his. He forced her lips open and caressed her tongue with his own, causing her to experience a melting, burning sense of excitement throughout her entire body. She hated herself for feeling such a sense of willful surrender, but she simply could not seem to fight against it. She was completely powerless against such overwhelming emotions and sensations.

Adam now began exploring her bare flesh as he continued to kiss her, his fingers leaving a trail of fire as they traveled downward across her curves, causing her to quiver as they moved across her full breasts, her stomach, her firmly rounded bottom, and then her soft thighs. He gently parted her thighs with his hand and began caressing the very core of her womanhood.

Sarah arched her back in surprise, then felt her thighs opening further as Adam continued his tender assault upon her unsuspecting body. She could feel an unknown yearning building to a fever pitch inside her, and she instinctively sought satisfaction by wrapping her arms about Adam and clasping him even tighter against her.

"Sarah, lass, my beautiful Sarah," Adam spoke against her ear. He reached downward and unfastened his trousers. Before Sarah fully realized what was happening, she felt something hard and alien probing between her parted thighs. She uttered a small cry as Adam plunged into her.

The first sudden, sharp pain rapidly subsided, to be replaced by a growing pleasure as Adam began slowly moving deep within her. Her breath was coming in short, uneven gasps as he finally brought the two of them to a bursting climax, leaving Sarah totally astounded and bewildered by what had just occurred.

Adam gently moved off her and lay by her side,

keeping his strong arm flung lovingly across her slender waist. His expression was one of both joy and concern as he gazed at her.

"Sarah. Sarah, I'm sorry if I hurt you, but it won't be that way the next time. I love you. Won't you believe me now?"

Sarah didn't answer him. She turned her head away from his searching look, averting her face in embarrassment and humiliation as the sudden realization of what she had done washed over her. How had such a thing occurred? Why had she allowed her traitorous body to overrule her convictions? How could she face Adam. How could she remain here with him now?

"Sarah? Sarah, lass, are you all right?" Adam asked in a solicitous manner. He gently took hold of her shoulders and turned her toward him, but she still refused to meet his gaze.

"Sarah, what's done is done. You have no reason to feel ashamed. I love you. I think you love me, too."

"I don't!" Sarah protested tearfully, finally raising her eyes to his face. As he opened his mouth to disagree, she said, "I don't know what I feel! I don't know anything anymore! Please just go away and leave me alone!" Adam tried to take her into his arms, but she quickly pushed him away, then clutched at the quilt on the bed in order to cover her exposed nakedness.

"You are my wife. There's no reason you should feel this way. There was nothing wrong in what happened between us. Our lovemaking was a natural thing, Sarah." Adam tried reasoning with her, feeling increasingly perplexed by her strange behavior.

"Go away!" Sarah repeated with feeling, turning upon her side in order to escape his searching gaze. The tears began spilling from her eyes, and she buried her face in the enveloping softness of the pillow.

Adam started to speak again but decided against it. He judged that it would perhaps be best if he did leave her alone for a spell. He climbed from the bed and hastily readjusted his trousers, then headed for the doorway. He glanced back at Sarah, but saw that she was still huddled beneath the quilt, now pathetically sobbing into the pillow. He hesitated a moment, then turned and strode from the room, closing the battered door softly behind him.

Sarah heard him leave the room, then listened as he stamped out of the cabin. She sat up and tried staunching the flow of tears. She was furious with herself as well as with him. He had intentionally and skillfully seduced her, but, what was worse, she had shamefully responded to him when she should have fought him tooth and nail!

Swinging her bare legs to the edge of the bed, she lowered her bare feet to the floor and stood upright, keeping the quilt close about her. She nearly cried aloud in dismay as she viewed the telltale bloodstains on the sheet. They were a most unwelcome reminder of what had just taken place, so she dragged them from the bed with a vengeance and tossed them into one corner of the room. She would wash them later, but not yet. Now, she didn't wish to dwell upon the humiliating encounter.

She still couldn't believe what had happened, still couldn't believe that she was no longer a virgin. However, she thought with an ominous frown, her body made her all too aware of that fact! Her skin still tingled warmly from Adam's caresses, and her mouth was red and bruised from his passionate kisses. No, she reminded herself angrily, don't think about it!

Approaching the washstand, she allowed the heavy quilt to drop to the floor as she poured water from the pitcher into the matching porcelain bowl. She vigorously scrubbed her skin from head to toe until it was pink and glowing from her efforts. But she still didn't feel that it was enough. She felt the need to immerse her body in a hot tub of water, she needed to try and wash away all the disturbing feelings of Adam MacShane's lovemaking!

Hastily donning a cotton wrapper, she padded across the floor in her bare feet and hurried into the kitchen, where she set water on the stove to heat. She then went to the back door of the cabin and dragged the wooden bathtub inside and into her room. She proceeded to carry several buckets of hot, steaming water from the kitchen as she slowly filled the tub.

Closing the door to her bedroom, she inspected the damage done to the bolt and frame. She glanced about the room for something to place in front of the door, something that would not make it easy for Adam in case he entertained any notion of returning! She finally settled on the oak washstand, which she dragged across the floor and placed in front of the door.

She threw off the wrapper and eased her tired body

into the water's soothing warmth. Relaxing back against the tub, she sighed heavily as she forced herself to contemplate her altered situation.

She grew more and more confused as she thought about the relationship that was supposed to have been nothing more than a business partnership between Adam and herself. He had probably been lying to her from the very beginning, had probably planned to make her his wife in every sense of the word while all the while agreeing to her terms. Oh! she fumed. If only she could escape him, never think of him again. But no, leaving now would defeat her entire purpose in coming to Texas. What was she to do?

She refused to admit to herself that Adam's lovemaking had aroused her more than she had ever believed possible. She refused to admit that she had never experienced such overwhelming satisfaction. Instead, she sought for ways to repay him for what he had done to her. The more she thought, the angrier she became, so angry that she almost, but not quite, wished she had shot him when she had had the opportunity!

Adam's thoughts were equally preoccupied as he splashed his tanned, muscular body with the cool water of the rushing stream. He took up the cake of lye soap and scrubbed his skin and then his scalp, being careful not to cause his wound to begin bleeding again. It had already soaked through the bandage, and Adam ruefully thought to himself that Sarah certainly wouldn't be feeling generous enough toward him to tend to it again any time soon!

For all her ranting and raving, he believed that she

felt something for him, something that ran as deep and strong as his own feelings for her. He knew that she had enjoyed their lovemaking, even though things had progressed too swiftly for him to take his time and concentrate on pleasuring her. Yet she had obviously experienced the emotions of a passionate woman, her protective shell forgotten as her enticingly beautiful body responded to his masterful touch.

He still felt a powerful exhilaration whenever he recalled the feel of her warm, soft curves against him. She had been even more perfect and ravishing than he had ever dreamed possible, despite that brief glimpse of her body he had been afforded the time he had burst into her room during her bath.

He knew Sarah well enough to realize that she would refuse to admit just how much she had been affected by what had occurred between them today. Her tears of shame and humiliation proved that to him. She wouldn't be prepared to admit that she loved him, not yet. He must teach her that their love was a glorious thing, that it was nothing of which to be ashamed, that they were husband and wife now in every sense of the word. There would be no returning to that impersonal business partnership after today!

It wouldn't be easy, Adam reflected as he heaved a sigh, but at least it was a start. Now that Sarah was no longer an innocent and frightened virgin, she would perhaps be more receptive to him from here on out. At least, he told himself as he stepped from the water, he damned sure hoped so.

Chapter Eleven

When Sarah finally opened the door to her room the following morning, she was visibly relieved that Adam was nowhere in sight. She had not ventured from her room after her bath the day before, preferring to postpone the inevitable confrontation between herself and Adam. He had not bothered her further, for which she was inwardly grateful. She dreaded facing him again, dreaded seeing the triumphant gleam in those green eyes that she was certain would be there.

Famished after missing her dinner the night before, she entered the kitchen and immediately set the coffee on to boil. She had detected the delicious aroma of frying bacon last night as Adam had apparently cooked his own dinner, but she had steadfastly refused to leave her room, no matter how hungry she was. Now, she set about preparing her breakfast, her thoughts preoccupied as she worked.

She wondered where Adam could be at this hour of the morning. Today was Sunday, the day he always allowed his men to spend as they wished. It certainly wasn't as if she relished the disagreeable prospect of seeing him again, she told herself as she cracked two fresh eggs into the hot iron skillet. No, she merely wanted to get a few matters straightened out between them. She wanted to make it clearly understood that what happened between them the day before was to be totally forgotten and definitely never repeated!

She still despised herself for giving in, for responding the way she had. Her traitorous body had made her cast aside all of her convictions, all of her caution. She would never be able to completely forget, but she would certainly endeavor to push it all to the back of her mind. Her body was bruised and sore this morning, another hateful reminder of what Adam had done to her.

Oh, she reflected bitterly as she scrambled the eggs, why had she ever come to Texas? Why had she ever met Adam MacShane, ever agreed to his proposal? Her life had been so uncomplicated and orderly back in Philadelphia. There certainly had been no men such as Adam to take advantage of her, to make her feel so humiliated and ashamed. Why couldn't Uncle John have stayed where he belonged?

Scraping the cooked eggs onto a plate, she paused as she heard the sound of hoofbeats approaching the cabin. Thinking it must surely be Adam returning from only God knew where, she set the eggs aside and hastily straightened her dress and apron, preparing to do verbal battle with him once again. We might as well get it over with right now, she thought as she mentally mustered her courage.

She was surprised when she heard a brief knock sound upon the door. She hurried to open it, wondering why in the world Adam would choose to knock upon his own cabin door. Who else would be out here this time of morning? she asked herself as she swung open the door.

"Good morning, Sarah. May I come in?" asked Clementine Patterson as she swept arrogantly inside without waiting for a reply.

"Why, Clementine," Sarah responded in amazement, stepping mechanically aside as she noticed the blond girl's astonishing appearance. Clem's blond curls were piled high atop her head in an elaborate coiffure, adding several inches to her already tall frame. Her trim figure was encased in a brightly printed cotton dress, delicately trimmed with several yards of lace and flounces. Sarah had never seen the young woman in anything but her rather drab attire, so her appearance was doubly shocking. Clem looked very lovely and feminine, and, for some reason, thought Sarah, very dangerous.

"Where's Adam?" Clem burst out rudely, whirling about to face Sarah.

"He isn't here. May I ask what you're doing here?" Sarah replied, her tone one of icy politeness. Of all the mornings, Clem Patterson had to pick this particular one to show up on her doorstep!

"Well, if you must know, I heard about the well accident yesterday," Clem replied with a frown, her eyes darting suspiciously about the cabin as if expecting that Sarah was somehow hiding Adam from her. "I just thought Adam might like to know that Cade's going to pull through. I saw the doctor last night and he told me so. Was Adam hurt?" she demanded abruptly.

"You needn't concern yourself with Adam. He's quite all right. He received a rather nasty wound on his shoulder, but I took care of it. I'm very relieved to hear that the shooter is going to be all right. I'll be certain to relate your message to Adam when he returns," Sarah told her, making it all too clear that Clem's presence was unwanted. Inwardly, she was wondering precisely what had brought the jealous girl all the way out to the cabin, and dressed the way she was. It certainly wasn't merely to talk about the well accident!

"I'll tell him myself!" Clem snapped, then added, "Where is he, anyway?"

"I don't know," Sarah answered without thinking.

"Why, Sarah," Clem purred, a malicious smile appearing on her face, "you're his wife, aren't you? You mean to tell me that you don't even know the whereabouts of your own husband? Well, I should have expected as much, seeing as how you two don't have a real marriage at all! That's something else I've got to talk to Adam about. I think it's high time you and he put a stop to this ridiculous little arrangement of yours!"

"Our arrangement is none of your business, and I'll thank you to remember that!" Sarah commanded imperiously, her color rising as the blond girl goaded her into anger. "I've told you that I do not know where Adam is, nor when he'll return. I'll give him your message, I assure you. I think you should be leaving now."

"This isn't your cabin, Sarah! This is Adam's place, not yours. It would belong to his wife, his real wife, if he had one. And I mean to see to it that he has a real wife, not a cold-blooded business partner! By the way," she suddenly interjected, smiling with apparent satisfaction, "I heard some other interesting news in town yesterday. It seems that Frank Mead, your uncle's partner, is coming back real soon. He should be here any day now, from what I hear. Then you can get whatever it is you're waiting for from him and get on back to Philadelphia where you belong! You can get that annulment from Adam and leave him free to marry someone else!"

"You mean yourself, don't you, Clem?" Sarah retorted scornfully, her temper rising measurably at the young woman's derisive words. "Thank you for your information concerning Mr. Mead. As for the rest of your advice, you have no right to concern yourself with my affairs. Whatever is between Adam MacShane and myself is our own business," she informed Clem, silently reflecting that the spiteful vixen would be extremely upset if she knew what had taken place in this very cabin yesterday!

"Now, will you kindly leave this cabin?" Sarah asked coldly, thinking what a great pleasure it would give her to be able to throw the young woman out on her ear!

"I told you before, anything that concerns Adam concerns me! Don't worry none, though," Clementine smirked as she swung open the front door and prepared to step outside, "I won't tell anyone else about your little secret, about you not having a real marriage. Of course, when the news of your annulment gets around, everyone will know that you and Adam weren't ever truly husband and wife, that you weren't woman enough to keep him!" With that parting shot, she flounced triumphantly outside, slamming the door resoundingly after her.

Sarah felt an overwhelming urge to scream after

her but succumbed to stamping her foot instead. She whirled about to return to the kitchen, her appetite completely vanished now, when her steps were arrested by the sound of voices outside the cabin. Flying to one of the front windows, she cautiously peered outward, only to discover that Adam had returned and was involved in a conversation with Clementine.

As she secretly watched them with great interest, she saw Clem suddenly laugh, then grasp her pretty skirts and whirl gaily about, evidently in order to show off her unaccustomed finery to Adam, who responded with an answering grin and appreciative eyes. Sarah frowned as Clem linked her arm with Adam's and drew him with her toward her waiting wagon, where the two of them stood and talked for a few moments longer. Then, before Sarah's astonished and indignant gaze, Clementine suddenly wrapped her arms about Adam and bestowed upon him a passionate kiss.

"Oh!" Sarah exclaimed aloud, jerking her head away from the window so that she was unable to see Adam gently disengage Clem's arms and set her resolutely away from him. He helped her up into the wagon, then stood watching as she flicked the reins and drove away at a brisk pace.

Sarah discovered, much to her dismay, that she was enraged enough to scream! How dare that disgraceful hussy throw herself at Adam that way, she fumed silently. How dare he accept that amorous embrace! No doubt the two of them had shared quite a number of such kisses! And she, Sarah Bradford, was actually married to such a womanizing rake!

Oh yes, she reflected bitterly as she stalked back into the kitchen, yes, Adam MacShane spoke honeyed words of love whenever it suited his purpose, but he had shown his true colors to her now! Not only had he so savagely forced himself upon her yesterday but he was apparently enjoying the conquest of Clementine Patterson the very next day! Well, she wouldn't stand for it! She wouldn't allow him to make a fool of her in such a manner!

She was startled out of her intense reverie when she heard the front door open and close. She could hear Adam's boots stepping loudly across the bare wooden floor until he was standing in the doorway of the kitchen. Sarah staunchly kept her back to him as he stared toward her.

"Good morning, Sarah, lass," his deep, resonant voice spoke in a cheerful tone. He made no move to enter the room, and Sarah finally took a deep breath as she turned about to face him.

"Is it a good morning?" she angrily retorted. "I suppose Clementine has gone?" Why was it so difficult to face him, even to be in the same room with him? she asked herself. She was finding it hard to breathe, hard to concentrate with him standing there so nonchalantly before her, a disarming grin on his handsome face.

"She has. She told me Cade's going to be fine, but I guess you're already aware of that fact," Adam answered, observing her face closely. He wanted nothing more than to cross the few feet of space between them and crush her in his arms. The urge to kiss her was immensely powerful as he gazed lovingly at her beautiful face, at her softly curved figure that he recalled so well.

"Yes, Clem told me," Sarah replied coldly, striving to control her temper, not wanting to give him the satisfaction of knowing how furious she was. "She had quite a lot to say to me." She turned and busied herself with pouring the steaming coffee, feeling nervous and on edge as her hands shook uncontrollably. She mentally steeled herself to try and behave as if she hadn't seen Adam and Clem locked in that passionate embrace, as if she hadn't experienced the overwhelming desire to fly at them and tear them apart!

"What's the matter, lass? Are you still upset about what happened yesterday?" he asked with genuine concern.

"I'd prefer it if you never mentioned that horrible episode again!" she responded frigidly, gazing at him with daggers in her opal eyes. "I want to forget about what occurred, forget what you did to me. Otherwise, I should find it impossible to continue with our business arrangement. Is that understood?"

"I understand perfectly," Adam said with a sardonic grin. "You're still too proud and prudish and stubborn to admit that you enjoyed our lovemaking, that you responded with a woman's natural passion. But you won't forget about it, Sarah. I don't believe even you could do that, no matter how hard you might try."

"I will forget!" Sarah cried, then regretted her childish outburst. Composing her features once more, she remarked, "As for Clementine Patterson, I'm quite sure she can help you forget about it as well!"

"What the devil do you mean by that? There's never been anything serious between us," Adam replied, the grin replaced by a tightening frown.

"I saw you two together just now! Yes, and what's more, Clementine herself has made it all too clear that you two belong together. As a matter of fact, I believe that I agree with her. You two certainly deserve each other!"

"What nonsense is this?" Adam demanded gruffly. "What has Clem been telling you?"

"Only that she means to marry you once we get an annulment. I'm sure the two of you will be very happy! The sooner I obtain that annulment the sooner you'll be free to wed your precious Clem!"

"I don't know what the hell you're talking about! I love you, Sarah, lass, I've never loved anyone else. I don't intend to get an annulment no matter what pack of lies Clem's been filling your pretty little head with! I love you, damn it, and I wish you'd open those beautiful blue eyes of yours and face the truth!"

"Don't you dare to speak to me about love! Not after what you did to me, not after I saw you and Clem kissing just now! You could at least have had the decency to wait until I had gone back to Philadelphia before you started again with your little affair!" Sarah spat at him, too angry to question why she was so upset about Clementine.

"I didn't kiss her, she kissed me!" Adam thundered, losing all patience now. His green eyes glinting dangerously, his brow suddenly cleared as something occurred to him. "You're jealous of Clementine!"

"I most certainly am not!" Sarah protested

vehemently, her bosom heaving as she tried to sweep past him. He caught her arm and pulled her to a halt.

"Let go of me!"

"I will not. Not until you listen to me." He gazed down into her angry, flushed little face, and his expression softened. "I love you. Whether you choose to believe it or not, it's the truth. There was never anything between Clem and me, no matter what she might have told you. Furthermore, you are my wife. There'll be no annulment, lass."

"No annulment?" Sarah repeated, eyes widening at his words. "There most certainly will be! If you think that I'm . . ."

"No, Sarah," Adam cut her off, "you are mine, you will always be my wife. I'll never let you go. The sooner you face your own feelings for me, the better."

"Feelings for you!" she said as she uttered a short, humorless laugh. "I despise you! I'll never forgive you for what you've done to me! I should have known that you wouldn't keep our bargain!" she raged, tears starting to her eyes as she squirmed and twisted in an attempt to escape him.

"No, lass, you don't hate me. Right now, you only hate yourself. You hate yourself because you've realized that you're human after all, because I've made you feel like a woman, because I've dared to love you. You'll soon get used to the idea that we're husband and wife, that we were meant to be married in every sense of the word."

"You're insane! I have no intention of remaining your wife. As a matter of fact," she told him, remembering what Clem had told her, "Frank Mead will be returning soon. I intend to see to it that my business here is concluded very shortly afterward, at which time I'll return to Philadelphia and never see you again!" she pronounced, her eyes flashing fire.

"For your information, Mrs. MacShane," Adam said with a dangerous gleam in his eyes, "there can be no annulment now. Have you forgotten what an annulment entails? A man and wife must not have consummated their marriage in order to meet the terms of an annulment."

Sarah stared at him in abject horror as the meaning of his words slowly sank in. She turned a stricken face up to him, then angrily dashed away the tears that had now begun rolling down her flushed cheeks.

"Very well then," she spoke calmly, her expression guarded as she faced him. "If you plan on using such disreputable, dishonorable tactics, I shall seek a divorce. Either way, I shall most certainly escape from this distasteful predicament!"

"No, Sarah!" Adam replied through tightly clenched teeth as he roughly pulled her against him, causing her to cry out in alarm. "No divorce. I'll never let you go."

"You'll have no say in the matter, sir!" Sarah cried indignantly, endeavoring to free herself from his bruising grasp, feeling faint at such close contact with him, growing a bit fearful at his savage expression.

"If it's a fight you want on your hands, you have it. I'll not give in, lass," he responded with a steely gaze. He released her arm without warning, causing her to stumble backward. She quickly regained her balance and glared defiant at him once more before turning about and hurrying to seek refuge in her room.

Adam stood staring after her, reflecting angrily that things were going to be a hell of a lot more difficult between them now than before. He knew that she was jealous of Clementine and also that she would somehow blame him for that jealousy.

Thinking of Clem, he sighed heavily. She was definitely a problem. He knew that she must have deliberately provoked Sarah in some manner, for it was just like her. She had probably kissed him that way because she knew Sarah would be watching.

Aye, he thought as he pulled his hat down onto his head and strode outside, he certainly had more than a handful of trouble to contend with. But, one thing was certain, he vowed silently, there would be no annulment, no divorce between him and Sarah. He would fight against it with his very last breath.

Sarah, meanwhile, was also thinking of a fight. She would write to one of her acquaintances back in Philadelphia, a lawyer who had been a close friend of her late uncle's. Though she was reluctant to disclose the humiliating details of her relationship with Adam, she felt that her uncle's friend would be able to advise her about a divorce, or tell her whether an annulment was somehow still possible. She would show Adam MacShane that she would never give in, either, that she would never rest until she was free of him!

Chapter Twelve

Sarah rose earlier than usual the following morning and dressed in one of her more stylish dresses, a light-green muslin accented by a large, fashionable bow of the same fabric that formed the bustle. She had made her plans the night before, after lying awake and restless for several hours. She planned to drive the wagon into town, where she would post the letter she had written to her uncle's lawyer friend, as well as pay a visit to the bank. Adam had informed her during dinner the night before that he had established an account for the profits from her wells at the bank in town. Although she had remained stubbornly silent throughout the course of the meal, she had later recalled his words. She also planned to do a bit of shopping, and perhaps even pay a visit to Mrs. Patterson, whom she felt was her only friend in this wild country. Of course, she thought now as she methodically brushed her long hair, she had no desire to encounter Clementine Patterson again after what had happened the day before!

Thinking of Clem and the events of the day before, she found herself growing angry again, something she had sternly vowed not to do. She would never

155

again give Adam MacShane the satisfaction of knowing he was capable of arousing any emotion in her whatsoever! As for Clem, she would coldly ignore the forward hussy in the future!

It was extremely difficult to forget, however, she thought with a slight frown as she finished pinning up her thick, curly tresses. It was difficult to forget all of the things that had happened since she had met Adam MacShane, particularly his reprehensible treatment of her on that day when he had forced himself into her room and forced his lustful attentions upon her. But she reminded herself with a determined sigh as she opened her bedroom door, I will forget everything about it!

Climbing up to the wagon seat, she suddenly remembered that she had neglected to inform Adam of her plans for the day, and he was obviously already gone. Well, she told herself as she defiantly tossed her head, her black curls bouncing riotously in the sunlight, it was none of his business what she chose to do! Besides, she thought as she settled her skirts and slapped the reins, I certainly do not intend to see him enough in the future to engage in much conversation with him!

The drive into town was fortunately short and uneventful, and Sarah finally slowed the horse to a halt in front of the town's lone bank. She would take care of her financial business first, then see to posting the letter to Philadelphia. It had been a most difficult letter to compose, but she prayed that the results would be worth any embarrassment.

She climbed down from the wagon seat and tied the reins to the hitching post, then straightened her shoulders, adjusted her bustle, and strolled gracefully inside the bank, wryly reflecting that it was hardly the sort of structure that would be classified as a bank in Philadelphia. However, she thought with a sigh as she swept inside the rustic wooden building, it was precisely in keeping with the rest of this wild, uncivilized town.

She was uncomfortably aware of the many heads that turned in surprise as she swiftly walked across the dirty wooden floor and approached the teller's window. A quick, sideways glance told her that there were no other women present, and she drew herself up proudly as she forced herself to ignore the stares and remarks of the handful of coarse men watching her so avidly.

"Pardon me," she spoke assertively as she stepped closer to the barred window, "I have an account here and I wish to make a small withdrawal."

"An account?" the young red-faced teller repeated stupidly, eyeing her curvaceous figure appreciatively, at least what he could see above the edge of the tall counter. He gulped noisily as he raised his surprised eyes to her face and encountered her frigid gaze.

"Yes," Sarah said, striving to remain polite and calm, "I wish to make a withdrawal."

"Yes, ma'am," the teller hurriedly replied, passing her a piece of paper and a pen beneath the window. "If you'll just fill out this little card here and sign your name, ma'am."

"Very well." She wrote down the necessary information and started to sign her name when it suddenly occurred to her, after all, it had been Adam who had arranged the account for her. And it would be just like the man to have set it up in the name of Mrs. Adam MacShane instead of Sarah Bradford!

As she was silently pondering which signature to use, one of the onlookers remarked in a loud voice, "Well, now, if this here's an example of what Jim Oliver's gonna have in his bank, I'll just have to come on in here more often!" His words were accompanied by laughs and other comments from the men, and Sarah stiffened in anger, fighting down the impulse to turn and soundly berate the impertinent fellow. Instead, she turned her attention back to the card and purposely ignored the impudent man, heaving a dissatisfied sigh as she finally scrawled her married name. She slid the paper and pen back across the counter to the admiring young teller.

"You're Adam MacShane's wife?" he exclaimed, glancing quickly from her signature back to her face.

"Yes, I am," Sarah answered curtly, hating to admit to the fact. "Would you please hurry? I have other matters to attend to today."

"Yes, ma'am. Sure thing, Mrs. MacShane, ma'am!" he responded, placing a special, loud emphasis upon her name. There were several surprised murmurs behind Sarah's back as the teller turned to do her bidding, nearly stumbling over his feet in his haste.

Sarah tapped her foot impatiently while he was gone, still aware of the stares directed her way as she resolutely kept her back to the men in the bank. She was, however, unaware of their altered attitudes toward her now, unaware of the impact of Adam

MacShane's name upon them. She was merely hoping that there would be no further disagreeable incidents while she was in town for the day, for she was out of all patience with the crude, ungentlemanly manner of the men she had so far encountered in Wildcat City!

"Here we are, Mrs. MacShane. Now, how much do you want to withdraw?" the teller inquired with increased deference when he finally returned.

"How much has been deposited in the account?"

"Well, you've got almost five hundred in here, ma'am."

"Five hundred?" Sarah repeated, obviously surprised with the amount. "Well, then, I suppose fifty dollars would be enough for now. You see, half of this money belongs to someone else."

"All right. Fifty dollars it is," the teller said, then proceeded to count out the money, placing it into Sarah's outstretched hand. She thanked him politely and turned about, stuffing the money into her bag.

She was half expecting another rude outburst from the crowd of men but she was pleasantly surprised when no one made any further gesture or comment as she headed for the doorway. She reflected that it was indeed a bit strange, the manner in which they had treated her earlier contrasting markedly with their behavior now, but she gave it no further thought as she paused outside the door and contemplated her good fortune.

It had been little more than a week, and already the one producing well had earned her nearly five hundred dollars! Of course, she reminded herself, half of it rightfully belonged to her uncle's partner.

And, if Clementine's news was correct, she would be able to square accounts with Mr. Mead within the next few days. At this rate, she thought as she directed her steps toward the general store and post office, she would soon have enough money to insure a decent burial for her uncle in Philadelphia, as well as fulfill his dream of a successful oil venture. She would also soon be free of Adam MacShane, free to return to Philadelphia and her quiet, orderly life there. Suddenly, for some unknown reason, she was forced to admit to herself that such a prospect had somehow lost some of its appeal for her. Briskly shaking off such ridiculous thoughts, she quickened her steps down the boardwalk.

She posted the letter, then purchased a few items. She was unable to resist selecting a beautiful divided skirt of soft, sueded leather, telling herself that it would come in handy whenever she chose to accompany Adam to the wells again. It wouldn't be at all proper for a young woman to wear such a thing back home, she thought with just a twinge of guilt as she had the man behind the counter wrap the skirt in a neat package for her. But, she consoled herself decisively, things were different out here in this untamed land. She would definitely be more comfortable when sitting out in the hot sun or riding in the wagon, not having to worry about her cumbersome skirts and petticoats. All the same, she mused ironically as she left the general store, she never would have thought of wearing such scandalous attire a month ago!

Strolling down the walk toward Mrs. Patterson's house, she slowed her steps to a halt as she caught sight of two wagons approaching the center of town. Their occupants, she noted with a quick glance of perusal, were obviously families. There were several children laughing and talking, women riding alongside their husbands on the wagon seats. Sarah realized that these people must actually be new settlers for the area. She was glad to see that Wildcat City was finally to have some decent, civilized inhabitants, especially some other women. The only other women she had encountered thus far, with a few exceptions, had been those who worked in the saloons! Perhaps if a few more families were to move into the territory, she thought, the town might actually begin to resemble a real settlement, a city with a church and a school and other evidences of permanence.

She turned her gaze away and approached the boardinghouse, climbing the front steps and knocking on the front door. The door swung open to reveal the lady of the house, who greeted Sarah with a warm and friendly smile.

"Sarah! I was beginning to wonder when you'd get into town and come on by to see me again!" Mrs. Patterson said, adding, "Come on in here and set a spell." She ushered Sarah inside the cheerfully decorated abode.

"Thank you, Mrs. Patterson. I'm afraid I can't stay very long, though. I just wanted to stop by and say hello before I returned to the cabin."

"Sure, honey. But, you can come on into the parlor and visit for a few minutes, can't you?" the older woman replied, making it apparent that she wouldn't accept a refusal of her offer.

"Is Clementine at home?" Sarah suddenly asked, taking a seat near the gingham-curtained front window.

"No, she's not. Why? Did you want to talk to her about something?"

"No," Sarah replied a bit too quickly, her expression tightening. "I most certainly do not wish to speak with her." Then, smiling again, she said, "I've just purchased some new dress lengths. Would you care to see them? I simply must make myself some new, cooler dresses. I'm afraid I'm not used to your warm, rather humid weather here."

"You'll get used to it in time," her friend responded kindly, her face lighting with pleasure as she came to sit beside Sarah on the sofa. "These are just beautiful, Sarah," she remarked as Sarah removed the fabrics for her inspection.

"Well, I thought that simple fabrics such as gingham and calico would be more in keeping with the environment. Everything here is so very different from what I'm accustomed to," Sarah commented with a sigh as she wrapped the fabrics again.

"While you're at it, you'd do best to make those dresses without a bustle, Sarah," the older woman advised her. "They may be right stylish back where you come from, but, out here, they ain't nothing but something more to get in a body's way."

"I suppose you're right," Sarah admitted with a laugh. "By the way, I just saw two covered wagons driving into town, obviously bringing new settlers. It seems that this country is to be made a bit more civilized after all."

"Oh, yes, there's more and more families coming

all the time. The boom's bringing some of them in, but others are coming for the land. It won't be long till we have us a real town, Sarah. I've waited a long time to see it, and now it's finally going to happen. Makes you sort of proud, don't it?"

"I'm pleased for you, Mrs. Patterson," Sarah responded, purposely not answering for herself. "Well, I really must be going," she announced as she stood up.

"Before you go," Emma Patterson said, gazing seriously into Sarah's face, "well, I hope you don't think I'm meaning to interfere or nothing, but I was wondering how things are going between you and Adam now."

Sarah hesitated, suddenly feeling as if the older woman could see clear through to her innermost thoughts and secrets. She shook off the uneasy sensation and answered, "Nothing has changed. I would still like to locate other accommodations as soon as possible."

"Sarah, I don't mean to be doubting your word, but, well, I can tell that something has changed. You seem different, child, especially when I mentioned your husband's name just now," her friend insisted, her kind face registering concern, her eyes soft and serious.

"I don't know what you're talking about," Sarah lied, knowing that her friend was speaking the truth. She knew that she was different, that her life had been forever altered. And, she thought with renewed anger, she had none other than Adam MacShane to thank for turning her world upside down!

"I really must be going now," Sarah repeated

briskly, heading for the doorway, wanting to escape the other woman's probing eyes.

"All right, Sarah, honey. Just remember," Mrs. Patterson said, opening the front door ahead of Sarah, "I'll be here if you ever need or want to talk to me about anything, anything at all."

"Thank you," Sarah replied earnestly, nearly softening. She reflected upon how easy it would be to tell this kind woman all of her troubles, to reveal all of her innermost secrets. But she was unaccustomed to sharing her confidence with anyone else. Smiling again, she left the house and hurried back down the front steps, leaving a thoughtful Emma Patterson behind.

Yes sir, Emma told herself as she watched Sarah hurry back down the walk toward her wagon, that gal is in for a big surprise whenever she finally gets up enough gumption to face her own feelings. And Adam MacShane will be mighty glad when she finally does, if I know him at all. He darn sure wouldn't have gone and married her if he didn't care for her, no matter what she said about it being for business reasons and all. It's a real shame my Clem couldn't have gotten him to the altar first, she thought with a heavy sigh as she shut the door and went about her business.

Sarah climbed up onto the wagon seat and flicked the reins, then guided the horse back along the road out of town. She gradually allowed the animal to slow to a more sedate pace once outside the town's limits, and she allowed her thoughts to wander back to her visit with Mrs. Patterson.

If only her wise friend had known the entire truth

of her words! Sarah told herself with a short, humorless little laugh. She was changed all right, changed from being an innocent maiden into a despoiled, dishonored woman! She refused to admit to herself that she was changed in other ways as well, and that those other changes also owed their origin to Adam MacShane.

Approaching the turn in the dirt road where her late uncle's small cabin was situated, she abruptly pulled the horse to a halt as she spotted a saddled horse tied in front of the cabin, happily grazing as it patiently waited for its owner to return.

Who on earth would be at Uncle John's old cabin? Sarah asked herself as she quickly scanned the surrounding grounds for any sign of the intruder. She hurriedly contemplated the situation, then briskly flicked the reins as she slowly drove the wagon a bit closer. Climbing carefully down from the wagon, she warily approached the cabin, her hand closing tightly upon the small pistol concealed in her skirt pocket.

Cautiously advancing toward the front door, which had been left slightly ajar, she wondered again why anyone would possibly be interested in examining her uncle's deserted cabin. Without pausing to rationally consider the possible consequences of her actions, she slowly edged the front door completely open and stepped across the threshold.

Sarah quickly satisfied herself that there was no one inside at the moment, and she closed the door behind her quietly. She looked about to ascertain if anything in the cabin had been disturbed. Then, keeping a wary eye upon the door, she approached the back window of the cabin in order to peer outside and perhaps spot the mysterious rider.

Suddenly the front door swung noisily open, and Sarah stifled a scream as she instinctively drew out the pistol and jerked about, prepared to defend herself against the intruder. The man she perceived standing calmly, and almost casually, in the doorway, the bright rays of sunlight outlining his masculine figure, stared back at her across the short distance between them.

"I don't really think that little old gun there will be necessary, ma'am," the young stranger spoke with a soft drawl, his words accented by a sardonic grin as he nodded toward Sarah's pistol. She quickly noted that he was both young and reasonably attractive, that his clothes were a cut above those she was accustomed to seeing in Wildcat City. She noted the way his brown eyes sparkled at her, the way his dark-brown hair waved close to his head, that he was only several inches taller than herself, and that he was now smiling at her in a very familiar manner.

"You!" Sarah exclaimed. It couldn't be true! How on earth did he, of all people, come to be here at her uncle's cabin in Texas?

"Who are you?" Sarah asked, beginning to calm down a bit from the initial shock.

"I just might ask you the same thing, young lady," the stranger responded, smiling nonchalantly as he leaned against the doorway, his eyes twinkling irrepressibly as he continued to gaze at her in a most disconcerting manner.

"I asked you for your name, sir," Sarah repeated sharply, her hand motioning toward him, the loaded pistol still aimed straight at his heart.

"My name, dear lady, is Frank Mead. And I can assure you I mean you absolutely no harm, so you may put away that gun," he said, smiling again.

"Frank Mead?" Sarah exclaimed in surprise, lowering the pistol to her side. "My uncle's partner?"

"Your uncle?" he replied, appearing a bit puzzled. Then, as realization suddenly dawned on him, he said, "So, you're John Bradford's niece!"

"Yes, John Bradford was my uncle," Sarah responded, then stiffened as all of the questions she had been storing up for this man now came flooding into her mind.

"Well then, that explains why we were fortunate enough to meet each other back in Philadelphia. I had been there at the hotel to talk to your uncle about some business matters earlier that same evening."

"I had no idea you were Uncle John's partner," Sarah murmured, half to herself.

"And I certainly had no idea you were his niece! But I'm pleased to make your acquaintance at last, Miss Bradford, at least in the proper sense. Your uncle used to speak of you quite often, but then, I never could have guessed that it was you he was talking about."

"How did my uncle die, Mr. Mead?" Sarah shot at him, her expression tightening as the well-dressed young man stepped closer.

"Don't you know?" he asked, sauntering across the dusty floor to stand directly before her now.

"Of course I don't know!" Sarah snapped irritably. "No one seems to know much about it, or at least they aren't willing to talk. But I've been waiting for the opportunity to ask my uncle's partner!"

"Well then, Miss Bradford, to answer your question, your uncle was killed in a drilling accident. I gave you all of the details in my letter to you."

"Your letter? I received no letter from you," she told him, then recalled the short, anonymous note she had received. She realized with a certainty that it hadn't come from this particular man. Besides, she thought, it had given no details whatsoever, only informed her that Uncle John was dead.

"I wrote you the day after the tragedy occurred. I'm sorry about your uncle, Miss Bradford," he said, his brown eyes gazing intently down into her blue ones. Sarah cautioned herself not to trust him, not until she had received sufficient answers to all of her questions.

"How did it happen? And why was everything about my uncle's death so mysterious? Why hasn't there been anyone willing to supply the details to me, instead of behaving as if it was none of my business?" Sarah insisted, eyeing him suspiciously.

"Just as I told you, it was a drilling accident. There was nothing mysterious about it, I can assure you. If no one wanted to talk about it, it's probably just because they wanted to spare your feelings," Frank Mead answered, his Southern drawl only slightly less pronounced than before.

"Your uncle was working on the drilling platform with some other men when it happened," he told her quietly, "and I was several yards away at the time. It all happened so fast, there wasn't any warning at all, no way of knowing what was going to happen. A cable suddenly broke and struck your uncle in the head, killing him instantly. There was nothing we could do. At least he didn't suffer, Miss Bradford," he told her consolingly, his brown eyes full of sympathy.

"Yes, at least he didn't suffer," Sarah softly repeated, her eyes filling with tears. Drawing out her handkerchief, she impatiently dabbed them away. "I still wish I had received your letter, Mr. Mead. It would have saved me a lot of trouble."

"I truly am sorry that it seemed as if there was something amiss about your uncle's death, Miss Bradford. It saddens me that you didn't get that letter. John was my friend as well as my partner."

"I understand. But tell me," Sarah asked, still not quite willing to trust him completely, "how did you and Uncle John come to be partners? He made no mention of a partner in any of his letters to me."

"I guess he didn't think it was important enough to bother you about. I put up the capital for his last two wells, in return for becoming his equal partner. I suppose he wanted to surprise you when everything started paying off," he explained, still gazing at her in that same disconcerting way.

Sarah felt uncomfortable beneath his perusal, and she stiffened as she said, "Mr. Mead, there are a few business matters that we need to discuss as soon as possible. This has all happened so fast. I had heard that you would be returning here within a few days, and I was planning to be prepared to present to you the latest details about the wells. I don't know precisely what the agreement between yourself and my late uncle was, but I am prepared to honor whatever contract was between you."

"You needn't worry about that, Miss Bradford. I'll be more than happy to take care of all the tiresome business details. I'll be sure and see to it that you receive your uncle's share of everything."

"I'm afraid you don't understand," Sarah persisted, feeling herself grow more obstinate, reflecting that he was obviously just as bullheaded as Adam when it came to women in the oil business. "I've already seen to it that one of the wells is successfully producing again. Another one should be in production within the next week or so. Your share of the profits thus far is safely deposited in the bank, in an account established in my name."

"What are you talking about?" Mead asked her in puzzlement.

"The wells. I know Uncle John would have wanted us to continue with this oil venture, Mr. Mead, and I fully intend to try and fulfill his dream. I shall then use the money to insure him a proper burial back in Philadelphia, as well as honor any debts which he may have incurred."

"I see," the young man responded, unsmiling. Sarah briefly wondered why he didn't seem more pleased at the news, then decided that it was probably as she had suspected, that he didn't approve of her taking over the business in his absence. He was most probably as narrow-minded about women in business as other men!

"You don't approve?" she asked him.

"Oh, it isn't that, Miss Bradford," he hurried to reassure her, smiling down at her again. "It's just that all of this comes as a surprise, that's all! Just how, may I ask, did a beautiful young lady such as yourself manage to get those wells producing again?"

"With the assistance of an acquaintance of yours, a neighbor of yours, I should say," she amended. "Adam MacShane."

"MacShane?" he repeated in surprise, then ruefully added, "He and I aren't exactly what you'd call 'neighborly,' ma'am."

"Oh? Well, that is beside the point. Mr. MacShane and I made a bargain, and he agreed to work the wells for us." She was hesitant to reveal her true relationship with Adam. It certainly wasn't something she was proud of, being married to such a scoundrel!

"I see. Well, I certainly don't wish to pry into your private affairs," he gallantly remarked, then asked, "But, Miss Bradford, would you mind telling me exactly how you persuaded MacShane to agree to such a thing?"

Sarah colored at his question, pondering precisely how she would answer him. She decided to tell him the truth, and squarely faced him as she answered, "Mr. Mead, you and I are business partners, so I suppose you should be apprised of the true situation. My personal life is really none of your concern, but this arrangement does involve business, and nothing more. You see, I had to agree to marry Mr. MacShane in return for his assistance. It was, and is, a business arrangement and nothing else. I don't feel that I should reveal Mr. MacShane's reasons for entering into such an arrangement, but suffice it to say that it was strictly business on his part as well."

"So yours is merely a marriage of convenience, then?" Mead probed, obviously interested in her answer.

"Yes. Purely for business reasons," Sarah insisted vehemently, wondering why it should matter to her whether this young man believed her or not. She felt a small twinge of guilt as she thought of what had occurred between herself and Adam, but she resolutely pushed it to the back of her mind. She wanted nothing more than to forget what that man had done to her! And Frank Mead would certainly never understand if she endeavored to tell him the truth of the matter.

"I am extremely sorry I wasn't here when you first arrived, Miss Bradford," he told her, purposely still addressing her by her maiden name. "I could have saved you all that trouble."

"Thank you, Mr. Mead," she responded, wanting to question exactly why he hadn't been around when she had first arrived. She decided to put that particular question to him later, when they discussed several other details that were still on her mind.

After a moment's pause, Sarah raised her eyes to his face once more and said, "I really must be going now, Mr. Mead. I must say, I certainly never expected to make your acquaintance under such circumstances. When would you like to meet and discuss our business matters?" she asked him, beginning to stroll toward the doorway now, his hand closing firmly upon her elbow as he escorted her.

"Anytime you please. Just say the word," Mead gallantly replied, then added, "I'm staying at the hotel in town. Perhaps you'd care to have dinner there with me tonight and discuss these business matters?"

"Well, I . . . I don't know," Sarah hesitated, an unbidden image of Adam coming into her mind. She realized that he would be furious if he knew of Mr. Mead's flattering attentions to her. At such a thought, she decided to accept, defiantly answering, "I think that would be very nice, Mr. Mead."

"Good! Where are you staying?"

"At Mr. MacShane's cabin," she replied, then blushed furiously beneath his shocked gaze. "You see, I have been unable to locate accommodations in town. Until I can do so, I am forced to remain in his cabin. In separate rooms, of course," she hastened to explain.

"I have an excellent suggestion then, Miss Bradford," Mead said with an engaging smile. "Why don't you take my room at the hotel? I had already thought of staying out here in the cabin, so the situation could be remedied quite easily."

"Oh, no, I wouldn't want to take your room," Sarah hurriedly declined, silently telling herself that she was a fool to pretend a refusal under such circumstances!

"I insist. Why don't you allow me to accompany you back to MacShane's right now and we'll get your things. Then, I'll be happy to escort you into town."

"Thank you," Sarah warmly responded, smiling graciously up at him. "I can't tell you how relieved I am at your suggestion, at your generous offer. I was beginning to believe that I would never esca . . . that

I would never be able to find other accommodations."

Her intended use of the word "escape" didn't go unnoticed by Mead, but he chose to ignore it, instead smiling to himself as he escorted her from the cabin and back toward her waiting horse and wagon.

Chapter Thirteen

During the brief wagon ride to Adam's cabin, Sarah and Frank conversed quite amiably. He told her of his reason for leaving so soon following her uncle's death, that he had been forced to attend to some urgent family business elsewhere. He said that he had not even considered visiting her in Philadelphia in order to give her the sad news in person, but that he had decided to write her the letter instead. Now, he had returned to Wildcat City to oversee the production of the wells once again and resume his life there.

Sarah told him that she had come to Texas in order to discover the truth of her uncle's death, but that her desire for such knowledge had soon developed into another desire as well, that of fulfilling her uncle's dream. She couldn't help noticing that Mead appeared to understand her desire, his smile sympathetic and his brown eyes soft and full of concern.

Arriving at the cabin, Sarah politely asked him inside to wait while she gathered up her belongings. He assisted her down from the wagon, causing her to blush as his hands lingered a moment longer than was necessary upon her trim waist. She turned away from him and started toward the cabin, while Frank remarked, glancing about, "Where is MacShane, anyway?"

"Oh, I suppose he's out at one of the wells. He usually doesn't return home until late evening."

"I guess that's pretty convenient for you, then, his being absent so much of the time," he told her with a caustically raised eyebrow.

"Yes," Sarah answered simply.

Stepping inside the cabin, she said, "Please take a seat while I see to my things." She hurried into her bedroom while Mead sat down on one of the wooden chairs in the large central room. Sarah returned several minutes later.

"Very well, Mr. Mead. I believe I have everything. Shall we go?"

"Of course. Here, let me carry those for you," he gallantly offered, taking charge of her baggage. At the doorway, Sarah hung back, suddenly hesitant.

"What is it?" Mead asked her, gazing curiously at her pensive face.

"Mr. Mead, if you don't mind, would you please go on out to the wagon? I will join you in just a moment."

"All right. Don't be long now," he replied with a smile, disappearing through the doorway, still wondering what was on her mind.

Sarah waited until he had gone, then softly closed the door behind him. She stepped into the kitchen, taking one last look at the surroundings that had become so familiar to her. It had almost seemed as if the cabin had belonged to her, as if it had taken the place of the home she had never had.

She toyed with the idea of leaving Adam a terse

little note, informing him of her departure and subsequent whereabouts, but she suddenly hardened as she recalled his treatment of her and his behavior with Clementine, still fresh on her mind.

No, she thought obstinately, I won't give him the satisfaction! Let him simply believe that she had gone, that she had finally made good her threat to leave and never see him again. She would arrange an annulment as soon as she received a reply to the letter she had posted earlier today. Beyond that, she indeed never intended to either see or correspond with Adam MacShane again! It shouldn't be much longer until she could completely forget that she had ever heard of the man!

Whirling about, she marched from the kitchen and out of the cabin. Clutching her skirts firmly in one hand, she allowed Frank Mead to lift her up to the wagon seat. He took a seat beside her, snapped the reins, and they drove away from the cabin at a brisk pace. Sarah, however, couldn't refrain from taking one last look as they drove away.

So much had happened, so much had occurred to confuse her, she reflected, sitting in silence beside her newfound friend. Would she ever truly be able to forget it all? Heaving a deep sigh, she turned her head about and proceeded to give her full attention to Mead, who was once more attempting to engage her in conversation. She bestowed upon him a bright smile, and the two of them happily passed the time as they drove toward town.

Mead pulled the horse to a halt in front of the hotel and said, "Here we are, Miss Bradford. I know it isn't too fancy, but it's about the best you'll find in a boomtown like this," he remarked with an apologetic smile as he helped her down and took up her baggage.

Sarah didn't answer him, for she had immediately noticed that the hotel was the very same one in which she had attempted to rent a room on that first day she had arrived in Texas. It was the same place where she had been so rudely accosted by that huge fellow, then had been so heroically rescued by Adam. No, she furiously chided herself, don't think about him at all!

She smiled up at Frank as she strolled inside with him, determined to put all thought of Adam behind her. After all, she told herself, Frank Mead was a very attractive young gentleman, a true gentleman in every sense of the word, and it was quite obvious that he admired her.

Indeed, he appeared quite proud as he entered the hotel with her upon his arm. She noted the curious, interested glances that were directed their way as they approached the front desk. It was manned by the same desk clerk who had so rudely turned her away once before, and she smiled sweetly at him as she stepped forward with Frank Mead, causing the poor clerk to color brightly and appear a trifle shamefaced.

"There's been a change in my plans, Sam. Miss Bradford here will now be occupying my room. I want her made as comfortable as possible for as long as she wants to stay. Is that understood?"

"Yes sir, Mr. Mead. Anything you say," the clerk hurried to agree.

"Good. Now then, Miss Bradford, I'll escort you up to your room." He tucked her hand under his arm and led her up the steps to the second floor, instructing the clerk to have the baggage sent up after them.

"This is really very kind of you, Mr. Mead," Sarah repeated as he took out the key and unlocked the door.

"It's my pleasure. By the way," he commented, ushering her inside the room, "I think that, seeing as how we're business partners and, I hope, friends, that we should call each other by our first names, don't you?"

"Well, I suppose it would be proper enough, under the circumstances," Sarah replied as she stepped inside the room. She noted that there was a large, iron bedstead against one wall, a chest of drawers in one corner, and a washstand in the other corner. It was hardly the sort of room she would have expected to find in a hotel, she reflected wryly, but it was in all probability the best she would find in Wildcat City!

"I hope this will suit you? I know it isn't much, but it is clean and you'll be undisturbed, I'll see to that," Mead assured her as he softly closed the door.

"It's fine. I do hope you won't mind, but I'd like to be left alone for a while in order to freshen up."

"Of course. I'll call for you at, say, six o'clock this evening?"

"Very well, Mr. Mead."

"I insist that you call me Frank, Sarah," he reminded her with a compelling smile.

"Six o'clock, then, Frank," Sarah responded, smiling in return. She followed him as he left the room, then closed the door and drew the bolt.

Sitting down upon the bed, she contemplated all that had happened in such a short period of time that day. Here she was, finally away from Adam MacShane, safely away from his cabin and such close contact with him. She had a hotel room, she had acquired a new friend and business partner, as well as a new admirer. She had finally received the answers she had sought concerning her uncle's death. It had all happened so quickly, she thought once more as she rested upon the bed.

Frank Mead was certainly a charmer, she thought as she arose several minutes later and began to undress. He was precisely the sort of young man one would wish to encounter amid all the wildness and brutality of the boomtown. He was also very attractive, very polite and attentive, she told herself with a slight smile. She couldn't help being pleased at his attention.

And yet, before she was fully aware of what she was doing, she was comparing him to Adam. He was certainly several inches shorter than Adam, as well as being much slighter in build. He possessed none of Adam's healthy tan, and he didn't appear at all to be the sort of young man one would find working in the oil fields. No, rather, he appeared to be the sort who would allow someone else to do all of the labor!

Realizing that she was perhaps being unfair to him, she sternly commanded herself to stop judging him, to stop comparing him to Adam or anyone else. What mattered most to her was the fact that he had shown himself to be a sympathetic and understanding friend. He was certainly a refreshing change from the uncouth, uncivilized men she was accustomed to seeing in Wildcat City.

After undressing completely, she poured the water

from the pitcher into the washbowl and proceeded to vigorously scrub her skin, using the harsh soap she found on the washstand. When she was satisfied that she was as clean as she could hope to be using such methods, she proceeded to brush her thick black hair and arrange it becomingly once more.

She was ready and waiting when Frank Mead came to call for her that evening. "Sarah, you're even more beautiful than before, if such a thing is possible," Frank told her with an admiring smile and a certain gleam in his eye as she opened the door.

She was wearing her best blue muslin dress and had piled her shining curls high atop her head, allowing a few tendrils to escape and curl invitingly about her face. The dress showed her curvaceous figure to the best advantage, and it was obvious that it had achieved the desired effect upon Frank Mead.

"Thank you," Sarah murmured in reply, suddenly wondering if she had done the right thing in wearing the dress. "I must say that you are certainly punctual," she told him, changing the subject. "Just allow me to get my bag." She picked up the handbag and said, "Shall we go?"

"Certainly." They stepped outside the room; Sarah closed and locked the door, then took Frank's arm as they walked back down the narrow hallway to the stairs.

"Where are we going to dine?" she asked as they reached the bottom of the stairs.

"Well, the restaurant here at the hotel is pretty good. If that's all right with you?"

"That sounds just fine."

The restaurant was crowded and noisy, but Frank

was able to procure them a table in a darkened corner, where they would be off to themselves and be able to speak a bit more privately. Sarah saw that there were few women inside, and that many of the men were avidly watching her as Frank graciously pulled out her chair, then took a seat across the table from her. My goodness, she thought to herself, I don't believe I'll ever get used to being stared at so much!

Clasping his hands on the table, Frank said, "I hope you don't mind, but I've already taken the liberty of ordering dinner for us. I've eaten here several times before, and the roast beef is excellent."

"That sounds perfectly delicious. For the past few days, I've only sampled my own cooking," Sarah confessed with an answering smile.

"Poor Sarah, don't tell me you had to do all the cooking out there at MacShane's?"

"Yes, as well as all of the housecleaning. Oh, but no one forced me to," she hastened to add, seeing his frown of displeasure. "You see, there really wasn't much else to do, no other way in which to occupy my time. To tell the truth, though, it was rather enjoyable. I've never had much of a chance to cook at home, since I live in a boardinghouse. And all of the cleaning is done by a housekeeper. So, you see, I actually relished the opportunity to improve my domestic skills. It was such a novel experience. But, of course, cooking and cleaning should definitely not be considered the only talents a woman should perfect," she pronounced decisively.

"It sounds as if you agree with those suffragettes or something," Frank remarked with a grin.

"And what's wrong with that?" she demanded,

frowning, her blue eyes sparkling defiantly.

"Oh, nothing, nothing at all," he rushed to say, realizing that his careless words had made her angry. "I think women should be able to do whatever it is they want to do."

"I quite agree. It is very nice to hear a man make such a comment, for a change," Sarah told him, her frown disappearing. "I only wish other men felt as you do on the matter."

"Well, give them time," he replied with a consoling smile. "If all of the suffragettes were like you, they'd come around a lot quicker!" he said with a mischievous grin.

"You are impossible!" Sarah retorted, unable to resist smiling at him.

Throughout the meal, Frank asked her more about herself, about her life in Philadelphia. When she felt that she had told him all that he could possibly wish to hear, she insisted that he speak about himself.

"Well, as I'm sure you can tell, I'm from the South. Originally from South Carolina, but I've been schooled in Georgia and Tennessee, and then in Boston."

"Oh, so that's why your accent is only faintly detectable at times," she remarked.

"Yes. It comes and goes, depending on whether or not I feel at ease with a subject, or with a person," he admitted with a chuckle.

"What about your family? Do they still live in South Carolina?"

"No. That is, they're all scattered about now. As I told you, I had to leave after your uncle's death on some family business. I had to return to South

Carolina first, then on to Boston, but it's all settled now."

"What brought you to Texas and to Wildcat City in the first place?" she asked, curious as to why such a well-educated and well-traveled young gentleman would choose to come to such an untamed wilderness.

"I suppose it was the same thing that brought everyone else out here—oil. I saw a chance to make a good investment, so I came."

"And that's why you were in Philadelphia that night we met? Because you wanted to persuade my uncle that this was a good investment?"

"Yes, at least partly. I met him through a mutual acquaintance, and I was already there in Philadelphia on some other business, so it was no trouble to see your uncle while I was there. I told him all I knew about the deal, and he sounded interested, very interested. When he finally arrived here, I made contact with him again. We had liked each other immediately, so we decided to become partners. You're very much like your uncle in so many ways, Sarah," he told her softly, leaning back in his chair as he pushed his empty plate away and brought the napkin to his lips.

"I suppose I inherited some of his characteristics. He was my father's younger brother, you see. Uncle John may not have been the best guardian by most people's standards, but I absolutely adored him," she said with shining eyes. "I was only able to see him a few times a year. I'm afraid I still can't quite believe that he's gone," she remarked with a heavy sigh.

"I'm sure he would have been pleased to know that

you and I managed to get together on his oil venture. By the way, I suppose it's time we got down to discussing those business matters."

"Yes, of course. As I've already stated, one of the wells is successfully producing once more. Mr. MacShane," she said, feeling decidedly uncomfortable at having to mention his name, "Mr. MacShane assured me that another one would be operating within the next week. Of course, now that the business agreement between he and myself is no longer valid, we will certainly need to employ new workers to work our wells."

"Why do you say that? Couldn't we have MacShane and his crews continue working for us?"

"Suffice it to say that I have broken my part of the bargain between us, as has he. Therefore, we will have to hire the men on our own," she patiently explained, not wishing to reveal too many details.

"All right, if that's the way you think things should be. I'll see about some new men the first thing in the morning. It may not be too easy to find them, though. Are you absolutely certain you wouldn't consider keeping MacShane a part of the deal for a while longer?" Frank queried suggestively.

"Certainly not," Sarah said firmly.

"The idea is apparently distasteful to you?" Mead probed.

"It most certainly is! I want nothing further to do with that particular man! I insist that we hire new workers!" she told him with a most determined expression, her blue eyes flashing with emotion.

Frank couldn't help noticing how upset she appeared to become at the mere mention of Adam's name, but he chose to remain silent on the subject. He had plans for Sarah, definite plans that didn't include a husband! If she behaved so vehemently whenever his very name was mentioned, then it would perhaps be for the best if they did exclude him in their business dealings. He didn't care for MacShane anyway, he never had. He smiled graciously and said, "All right, Sarah. We'll do things your way. After all, you are my partner now. And a beautiful and charming one at that," he remarked, reaching across the table to place his hand gently on top of her own. She blushed and removed her hand, clasping it with her other in her lap.

"Thank you. I'm terribly sorry if this makes things difficult, but I really must insist. There are still a few other matters that we must discuss," she said, drawing a piece of paper and a pencil from her handbag.

"Of course," Frank agreed, gazing at her intently. He was thinking that he had never before encountered such a bewitching creature. Things were definitely going even better than he had planned!

After discussing their business for nearly an hour, Sarah and Frank rose from the table and left the restaurant, both pleased with the outcome of their meeting. Sarah turned to face him as they paused in front of her door. "Thank you for the dinner, Frank. I'm glad that we were able to come to such an amiable agreement on all of these matters."

"So am I. I think that our partnership is going to be one of the best things that's ever happened to me. In more ways than one," he commented, his expression serious.

"I had better say good night," Sarah said, lowering her eyes before his disturbingly intense gaze as she turned to unlock the door. "I'll see you in the morning, then?"

"Of course. Wait a moment, Sarah," Frank suddenly commanded. "Let me check your room first, to make certain no one has been inside."

"What on earth are you talking about?" she asked. "The door was locked."

"I know, but a lock like that is very easy to tamper with. I won't be but a moment. I just want to make certain everything is all right before I leave you here alone," he insisted, brushing past her and into the room. He glanced about, then hurried to light the lamp on the table beside the bedstead. Holding it high, he made a quick sweep of the room, then turned back to Sarah, who had now followed him into the room.

"I'm glad to say that everything appears to be fine," Frank assured her.

"I really don't understand why you believed this necessary," Sarah told him, puzzled by his actions.

"In a wild town like this one, Sarah, anything can happen to a beautiful young woman who's alone. Someone could have managed to get inside your room and could have been lying in wait for you. Anyway, be sure to draw the bolt when you close the door," he cautioned her, placing the lamp back beside the bed.

"I will. Thank you, Frank," Sarah said, smiling as they approached the door again. Frank paused before stepping out into the hallway.

"Sarah, if there's anything you need, anything at

all, just tell the clerk downstairs. He's under the strictest orders to take good care of you."

"Please don't worry about me. I'll be fine," Sarah insisted, holding the door open as she waited for him to leave. Her eyes widened in surprise as he suddenly stepped back inside the room and placed an arm about her shoulders, drawing her close. "Frank, what on earth are you doing?" she uttered breathlessly, before being silenced by the pressure of his lips on her own. She pushed weakly against him, shocked by his unexpected actions.

"Get your blasted hands off of my wife!" Adam's deep, resonant voice spoke from the direction of the doorway.

Frank and Sarah sprang apart abruptly, both gasping loudly as Adam's words startled them both. Sarah immediately noticed that Adam was angrier than she had ever seen him before, that the expression on his face and the light in his eyes were both dangerous and savage.

"MacShane!" Frank exclaimed, then demanded, "What are you doing here?"

"I've come to fetch my wife and take her home with me where she belongs," Adam muttered viciously, his eyes seeming to bore into Sarah as she stood beside Frank. She finally recovered her voice enough to say, "You have no right to behave in such a disagreeable manner! Get out of here at once!"

"You heard the lady," Frank chimed in, placing himself between Adam and Sarah. "She has no wish to go with you, now or ever!"

"Get out of my way, Mead!" Adam growled, his expression growing even darker and more menacing.

"Adam, please leave," Sarah implored now, afraid that he might just kill Frank. She had never seen him looking so enraged, and she felt a fear descend upon her as she gazed up at him.

"I told you to get out of my way," Adam repeated quietly. As Frank made no move to comply with his command, Adam's right fist shot out and caught him on the chin, knocking him dazedly to the floor. Sarah glared murderously at Adam, then flew to kneel beside the prone Frank.

"How could you do such a thing? Why, you know he's no match for you! What a perfectly cowardly thing to do!" she raged at him, lightly slapping Frank's face in an effort to restore him to full consciousness.

"Sarah," Adam ground out through tightly clenched teeth, "I'm much too furious to stand here and argue with you right now. I've been all over the damned countryside looking for you ever since this afternoon! I only managed to find you because a friend of mine happened to see you come here to the hotel with Mead. You're coming home with me, now!" he stated tightly, his Scottish brogue more pronounced than ever before.

"I most certainly will not!" Sarah snapped defiantly. She cried out sharply as Adam strode toward her and took hold of her arm firmly, yanking her roughly to her feet.

"Let go of me! You're hurting me! How dare you treat me in such a manner! I won't go with you, I refuse to go with you! And I am not your wife!" she railed at him, striking him about the chest and shoulders with her clenched fists and kicking vainly at his legs with her feet. She vaguely wondered if anyone would perhaps come to her assistance, but realized that no one would interfere. She knew that it was useless to scream for help.

"You are my wife," Adam growled, before grasping her by the wrist and pulling her toward him. He slung her over his broad shoulder, like a sack of grain, and proceeded to march from the room, not pausing to close the door after him.

Sarah beat at his muscular back, squirming and twisting to try and force him to release her, but to no avail. The few people standing about in the hotel lobby all looked upon the ensuing scene with curious eyes as Adam MacShane strode with his unwilling burden out of the hotel and down the boardwalk to where his horse was tethered.

Sarah felt as if she would die of the humiliation as everyone turned to stare at them, and she pounded vigorously upon Adam's broad back with renewed strength.

"Put me down! I won't go back with you! I never want to see you again, and I'll never forgive you for doing this to me! I hate you, Adam MacShane!" she cried, twisting helplessly about. She was thrown up onto the back of his horse while he swiftly mounted behind her, clasping her tightly against him as he urged the horse back down the road and out of town, the bright moonlight illuminating their path as the animal galloped along the hard-packed road.

Chapter Fourteen

Sarah burst into angry tears of frustration and humiliation as they rode, too overcome by the tumultuous emotions she was experiencing to struggle any longer, at least for the moment. She hung her head dejectedly and wept throughout the furious night ride, only raising her eyes once again as Adam finally pulled the lathered, snorting horse to a halt in front of the moonlit cabin.

"I will not remain here. I will leave again just as soon as the opportunity presents itself," she threatened loudly with determination as Adam took hold of her slim waist and roughly pulled her down into his muscular arms. He carried her swiftly toward the cabin as she renewed her struggles.

"You'll never leave me again, Sarah, lass," Adam told her, his expression still dark and foreboding as he kicked open the cabin door and strode into the darkened interior with her. He set her on her feet, then slammed the door shut. Turning back to her, he advanced slowly upon her, his rugged, handsome face intense and purposeful.

"I will never forgive you for what you have done tonight! Frank Mead did not deserve the brutal treatment he received at your bullying hands!" she angrily accused him as she faced him squarely, clenching her fists at her sides, refusing to back down in the face of his anger.

"He deserved a good deal more than what I gave him, from what I could see! Damn it, woman, you were kissing him when I came upon you, remember?" Adam roared at her, appearing as if he wanted to strike her. His handsome, scowling face was clearly discernible with the bright moonlight streaming in the back window of the cabin.

"I was not kissing him, he was kissing me! A goodnight kiss and nothing more, as if it were any of your business! You're certainly a fine one to talk, Adam MacShane, after the way I saw you and Clementine Patterson carrying on yesterday! Besides that, you had absolutely no right to come bursting into my room at the hotel that way! You had no right to treat me as if I were some sort of wayward possession of yours. I do not belong to you!" Sarah stormed furiously, glaring defiantly up into his face as he towered ominously over her.

"You are mine, Sarah. You will always be mine. And you have behaved in a foolish and childish manner. Don't you know that I was crazy with worry for you? I came home and couldn't find you anywhere; looked and saw that all of your things were gone as well. I thought you had returned to Philadelphia. Damn it, woman, you had no right to do such a foolhardy thing!"

"I had no right?" Sarah repeated in a voice that grew increasingly shrill. "You say that I had no right to do anything I wished to do? How dare you! You do not own me. No man will ever own me. And the sooner you realize it, the better! No matter what you think, no matter that you have a mere slip of paper stating that we are husband and wife, I am not yours! I refuse to be treated as if I were!"

"We are husband and wife, lass, in every sense of the word. That entitles me to certain rights, to authority as your husband," Adam ground out.

"I have taken care of that particular matter," she informed him with a triumphant smile. "I have written to a lawyer in Philadelphia concerning an annulment of our marriage, and I expect a reply very shortly. Then this so-called marriage of ours will be legally dissolved, and we will both be free to resume our lives. As for our business agreement, consider it terminated here and now! I no longer have any need of your services in the working of my wells, now that Mr. Mead has returned. As for your inheritance and the stipulation of your grandfather's will, find someone else to marry! I refuse to remain shackled to you any longer!" Her blue eyes seemed to flash fire as she brushed past him and headed for the doorway.

"You're not going anywhere!" Adam commanded tightly, grasping her arm as she attempted to wrench open the front door.

"Let go of me!" Sarah insisted, endeavoring to twist free of his bruising grip.

"You are my wife, once and for all! You will do as I say!"

"I will not! Oh, I wish I had never set eyes on you, you . . . you Scottish scoundrel, you! I hate you, Adam MacShane!" she raged at him, her face flushed bright red and her thick, black hair streaming down about her shoulders as she faced him.

"You can say it all you damn well like, my Sarah, but you know it isn't true," Adam quietly countered, suddenly reaching out and drawing her into his powerful embrace.

"Let go of me! Haven't you humiliated me enough for one evening?" Sarah tearfully responded, struggling against him, feeling a familiar weakness descend upon her as she viewed the naked desire in his eyes.

"Be quiet, woman," Adam calmly ordered, before lowering his head and taking her lips with his own. Sarah sought frantically to escape him, but she found herself powerless against the pressure of his warm lips, the pressure of his hard, masculine body against her own.

As he continued kissing her, Adam's hands began to slowly unfasten her dress, and Sarah gasped as she felt cool air on her naked back and shoulders, as her dress slipped quietly to the floor. She attempted to speak, but Adam's lips captured hers once more, and he pressed harder against her softness as he pulled the straps of her chemise down and began untying the strings of her corset. Soon, before she fully realized what had happened, Sarah discovered that she was nearly naked beneath his strong, supple hands, clad only in her chemise and drawers. She tore her lips away from his and breathlessly protested, "No! Please, not again!"

"It will be different this time, Sarah, lass. You'll see," Adam softly assured her, his eyes full of love and passion. He scooped her easily up in his strong, muscular arms and carried her into her bedroom, ignoring her tearful protests and ineffectual struggles as he placed her upon the bed. He quickly removed his boots and divested himself of his own clothing, returning to Sarah and placing his naked body on top of hers, tugging at her chemise and drawers until she too lay completely naked beneath him.

"Sarah, Sarah, lass, I love you so much," he whispered softly against her ear. "I never wanted to hurt you, but you made me so blasted furious! I thought I would go mad with jealousy when I saw you and Mead kissing," he told her as his loving lips roamed gently across her face and neck. Sarah moaned softly as his lips traveled lower to touch her breasts, as his hands caressed her naked flesh.

Adam gently parted her thighs with his hand as his lips fastened on one of her quivering white breasts, drawing the nipple into his warm mouth and teasing it lightly with his tongue. Sarah gasped loudly and arched her back as the most disturbing, turbulent emotions shot through her entire being. His lips moved across to her other breast, while his fingers continued caressing her gently, bringing her to passionate response. Sarah caught her breath in a gasp, then couldn't refrain from opening her thighs further, from suddenly grasping Adam's head where it lay upon her bosom, from running her fingers through his thick hair.

"Adam," she whispered, unable to think any longer, unable to resist the powerful, overwhelming sensations she was experiencing. She had never felt so completely alive, never felt so completely and desirably a woman.

Adam kissed her upon her lips now, driving her mindless with his persistent caresses, making her yearn for something she could not name. She moaned softly beneath his lips, clasping him tighter against her softness as he now teased her tongue with his own.

When Adam sensed that she was finally ready for him, he positioned himself between her thighs and gently entered her, beginning to slowly thrust back and forth as Sarah gasped aloud at the delicious, searing fires that threatened to drive her insane. She moaned louder as he continued thrusting, as he took them both to a rapturous fulfillment at last.

"I love you, lass," Adam whispered against her hair as he finally rolled off her and lay by her side, holding her close and gently stroking her forehead as he lovingly smoothed the hair from her flushed face.

Sarah remained silent, seeking to recapture her breath, not knowing exactly what to say to him, only knowing that she had never felt this way before. Her whole body tingled with the lingering sensations, and she suddenly realized that she was experiencing a sense of well-being that she had never felt before. She averted her eyes from Adam's searching gaze, not entirely sure how she could face him again after exhibiting such wild abandon, not knowing how she could speak to him after their wildly loving union.

"Sarah, it's all right. The way you felt was perfectly natural for a woman. I told you it would be better this time. And, with more practice, it will continue to improve," Adam said with a twinkle in his eye and a disarming grin upon his face as he drew her unresisting softness even closer into his arms.

"Sarah, please say something," he entreated,

holding her comfortingly against his hard, muscular body.

"Adam," Sarah whispered tremulously, falteringly. "I . . . I'm so confused."

"I know, lass, I know. You've kept telling yourself that you hated me, tried to convince yourself that you wanted nothing more to do with me. Only, it isn't the truth. I know you care for me, Sarah, and I think, deep down, you know it, too. What we just experienced together is only a part of it, my love."

"I don't know. I just don't understand, I just don't know," Sarah lamented tearfully. "I don't love you, I don't love anyone!"

"Aye, lass, you do, but I suppose it'll take more time for you to realize it," Adam responded with a sigh as he caressed her lovingly.

Sarah was too exhausted, both physically and emotionally, to argue with him, to think about any of it for the time being. She closed her eyes and sighed heavily, snuggling closer to the warmth of Adam's body as sleep began to overtake her. She was so tired, so very tired.

Adam chuckled quietly to himself as he gazed down at the sleeping form beside him. He carefully drew the covers up over the two of them, then positioned Sarah's head on his shoulder as he too closed his eyes. He drifted off to sleep happily, encouraged that things were definitely taking a turn for the better.

The next morning, Sarah sleepily opened her eyes as the bright sunlight streaming through her bedroom window awakened her. She began to stretch lazily, then gasped and jumped sharply as her arm came into contact with Adam's bare, sleeping body beside her.

As the memory of what had occurred between them the night before came flooding back to her, she blushed a fiery red and edged away from Adam's naked maleness beside her.

How could I have allowed such a thing to happen again? she berated herself furiously. How could I have behaved in such a wanton fashion? Twice now, twice she had given in to her traitorous body and betrayed her principles. She was so thoroughly enraged with herself, she could have screamed!

Of course, she reminded herself consolingly, Adam was partially to blame, certainly much more so than herself! Oh yes, it was he who had known precisely how to conquer her better judgment, he who had been the expert lover, the learned seducer. How could she have allowed him to make love to her again, though? she asked herself in bewilderment.

Refusing to face the truth, that she had totally enjoyed the lovemaking between them, Sarah slowly edged herself farther away from Adam and out of the bed, being careful not to awaken him. She quickly gathered up her clothing, then crept quietly from the room, closing the door softly behind her.

She dressed hurriedly, noting with dismay the damage Adam had done to her chemise and dress, then opened the front door of the cabin and ventured outside into the crisp morning air. She turned her steps toward the stream in the nearby woods, knowing that she could be alone there to bathe and consider her predicament.

Arriving at the stream, she glanced about to make

certain that she was unobserved, then drew off her clothing. She waded slowly into the inviting coolness of the rushing water, stopping when the level of the water was even with her shoulders. She relaxed and allowed the water to soothe her, then scooped some sand from the bottom of the stream and began vigorously scrubbing her skin until it glowed a healthy pink, an old method of bathing she had learned from a book she had read while still in school. Bending over, she proceeded to wash her long, silky tresses, then decided to swim for a few moments before heading back to the bank.

She found herself thinking how strange it was, bathing and swimming in a stream out in the middle of nowhere. She had really changed so much, had become so confused, since leaving Philadelphia and coming to Texas. She knew that it was Adam who was causing her confusion, who was the source of most of her change. It was he who was forcing her to admit that she had changed.

Recalling their lovemaking of the night before, she blushed once again. How had it happened? Why had she surrendered to his desires? Why had she surrendered to her own longings? Adam had been right, though. It had been very different from the first time he had taken her so savagely.

This time, there had been no hurry, only a growing fire deep within her as he had fanned the flames of passion between them. He had been gentle, but masterfully seductive. Oh, how could I? she bewailed silently as she paddled about in the cool water.

Sternly ordering herself to try and put the night before from her mind, she slowly approached the bank and stepped from the water, twisting her long hair between her fingers in order to remove most of the water from its tresses. She stepped toward the spot where she had left her clothing neatly folded, and reached a hand downward to take up her drawers, when she thought she detected a movement beneath the fabric. Withdrawing her hand sharply, she was unable to stifle a piercing scream as she saw a long snake crawl out from under the pile of clothing.

Sarah remained perfectly motionless, watching the snake with wide-eyed horror as it inched its way slowly toward the spot where she stood. Not knowing what to do, whether to attempt to run from it or to remain where she was, she simply gazed at it, her hand tightly clamped across her mouth to prevent herself from making any further sound.

"Don't move, Sarah," Adam's voice spoke calmly behind her. Sarah could have fainted with relief, so glad was she to hear him. Before she knew what was happening, Adam had aimed his pistol and deftly shot the snake. It twisted and wriggled about for a few more seconds, then lay still and lifeless, mere inches away from Sarah's bare feet upon the ground.

Sarah let out a long sigh of relief and turned to face Adam, clutching at him for support as he quickly covered the distance between them.

"It's all right now, Sarah, lass. There's no need to be afraid any longer," he softly whispered, holding her close, then frowned as she suddenly pulled away from him.

When she perceived that he was looking at her in a most disturbing manner, she suddenly realized that she was standing there completely naked before him. She reached down and snatched up her chemise, holding it up against her body to shield her nudity from his admiring eyes.

"How long have you been there?" she managed to demand.

"I guess you could say 'long enough.' I followed you when you left the cabin," he told her, his smile making her most uncomfortable.

"Why didn't you warn me that you were here?" Sarah protested indignantly, realizing that he must have been watching her all along, watching as she swam naked in the stream!

"I didn't see any need," Adam responded nonchalantly, still smiling. "Besides, if I had let you know of my presence, I would have missed a most charming, delectable sight," he remarked with a twinkle of mischief in his green eyes.

"Oh!" Sarah muttered with a frown, then shivered as a sudden breeze swept across her naked backside.

"You'd better get dressed before you get chilled," Adam suggested, still watching her with an increasing desire apparent in his eyes.

"Will you please turn around, then, and at least allow me some privacy?" Sarah demanded hotly, flushing beneath the expression on his handsome face.

"Sarah, lass, you certainly have nothing to hide from me now!" he remarked with a wicked grin as his eyes swept up and down her partially exposed figure.

"You are the most . . . the most ungentlemanly man I have ever known!" she informed him, before resolutely turning her back upon him and quickly drawing on her clothing.

Adam's eyes glowed with a passionate light as he stood staring at her womanly curves, his gaze traveling leisurely over her graceful back, her firmly rounded bottom, her shapely legs. He was disappointed when she pulled the chemise over her head and pulled on her drawers, then donned her dress, not bothering with her corset for the moment.

Turning defiantly back to face him, Sarah suddenly found herself growing weak beneath his gaze, and she hurriedly clutched her skirts and headed back toward the cabin, turning away from the dead snake with an involuntary shudder. Adam followed after her, still fighting down the waves of desire that now rushed over him.

When they reached the cabin, Sarah immediately stepped into her bedroom and shut the door. Adam decided that it would perhaps be best to wait and speak with her again later. He pulled his hat down over his head, glanced back once more toward the closed door of Sarah's room, then stepped back outside and quietly closed the front door after him.

Striding to the barn, he quickly and expertly saddled his horse, then mounted up and reined the horse toward town.

Sarah heard the sound of hoofbeats and flew to her window, watching as Adam rode away. Where could he be going? she asked herself. She knew that he was certainly riding in the wrong direction if he planned on riding to one of his wells. It suddenly occurred to her that he just might be contemplating going in search of Frank Mead and doing him further bodily harm!

She hurried out of the cabin and to the barn but was dismayed to discover that there were no other horses within. And her wagon was still in town. She would just have to wait until Adam returned, at which time she would demand an account of his journey into town!

Chapter Fifteen

Adam cantered along the dirt road toward town, lost in his own thoughts as he allowed the horse to set its own leisurely pace. His thoughts were centered almost exclusively upon his relationship with Sarah as he rode.

Recalling their rapturous lovemaking of the night before, Sarah's innocently passionate response, his own exhilarating sense of fulfillment, he smiled broadly to himself. There had never been a woman such as Sarah in his life before, and he knew that he was damned fortunate to have found her. He was more than ever certain that he would always love her to distraction, and that he would never give her up, never.

When he had seen her and Frank Mead together in that hotel room, he had come closer to committing murder than he had ever done before! Even now, he realized that he must take care to keep a rigid control upon his temper whenever he saw Frank Mead. As for the manner in which he had treated Sarah last night at the hotel, he was feeling a bit guilty. He knew that she was still almost a complete innocent, that she had most likely never even suspected Mead's designs upon her.

This morning, when he had stealthily followed Sarah to the stream, he had thought his heart would burst with both love and pride as he had watched her bathing. And then, that brief moment when she had carelessly flung herself into his arms with relief, he had felt an overwhelming urge to take her right there on the grass! But, he thought now with a sigh, she was behaving stubborn again this morning, still refusing to face up to facts, still refusing to accept their passionate night together.

Sooner or later, he vowed silently as he maneuvered his mount along the road, she would be forced to admit her love for him, forced to admit that the emotion she was feeling was completely opposite from the hate she tried so hard to convince herself she felt.

His thoughts suddenly turned in another direction, as he realized he still hadn't heard any news from his grandfather's solicitors in Scotland. He hoped that his letter had reached them, that the will would be settled soon. Too much had been happening to him lately to even think about the inheritance he would be receiving. He suddenly realized that he was in no hurry for the inheritance, that it might just possibly add more fuel to Sarah's insistence that their marriage be immediately annulled. And, he grimly reflected, there was no amount of money in the world to compensate him for the loss of the stubborn, willful, totally ravishing woman he loved!

True, he had told her that he must be legally married for about six months before he could meet the terms of his grandfather's will. But, he thought sheepishly, that had not been completely true. He had known all along that there was no stipulation whatsoever concerning the period of time his marriage lasted. He admitted to himself that something deep inside him must have made him tell her that particular untruth, that he must have unknowingly loved her even then. She would be furious with him if she ever discovered that he had lied to her. He didn't intend to allow her to learn of it, though.

Finally reaching the outskirts of town, he pulled upon the reins and firmly slowed the horse's pace to a walk as he neared the center of town. Pulling to a halt in front of the hotel, he dismounted and went inside to fetch Sarah's baggage. He ruefully thought to himself that she would probably never forgive him for leaving her clothing at the hotel!

Striding up to the front desk, he said, "I'm here to collect my wife's baggage. Is it still up in her room?"

"Yes sir, Mr. MacShane. But, well, Mr. Mead is occupying the room now," the clerk replied cautiously, carefully observing Adam's expression for any sign that there would be further violence. That was one thing he didn't want, his hotel being torn apart by a vengeful husband!

"Thanks." Adam swiftly climbed the stairs and headed for the room, then pounded upon the door.

"Who is it?" he heard Frank Mead's voice call out from inside.

"Open the door, Mead," Adam boomed, wondering if he was going to be forced to break down the door.

"I've got a gun, MacShane!" Mead threatened.

"And I said to open this blasted door!" Adam repeated ominously, fighting a losing battle with his temper once more.

The door was slowly edged open to reveal Mead, his boyish face bruised and swollen. He aimed the gun directly at Adam as he swung the door open wider. Adam contemptuously ignored him and strode inside the room, spotted Sarah's things, and hoisted the valise and bag up onto his shoulder. As he turned to leave the room, Mead said, "I plan to pay you back for last night, MacShane, make no mistake about that!"

"I'm sure as hell not the one who made the mistake!" Adam gruffly countered, an almost overwhelming urge to beat Frank Mead to a pulp threatening to override his better judgment. "You'd better stay away from my wife. You're damned lucky I didn't kill you!" he ground out.

"Your so-called 'wife' happens to be my business partner. That means I'll certainly have to see her again. You might as well get used to that fact, MacShane!" Frank insisted, feeling braver behind the protection of his gun. He warily observed Adam as he turned back to face him upon reaching the doorway.

"Mead, I've got a few things to say to you on the subject of your partnership with my wife. But now isn't the time. Just be forewarned that I intend to seek you out someday soon and have a little 'talk' about your business dealings," Adam warned, his face tightening. He left the room then, still fighting down his temper. Right now, he reminded himself reasonably, he wanted Mead alive and well; he wanted some answers about certain matters.

Outside again, he tied Sarah's baggage to his

mount, then led the horse down the street to Mrs. Patterson's. He looped the reins over the hitching post, then climbed the steps and knocked loudly on the front door.

"Why, Adam, what brings you here?" Mrs. Patterson remarked with a warm smile as she opened the door to admit him. "You haven't dropped by for quite a spell now. I guess you've been a mite busy, what with just getting hitched and all," she commented with a broad wink.

"Hello, Emma. Is Clem here? I'd like to speak with her," Adam replied, ignoring her remark about his recent marriage. He removed his hat and entered the parlor to wait.

"Sure thing, Adam. I'll go on up and tell her you're here," Mrs. Patterson responded. As she climbed the staircase, she thought to herself that something was obviously on Adam's mind, something that was making him behave a bit unlike himself.

A few moments later, Adam rose from his seat as Clementine entered the room, her blond curls freshly brushed and pinned, her dress a pretty sprigged cotton he hadn't seen before. She smiled impishly at him as she approached.

"Adam MacShane, you no-account rascal! Why in tarnation haven't you been to see me lately?" she asked, pouting prettily as she sat down on the sofa and patted the place beside her.

"Clem, you're looking prettier every day. You keep on this way, and you're going to be the most sought-after young lady in town before too much longer," Adam remarked with a friendly grin, taking the seat she had indicated next to her. "I stopped by because I felt it was time you and I had a talk about a few things."

"I was wondering when you'd get around to that," Clem responded, smiling happily with undisguised pleasure and satisfaction as she inched closer to him. "I knew this whole thing between you and that Yankee schoolteacher was nothing that really mattered. I knew it, just like I told you the other day when I was out at your cabin."

"Clem, it isn't like that at all," Adam protested, trying to explain. He was interrupted by her next words.

"Nothing's changed between us, Adam. I forgive you for marrying her, though I still can't for the life of me figure out why you didn't just come to me when you found out about that will and all. We'll just have to try and put all that behind us now," she informed him with a magnanimous air.

"Clem, please let me explain. I didn't marry Sarah for the reasons you seem to believe. It may have started out that way, but it isn't like that now . . ."

"You don't have to say another word, Adam!" Clem rushed on to say. "I know you must have felt sorry for her, too, besides needing someone to go along on a business arrangement. I guess you didn't want to approach me on those terms; you must have felt it would have been dishonorable or something. That's all right. You've known all along that I was just waiting for you to ask me to marry you, though. Well, I'm saying here and now that I'll still marry you just as soon as you can get free of that scheming little witch!"

"Clem," Adam said, searching for the right words.

"Clem, it is no longer merely a business arrangement. You see, I happen to have fallen in love with Sarah. I suppose I've loved her almost from the first moment I saw her. No matter what you think, no matter what she may have said, we are husband and wife now in every sense of the word, and I mean to keep it that way."

"You can't mean that!" Clementine cried vehemently, rising abruptly to her feet and glaring down at him in disbelief. "You're just saying that for some reason, because you feel sorry for her and want to protect her honor or something silly like that! Or maybe because of your inheritance. That's it, isn't it, Adam?" she asked, smiling once more as she sat back down. "You need to make everyone think you and Sarah are happily married so you'll get that money your grandfather left you, is that it? Well, there's no need to pretend with me! I'll keep your little secret, Adam, and I'll still be here for you whenever you're through with this little game of yours!"

"No, Clementine," Adam declared quietly, taking her hand gently and clasping it between his two larger ones. "What I told you is the truth. I love Sarah, and I intend to keep her for my wife from now on. I believe she loves me, too, even if she isn't quite ready to admit it yet. Whatever the case, you know there was never really anything between you and me, no commitments, no promises. You and I never spoke of serious things; we were simply two people who enjoyed each other's company, two good friends."

"Good friends?" Clementine burst out, growing

angry once more. "I would say we were certainly much more than that! You knew how I felt all along, Adam MacShane! And you led me to believe you cared for me as well!"

"That's not true, and you know it," Adam denied calmly. "I'm sorry if things didn't work out the way you wanted them to, but that's just the way things are. I never told you I loved you; I never encouraged you in that way. I love Sarah, she is my wife, and it's going to stay that way. Please try and understand, Clem. I'm truly sorry if you've been hurt. I never meant to hurt you," he implored, trying to remain kind and understanding in the face of her obstinate refusal to agree.

Clementine frowned, her mind flying to think of some way she could convince Adam that Sarah was not for him. He was obviously laboring under a strong misconception about the whole thing! Sarah didn't love him. No, she, Clem, loved him, would always love him. She'd have to make him see that, make him forget his little infatuation with the Yankee hussy!

And yet, she told herself, Adam had said that they were man and wife in every sense of the word now. Well, she was every bit as much of a real woman as that little tramp. No, she was more of a woman! She would have to think of some way to prove that to Adam.

"Clem, are you listening? I've got something else I need to ask you. I know the timing isn't quite right, but I need your help."

"What are you talking about?" she asked, her mind

211

returning from its silent reverie.

"Are you sure you want to know?" Adam questioned.

"Yes, of course, Adam. You know I'd help you anyway I can." She told herself that she would not give in, she would find some way to win him back yet! For now, though, she silently plotted, she would appear to accept it. She would be his "good friend" and she would do what he asked, if that's the way he wanted it. But, in the long run, it was she who would be his loving wife!

"Well, there's something I need you to do for me. It has to do with Frank Mead."

"What is it, Adam?" Clementine responded, forcing herself to smile at him. Just you wait, Adam MacShane, she declared silently.

"I know you've met him once or twice. Now that he's back in town, I want you to get to know him a whole lot better."

"Why?"

"Because, well, let's just say I've suspected him of something ever since John Bradford's death. And now that he's returned here, well, I thought he never would. Besides all that, he's convinced Sarah that they're business partners."

"Why should I want to help Sarah?" Clem protested loudly.

"It won't be for Sarah, it will be for me. I need you to try and get some information from Mead," Adam patiently explained.

"What sort of information?"

"Well, first of all, try and find out why he returned here. And why he left in the first place, though I must say I already suspect the answer to that one. Nevertheless, I want you to be friendly to him and see what you can discover about him. Anything at all about him that you think I might need to know."

"Why can't you have your 'wife' get your information for you?" Clem suggested caustically.

"I don't want Sarah involved in this any more than absolutely necessary!" Adam insisted.

Clem appeared to digest his words, then grudgingly agreed.

"All right, Adam. I'll do it for you. But are you really sure you want me to be so nice to him? Won't you be the least bit jealous?" she suggested, placing her hand gently upon his strong arm and gazing up at him with adoring eyes.

"Clem, you're an original!" Adam remarked with an amused chuckle, refusing to take her seriously. "Just make him think you're interested in him, that's all. I have a feeling our fine and dandy gentleman cannot resist flattery!"

"Very well," Clem said, drawing her hand away in disappointment. "You want me to find out anything I can about John Bradford's death, about why Mead left and then came back. You want to know all about his business dealings, right? Is that all?" she asked, growing a bit impatient with the entire subject.

"That just about covers it. I really appreciate this, Clem. If there's anything I can do for you, ever, don't hesitate to ask," Adam offered gallantly. "And, by the way, don't get too friendly with Mead, if you know what I mean," he told her, standing up and pulling on his hat.

"So you are jealous, aren't you?" Clementine

taunted playfully, walking with him to the front door. "I know you care, Adam. And someday, you'll look back on this and wonder how you could have been so blind and stupid. Honestly, I don't guess I've got any pride at all, offering to wait for a man who thinks he's involved with another woman!" she declared dramatically.

"Clementine, I do love you," Adam stated suddenly, opening the door and stepping across the threshold. Turning back to face an astonished, open-mouthed Clem, he added, "Just like a sister!" He laughed as she slammed the door.

Riding back toward his cabin, he reflected that Clem might just become more of a problem than he had earlier believed. He had known all along that she had fancied herself in love with him, but he knew it wasn't love at all, merely a passing infatuation. Clem had never known her father, and she needed a strong man around to keep her under control. He knew that she'd get over him in time. He also knew that he had never led her on, had honestly never offered her any encouragement, had never even so much as kissed her good night. Now, he knew that she'd do what he had asked of her, if only because she still believed she was in love with him.

Thinking back to his conversation with Clementine, he thought of Frank Mead once more. There had always been something not quite right about his story concerning the death of Sarah's uncle, especially the way he and his workers had disappeared shortly after the accident. And then, there was the curious matter of the wells being shut down. It just didn't make sense for a man to shut down his wells, wells that had been producing so much. Besides that, he knew that Mead hadn't even bothered to contact Sarah, John Bradford's legal heir, after it had all happened. And now, he had returned. But for what reason?

Actually, he admitted to himself as he neared the cabin, there had been another reason for his asking Clem to play up to Mead. It might just serve to divert Mead's attention away from Sarah! He felt certain that Frank Mead was smitten with her, that he would probably stop at nothing to win her away from him. It had been perfectly obvious what Mead had been trying to pull last night at the hotel, even if Sarah hadn't realized what was going on.

Sarah. He smiled to himself again. Just the mere thought of her brought the most wicked, delectable thoughts to his mind, caused a growing tightness in his loins! He knew that she would probably be angry with him for riding off and leaving her alone. Someday, someday he told himself, she would greet him with love in her beautiful eyes whenever he returned home. Someday she would speak the words he had waited to hear from her soft lips. Someday she would be his, completely and in every way.

He pulled the horse to a halt and led it inside the weather-beaten barn. After unsaddling the tired animal and rubbing it down with some hay, he headed back toward the cabin. He opened the door and stepped inside, then glanced about for Sarah.

"Where on earth have you been? You haven't done anything else to Frank Mead, have you? If you have, if you have harmed so much as one hair on his head, I'll never forgive you!" Sarah said angrily as she appeared in the doorway of the kitchen. Drying her hands on a towel, she stepped closer to Adam, bristling angrily as he smiled down at her disarmingly.

"Sarah, lass, nothing happened. You can rest assured about that. Your friend Mead felt the need for a gun in his hand this morning, so he's perfectly all right. Not that the gun stopped me. Anyway, I brought your baggage from the hotel," he told her, sauntering across the floor to deposit her belongings in her bedroom. Sarah followed after him quickly, still not satisfied with his answer.

"Why did you ride off like that, without so much as a good-bye? The least you could have done would have been to inform me of where you were going."

"Why, Sarah my love, don't tell me you were concerned about me?" Adam teased unmercifully, his eyes twinkling with mischief as he turned to her and attempted to take her into his arms.

"Don't be absurd!" Sarah retorted, slapping away his hands and retreating across the floor to what she judged to be a safer distance. "I simply do not like being left alone here, without any means of transportation. Did you happen to remember to retrieve the horse and wagon I rented?"

"No. I decided that you'd be better off not having them here. At least not until I can trust you to stay put."

"Adam MacShane, you had no right to make such a decision! What am I supposed to do all day long?

Am I not even permitted to take a ride now and then? You are being utterly impossible and overbearing! I refuse to be treated like this! You have no right to keep me here against my will!" she stormed at him.

"Well, I suppose I can leave you a horse in the barn, if you really feel the need to take a ride. But I want your word that you won't use it to leave here again, is that understood?" he demanded with a stern look.

"This is blackmail!" Sarah cried with an indignant gasp. "You have no right to force me to remain here as some sort of prisoner!"

"I don't want you to feel like a prisoner, lass. I just want your word that you won't leave me again if I permit you the use of a horse," Adam reasoned quietly, gazing down into her upturned, angry little face with a loving smile.

"Very well, I will not attempt to leave, at least for now!" Sarah responded, obviously unwilling to prolong their distasteful discussion any longer. "However, I certainly do not promise that I will never leave you! As soon as I can, I will leave here and never come back!" she threatened.

"No, you won't. You'll come to your senses before that happens," Adam replied maddeningly.

As he turned away from her, Sarah said, "By the way, I meant what I said to you last night. Frank Mead and I are business partners, and we no longer have any need for your services on our wells. Therefore, you may return to working your own wells and leave us to ours. I assure you, if there were any way I could possibly manage to never see you again right now, I would not hesitate to do so!"

"Sarah," Adam said with a heavy sigh, "didn't last night teach you anything?"

"It only taught me that you are an experienced rake, a man who does not hesitate to take his pleasure whenever he chooses! I swear to you that I will never again be taken in by your wiles! I demand that you promise never to touch me again!" she told him, a very determined look on her beautiful face. She refused to admit to him that she blamed herself for what had occurred every bit as much as she blamed him.

"No, lass. I won't make you that promise, not now, not ever. You are my wife, and I will try every way I can, do everything in my power, to make you realize that we belong together!" Adam ground out, before wrenching open the door and marching outside.

"Oh!" Sarah uttered aloud. She slammed the door after him, then stalked back into the kitchen where she continued with her bread making, pounding the soft dough with a vengeance. As she worked, she reflected that she had never before lost her temper as often as she had done since meeting Adam Mac-Shane. She was thoroughly ashamed and disgusted with the termagant she had become, with the emotional woman she now saw herself to be.

What she had told Adam was true. She wouldn't attempt to leave again just yet, for she realized that she really had nowhere else to go. She knew with a certainty that if she attempted to return to the hotel Adam would merely come after her again, merely creating another humiliating scene! For the time being, she was forced to remain in his cabin, forced to remain legally tied to him. But just as soon as she received a reply to that letter, she told herself, she would attempt to erase the entire memory of Adam MacShane from her mind forever!

As she punched and then formed the bread dough, a tiny voice at the back of her mind asked her if she could ever erase what Adam had done to her, if she could ever truly forget the things that had happened to her since meeting him. She surely could not pretend she was an innocent virgin any longer! No, that was something that could never be reversed, something she would simply have to live with for the rest of her life.

Why do I become so weak when he takes me in his arms, when he caresses and kisses me as he did last night? she silently asked herself with a last angry punch at the unresisting dough. What is it about him that makes him so impossible to resist? She told herself that it was nothing more than pure animal lust, that she was nothing more than a disgraceful, dishonorable creature who did not deserve any self-respect.

And yet, the tiny voice insisted before Sarah finished with her task, what if he tried again, as he surely would? What if he attempted to make love to her again tonight? What would she do? Would she really be able to resist him, to remain strong against the temptation to surrender? Would she really be able to keep from surrendering to her own deep, overpowering desires, desires that she hadn't even known existed until she'd met Adam?

That was a prospect she didn't wish to face. She didn't intend to give him the opportunity to seduce her ever again! She would be on her guard at all times; she would be strong, no matter what he said or did. Adam MacShane, she vowed to herself, must not be allowed to become an integral part of her life!

Chapter Sixteen

Sarah lay in almost breathless anticipation that night, listening intently for any sound that would indicate to her that Adam planned to enter her bedroom and attempt to make love to her again. She breathed a long sigh of relief and leaned back against her pillow as she finally heard him come home late that night and go directly to his room. He closed the door softly, and then there was silence.

She refused to acknowledge the increasing restlessness she felt, the certain anxiety she was experiencing as she realized that he apparently had no intention of bothering her that night. He was probably staying away simply to put her off guard! She turned over upon her side resolutely and pounded the softness of her pillow with her fist but could not completely ignore the strong yearnings deep within her as her body refused to surrender to sleep.

The next morning Sarah slept much later than was her custom, not having been able to drift into sleep until the very early hours of the dawn. She awakened long after Adam had left for his day's work at the wells, and she crawled lazily from the bed and shuffled into the kitchen to make herself a fresh pot of coffee.

After preparing herself a bit of breakfast as well, she returned to her room and dressed in her new split riding skirt, a lightweight white cotton shirt, and her oldest pair of leather boots. She pulled back her thick hair and tied it with a red ribbon at her neck, allowing its luxuriant mass to cascade down her slender back.

Stepping outside into the late-morning sunshine, she hurried inside the barn and saddled the horse she had hoped she would find there. At least Adam had made good his word to allow her some means for riding!

Climbing up into the saddle, she gently kicked the horse and turned it down the road toward town. She knew that she must find Frank Mead and endeavor to explain the disastrous events of the night at the hotel. She also wanted to discover if he had been successful in locating a crew to work their wells. The one thing she most certainly did not want was for them to be forced to rely upon Adam for their workers!

Riding leisurely along the road toward town, Sarah reflected that the soft leather riding skirt had definitely been a wise investment. For the first time, she was able to enjoy horseback riding, able to ride astride, unimpeded by her long, full skirts and cumbersome bustle. She suddenly glanced overhead as she thought she perceived the distant sound of thunder. She saw that the sky was indeed beginning to appear quite overcast now, that it was gradually becoming darker by the minute. It was obviously going to rain, or perhaps even storm, and she urged the horse to step livelier as she neared Wildcat City.

Once there, she pulled the horse to a halt in front of

the hotel and quickly dismounted, stealing another concerned glance upward at the darkening sky and threatening clouds. Striding inside the hotel, she inquired of the clerk if Frank Mead was still occupying the same room there. Receiving a terse but affirmative reply she ascended the stairs and proceeded down the narrow hallway to the appropriate room. Knocking on the door, Sarah called, "Mr. Mead? Frank, are you there? This is Sarah Bradford."

Just as she began to turn away and leave, the door opened. "Sarah, how good of you to come!" Frank told her, drawing on his coat and straightening his tie. "Would you care to come in?"

Sarah immediately noticed his bruised face, his blackened eye, and she winced inwardly as she recalled the embarrassing incident that had taken place inside the room. She hesitated for the space of a few seconds, then suggested, "Frank, I think it would perhaps be best if we spoke downstairs in the lobby, or maybe in the restaurant. I'm terribly sorry if I've come at an inopportune moment. I feel perfectly dreadful about what happened the other night," she said with sincere regret.

"It wasn't your fault, Sarah," Mead hurried to assure her, smiling as he came out into the hallway and shut the door to his room. "Of course, I understand that it would probably look better if we spoke elsewhere. Shall we go?" He offered her his arm, and she took it with an answering smile as the two of them walked down the hallway and back down the stairs.

Sitting at a table in the hotel restaurant, Sarah again apologized for Adam's actions. "Frank, I truly am sorry for the way Mr. MacShane behaved. It was thoroughly inexcusable and completely unforgivable for him to treat you in such a brutal manner! I can assure you, I certainly informed him of such!" Sarah remarked emphatically, frowning as she glanced across at Mead's discolored face.

"Now, now, Sarah," he reassured her, patting her hand in a comforting gesture, "it wasn't your fault. I only wish you had never become involved with MacShane! I never did find out what happened after he threw that lucky punch at me, you know," he remarked, appearing a trifle confused.

"Oh, well . . ." Sarah faltered, coloring beneath his gaze. How on earth could she tell him about what had happened after Adam had carried her from the hotel and taken her back to his cabin? How could she reveal to him the humiliating, intimate details of what had taken place between herself and Adam? She finally said, "Nothing much happened. He simply forced me to ride back to his cabin with him. We are still occupying separate rooms, and it is as if we are two strangers in the same house." Let him believe that there was nothing more involved in the matter, nothing such as a wild, abandoned night of passion between herself and Adam!

"Well, I'm relieved to hear that he didn't hurt you. I could kill him for treating you in such a shameful way!" Frank declared with a darkening glint in his usually friendly eyes. Sarah felt a sudden uneasiness as she observed the ruthless expression that had now appeared upon his well-bred features, and she quickly sought to change the subject.

"Have you been able to locate enough men to work

our wells?"

"Yes, I have. I signed them up earlier this morning, as a matter of fact. They're due to start the first thing tomorrow morning."

"Excellent!" Sarah commented with a pleased smile. "It appears that our business partnership is going to be successful after all." And she would be done with the business arrangement with Adam!

"Of course, Sarah, dear. The two of us should have a long and properous partnership!" Mead answered, the deadly gleam in his eyes replaced now by a pleasant sparkle. "I think the two of us should celebrate our future success. Do you think you could possibly get away from MacShane long enough to have dinner with me here tonight?"

"Oh, Frank, I don't really think so," Sarah answered regretfully. "You see, Adam has this idea that I am truly his wife, no matter how much I try to convince him that our arrangement is still nothing more than a business contract. But, of course, now that you've returned and our wells will be worked, there is no longer any need for my business partnership with Adam. As a matter of fact, I have already written to a friend of my uncle's, a lawyer in Philadelphia, in order to begin the necessary proceedings for an annulment from Mr. MacShane. If everything goes as smoothly as I hope it will, I will have my annulment within the next month or so. Then I can resume my own life once more!" she remarked with determination.

"I see. Well, I can tell you that I'm very pleased that you intend to take care of that matter as soon as possible. I myself will be glad when you're finally free of Adam MacShane! A woman as beautiful and spirited as you, Sarah, certainly wasn't meant for the likes of that ruffian," Frank told her with an admiring gleam in his eyes and a slight, meaningful smile on his face. Sarah shyly smiled in response and cast her eyes downward.

"I suppose I really must be going now. I have other errands I must see to before I return to the cabin. May I count on you to meet me at my uncle's cabin early tomorrow morning then?" Sarah asked.

"Certainly. I'll be more than happy to come and escort you personally, if you wish."

"No, I don't think that would be such a good idea. I'll just meet you there. Until tomorrow then," she said, rising to her feet beside the table and gracefully extending her small hand.

"I hope there will be many more tomorrows between us, Sarah," Frank replied, his bruised face very serious as he took her hand and clasped it between both of his own.

Sarah lowered her eyes beneath his gaze and slowly withdrew her hand, then turned and hurried from the restaurant. She was not accustomed to such open flattery, to such meaningful glances.

Mead stood motionless, watching her with a fierce light in his eyes as she soon disappeared from his view. Sinking back down into his chair at the table, he took a cigar from his coat pocket and lit it, then sat and contemplated all that had occurred since he had returned to Wildcat City.

One thing was certain, he thought as he stared downward toward the cigar he held in his hand,

Sarah Bradford was the type of woman he wouldn't find so easy to put from his mind. As a matter of fact, he told himself, she was exactly the sort of woman who would be downright impossible to forget. But then, he definitely didn't intend to forget her!

Sarah had left the hotel and returned outside to her waiting horse when she was halted by Clementine's voice calling to her. "Sarah! Sarah, wait a minute!" She hurried down the boardwalk toward Sarah, her boots connecting noisily with the bare wooden boards.

"Yes, what is it?" Sarah asked frostily, torn between a desire to mount up and ride away from the catty young woman and her natural curiosity to discover why Clementine was hailing her at all.

"I just wondered if Adam has mentioned his coming to see me yesterday," Clementine told her with a broad smile. She would try her darnedest to cause trouble between Sarah and Adam and she saw her opportunity to cause some trouble right now!

"I do not know what you are talking about, nor do I wish to know," Sarah replied icily, turning back to her horse and preparing to mount. She swung up into the saddle, but Clem's firm hand on the reins prevented her from riding away.

"Remove your hand at once!" Sarah ordered imperiously, treating Clementine as if she were one of the pupils back at the school. She had learned at the very beginning of her teaching career that because she was small in stature, she would have to compensate for that fact with a rigid air of command whenever necessary.

"I can see he didn't," Clem remarked with a malicious smile. "I can see right off that he didn't tell you about his coming to see me. I guess he doesn't tell you very much, does he? He and I are just as close as we can be, and yet he doesn't even bother to tell you, his own 'wife' what goes on in his life," she gloated, taunting Sarah with an obvious enjoyment of the situation.

"If you do not remove your hand at once, I shall force you to do so!" Sarah threatened tightly, growing increasingly angry.

"Well, I guess I don't see no need to keep you here any longer. Why don't you just come right out and ask Adam about his coming to see me? Why don't you ask him about the plans we made? Plans that surely don't include you!" Let her think the plans were of a personal nature, Clem thought to herself with smug satisfaction.

Sarah felt herself become nearly as furious as she had ever been, and she didn't pause to reconsider the rashness of her actions as she took up the other end of the reins and brought them whistling down through the air, connecting with a loud slap across Clementine's wrist. Clem yelped in stunned surprise and pain, as Sarah turned her mount and swiftly galloped away.

Clementine stood vigorously rubbing her throbbing wrist, glaring murderously after the retreating figure of the hated Sarah. If it was the last thing she ever did, she would get even with that little witch for daring to hit her! That little Yankee would soon regret the day she had raised a hand to Clementine

Patterson! And she'd be doubly repaid when she, Clem, finally won Adam away from her!

Sarah inexorably urged the horse faster, too upset by Clem's taunts to exercise caution as she rode. She could not deny the powerful effect Clem's jibes had had on her. So, she thought angrily as she used the reins to increase the animal's speed, Adam had been to see Clementine. What sort of plans had the two of them made? she wondered silently. Should she believe Clem's words? Should she believe that Clem and Adam were making plans for a future together?

Could it possibly be that he had been lying to her all along, that he had been declaring his love and devotion to her while playing up to Clementine at the same time? He had probably only told her his deceitful lies to achieve his own lustful purposes, just as she had always suspected!

Oh! she fumed to herself as she rode. She could tear Clementine's blond hair from her head, could hit her a dozen times harder than she had just done! As for Adam MacShane, she would tell him precisely what she thought of him just as soon as he returned to the cabin this evening! She would thoroughly berate him for using her, for forcing his attentions upon her while all the while keeping Clementine Patterson waiting for him on the side! She would show him once and for all that she was not to be trifled with, that she was made of much sterner stuff than either he or that hussy, Clem, had counted on!

Sarah pulled on the reins then, finally allowing the wheezing horse to slow its breakneck pace. A loud clap of thunder rang out, causing her to shiver involuntarily. As she peered overhead at the ominous clouds, she happened to turn her head about and discover that there were three horsemen following her. She instinctively reached for her gun, then realized that the riding skirt she had purchased did not have a pocket, that her pistol was still lying on the washstand in her room back at the cabin.

As she felt a growing uneasiness descend upon her, she told herself that she was being utterly ridiculous. There had been other riders on this road many times when she had been to town. It was only the approaching storm that caused her to feel the uneasy fear.

As she kicked the horse to make it go faster once more, she heard one of the three men behind her loudly remark, "Hey, ain't that the little gal we seen at that auction that time? By damn, I wanted to bid on her myself! Maybe it ain't too late yet to make her acquaintance now!"

The other two men laughed in ribald accompaniment, and the three of them began swiftly closing the distance between themselves and Sarah. Sarah gulped as she realized that they might attempt to do her harm, and she kicked her mount harder as she sought to try and outrun them.

"Hey there, missy! Where you going in such a all-fired hurry? We just want to have a little fun!" one of them called out as they continued in pursuit.

Sarah glanced backward, then uttered a desperate gasp of fear and growing dismay as she realized that they were gaining on her. She knew that it might not be possible to outdistance them, and she frantically wondered if someone else would be coming along to help her. She searched the surrounding countryside for any sign of other people, then bent even lower over the horse's neck in an attempt to gain even more speed.

She screamed loudly as she suddenly felt a large, calloused hand closing upon her upper arm, as the reins were jerked roughly from her grasp. Her horse was pulled to an abrupt halt, and the man who had grabbed her arm now yanked her down from her lathered mount and forced her to stand beside him upon the ground.

"You ain't got no call to go and act so uppity with us! We just want to have a little talk with you, honey, that's all!" the man who imprisoned her assured her with a leering smile. The three coarse men surrounded her, and she was roughly pushed and then shoved from one to the other as they laughed and jeered at her frantic efforts to escape. She could feel their dirty, pawing hands everywhere upon her body, and she screamed again and again as she tried to fight them off.

"Stop it! Let go of me! How dare you!" she cried. Suddenly, the front of her cotton blouse was savagely ripped open, revealing her partially exposed breasts to their lustful gazes. She shrieked piercingly as the blouse was then ripped completely from her body and they tried to tear off her skirt as well.

One of them held her now, forcing her face upward toward his own crazed one as he brought his savage, bruising mouth down upon her opened lips. She struggled violently, her mind reeling as she tried to think of some way to escape them, to prevent her body from being brutally violated by such animals!

"Leave some of the fight in her, Ben!" the man's companions chimed in, their eyes wide and crazy with their lust. Sarah finally managed to break free from her captor, but she was soon laughingly imprisoned by another. She freed her lips and screamed as loud as she possibly could, using the very last of her breath.

Suddenly she heard a loud boom and took it to be another burst of thunder. But it was quickly followed by an identical sound, and she gratefully realized that it was gunfire. She nearly fainted with relief when she was suddenly released; she sank to her knees upon the hard earth, clutching the torn remnants of her chemise about her exposed bosom.

"All right, you filthy bastards, get out of here before I kill you!" Frank Mead threatened viciously, an evil-looking pistol pointed toward the astonished group of men. Without another word, the three attackers mounted up and swiftly rode away, back toward town, leaving a stunned and humiliated Sarah alone with her rescuer.

"Sarah! Sarah, my dear, are you all right? Are you all right?" Frank demanded as he quickly dismounted and rushed to her side.

"Yes. Yes, I think I'm all right," Sarah managed to utter, still clutching her clothing about her with shaking hands. "Oh, Frank, those terrible men were going to . . . they were going to rape me!" she cried tearfully, as the full impact of what had almost happened dawned upon her.

"I know. But it's all right now, Sarah. They'll never bother you again," Frank assured her as he knelt beside her. He drew off his own jacket and placed it about her naked shoulders. Sarah smiled up at him in tremulous gratitude as she allowed him to help her to her feet.

Another flash of lightning and an answering clap of thunder rang out as Frank placed a comforting arm about her shoulders and said, "Sarah, I'm so sorry this had to happen. You should never have been out riding alone like this. That's why I was coming this way, to make certain you got home safely."

"I usually have a gun with me, but I didn't today. I can only thank God you happened to be following me and were able to arrive in time!" Sarah said with a violent shudder. She pushed the thick strands of hair away from her face and leaned against Frank, allowing him to support her as he helped her to her horse.

"You'd better let me take you into town to see the doctor. I want to make sure you're really all right," Frank told her with genuine concern. His kind face was such a welcome sight, she nearly cried aloud with the intensity of her gratitude to him.

"No. I'm fine, really I am. I'm just a little bruised, that's all, and slightly dirty. A hot bath will do wonders for me, I'm sure," Sarah calmly replied. Then, as they reached her horse, she suddenly turned to Frank and threw herself into his arms as the tears finally came.

"Oh, Frank, it was so horrible! So unspeakably degrading! How can I ever thank you for saving me?"

"Sarah, you know you don't have to thank me. Surely you can sense how I feel about you? Now there, there, it's all right now. I'm going to take you home now. You'll be just fine after a bath and a good night's sleep," Frank consoled her. He lifted her up into the saddle, then went back and mounted his own waiting horse. He took the reins and led her horse along after his.

Sarah slumped forward in the saddle, still modestly trying to cover herself as she rode. She vaguely thought of how she could smell the gathering rain, of how uncomfortable it would be if they were unable to reach the cabin before the downpour started. She only hoped that Adam hadn't returned from the wells yet, for she knew he would be uncontrollably furious if he knew what had happened to her. She certainly didn't feel up to any explanations just yet, so she hoped that she would be able to bathe and rest a bit before he returned for their evening meal.

She thought again of how miraculous it had been for Frank to arrive in time. She must try and forget about the entire incident, and yet she knew she would never forget Frank's help, nor his unfailing kindness to her afterward.

When they finally reached the cabin, Frank lifted her down and said, "Sarah, I'd better see to your horse before it begins raining. You go on in and see to your bath. I'll stay around if you want me to, at least until MacShane comes home," he offered solicitously.

"No, that really won't be necessary, but thank you all the same. I'd rather be alone for a while now, if you don't mind. I'm sure I'll be almost completely recovered by morning. I'll see you at the cabin tomorrow morning, just as we planned."

"Very well. Now you get on in the cabin and get some rest," Frank commanded gently with a comforting smile.

"Of course. Frank, I can never express to you the full extent of my gratitude . . ." Sarah began, only to be cut off by him.

"That's not necessary. I'd do anything in the world for you, Sarah," he told her. She smiled tremulously once more, then turned away and headed for the cabin.

Frank watched her go inside, then took her horse into the barn and unsaddled it. Striding back outside, he mounted up and hurriedly rode away.

Sarah immediately set the water on to heat for her bath, then went into her bedroom and carefully drew off her tattered clothing. She shivered as she viewed the damage done to her blouse and chemise. She tossed them onto the bed, then drew off her skirt, which she was glad to see had remained unscathed. She removed her drawers and donned a lightweight wrapper as she padded barefoot back across the floor to fetch the hot water.

After she had filled the wooden bathtub, she closed her bedroom door and took off her wrapper. Acting on a sudden impulse, she approached the mirror hanging above the washstand and stood before it, completely naked, as she viewed the evidences of the attack.

There were already several colorful bruises appearing on her arms, as well as several swollen areas on her tender breasts and back. She grimaced as she viewed the painful areas, then, turning away from the mirror, she hurried back to immerse her aching body into the soothing warmth of the bath water.

Schooling her thoughts away from the terrifying ordeal she had endured, she relaxed back against the tub and closed her eyes. She soaked for several minutes, then took up the cake of soap and vigorously soaped and scrubbed her entire body. She stood up and climbed out of the tub, then bent over it and washed her dust-caked tresses of hair. Soon, she felt clean once more, and she donned a fresh nightgown and wrapper.

She piled her still damp hair high atop her head as she opened the door and dragged the tub back across the floor to the rear entrance of the cabin. She decided that she would empty it later, and she returned to her room and took up her torn blouse and chemise. Frowning as she realized that they were beyond repair, she contemplated what she should do with them, then decided that she would burn them.

Entering the kitchen, she placed the torn clothing on the floor beside the stove and turned to make a fresh pot of coffee. She jumped as she heard the front door open and close and Adam's boots stomp across the floor.

"Sarah, where did you go today? Your horse is lathered and tired. Didn't you even bother to rub him down?"

"I went for a ride. I'm sorry about the horse. I suppose I forgot," Sarah retorted stiffly, turning away from him as she put the coffee pot on top of the stove.

"What's the matter, Sarah? You don't act as if you're feeling well. Did you get caught out in the rain? It's sure storming now," Adam said, frowning as she still refused to face him.

"No, I'm fine. I simply took a bath and didn't wish to dress again. I'll have our dinner prepared in less than an hour. I didn't expect you home so early," she answered calmly. However, her hand trembled uncontrollably as she turned to take up a plate of bread, and she cried out as the plate clattered to the floor.

"Something is wrong. What is it? What's happened?" Adam demanded sternly, striding across to grasp her by the shoulders. He removed his hands as Sarah couldn't refrain from wincing with the pain. "What is it? I demand that you tell me at once!" he repeated authoritatively, scrutinizing her face.

"Nothing is wrong," Sarah denied, walking away from him. She left the kitchen and went back into the privacy of her bedroom.

Adam glared after her, knowing deep within that there was definitely something not quite right. He bent down to retrieve the fallen platter of bread and his gaze lit upon Sarah's discarded blouse and chemise, where she had carelessly left them lying on the floor beside the stove.

He snatched up the torn garments and hastily examined them, then threw them back onto the floor with an oath and stalked from the kitchen to Sarah's bedroom. He entered without knocking, surprising her as she turned from the mirror where she was brushing her long hair.

"How dare you! I've told you on several occasions, you have no right to enter my room in such a manner!"

"Sarah, don't lie to me any longer!" Adam spoke through tightened lips. "I found your clothes on the floor in the kitchen, your torn and dirty clothes! What in the world happened to you?" he roared at her, towering over her as he demanded an answer.

"It's none of your business!" Sarah retorted, whirling about and presenting him with her back. She fought the tears that threatened to spill over.

Adam firmly clasped her shoulders and forced her about to face him. "Sarah, lass, tell me what happened! Damn it, woman, something's happened to you! What was it? Was it Mead? Did he attack you?" Adam probed, growing more and more deadly as the thought of Mead entered his head.

"No!" Sarah hurried to deny. "Frank had nothing to do with it. Except for the fact that he saved me from a horrible fate! I don't want to tell you, I don't want to worry about what you'll do if I tell you the truth!" she cried, the tears spilling over now as she averted her face.

"Sarah," Adam spoke softly now, placing a gentle finger beneath her trembling chin and firmly forcing her to face him. "Sarah, lass, what was it? I promise you that I'll hear you out before I take any action. What happened to you?"

Sarah gazed upward at him in anguish, realizing that she must tell him. She was afraid that he would attempt to find her attackers, that he would attempt to avenge her in some way. She realized that he would be up against three vicious men, that he might possibly be killed because of her, a prospect she did not wish to face. She swallowed hard and told him reluctantly. "There were three of them. They rode after me on the road back from town today; they forced me from my horse and attacked me! They were going to rape me, and they would have succeeded if it hadn't been for Frank!" she said, the tears running freely down her flushed cheeks.

"Mead? What did he do?" Adam asked, the rage building to a fever pitch inside him at the thought of his Sarah being attacked.

"He came riding along just in time. He had a gun, and he ordered them to ride off or he'd shoot them. There!" she declared defiantly, sniffing back the tears. "I've told you the whole of it. Please, please don't do anything! I'd just like to try and forget the whole terrible ordeal!" she pleaded with him, pulling away from him now as she sank down upon the bed. She pulled a handkerchief from the pocket of her wrapper and dabbed at her eyes, then blew her nose.

Adam stood for a moment looking down at her, torn between his vengeful fury and his desire to comfort his beloved wife. He loved her so very much, he knew he could never forget, or forgive, what those men had done to her today. He knelt beside her, drawing her gently into his strong arms as he said, "Sarah, I'm sorry. Oh, lass, I'm sorry if I upset you even more. Heaven knows you've been through enough today. Don't worry, I promise you I won't do anything hasty. I promise you that I won't hurt you further. Now you just lie back and get some rest. I'll see to our dinner tonight. Are you certain you're unharmed?'' he asked, drawing back to search her tear-streaked face with loving eyes.

"I'm all right. I'm bruised and exhausted, but I shall recover," Sarah replied. She sniffed once more as she allowed Adam to pick her up and place her between the covers of the bed.

He lovingly tucked them up around her neck as he whispered softly, "Sarah, I love you. I'd give anything in the world not to have this happen to you." He brushed her cheek with a light kiss, then quietly left the room and headed back into the kitchen.

He was far from feeling the calm rationality he hoped he had displayed to Sarah! He had never felt so murderous in his life! He intended to find Sarah's attackers, and he intended to question Mead about the incident as well.

Thinking of Mead, he felt a tiny doubt suddenly lodge itself in his mind. Why had Mead allowed those men to escape unharmed? Why had he not taken them into town to the sheriff? Out in this part of the world, if a man attacked a woman the way those three cowards had, they were more times than not killed upon the spot. Why, then, had Frank Mead allowed them to go completely free?

Whatever the reason, Adam promised himself, he damned sure intended to find out. He would keep his word to Sarah, for she had been through enough. He would attempt to behave calmly and rationally, even though, right at this very moment, he desired nothing more than to fly out of the cabin and ride like hell into town to find those bastards and exact his vengeance upon them! But, thinking of Sarah, he forced himself to keep his word to her. He loved her more than life itself, and he never wanted to do anything that would hurt her. But he'd be damned if he'd allow anyone else to ever hurt her again!

Chapter Seventeen

Clementine put the finishing touches to her painstaking toilette, then advanced to the full-length mirror located behind her bedroom door in order to survey the end result of her efforts. She preened in satisfaction, obviously pleased as she critically viewed her blossoming young figure encased in the form-fitting white cotton dress, its heart-shaped neckline a trifle lower than her mother would approve. Smiling wickedly at her reflection, she tugged it even lower, exposing a bit more of her ripe young bosom.

Her shining blond hair had been carefully arranged atop her head, a few loose tendrils curling naturally about her attractive face. Turning away from the mirror, she drew on her gloves and caught up her matching bag, then opened the door and crept quietly downstairs and outside. She glanced back once more to make certain her mother had not observed her departure, then turned her steps toward the hotel, where she hoped her time and efforts would not be wasted.

Adam had instructed her to flatter Frank Mead, to act interested in him, and that was just what she intended to do. Besides, she thought as she quickened her steps along the boardwalk, it might just be fun. After all, Frank Mead was an attractive young fellow, though not nearly as handsome as Adam. But he did possess a certain likable charm, a decidedly well-cultured manner that was so different from most of the men she had encountered. Come to think of it, she told herself with a mischievous smile, the assignment Adam had given her might be very enjoyable after all. Perhaps she could even make him jealous of Frank Mead!

She took a deep breath of determination before entering the hotel, inhaling the freshness of the cool night air, which smelled clean and pure after the hard rain of the afternoon. She carefully lifted her white skirts higher as she stepped inside the building, taking care not to soil them with the traces of muddy footprints that lined the weathered boardwalk and the hotel's wooden floor.

Clementine disdainfully ignored the curious stares directed her way as she climbed the stairs to the second floor and marched resolutely down the narrow hallway. She had inquired earlier of the desk clerk as to which room Mead was occupying, and she now paused before his door. She hoped Adam knew what he was doing, asking her to try and get information from Mead. Taking another deep breath, she knocked loudly upon the door, then gave a last hasty pat to her hair.

"Yes? May I help you?" Frank Mead asked in puzzlement as he opened his door to reveal a very attractive young lady who seemed vaguely familiar to him.

"Frank Mead? Don't you remember me? I'm

Clementine Patterson. You stayed at my mother's boardinghouse when you first came to Wildcat City, remember?" Clem responded with a sweet smile and a seductive fluttering of her long eyelashes.

"Yes, I believe I do remember you, Miss Patterson," Frank replied, obviously pleased. "But what are you doing here? Is there something I can do for you?"

"Why, I've just come to see you, Mr. Mead. I heard you had come back, and I just, well, I just thought we might renew our acquaintance, if I may be so bold," Clem told him with a feigned coyness.

"Of course, Miss Patterson," Frank eagerly agreed, coming out of his darkened room now and taking up his hat. "Would you perhaps care to have dinner with me downstairs this evening?"

"Yes, I believe I would," she said, smiling again as she took his arm and walked so that her skirts gently swayed against him in an enticing manner.

Throughout their meal together, Clementine effectively flirted and simpered, totally intriguing the unsuspecting Frank. Sarah's image kept floating through his mind, but he consoled himself with the reminder that his attraction for Clementine had nothing whatsoever to do with his regard for Sarah. No, his feelings for Sarah were more than just mere desire or lust, for he believed he had fallen in love with her, that he would someday marry her. As for the delightfully entrancing, delectable creature sitting opposite him at the table, she was exactly the sort of pleasant diversion he was accustomed to dallying with on his many travels. She would make a very enjoyable companion for a brief period of time, and he would take special care to keep their "relationship" discreet so that Sarah need never know.

After dinner, Frank escorted Clementine back upstairs to his room and invited her inside, insisting that the two of them could certainly share a drink before saying good night.

"Why, Mr. Mead, what on earth must you think of me?" Clementine said in mock indignation as she paused outside the doorway to his room. "I know I must have appeared a bit forward, but you know good and well a young lady should never go into a gentleman's room alone with him, especially not at this late hour of the night," she playfully admonished him, a mischievous sparkle in her deep-blue eyes.

"Couldn't we perhaps make an exception to that old-fashioned rule just this once?" Frank asked with a meaningful smile, his gaze traveling downward to rest upon her swelling bosom.

"Oh, come now, Mr. Mead," Clementine responded with a flirtatious smile. "I really don't think I should, at least not tonight. However, you just might be able to persuade me to do so the next time we see each other," she remarked suggestively, leaning slightly forward so that even more of her enticing cleavage was laid open to his lustful gaze.

"Would you have dinner with me again tomorrow evening then, Miss Patterson?" Frank inquired, feeling his desire mounting, certain that he would be able to bed the delightful little baggage by tomorrow night, if he would only be patient now.

"Why, I'd be delighted. Until tomorrow evening

then, at about eight o'clock? I'll be more than happy to meet you here at the hotel again."

"That sounds fine. Thank you for a most enjoyable evening, Miss Patterson," Frank said, feeling confident that he had made a conquest. He smiled to himself as Clementine turned and walked away gracefully, her hips swaying gently as she inclined her head in order to look back at him once more with a provocative half smile.

Clementine hurried out of the hotel and back down the street to the boardinghouse, stealthily creeping inside the darkened house and back upstairs to her room. She quickly removed all of her clothing and unpinned her bright hair, then pulled a nightgown over her head and jumped into bed, hoping her mother hadn't realized that she had stayed out so late.

She certainly had a few interesting tidbits of information she would pass on to Adam concerning Frank Mead. She planned to ride out to Adam's place first thing in the morning, knowing full well that he would certainly want to hear what she had to say as soon as possible. And if that little schoolteacher happened to be around, so much the better! She would probably believe that they had planned the meeting to discuss their future together!

With a triumphant grin, Clem nestled down further between the covers and closed her eyes. Heaving a deep sigh of supreme satisfaction, she drifted off into a sleep filled with dreams of herself finally becoming Adam's wife.

Early the following morning Sarah awakened and

stretched lazily, then remembered that she was supposed to meet Frank at her uncle's cabin. She hastily rose and dressed herself in another cotton blouse and her riding skirt, then braided her thick hair and pinned it high on her neck. She saw that Adam had already gone, so she decided to miss breakfast and be on her way. She hurried out to the barn and saddled her horse, heading it down the road toward her uncle's old cabin a couple of miles away.

She suddenly realized that she had completely forgotten about the terrible thing that had happened to her the day before, and she resolved to keep it from her mind. She breathed deeply, inhaling the fresh morning air, reveling in the beautiful colors of the spring countryside. She wryly reflected that the landscape seemed even more familiar to her now than that back in Philadelphia, and she wondered anew how soon she would be leaving Texas. She was forced to admit to herself that she was in no great hurry to leave behind the beauty of this untamed country in order to return to the civilized, bustling world of the city.

She was glad to see that Frank was already waiting for her at the cabin when she arrived, and she allowed him to assist her down from her horse as she said, "Oh, Frank, this is so very exciting! Imagine, our own oil wells producing, possibly earning us both a great deal of money!"

"Well, we can't say for sure exactly how much we can expect to make just yet, Sarah," Frank cautioned her as he led her along toward the first well. "The crew is already at work. I thought you might enjoy watching them for a while."

"Of course I would. I want to know every detail of what is done to our wells!" They finally reached the well, and Sarah gazed curiously at the three workers Frank had hired, who seemed to be doing something around the area of the steam engine that usually operated the drilling mechanism. Today, for some reason, it had been shut down.

"Why are there only three of them? Surely it will take more than that? And why isn't the well working?" she questioned.

"Well, those men are all I could find right now, but they'll be sufficient. As for the well, we've developed a hole in the boiler of the steam engine."

"Is that serious?"

"Yes, it can be."

"But that well was doing fine. It's the same well that has already earned us more than five hundred dollars. It seems like such a waste to shut it down," Sarah remarked, obviously perplexed.

"They're trying to fix the boiler, Sarah. If they can't repair it, I'm afraid we'll have to send off for a new one. That could take some time, and the well will have to remain shut down for a while," Frank explained with an apologetic air.

"But that will cause us to lose money, won't it?" Sarah insisted. "If that happens, where are we going to get the necessary capital to begin work on the other two wells?"

"Now, Sarah, don't worry your pretty little head about that. We'll soon have everything working smoothly once more. These things are bound to happen now and then, you know."

"Frank, I must insist that I be kept informed about the entire matter. I am your business partner, remember? I refuse to be patronized, to be treated as a mindless child!" Sarah declared with a frown.

"Of course. I'm sorry if I appeared to sound condescending. Two things are for certain, Sarah: you are certainly not mindless, and you are not a child! On the contrary, you are one of the most fascinating and intelligent young women I have ever known!"

"Thank you," Sarah responded a bit stiffly, still wishing he wouldn't continue to treat her merely as a woman. Oh well, she thought with an inward sigh, at least he treated her better than Adam! Thinking of Adam, she wondered what he would think of this current problem with the well, if he would perhaps know of some way to repair the damage to the boiler.

"I really don't see any need for us to remain here any longer, Sarah. I really am sorry about this delay in our plans, but I'm sure it will all work out soon. It may take a few weeks to get that new boiler, but we'll have everything back to normal after that. Why don't you come into town with me and have some lunch?" he offered gallantly.

"No, thank you just the same. I need to return to the cabin and see to some matters there. However, if your offer still holds, perhaps we could dine together this evening?" she suggested with a smile. She absolutely refused to remain out at that cabin with Adam every single night!

"Well . . ." Frank hesitated, then said, "I'm sorry,

Sarah, but I'm afraid I've already made other plans for this evening. Just some personal business, nothing that concerns you."

"I understand. Perhaps some other time. You will let me know how things go with the wells?" she reminded him as she waved away his offer of assistance and swung up into the saddle by herself.

"Sarah, you can trust me. Surely you know that by now?" Frank replied with a rather hurt expression on his attractive young face.

"Oh, of course I know I can trust you! Why, I'll never be able to repay you for all your help."

"I'm glad to hear that, for there's something I've been wanting to say to you," he told her earnestly, gazing up at her in adoration.

"Please, not now, Frank," Sarah interrupted gently. "It's too soon."

"Very well. I don't want to rush you, Sarah dear. I simply want you to know that I'm waiting anxiously for you to get that annulment from MacShane, when you'll be free to entertain the possibility of a future with someone else, namely myself."

"I can't think that far ahead into the future just yet, Frank, but I truly appreciate your kindness. Well, good day now. I'll meet you here at the cabin again tomorrow morning, if that's agreeable?" she asked.

"I don't know if anything will have changed, but I suppose we'll have to discuss it anyway, so that will be fine. Good day, Sarah," Frank said with a tender smile. Sarah smiled in response, then reined her horse about and rode away.

Damn! he swore to himself as he watched her go.

Why had he made those plans with Clementine Patterson for this evening? He wanted nothing more than to spend time with Sarah, and yet he could not deny his desire for the charms of Clementine. Well, he consoled himself, there would be other times. He didn't intend to let anything stand in the way of his carefully laid plans, particularly his plans for Sarah!

Sarah was extremely disappointed in the delay of progress on the wells, but she was realistic enough to realize that there would indeed probably be several other setbacks before she and Frank enjoyed success. She sighed and allowed her horse to plod along at a leisurely pace.

As she neared the cabin, she decided that she would like to pay a visit to the stream, where she could sit and enjoy the beautiful spring day and have a few moments of privacy. She guided the horse away from the road and toward the thick clump of trees surrounding the wide stream. Dismounting, she tied the reins to a tree and ventured further into the cool forest, when her steps were suddenly arrested by the sound of voices coming from several yards away. She paused for a moment and listened, then heard the voices once again. She hesitated, not knowing whether she should turn and leave or whether to approach closer. Choosing the latter, telling herself that it must be Adam speaking with someone since they were so close to his cabin, she carefully picked her way through the trees and underbrush and crept closer to the voices, halting when she could finally make out the faces of their owners.

It was Adam all right, and he was speaking with

Clementine Patterson! What on earth was that girl doing here? Sarah angrily asked herself, her mind in a frenzy. She must have been telling the truth about herself and Adam after all. They must be having this secret little rendezvous to discuss their plans for a future together!

Sarah tried to calm her uneven breathing at such a thought, and she concentrated on attempting to overhear their conversation.

"Oh, Adam, why can't you be reasonable? Why don't you just come right out and admit that you're jealous of Frank Mead, jealous because he likes me so much!" Clementine said.

"Clem, don't be silly. Now, what else did you learn from him?"

"I've told you everything. Do you think we could forget about him for a while and just talk about us? Couldn't we talk about how glad you are to see me, how nice it is to be so close to me, to be alone with me out here in the woods?" Clem teased, stepping closer to him beside the stream.

"Clem, when will you ever learn?" Adam responded with an amused chuckle, which was abruptly cut off as Clem threw herself against his unsuspecting chest and drew his head down sharply for her kiss. He stepped back, trying to disengage himself from her passionate embrace. "Clem, you've got to stop carrying on this way. You know I'm a married man. Now behave yourself, you young scamp!" he said, turning her about and slapping her playfully across the bottom. Clem merely smiled mischievously and blew him another kiss as she grasped one of his hands and laughingly pulled him along with her as they strolled away from the stream and out of earshot of Sarah.

She had only been able to make out bits and pieces of their conversation, but she angrily told herself that she had certainly heard enough! How dare he! she silently raged, stalking away from the spot and back to the tree where she had tied her horse. How dare he pretend to love her while all the time retaining his relationship with Clementine!

It had been perfectly obvious to her astonished eyes that the two of them shared something very special! And she, Sarah Bradford, was made to look the fool!

Briskly swinging up into the saddle, she rode with a vengeance the short distance to the cabin, arriving there just as Clem and Adam emerged from the forest, still walking hand in hand. Sarah scowled as she jerked her gaze away from them and rode directly into the barn. As she hurriedly unsaddled her horse, she calculated the many ways she could seek to have her revenge upon the two of them!

"Sarah? Sarah, lass, where have you been?" Adam called out as he and Clem appeared in the doorway of the barn.

"None of your business!" Sarah retorted petulantly, seething with anger and indignation as she whirled about to face the two culprits. "I don't see how that could possibly matter to you, since it is quite obvious that you have been otherwise engaged during my absence!"

"What the hell are you talking about?" Adam demanded, puzzled by her stormy behavior. He turned to Clementine and said, "Clem, thanks for riding all the way out here. We'll talk again later, all right? Keep up the good work." He smiled apologetically at her, but she didn't seem in the least bit perturbed by Sarah's behavior. She smiled broadly before leaving, directing a last triumphant glance toward Sarah as she went. She reflected that there had been no need for words between herself and Sarah, that everything was going even better than she had planned!

"Now, what's all this about? Why are you acting this way?" Adam thundered, striding forward till he was mere inches from her.

"I have nothing to say to you," Sarah defied stubbornly, still fuming. Oh, the absolute gall of the man! Behaving as if he were completely innocent!

"Sarah, are you going to tell me or not? Has this got anything to do with what happened to you yesterday?" Adam asked, his handsome face suddenly full of concern.

"No!" she loudly exclaimed, flouncing away from him.

"Then what is it?" he demanded, following after her. "Why won't you just turn around and tell me?"

"Leave me alone! I do not wish to speak to you at all!" Sarah ground out, then gasped as Adam's large hands closed on her still tender shoulders and forced her about to face him.

"Does this by any chance have anything to do with Clem's being here? Is that it?" he asked with a fierce scowl.

"Why on earth should her presence here concern

me? You are perfectly free to do as you wish, Adam MacShane! And, before too much longer, you will be legally free as well!" she stormed at him, still breathing quite unevenly with the force of her emotions. She was much too upset to stop and question why she was behaving in such a violent manner, too overcome by an unidentifiable fury to listen to reason.

"You're jealous, aren't you?" Adam said, his brow clearing as the truth dawned on him at last. "You were jealous of Clem once before, weren't you? That day you saw her kiss me? And now you're jealous because you came home and found the two of us here alone together! Of course that's it! I knew you'd eventually realize that you cared for me! I knew something would eventually knock some sense into that beautiful little head of yours! Come on, Sarah, lass, admit it!" he told her with a pleased grin.

Sarah's eyes grew even wider as she grew even more enraged at his smug, insufferable words. Raising her hand, she suddenly dealt him a stinging blow with her open palm, catching him right across his left cheek, leaving a bright-red imprint upon his surprised face. Her eyes grew frightened as she viewed the savage expression that had now appeared upon his handsome features.

"I warned you never to do that again, Sarah!" he stated in a deadly undertone. Before she knew what was happening, he had picked her up and roughly flung her down into a large, cushioning pile of hay. She opened her mouth in mingled astonishment and fear at his actions while he merely stood and stared down at her for a moment with dangerously narrowed eyes, then turned upon his booted heel with a muttered curse and strode from the barn.

Sarah remained lying where he had thrown her, totally flabbergasted. She realized that she was most fortunate that he had not done more to her, judging from the terrible rage he had obviously been in, knowing the violent temper he possessed. Her own anger and fury had now begun to fade, and she picked herself up from the odorous pile of hay and began to pick the clinging pieces of it from her clothing and hair.

She was much shaken by what had occurred, by her own uncontrollable temper and by Adam's answering rage. And yet, it suddenly dawned on her that his words must have been true, that she must have been jealous of him and Clementine in order to have behaved the way she had.

But that's impossible! she hotly denied to herself as she adjusted her skirt. How on earth could she be jealous of a man she did not love, a man she professed to despise? But the facts were there, the evidence undeniable. She had been overwhelmingly, violently jealous of Clementine Patterson all along!

The realization of her discovery, the impact of her jealousy, came to hit her full force, and she slowly sank back down into the hay, an expression of both wonderment and dismay upon her beautiful features.

It simply could not be true! she told herself. She could not be jealous! And yet she was forced to admit that she was, that she must feel more than mere contempt for Adam if she experienced this jealousy every time she saw him and Clementine together, every time Clementine taunted her about Adam.

Still confused, still unable to understand the full importance of her discovery, she again wondered how she could possibly be jealous of a man she did not love. It made no sense to her at all, and she remained sitting in the hay for a long time before finally rising and walking slowly toward the cabin.

Chapter Eighteen

Frank and Clementine dined together again that evening, and Clementine did her absolute best to weave her charming web. She encouraged Mead to talk extensively about himself, and she pretended an avid interest in everything he told her.

"But whatever made you come to Wildcat City in the first place, Mr. Mead, a fine gentleman such as yourself?" she prompted with an engaging smile as the two of them sat having coffee following their dinner in the hotel restaurant.

"The very same thing that brought everyone else to this hellhole, if you'll pardon the expression. I saw the opportunity to make some fast money. As I told you last night, I never stay in one place very long. Yes, I've seen nearly all of the states," he boasted.

"I can imagine that a man of your talents and experience has surely found more profitable means of making money than becoming a partner in a few old oil wells," Clem responded, flattering him with her wide-eyed attention.

"Oh yes, Miss Patterson," he informed her arrogantly, "I have certainly learned many ways in which to turn a profit. But I've always wanted to continue broadening my horizons, which is why I decided to come to Texas and try my hand at the oil game. I finally found someone gullible enough to take me on as a partner!" he remarked with a contemptuous laugh.

"Wasn't your partner the uncle of that Yankee schoolteacher who married Adam MacShane?" Clem questioned innocently.

"Yes," Frank replied tersely, his expression suddenly becoming close and guarded.

"But you still haven't told me why you left here, and what made you come back all of a sudden," she said.

"Let's just say that I had my reasons for doing both, Miss Patterson," he answered, brushing aside her questions now with an impatient gesture of his hand. "Why don't we talk about something much more interesting than my business? I think we should concentrate on you."

"Me? Why there really isn't much to say about me. I'm just a little old Texas gal," she simpered, silently wondering why he constantly steered her away from the subject of his association with John Bradford. He had done the very same thing the night before, had cut her off in the same brusque manner. She realized that Adam's suspicions about this man must have a good basis after all.

"You happen to be one of the most charming, and desirable, young women I have ever met," he told her quietly, his gaze traveling slowly and insolently up and down the entire length of her feminine curves. "Would you care to come up to my room now, where we can converse a bit more privately? I'd like to get to know you even better," he suggested, his intentions obvious.

"Well, I don't see as how that could do any harm," Clem agreed, following a brief hesitation. She still hadn't thought about what she was going to do once she was alone with him up in his room, but she surmised that she still might be able to discover something else that would be of interest to Adam. Besides, she consoled herself, I still might be able to make Adam admit that he's jealous, especially when I let him know how I went up to Frank Mead's room alone with him!

"Good. Shall we go then?" He rose and politely pulled the chair out for her, then offered her his arm and escorted her from the restaurant and up the stairs to his room. Clementine hung back momentarily as he unlocked the door and swung it open, but she resolutely squared her shoulders and smiled a bit nervously as she preceded him into the dark room.

Oh, dear Lord, she frantically thought to herself, what have I gone and gotten myself into? What in heaven's name would her mother say if she knew her beloved daughter was alone with a strange man in his hotel room at this very moment? She suddenly decided that she didn't have the courage to remain a moment longer, that it wasn't worth taking such a chance in order to make Adam jealous!

"Would you care for a bit of sherry, Miss Patterson?" Mead asked, startling her. He held the glassful of aromatic liquid out to her.

"Thank you," she murmured with another nervous smile, taking a seat on the bed and holding the glass up to lips suddenly gone dry.

"There now," he remarked, finishing off his own drink. He set the glass down on top of the chest of drawers, then turned back to Clementine.

"I'm afraid I'm not used to such strong spirits," she admitted with a slight cough as she attempted to drink it.

"That's all right. Just take your time and sip it slowly. It gives you the most deliciously warm sensation as it goes down," he stated with a wicked smile. She nearly jumped as he sank down upon the bed beside her and placed an arm about her trembling shoulders.

"I don't think I can drink this after all!" Clem exclaimed, rising from the bed abruptly and escaping his embrace. She stood beside the chest, her back turned to Mead, who merely smiled, believing her to be playing hard to get. "Would you please light the lamp? I think it's getting even darker in here!" she said, barely able to make out his form in the moonlit room.

"Miss Patterson, I think I should call you 'Clementine' now, don't you? And you're to call me 'Frank.' After all, you and I have become very good friends, have we not?" he asked, standing up and slowly advancing upon her. "Why don't we stop this little game and admit that we feel something very powerful for each other, some uncontrollable force of passion?" he whispered gently against her ear.

Clementine gulped noisily, beginning to feel no small degree of panic set in. She'd better get out of there as soon as possible, before something terrible happened!

"Why, Mr. Mead," she responded in a shaky voice,

"I do . . ." Her words were effectively cut off as he swiftly placed his arms about her and brought his lips crushing down upon her mouth with bruising force. She pushed against him, screaming deep in her throat as he brought one of his hands up to roughly clasp her soft breast through the thin material of her dress. She was finding it increasingly difficult to breathe, and she finally administered a shove that sent him stumbling backward; he barely managed to catch himself before falling to the floor below.

"What the hell do you think you're doing?" he demanded angrily, his attractive features appearing quite ugly now. "Just what sort of a game is it you're playing?"

"Oh, I'm so sorry, Mr. Mead," Clem gushed, apologizing profusely as she readjusted her bodice. "I'm afraid I've suddenly developed a powerful headache! It's my nerves, you see. It happens any time I become overly excited. I think I'd better be going home now. I'm terribly sorry about the way things turned out. Maybe some other time. Good night, Mr. Mead!" she spoke in a breathless rush, wrenching open the door and scurrying from the room and back down the hallway.

She flew out of the hotel and toward home. Now that the whole ordeal was over with, she finally gave in to the strong urge to laugh out loud. Frank Mead had looked so utterly ridiculous tumbling backward that way! she reflected, clamping a hand over her mouth as she ran up the front steps of the boardinghouse. The high and mighty gentleman, brought low by a young, inexperienced maiden!

Stifling her giggles, she edged open the front door

and began creeping quietly up the staircase when a light appeared in the front entrance foyer and caught her attention. She whirled about to face the angry countenance of her mother.

"Where on earth have you been, young lady? Don't you know it's after ten o'clock at night?" Mrs. Patterson demanded. "Land's sake, girl, what's happened to your dress?" she asked in a high-pitched voice.

Clementine glanced downward, then saw with growing dismay that the bodice was slightly torn near the shoulder seam. She took a deep breath and started to explain the truth of the matter to her mother, when an idea suddenly occurred to her. She knew she was crazy to even think of such a thing, but it suddenly seemed like it just might be the answer to all her problems! She slowly descended the stairs as she opened her mouth and began telling her mother her tale.

As Clementine was relating her story, Sarah was sitting at the kitchen table, impatiently waiting for Adam to return to the cabin. She hadn't seen him since that morning, and she was becoming quite apprehensive, for it was quite late at night, much later than when he usually arrived home from a day's work at his wells.

She impatiently stood and marched to the stove and once again raised the lid of the iron pot in order to stir the red beans she had prepared much earlier in the evening. As she took up the spoon, it occurred to her that perhaps Adam wouldn't return to the cabin at all that night, that perhaps he was still angry with her. Perhaps she had finally driven him to his limit, had made him realize that the two of them were not meant to be together. Then he'd be free to openly enjoy the companionship of Clementine! she thought, taking the spoon and viciously rapping it on the side of the large pot.

No, she sternly ordered herself, don't let that ridiculous jealousy overpower you again! Just the mere thought of Clem and Adam together was enough to send her temper boiling! She still didn't understand, couldn't fathom how she could feel such a violent emotion over a man she did not love, but she forbade herself to think about it any longer. She returned to her seat at the kitchen table and plopped down to wait.

More than an hour later, she jumped to her feet as the cabin door swung open, then closed softly. She hastily replaced a pin that had loosened in her hair, then stood waiting to confront Adam and demand an explanation as to why he had kept her waiting until such a late hour.

"I'm sorry I'm so late, Sarah," Adam said simply as he entered the kitchen and went to wash his grimy hands at the sink.

"Is that all you have to say?" she demanded a bit shrilly. "I have been waiting for several hours! Why, anything in the world might have happened to you, and yet all you can say is that you're sorry for being late?"

"I said I was sorry, Sarah," he told her earnestly, drying his hands on a towel and turning about to face her with a rather sheepish grin of apology on his handsome face. "I'd also like to apologize for my treatment of you in the barn earlier today. It's just that I was afraid of what I might do if I remained there with you any longer. Sometimes my damnable temper gets the better of me. My old grandmother always said it would be my undoing!" he ruefully remarked with a twinkle in his eyes.

Sarah felt herself begin to soften, and she tightly closed her mouth upon her next words as she turned and proceeded to dish up a large bowl of the beans. He took a seat at the table and she set the bowl in front of him, along with the corn bread and apple pie she had baked. She poured him a cup of coffee.

"Why don't you sit down and have a cup of coffee with me? I suppose you've already had your dinner."

"Yes, hours ago," she admitted with a slight frown, but took his offer and sat down opposite him. "Would you mind telling me what kept you out so late? It isn't like you to come home at this hour," she said, more calmly now. What on earth is the matter with me? she chided herself in silence. Why am I behaving so on-edge? What concern is it of mine what he does, or when he chooses to come home? She realized with a touch of self-disgust that she was actually beginning to behave like a possessive wife!

"There was some trouble with one of the wells. Since there was a full moon and plenty of light, we decided to go ahead and see to it tonight. I'm sorry if you were anxious about me," he told her with a teasing grin.

Sarah was unable to resist an answering smile, and she laughed at herself as she realized how ridiculous she had been behaving. The two of them passed the remainder of the meal in a more companionable silence, their previous anger with each other momentarily forgotten.

When Adam had finished eating, he stood from the table and commented, "Sarah, lass, you have become quite an expert cook. That apple pie was the best I've ever tasted. I didn't know when I offered to marry you what a good bargain I was getting!" he remarked with a humorous chuckle.

Sarah's smile faded at his words, and she stiffly turned away from him as she began to clear away the dishes. Adam appeared puzzled by her abrupt change in behavior, and he stepped closer to her, wanting to clear the air between them concerning their temperamental encounter earlier that day.

At that precise moment, the heel of Sarah's boot suddenly gave way, and she uttered a sharp cry as she twisted her ankle and began to fall. Adam's strong arms shot out and caught her, and she breathlessly gazed up into his face, the pain in her ankle forgotten as she managed to utter, "Thank you."

"Oh, Sarah! Haven't we had enough of this stiff politeness between us? Damn it, woman, I love you! And I know you love me!" he spoke in an anguished voice before hugging her tighter and bringing his head down to hers. Sarah struggled for only a moment, then found herself melting against him in rapturous surrender. She admitted to herself that she could fight down her own answering passion no longer, and she kissed him back with an innocent sensuality that served to further entice him.

Adam was both surprised and fired by her response, and he gently lifted her in his powerful arms and swiftly carried her into her bedroom without another word. Sarah nestled her head against his shoulder as he walked, and she sought to control her suddenly uneven breathing as he set her down upon the bed.

"Sarah, lass, you are so sweet, so very lovely," Adam said softly in a husky voice full of love. He smiled as he slowly untied the sash of her wrapper, then slipped it from her shoulders. Sarah gasped as his fingers seemed to burn right through the delicate fabric of her nightgown, then it, too, was unfastened and pushed from her shoulders. Encouraging her with light kisses and caresses, he gently urged her to her feet, causing her wrapper and nightgown to fall to the floor in a heap. Adam's eyes shone with mingled desire and love as he swiftly removed his own clothing, until he, too, stood naked before her.

Sarah's eyes opened wide as they were irresistibly drawn to his throbbing maleness, as he reached out and pulled her tightly against him and the warm flesh of their naked bodies made delicious contact. Adam brought his lips tenderly down upon her own once more as he kissed her long and thoroughly, only raising his head for a brief moment in order to lay her upon the bed. He placed his own firm, muscular body on top of her softly rounded curves as his lips continued their tender assault.

Sarah caught her breath and closed her eyes as his hands gently parted her thighs, as his mouth traveled downward to fasten on one of her white breasts, as his tongue lazily circled a pert nipple. She arched her back as his fingers touched and softly caressed her most sensitive parts, and she instinctively sought to fill his mouth with even more of her tingling breasts as she clasped him even tighter.

Oh, she dreamily reflected as she felt the searing flames of passion building deep within her, it was indeed so much more wonderful when she surrendered, when she didn't fight him, didn't hold back her own blazing desires. She gasped aloud once again as his warm lips traveled gently downward to caress her belly, then back up to tease her other breast.

"Oh, Adam!" she whispered in impassioned torment. She thought she would faint with the overwhelming, all-powerful sensation as he returned his lips to hers once more, as his tongue pressed into her mouth to caress her own tongue.

Just as she thought she could bear no more, Adam removed his hand from between her thighs, and she opened them even farther as he gently grasped her rounded bottom and pulled her forward to meet his thrust. She moaned aloud as he thrust into her softness, her legs tightening about him, molding their bodies even closer. She thought she would burst with the fiery burning that had reached a fever pitch within her, and she screamed softly as Adam expertly brought them both to an earth-shattering fulfillment.

In the soft afterglow of loving, Adam held Sarah snugly against his muscular litheness and lovingly smoothed the damp strands of hair away from her flushed face. She shyly averted her face from his gaze as he said, "Sarah, lass. That's how it should always be between us, the way it can be."

Sarah remained silent. She was finally able to admit to herself that she was powerless to resist this man's embrace, powerless to resist the temptations she had tried to fight against, too weak to resist her own deep desires. It's true, she thought to herself with a touch of dismay, every time he touches me I tremble with the sheer force of my own passion!

"I love you, Sarah. I'm so glad you've finally realized that it's no use fighting against the inevitable, that we belong together as husband and wife."

"I only realize that we share a strong physical attraction for each other," she tightly responded, still refusing to face the truth of his statements.

"No, it's much more than that and you know it. Once and for all, face up to reality, my lass. Face the fact that we share a deep, all-powerful, all-consuming love for each other and not a mere physical desire. Face the fact that we were perfectly fashioned for each other, to live together as man and wife," he insisted, forcing her face upward toward his own. He held her head softly between his large palms, gazing intently into the depths of her very soul, or so it seemed to her.

"Oh, I don't know!" she cried. "I just don't know! I don't know if I truly know the meaning of the word love. You see," she tried to explain, "I've never had anyone to love. No one except Uncle John. I was too young to remember very much about my parents when they died. My childhood, the greater part of my life was spent within the confining walls of a girls' school, the school where I am now employed as a teacher. I formed a few friendships with schoolmates throughout the years, but I never truly loved any of them. I have had very little experience, very little acquaintanceship with the opposite sex, and I'm not certain that I am capable of feeling love for any man," she told him with a slight catch in her voice.

"Sarah, you may not be able to see it, but you do have a deep capacity for loving. I can see it, even if you cannot just yet. And what's more, I'm more than ever certain that you do love me. My poor lassie," he said, drawing her closer as he replaced her head upon his shoulder, "I wish I could erase that desperate loneliness of your childhood, but I cannot. Instead, I can promise you that I will do my very best to make the rest of your life as happy as I possibly can. You need never be lonely again, my beautiful Sarah. Only face up to the truth and allow me to love you the way you should be loved."

Sarah felt hot tears gathering in her eyes, and she was tempted to believe him, when the sudden image of Clementine's maliciously gloating face lodged itself in her mind.

"What about Clementine?" she coldly asked. "Have you spoken these same words to her? Have you also promised her that you will love and cherish her forever?" she demanded hotly, pulling away from him and facing him with an accusing glare.

"Clem? Whatever gave you such a ridiculous idea? I love only you, Sarah. I never promised my love or devotion to any other woman but you," he denied, frowning.

"Clementine herself told me what is between you! I also have the evidence of my own eyes and ears, remember? Surely you are not suggesting that I deny what I saw and heard for myself!" she reminded him, growing angry once again, as if the tender moment of a few seconds ago had never existed.

"Lass, there's no need for you to feel jealous of Clementine. She may have been leading you to believe that there is something between us, but that's simply because she's young and foolish and used to getting her own way. As for what you saw this morning, there is a perfectly logical explanation for that. Clem rode out here to give me some information I had asked her to discover for me."

"What sort of information?" Sarah asked, eyeing him suspiciously.

"Well, I suppose I might as well tell you. I asked Clem to find out all she could about Frank Mead, to play up to him in order to discover anything suspicious about him."

"Frank? Why on earth would you ask her to do such a thing? Why, Frank Mead is a fine, decent, honorable gentleman!"

"Let's just say that I have my particular reasons. I'm not quite ready to divulge them to you just yet. I simply wanted you to know that Clem's visit today was not a matter of personal business. You really shouldn't allow her to upset you so much," he reasoned with an amused chuckle, secretly delighted by her jealousy.

"I did not say I was jealous!" Sarah denied indignantly, then bit her tongue as she realized that she was not speaking the truth. Oh, Adam MacShane had the most disagreeable habit of forcing her to admit things she would rather not admit, not even to herself!

"All right then," Adam said in a conciliatory manner, "why don't we simply drop the subject? Why don't you come back here and put your beautiful little head upon my shoulder once more and let me show you that you are the only love in my life!" he suggested with a delightful sparkle and a wicked grin.

"Oh!" Sarah exclaimed in mock impatience, unable to resist him. Soon the two of them were once more locked in a passionate embrace, and the remainder of the moonlit night was spent in a secret world of shared rapture.

Chapter Nineteen

Sarah smiled to herself as she dressed the following morning, her spirits higher than usual. Adam had already left her bed by the time she had awakened, but memories of the wild, abandoned night of loving they had shared still warmed her mind. She was forced to admit to herself that her heart had been affected as well, though she still did not know if she could call it love just yet. For the first time in quite a while, she hummed softly to herself as she went about her morning routine.

When had the drastic change taken place? she mused as she brushed her silky tresses. When had she finally ceased to detest Adam, to begin to feel this unfamiliar longing to be with him? When had she ceased to experience a feeling of shame for her desires, for her seemingly wanton response? Had all of these things truly come about overnight?

No matter, she told herself as she faced her reflection in the mirror now. All that matters now is that I feel truly, exuberantly alive, and none of my troubles seem noticeable in comparison with this glorious feeling.

As she turned away from the mirror and opened her bedroom door, she detected the faint sounds of a horse and wagon drawing up in front of the cabin. Rushing to the front window, she peered out expectantly, believing it to be Adam perhaps returning from town with the wagon she had previously rented from the livery stable. A frown furrowed her brow as she perceived Clementine and her mother climbing down from the wagon seat.

What in heaven's name would the two of them be doing out here at this early hour of the morning? she wondered as she prepared to greet them. She certainly considered Emma Patterson to be a friend, but why would Clementine accompany her on a social call?

"Good morning, Mrs. Patterson, Clementine. Please come in," Sarah said with a slight welcoming smile as she opened the door to admit them.

"Morning, Sarah. Sorry to be driving up at your doorstep this early, but we need to speak with Adam right away, and it was just something that couldn't wait," Mrs. Patterson responded seriously. Clementine remained silent, causing Sarah to glance suspiciously in her direction as she and her mother stepped inside.

"I'm afraid Adam isn't here, Mrs. Patterson. He's apparently already departed for work at his wells," Sarah explained. "Perhaps I can be of some assistance to you. What was it you needed to speak with him about?"

"Sarah, I don't mean to sound unkind, but it really is a private matter just between us and Adam. It's also kind of urgent, so maybe you could tell us where we might be able to find him." Her usually smiling features were drawn into a severe frown, and Sarah was extremely puzzled by her manner.

"Yes, it's private all right, but maybe you have a right to know, seeing as how you're his wife and all!" Clementine spoke with a look that indicated her disgust for Sarah.

"Clem, that's enough!" her mother reprimanded sharply, with a quick sideways glance at Sarah.

"What are you talking about?" Sarah demanded to know, becoming increasingly curious at their strange behavior.

"I'm talking about me and Adam!" Clem declared with a triumphantly exultant smile. "I'm talking about how he and I are in love with each other, and how you'd be wise to let him go so he can marry me! He doesn't love you, he never did, he only married you because of that will!"

"You are certainly entitled to your personal opinion, Clementine," Sarah responded with an icy politeness, "but Adam himself has told me that he does not love you, that there was never anything between you that could possibly be construed as a serious romance. As for his reasons for marrying me, they are none of your business." Her stomach had fluttered uncomfortably at Clem's hateful words, and the seeds of doubt that had already been planted now began to grow in her mind.

"He'd tell you anything so he can get that money from his grandfather's will, and you know it! What's more, you'd do or say anything to hang on to him, to keep him from me!"

"Clementine Patterson, if you don't hush up right this instant, I'll tan your hide, no matter how grown-up you think you've gotten!" her mother warned, shaking a finger at her daughter.

"No, please, allow her to speak, Mrs. Patterson," said Sarah, her face tight and flushed, her temper rising immeasurably, a feeling of dread beginning to descend upon her as she knew that she must listen to Clem's speech.

"Adam and I were together last night, just like we've been a whole lot of other times!" Clem pronounced with a gloating smirk. "Ma caught me coming in late last night, and I had to finally tell her the truth, that I had been with Adam. There's no use denying it any longer, for I was meant to be Adam's wife, not you! So you might as well pack your bags right now, schoolteacher, because there isn't any use in you hanging around here any longer!" she remarked with a malicious smile.

"What you are saying is absolutely preposterous, as well as being a complete and total untruth! Adam was here at the cabin with me last night," Sarah attempted to speak calmly, an overpowering urge to fly at the lying little cat threatening to overtake her.

"Was he? Well, I expected as much from you. You'd say that no matter what, because you want him for yourself, just like you've wanted him all along, only you were just too high and mighty to tell the truth! Adam was with me last night, and you know it!" Clementine retorted, the lies coming easily to her taunting lips. She knew that she was taking an awfully big chance, but she also knew that she could bluff her way through it all. She must, if she was to get Adam back!

"I do not believe you!" Sarah gasped, a terrible realization beginning to dawn on her. Adam had indeed arrived home quite late, offering a rather simple explanation of his whereabouts. Dear Lord, don't let it be true! she fervently prayed in silence. And yet, it was possible, it was definitely possible that he had been with Clem before he had come home to her! Her mind was in a whirl, and she pressed a hand to her forehead.

"It's the truth!" Clem smugly insisted, refusing to glance toward her mother, who was full of concern for Sarah. She could see some sort of hesitation in Sarah's face, could see the doubt apparent in her eyes. Her bluff had worked, her words had done their job! She was immensely pleased with the outcome. Now Adam would finally be rid of this interfering little Yankee bitch, free to marry her! Heaven help her, though, she thought with a sharp glance at her mother now, if Ma ever found out she was lying!

"I'm sorry, Sarah, sorry you had to find out this way," Mrs. Patterson apologized sincerely, coming up to Sarah and patting her shoulder in comfort.

"It isn't true, your daughter is lying, she must be lying!" Sarah murmured in disbelief.

"Well, I don't know for sure if what Clem's been saying is the truth, but I thought we'd best come on out and talk to Adam about it right away. If it isn't true, well, then, I'll take care of the matter. But if it is the truth, then there's going to be hell to pay for Adam MacShane!" she stated with a fierce scowl.

"Mrs. Patterson, you know Adam. You've known him much longer than I have. You must know that what your daughter is saying cannot possibly be true of him. He simply isn't that sort of man, and I believe you know that. However, I do agree that you should speak to him about this, and that you should do so immediately. I believe you can find him about a mile from here, by driving south on the road," she offered, still stunned by Clem's accusations. It cannot be true, it cannot be! her mind insisted.

"He might deny the whole thing, you know," Clem piped up, wanting to make certain that she had covered all the angles. "He might deny it just to keep from having to maybe lose that money he's got coming."

"I'll get the truth from him, don't you worry," her mother retorted, then said, "Come on, Clem, you've done your worst here!"

Clementine shot Sarah one last maliciously triumphant smile, then followed her mother out of the cabin. Sarah heard them drive away a few moments later.

She must be lying, Sarah told herself as she paced the floor frantically. She must have concocted this little story in order to drive me away, in order to get Adam for herself. That simply must be it!

I don't want to even consider it as truth, she thought as she opened the door and hurried to the barn. I refuse to consider it as anything more than a last attempt by a jealous girl to snatch a man for herself!

But, as she mounted and rode away from the cabin in order to keep her rendezvous with Frank at her uncle's cabin, a tiny voice at the back of her mind said, what if there is even one ounce of truth to her story, what if Adam had indeed been with her last night, had been with her other times as well?

Dear Lord, she suddenly thought as a decidedly upsetting idea occurred to her. What if she had willingly given herself to a man who had been leading her on, who had actually been deceiving her all along in order to achieve his own lustful desires? What if Adam truly did love Clem, was only lying to her in order to get what he wanted? Had she surrendered her body, her dreams, and possibly her heart to a man who was a deceitful, lying rake?

These thoughts jumbled in her mind as she rode, causing her more and more anxiety as she finally arrived at her uncle's cabin. Frank was waiting for her again, and she dismounted with an obvious air of distraction as he came forward to meet her.

"Sarah! I was beginning to get a little worried about you. Don't you realize that you're more than an hour late for our meeting?" he chastised her mildly, his face smiling as he took her arm and led her toward the deserted cabin.

"Oh, Frank!" she cried, her own face appearing strained. "I don't know what to do!"

"What's the matter? What is it that's made you look so upset?" he asked sharply.

"I don't want to burden you with my problems Frank, but I simply must talk to someone about it!" she tearfully replied, too emotional to think rationally about any of it.

"Let's go on inside the cabin and talk there. We'll have a bit more privacy there." He gently led her inside the building, then softly closed the door after them. Gently pushing her down onto a bench, he then took a seat across from her, placing his hands upon the wooden table and grasping her smaller, shaking hands in his.

"Now what is it? What's happened to cause you

such distress?" he inquired, his features mirroring his concern for her.

"It's Adam," Sarah stated simply, searching for the right words with which to explain the situation to him.

"MacShane? What's he done to you now?" Frank questioned sharply, his eyes gleaming with a sudden, savage light.

"It isn't what he's done to me, Frank, but well, it's what he has possibly done with another woman!" she burst out.

"What other woman?" he asked, his features relaxing a bit as he smiled inwardly. Things might just be working out even better than he had hoped.

"Clementine Patterson."

"Clementine Patterson?" he echoed, feeling very uneasy at the mention of her name. He frowned, then prompted Sarah to continue.

"It seems that my so-called husband has possibly been unfaithful to me, that he has been deceiving me all along. Oh, what a fool I must have appeared!" she spoke with disdain, the tears gathering in her stormy eyes.

"You're saying that MacShane has been involved with Miss Patterson?"

"I don't know!" she wailed, angrily dashing away the hot tears that now coursed down her flushed cheeks. "I don't know if she was speaking the truth or not, but there is some evidence, something that makes me doubt Adam, makes me realize that her story could be true!"

"But my dear Sarah," Frank delicately pointed out, "I don't wish to seem callous, but you yourself have told me that your relationship with Adam MacShane is nothing more than a mere business arrangement, though the two of you are legally wed. Therefore, I really fail to see why his affair with another woman should upset you at all. From what you have told me, the two of you go your separate ways," he added.

"I know what I've told you!" she responded angrily, jumping to her feet and continuing with her pacing, wringing her hands anxiously as she walked. "I know what I've been telling myself these past few weeks! That doesn't alter the fact that the two of us are husband and wife, that he has absolutely no right to make me appear the fool! No matter what our arrangement, we are married, and he should at least have had the common decency to wait until our marriage was officially annulled before taking up with Clementine Patterson once more!"

"I agree," Frank said consolingly, rising to his feet and quickly going to her. "However, I shouldn't let it bother me if I were you. Now that you have seen his true colors, you know what a scoundrel he really is. It will seem even better than before when you get that annulment from him, won't it?" He placed an arm about her shoulders and drew her unresisting body against his. "Besides, I do believe I have heard rumors to the effect that MacShane and this Patterson girl were indeed quite involved. It seems that they have been seen about town with each other on several occasions," he lied, adding fuel to the fire. He wanted nothing more than to destroy any feelings she might have for MacShane, and he saw the perfect opportunity to do so at this time!

"What?" Sarah gasped, gazing up at him in horror. "Are you saying that everyone else knows what has been going on, everyone except for myself? Oh, how could he!" she raged. "How could I have been so blind? How could I have believed him, have surrendered . . ." she caught herself as she almost told Frank about the wanton behavior she had exhibited the night before. "Oh, I don't know what to believe!"

"Of course you don't. But don't worry, dear Sarah, I'm here to comfort you," Frank murmured against her hair. Sarah suddenly became aware of the fact that he was no longer holding her in mere consolation, that his other arm had now crept about her and he was pulling her even closer as he slowly brought his head down to hers.

Why not? she asked herself bitterly, fighting back her tears. If Clem's story was true, if the rumors Frank had overheard were true, if Adam had indeed been unfaithful, if she herself had given herself to a man who was both a liar and a cad, then why shouldn't she repay him in kind? Why shouldn't she show him that she, too, was capable of breaking their trust? she thought childishly, not thinking clearly enough to consider the consequences of her rash behavior. All she knew was that she was hurting dreadfully, that she could barely contain her anger and jealousy.

"Sarah, Sarah, I love you so very much! I've wanted you for so long!" Frank whispered intensely, before lowering his lips to hers. Sarah instinctively stiffened, then forced herself to surrender, melting against him as she began to return his kisses with a fervent response. She experienced a mild shock as

Frank's hand crept up to the buttons of her blouse, as he began gently undoing them, as his hand gently insinuated itself inside her blouse. His hand firmly squeezed her soft breast, and she gasped as he now began trailing his passionate kisses down her slender neck, whispering words of love, kindling his desire.

Sarah suddenly awakened from her momentary trance, beginning to wriggle and push against him as a blinding revelation came to her. When Frank refused to relinquish his hold upon her, she pushed even harder, succeeding in extricating herself from his embrace as she stumbled backward, her bosom heaving as she clutched her blouse about her and stared across into Frank's astonished face.

What was she doing? she asked herself. She couldn't allow him to kiss her this way, to touch her this way. She couldn't allow any man to touch her at all, any man except Adam. For she now realized the very thing she had been fighting against, the thing she had persistently refused to face. She was in love with Adam; she loved her husband!

"Sarah? Sarah, what's wrong? Did I frighten you? I'm sorry if I did, it's just that I love you so desperately, I want you so very much!" Frank declared dramatically, closing the distance between them as he tried to take her into his arms once more. Sarah turned away from him, still dazed by the overwhelming realization of her love for Adam.

That was why Clem's story had upset her so much, why she had been powerless to resist Adam's lovemaking! That was the reason she had been so jealous of Clem, why she had felt so furious at her words!

"Sarah, oh darling!" Frank whispered, turning her about in his arms and attempting to kiss her while she continued to squirm and twist away from him.

"No!" she exclaimed loudly. "I can't! I simply can't! I'm sorry, Frank, sorry I let you kiss me that way. It was wrong! All of this is wrong! I'm sorry if I have hurt you, but this is all wrong! I have to go, I have to find Adam!" she burst out, her eyes full of remorse as she silently implored him to understand, as she turned away and quickly fled the cabin.

Frank ran after her, only to stand helplessly by as she galloped away. Why had things changed all of a sudden? he wondered silently, perplexed and bewildered by Sarah's abrupt change of attitude. Why had she allowed him to kiss her, to fondle her breast, only to turn around and fight him, to utter something about Adam, about having to find Adam? There must be an explanation, and he knew that it had something to do with Adam MacShane! His eyes glowed murderously as he whirled about and stalked back inside the cabin.

Damn! he cursed silently. He had waited long enough, he would not wait any longer. Sarah would be his; she would surrender to him willingly, would cry out in the tempestuous depths of passion as he took her, as he caressed her soft, white curves. Adam MacShane would be completely erased from her mind, as well as completely erased from the face of the earth!

Sarah had apparently not had a man yet, she was still pure and virginal and innocent, and he would be the one to awaken her, to delight in teaching her the ways of love. Yes, she was the only truly innocent woman he had ever known, the only one worthy of his love. She would be his, she would do anything she could to please him! He must make his plans, he must take action soon.

Sarah kicked the horse into a faster gallop as she headed back toward the cabin, her thoughts in a tumultuous jumble. She was in love, she actually loved someone for the first time in her life, and that someone had turned out to be none other than the very man she was married to, the very man who had continuously declared his own love for her! If only it were true, she thought with a touch of despair. If only Clem's story were indeed false, then everything would finally be resolved between herself and Adam.

She realized that, even if Adam had indeed been seeing Clem, had been involved with her, had been making love to her, she would still love him! She knew that nothing could ever destroy her love for him, that she would never willingly give him up! She would not give in, she would fight before she would ever hand him over to that liar, Clementine! She loved him, she loved him more than she had ever believed possible, and she knew that she would always love him, no matter what the outcome of this present trouble.

But, she reasoned with herself, what if he doesn't love you? What if Clem's words were true? What if it is Clementine he loves? Could she face it if she discovered that he did not love her, that he loved another woman?

She realized that she loved him so much, she wanted his happiness, though she selfishly wanted only to be with him, whether he truly loved her or not. She also realized that such a situation would be intolerable, that she could never remain with a man who did not love her in return.

Oh God, she silently prayed as she drew the horse to a halt at the cabin, don't let it be true! Keep Adam's love for me, only for me!

Chapter Twenty

Sarah sat alone in the cabin, her feet tucked under her skirts as she waited in the kitchen for Adam to return. She had been attempting to sort out her disturbing thoughts and emotions, but she felt even more perplexed than before, even more tormented. If only Adam would return and tell her what had transpired between himself and the Pattersons. The suspense was beginning to take its toll on her, and she stood for the hundredth time and peered out of the kitchen window, sighing heavily with disappointment when she spotted nothing worthy of her attention.

Why should her newly discovered love for Adam cause her such grief? she reflected ironically, smiling without humor. After all of her confusion, why should a resolution to her problem cause her to feel so despondent? She would be able to ascertain the outcome of Adam's meeting with the Pattersons soon after he walked through the cabin door, after she had closely scrutinized his handsome face for any sign that would serve to tell her that Clem's taunts and derisive jibes had been founded on truth, that it was she whom he loved.

Please let him come soon, she silently beseeched,

sinking back down into her seat at the kitchen table with a despairing sigh. The anxiety was beginning to wear heavily upon her already tattered nerves.

Adam rode toward the cabin at a moderate pace, his face pensive as he thought back to his encounter with Clementine and her mother earlier that day. He had been supervising the drilling of a new well when he had noticed them drive up in the wagon and hail him from a short distance away. He had instructed one of his top hands to take over for him, then had strode away from the platform, a frown on his face as he wondered what the two women would be doing out that far, at that hour of the day. He decided that it must be important, for Mrs. Patterson would never dream of disturbing his work if it were not.

"Emma, Clem, what are you two doing way out here? Is there something wrong?" he asked in a voice full of genuine concern, hastily wiping his soiled hands on the sides of his heavy denim trousers. His hair was tousled and sweaty, his handsome features were caked with dust and grime, but he had never appeared so utterly attractive to Clementine as she sat silent beside her mother, a secret smile lighting her blue eyes.

"Adam, I'm real sorry to have to bother you while you're working, but this is something that just couldn't wait until later. I just got to know right here and now so we can get this thing settled once and for all," Mrs. Patterson told him as she climbed down from the wagon, impatiently waving away Adam's offer of assistance. Clem, however, graciously accepted his offer, smiling with obvious pleasure as his large hands grasped her waist and swung her easily to the ground. She still didn't speak, causing Adam to eye her suspiciously, musing to himself that it was very unlike Clem to hold her tongue for so long a time!

"All right. What's this all about?" he asked, smiling mildly as he faced the two of them.

"It's about you and Clem, Adam. It's about the fact that she came in awful late last night, looking downright guilty, her new dress torn and rumpled. She said that she had been with you, and that this wasn't the first time. Now what I want to know is, was she telling the truth?" demanded Emma Patterson, her words coming out in a rush. "I want some straight answers from you, Adam MacShane, and I want them right now."

"What?" Adam ejaculated, his face registering mingled surprise and disbelief at her words. "Why, you know it isn't true! There's never been anything like that between myself and Clem," he denied strongly. He then jerked his head about toward Clementine and commanded, "Clem, tell your mother the truth, that you lied to her about us. Tell her where you really were last night, that you were probably with Frank Mead, that you were only seeing him as a favor to me."

"Why, Adam," Clementine literally purred, linking her arm through his as she stepped closer and gazed adoringly up into his angry features, "I don't know what you're talking about! I was with you last night, remember? And it certainly wasn't the first time, was it? Now, darling, there isn't any reason for us to hide it from Ma here any longer. I told her everything."

"Clementine Patterson, this is nothing more than a childish, harebrained little scheme of yours, isn't it? Well, I'm telling you that it won't work!" he thundered, causing Clem to experience a twinge of fear as she viewed his growing fury. Well, she told herself with stubborn determination, I've got to see it through now, I've just got to make it work! Adam's just got to face the facts!

"Clem, it seems Adam here is saying that you weren't being honest with me about last night," Mrs. Patterson spoke up, her gaze seeming to bore through her daughter's. Clem suddenly averted her eyes as her mother asked, "Are you sure you told me the truth? Are you so all-fired sure you aren't just making this whole thing up out of the blue?"

"No, Ma," Clem countered, refusing to back down. "I wasn't lying. I was with Adam last night, and I've been with him lots of other times, too. Why, if it wasn't for that Yankee schoolteacher, we'd have been married by now for sure!"

"Then how come he didn't just go and marry you when he found out he needed a wife?" her mother demanded sharply, knowing her troublesome daughter well enough to sense that there was something not quite right with the whole matter.

"Because he didn't want to make it look like he was marrying me just to get that money from his grandfather's will, isn't that right, Adam?" she insisted, turning to Adam and flashing him what she hoped was a tantalizingly seductive look.

"No, that is not right!" he spoke through clenched teeth, trying to maintain control over his temper. "I don't know where you got the notion that this little scheme of yours would work, Clem, but you are not going to succeed! I've already told you that I married Sarah because I truly loved her, even if I didn't realize it at the time. But I'm telling both you and your mother now, that I love my wife, that she loves me, that we are husband and wife for eternity, that I certainly do not need to go about carousing with other women, and that includes you, Clementine!" he roared, growing so enraged with the whole thing that he was beginning to experience a slight tendency toward violence as he glared at Clem, who merely responded by innocently smiling up into his frowning countenance.

"Adam, there's one way you can maybe prove that you weren't with my daughter last night," Emma Patterson suggested, beginning to doubt her own wisdom in ever listening to her mischievous daughter. "Clem came in about ten-thirty last night and said that she had just left you. Well, tell me, is there any way you can prove that you weren't in town last night?"

"As a matter of fact, I can!" he answered with a relieved grin and a slight chuckle. "I was out here at the well, where we worked until well after eleven o'clock last night. Any of my men will testify to that fact!"

"Of course they will!" Clem cried sarcastically. "They'll do anything you say. They'll tell us anything you want them to because they'll be afraid of losing their jobs if they don't! Come on now, Adam darling, just admit the truth, that you love me, that I love you, that we've been sharing a lot more than just a casual friendship!"

"Clem," her mother said, the truth beginning to dawn on her as she realized that Adam was telling the truth, that he couldn't possibly have come up with such an excuse all of a sudden like that, "Clem, you lied to me about you and Adam, didn't you?"

"No, Ma, I did not!" she hotly denied, beginning to dread that her plan had backfired after all. "I told you the truth, Ma! Adam's the one who's lying to you!"

"Why would he lie to me about this, if he really loves you like you say he does?" her mother asked.

"Because, well..." she faltered, searching for some sort of explanation, suddenly acutely aware that she was beaten, furious that Adam had possessed an alibi more concrete than Sarah's word that he had been at the cabin with her last night. "Well, because he feels sorry for that snooty little wife of his, because he doesn't want to do anything to hurt her, or because he doesn't want me to look like a homewrecker! Yes, he cares about how it's going to look if he gets rid of her too quick!" she finished triumphantly, much pleased with herself. However, Clementine Patterson had a great deal to learn.

"Wait a minute, Mrs. Patterson," Adam said, his face smiling pleasantly now, "there's another way we can prove that Clem was with someone else besides me last night. Since I'm almost certain your daughter was with Frank Mead at the hotel last night, then there must have been plenty of people who saw them there together. As a matter of fact, we might just go pay a little visit to Mead and get the truth from him. After all, it was my idea that Clem become friends with him in the first place," he admitted with a wicked grin, his anger fading as he was forced to see the humor of the whole situation.

"Why on earth did you go and tell her to do that? Why did you tell her to be friendly to that fancy dude?" Mrs. Patterson demanded in puzzlement.

"I had my reasons. I asked Clem to get some information from him, information that I might find very helpful. But I must say, I had no idea that she would stay at the hotel so late with him," he told her mother, his eyes still fastened on Clementine, who had begun to exhibit a small portion of the worry she was experiencing at his tone. Things weren't going at all the way she had planned!

She had been hoping that Adam would come to his senses when her mother confronted him, that he would realize that this was the way he could finally rid himself of that cold-hearted Yankee vixen he had married! Oh, she wailed silently, why did he have to go and spoil it this way? Why couldn't he have played right into her hands the way she had planned? Why had she come up with such a stupid plan in the first place? she now furiously berated herself, realizing that she had been caught in her own trap.

"Clem, is what Adam's telling me so? Were you at the hotel last night with that Mead fellow?" her mother asked, marching toward her daughter with growing anger apparent on her usually kind features.

"No!" Clem denied, backing away. "He's just saying all this to keep from admitting that he was with me!" she contended. She turned to him and placed her hands imploringly upon his muscular chest as she gazed upward into his grinning face.

"Adam, please tell her that you were with me, please! Don't you see? This is the perfect opportunity for us to be together, for you to be free of your wife, for you to marry me! I love you, Adam, and you know I'd do anything in the world for you! Please, Adam, tell her that you were with me last night!" she begged, her face stricken as she perceived the unholy amusement lighting up his green eyes.

"Clementine Patterson, you are the most bedeviling little wildcat I have ever known!" he remarked as he laughed aloud. Stifling his laughter, he turned to her mother and said, "Emma, don't be too upset about all of this. After all, Clem is still very young, and still very headstrong. What she needs, what she's needed all along is a strong, masculine hand to tame her. And now, with your permission," he declared, beginning to roll up his sleeves, "I'll be more than happy to teach her a good lesson!"

"Ma!" Clementine shrieked frantically, flying to her mother's side for protection as her eyes widened in horror at Adam's obvious intentions. "Ma, you aren't just going to stand by and let him do this to me, are you?" she cried, trying to hide behind her mother now as Adam slowly and purposefully approached.

"You deserve a good deal more than you'll get from him, you little troublemaker!" her mother stated with an answering nod and grin at Adam.

"Ma! Adam MacShane, don't you dare! Don't you touch me! I only did it because I love you!" Clem exclaimed breathlessly, screaming as Adam's large hand closed upon her wrist and pulled her none too gently along with him and over to a large rock jutting up from the ground. He took a seat upon the rock, then pulled Clem's wildly struggling form across his lap, maneuvering so that he held both of her flailing wrists in one of his large hands. Then, while she alternately screamed and pleaded with both him and her mother, he proceeded to bring his strong hand down upon her squirming bottom, causing her to squeal in both pain and indignation. He held her down easily and continued to spank her resoundingly several more times.

"There. And there! Now, we won't be hearing any more lies from your lips, will we, my fine young lady!" He laughed at her futile efforts to escape his punishing blows, then finally stood to his feet, causing her to tumble unceremoniously to the ground, where she sat with her skirts fanning out about her in complete disarray, her shining blond curls streaming about her flushed and tear-streaked face.

"Oh! I hate you, Adam MacShane!" she declared passionately, for the moment entirely forgetting that she had just a few moments before declared her undying love for him. "I'll never, ever, forgive you for this!" she threatened, stumbling to her feet as she tightly clenched her skirts and literally ran back to the wagon, her hand rubbing across her smarting derriere.

"Well, I guess she's been needing that for a long time," Emma Patterson remarked with a heavy sigh. "I guess I haven't done as good a job in raising her as I thought, but it's been mighty hard without a man around to help."

"You've done as good a job as anyone could have under the circumstances," Adam told her gently.

"She's just willful and headstrong, but she'll grow up, she'll learn eventually. Someday, she'll be a fine young woman, just like her mother. I just hope she marries someone who can handle her!" he commented with another chuckle, rolling his sleeves back down as he prepared to return to his work. "I'm sorry about all this, though, about her staying at the hotel so late with Frank Mead last night. You really shouldn't blame her for that, because it was at my bidding that she began to see him."

"All right. But all the same, I don't think it's a good idea that you ask her to do any more snooping for you, if you don't mind," Mrs. Patterson replied with a frown. "I guess I should have known she was lying all along, but, well, being her mother and all, I thought it best if I asked you about it, anyway. Sorry to have bothered you, Adam. We'll see you later." She turned away and strode back to the wagon, where she didn't so much as glance at her sullen and silent daughter as she climbed up beside her on the wagon seat and flicked the reins.

"Good day to you both!" Adam laughingly called as they drove away. He grinned to himself as he saw the murderous glance Clem directed toward him before the wagon drove away.

And now, as he unsaddled his horse and led it into the barn, a disturbing thought suddenly occurred to him. Mrs. Patterson and Clementine must have come by the cabin first this morning, looking for him. Had Sarah been there to greet them, or had she possibly gone out riding? How else would Emma and Clem have known where to find him, without first speaking with Sarah? Oh no, he thought as he finished rubbing down his horse and headed for the cabin. Had Sarah already heard Clem's story, and, if so, would she possibly believe it?

"Sarah! Sarah, are you home?" he called as he swung open the front door and strode inside. When he received no reply, he removed his hat and hung it on the peg, then walked across the floor to search her bedroom. Satisfying himself that she was not there, he turned and headed for the kitchen, where he saw her sitting at the table, her back turned toward the doorway as she sat alone in the gathering darkness of the evening.

"Sarah, lass, why didn't you answer me?" he asked softly, his worst fears realized as she slowly turned about to face him. He perceived the pain and despair written on her beautiful little face, the anguish apparent in her expressive eyes. "Oh, lass," he said, hurrying to her side as he knelt on the floor beside the bench and gazed into her opal eyes. "Mrs. Patterson and Clem did come here this morning, didn't they?"

"Yes," Sarah murmured quietly, unable to trust herself to say much more than that one simple word. She gazed at Adam as if seeing him for the first time, as indeed it was the first time since she had realized how much she loved him. Please, please say it isn't true, she implored him silently with her sparkling eyes as she stared into his face. Please tell me that Clementine was lying, that everything is all right, that it was just a silly mistake, a silly little lie.

"They came by to see me at the well this morning. I suppose you told them where they might find me?" he questioned, receiving a brief nod in return. "I can see by the expression on your face that you heard

Clem's accusations, didn't you, lass?"

"Yes," she replied again, still unable to take her eyes from his beloved face. Everything about him seemed so precious to her now, and she was reluctant to force herself to discuss Clem's story with him, yet she knew that she must.

"Well, it simply isn't true. You must know that I wouldn't do such a thing," he told her, his face very serious as he compelled her to look deep into his eyes. "You know that I love you, that what I said about Clem before was the truth, that there was never anything between us, that there certainly isn't now. You must see that her story was nothing but a vicious lie, nothing more than an attempt to try and force me to love her. She still doesn't realize that you can't force love, that it must come from deep within a person's heart, deep within their very soul. That's how I love you," he spoke softly, gazing at her with all the love he felt.

"And that's how I want you to love me in return. I don't want to force you to love me," he insisted. "As I just said, that would be impossible. But I know you care, I know you will someday realize that you love me as I love you. It was meant to be, my lovely lassie."

Sarah opened her mouth to speak, then abruptly turned away from him in confusion. She wanted to believe him, she desperately wanted to believe him! It was so very difficult to look at him, to question him at all when he looked at her in that manner! How could she ever think things through rationally, how could she consider the matter in a reasonable manner when he persisted in telling her that he loved her so much?

"Adam," she finally said, taking a deep breath as she returned her winsome gaze to him, "Adam, I know that Clem is nothing more than a jealous little girl, that she is foolish as well as immature. However, I cannot help but think that there must be some basis for her story, for she has consistently insisted that the two of you love each other, that you indeed share something. I only hope you were able to convince her mother that there was no truth to the story about you, for I fear that such a scandal would harm the poor woman quite a lot," she stated in a calm, almost chilly manner, though her heart was pounding and her mind was racing. She couldn't sit here much longer; she couldn't remain in the same room with him and not believe him, and not surrender herself to him once more. But no, she sternly commanded herself, I must have the truth; I must not allow my emotions to color my good judgment. Only, it was so very difficult to even breathe when he was so close to her!

"I can see that I'm going to have to tell you the entire story if you're ever going to believe me, if I want to erase the doubt from your mind. Very well," he remarked, taking a seat beside her now and clasping her hand between his.

"I asked Clementine to become friendly with Frank Mead in order to obtain certain information about him, certain information concerning your uncle's accident. As I have already told you, I have been suspicious of him for some time now, and I asked Clem to help me."

"Yes, you mentioned your suspicions quite briefly. And I recall that Clem was somehow involved. But I still fail to see what that has to do with this present difficulty," Sarah responded in confusion, still fighting to regain control over her uneven breathing.

"Well, I'm afraid that you won't like this next part very much. But I've been suspicious of Mead ever since your uncle died. I think that he had something to do with your uncle's death, that he may have even planned that accident in order to gain complete control of the wells. He left rather abruptly after John's death, Sarah, and he didn't leave word with anyone as to where he was going. What's more, all of the workers who had been employed by him and your uncle disappeared soon afterward as well."

"Frank Mead?" Sarah uttered in shock. "You're saying that he may have actually killed my uncle, that he may have planned to do so all along?" Yes, she silently answered herself, it all fit. Uncle John had never once mentioned a partner to her in his letters, and Frank had indeed absented himself very conveniently following Uncle John's death. But why? she asked herself. Why would he kill Uncle John? Surely there was not that much monetary gain from such action? Surely Uncle John would have been cautious enough to question him before agreeing to form a partnership with him. Oh, she thought, the idea of Frank having something to do with her uncle's death was very disturbing, and she was reluctant to consider the possibility further.

"I'm not actually saying that Mead murdered your uncle, lass," Adam amended, "but I am saying that the whole thing appears very suspicious. And then, all of a sudden, he returns here, with no reasonable explanations of why he either left or returned. There is simply too much mystery about the man. So I asked Clementine to do me a favor by playing up to him, to see what she could discover about his business practices, about his personal life."

"I see," Sarah responded, still somewhat dazed by Adam's words. "But I still fail to see how any of this affects Clem's story."

"It's very simple. Clem dined with Mead at the hotel last night, and apparently she returned home rather late. Her mother evidently caught her coming in, her dress torn, and Clem offered this impulsive tale concerning herself and me. She's had this fool notion that I am really in love with her, that I'll somehow finally come to her senses if she waits long enough. Well, she obviously concocted this little scheme in order to make me see reason, in order to seize the perfect opportunity to get you angry enough with me to leave," he patiently explained, searching her thoughtful face for any sign that she believed him, hoping she would at least consider his side of the story before making any final judgment.

"Yes, I can see how she would do such a thing, for it is decidedly just like her, isn't it?" Sarah admitted with a nervous little laugh as she began to experience a small degree of relief. She still didn't know what to think about Adam's suspicions, nor her own, concerning Frank Mead. And she still didn't know what she truly believed about Adam and Clementine. But for now, all that mattered was that Adam claimed to love her, and not Clem. For now, that was enough to put her mind more at ease, to make her feel a bit more jubilant, more encouraged about their future together.

I can't just come right out and tell him that I have finally realized that I love him, she chided herself as she found herself feeling suddenly shy with him. No, she decided that she would keep her precious secret a while longer, until she felt totally secure about his love for her, until she was certain that there was not indeed, and never had been, anything between him and Clementine Patterson.

"Sarah, I hope you believe me, for it's the truth. I've already satisfied Emma Patterson, so I hope we can put this ridiculous matter aside now. As for Frank Mead, I only hope that you will treat him with more caution than ever before, that you will question everything he tries to tell you."

"Well," she remarked pensively as she voiced a matter that had been bothering her, "there is the matter of the steam engine's boiler. Frank said that it would take several weeks in order to obtain a new one, and that the well would have to be completely shut down until then. It seemed rather strange to me that a successfully producing well should be kept inoperable for so long a period of time, but I did no more at the time than simply ask him the reason for such action." Her mind suddenly recalled her disturbing encounter with Frank at her uncle's cabin that morning, and she knew that she should never, under any circumstances, mention the incident to Adam. She was ashamed of her behavior, ashamed of the manner in which she had allowed Frank to kiss and caress her. But then, she consoled herself, it was because of that very incident that she had finally discovered just how very much she loved her husband!

"It is odd," Adam agreed, his face tightening almost imperceptibly. "It would have been a simple matter for them to patch the boiler until a new one arrived. I'm afraid I'm even more suspicious than ever," he admitted with a sigh.

"Well, I shall speak to Mr. Mead the first thing in the morning about the matter!" she declared with an angry frown. "After all, he is supposed to be my business partner, so I shall certainly demand an explanation!"

"No, lass," Adam sternly disagreed, then smiled to soften his words as he explained, "Don't say a word about this to him, not just yet. Let's just wait and see what develops. I don't want him to know that we suspect him of anything just yet. But I will admit that I'd feel a lot better if you avoided seeing him from now on."

"But I can't do that. He would certainly suspect something if I did that," she reasoned, her heart still quickening every time Adam looked at her. It was so difficult to sit and speak calmly with him when all she really yearned to do was fly into his strong arms and have him hold her and tell her that he loved her passionately!

"Aye," he responded with another sigh. "But I'll be watching out for you, so don't get angry with me if I tell you that you shouldn't see him at a particular time. Besides that, I don't want you seeing him at all! I must admit," he said with a rueful smile. "I am more than a bit jealous of the gentleman!"

Sarah experienced a sudden exhilaration at his words, and she impishly considered relating to him the details of her meeting with Frank that morning, but she knew that her earlier decision to remain silent about it was for the best. After all, she was afraid he would become exceedingly angry and march right off to confront Frank at that very moment. She certainly didn't want that. She wanted nothing more than to shut the entire world out, to be alone with Adam, to take time to consider her new situation. All she knew was that she loved him, she loved him desperately, and she wanted him to love her the way he professed to.

"Sarah, lass, what's wrong? Why are you being so quiet all of a sudden?"

"Oh, it's nothing. I suppose all of this has affected my thinking for a time." She rose from the bench, intending to begin preparing their dinner, when Adam suddenly caught her arm and pulled her back against him, then down into his lap.

"Adam, what on earth are you doing? I have to get our dinner!" she protested, secretly delighting at his masterful actions.

"Sarah," he spoke seriously, his gaze seeming to pierce her heart, "please don't let any of this nonsense about Clem upset you. I love you, only you, and I hope you'll believe me. I never want to let you go. I hope you'll forget about that silly annulment idea of yours, that you'll finally realize that you will always be mine." Before she could open her mouth to reply, he had silenced her with a searing kiss, his hands drawing her even closer against his masculine hardness.

No, Adam, she thought as she gave herself up to the rapturous sensations she experienced every time he kissed her, I don't want to let Clementine come between us. But there is still some disturbing doubt, still some lurking fear, that all was not as it should be. But for now, she told herself with a sigh as she felt his hand upon the buttons of her blouse, for now I won't think of anything but the fact that I love you, that I love you more than I ever dreamed possible.

Chapter Twenty-One

Sarah was pleasantly surprised when she awakened the following morning and discovered Adam still sleeping peacefully beside her. She smiled softly to herself as she leaned quietly over him, her eyes lovingly tracing the outlines of his tanned face and muscular body. The night they had shared together had been the most wonderful night of her life, and she could actually feel herself blushing as she recalled the wild, passionate, almost wanton abandon she had displayed with him. Adam had also noticed that there had been something decidedly different about her response last night, for he had even mentioned it to her following their rapturous lovemaking. She had been sorely tempted to reveal her love to him but had momentarily lost her courage and had simply flashed him a mysterious smile instead.

Carefully edging away from his warm body and out of the bed now, she threw her discarded wrapper about her shoulders and padded across the bare wooden floor into the kitchen. She felt so very happy, so wonderfully fulfilled, as if she had never really experienced life before. As she set about building a fire in the stove in order to prepare their breakfast, her thoughts unwillingly turned to Frank Mead.

If Adam's suspicions were true, if Frank did actually have something to do with Uncle John's death, then she couldn't help but wonder what other foul deeds he might be capable of. But no, she told herself reasonably, he isn't like that, or at least he doesn't seem that sort of person. He had been so kind to her, had even professed his love for her yesterday at the deserted cabin. How on earth could she think badly of such a charming young gentleman, a young man who said he loved her?

"Good morning, my lovely lass," Adam's deep voice spoke quietly from the doorway. Sarah turned to greet him with a shy smile as he came up to her and slipped his warm, strong arms about her slender waist, pulling her against him until their two bodies fit together perfectly.

"Adam! Stop it, you'll make me scorch the eggs!" she laughingly protested, then playfully sighed in mock anger as she reached out to set the eggs aside and raised her shining face for his kiss. When he finally allowed her to speak, she said, a bit breathlessly, "I thought you were still asleep."

"I missed you beside me," he murmured, before capturing her lips with his once again. Sarah mused that there would certainly be no breakfast if she didn't escape him soon! She finally pushed against him, and he released her with a heavy sigh. "After last night, I thought you'd at least be a bit more receptive to me!" he stated with a sardonic grin.

Sarah chuckled happily as she turned back to the

stove and told him, "You'd better go and get dressed and leave me alone for a while if you want any breakfast at all."

"Yes, madam, whatever you say, madam," he retorted with a comical expression on his handsome face. He winked broadly at her before leaving the room, and Sarah once more began to ponder her predicament.

She loved him so very much. She could not tolerate the thought of his loving Clementine instead of her! There must be some way she could discover the answer she sought so desperately, if he truly did love her in the manner in which he had ardently professed.

Sighing with just a touch of lingering despair, she scooped the cooked eggs from the iron skillet and took the boiling coffee pot from the stove in order to pour the aromatic brew into the waiting mugs. She didn't wish to contemplate the future any more for the moment. She would simply concentrate upon the present, for it always seemed to possess enough of its own difficulties!

Later, after Adam had left the cabin for his day's work, Sarah saddled the horse and rode into town. Pulling up directly in front of the general store, which also served as the town's post office, she dismounted and looped the reins across the hitching post. Walking inside the store, she observed that there were several other women inside, each purchasing a variety of goods. She reflected that Wildcat City was swiftly becoming more and more civilized, for one could now walk down the streets and see women and children, as well as the usual rough-looking men. Sarah discovered, much to her own surprise, that she had begun considering Wildcat City as a home of sorts, and she was not too displeased with her discovery. She was forced to admit to herself that Philadelphia seemed almost as if it belonged in the faraway past, even though it had been barely a month since she had left.

Her thoughts were rudely interrupted when she suddenly came face-to-face with Clementine Patterson. Good gracious, she complained silently, can't I go anywhere without encountering her? Mentally steeling herself for what seemed to be an inevitable confrontation, she waited for Clem to speak.

"Well, well, if it isn't Mrs. MacShane," Clem said in an exaggerated drawl, her attractive young face smiling maliciously.

"Good morning, Clementine," Sarah cooly replied, then started to sweep past the taller young woman. However, Clem reached out and tightly grasped Sarah's arm as she forced her to a halt.

"I'd like to have a few words with you, Mrs. MacShane," she declared contemptuously, placing a special, derisive emphasis upon Sarah's married name.

"I have nothing whatsoever to discuss with you, my dear Miss Patterson. Now, will you kindly release my arm so that I may continue with my errands?" Sarah asked with icy politeness, her glance quickly sweeping the store's interior. She saw that the ladies inside had now ceased their activity, that they were curiously staring toward herself and Clem. The few men inside the store were also watching with open curiosity. Sarah experienced a wave of embarrassment as she observed the attention she and Clem were attracting, and once more she said, "Let go of my arm." She tried to draw away, but Clem firmly held on.

"I said that I want to talk to you, you Yankee she-wolf!" Clem exclaimed viciously, her temper boiling at the mere sight of Sarah. It was Sarah who had caused all of this trouble between herself and Adam, Sarah who had stolen Adam away from her! She would be avenged, she would get even with her in some way!

"Clementine," Sarah now spoke sweetly, though her words were laced with a growing fury, "I think it best that, if you truly wish to speak with me, you do so in a more private atmosphere." She was feeling increasingly uncomfortable with the stares directed their way, and she finally brought her hand up and managed to pry Clem's fingers from her arm as she abruptly stepped away.

Clementine remained rooted to the spot for a few moments as Sarah walked over to the counter and began speaking with the clerk there. "I wish to inquire if there is a letter waiting for me. The name is Sarah Bradford, and the letter will be from Philadelphia."

"Yes, ma'am," the portly older gentleman replied. "I got that letter right here. It came in on this morning's train." He bent over and reached beneath the counter to retrieve the letter, then handed it to Sarah.

"Thank you," she politely replied. She pushed the letter into her bag and debated whether or not she should attempt to do her shopping while Clem was still present. Deciding that it might perhaps be best if she waited until Clem had left, she marched toward the doorway without a backward glance.

"Oh no you don't!" Clem spoke up with seething anger, her eyes glowing dangerously as she stalked after Sarah. Her hand shot out and grabbed hold of the back of Sarah's pretty gingham blouse. Sarah opened her mouth in shock, but was given no time to do more than gasp as Clem's other hand once more tightened on her arm and jerked her about. "I said I wanted to talk to you, and no one, especially not you, Miss High-and-Mighty, can get away with turning their back on me!" she spoke haughtily, very pleased with herself as she viewed the surrounding people avidly watching once more. She would show them, she would show everyone that Clementine Patterson was made of stronger stuff than this little schoolteacher apparently thought! Deep down, she realized that she was behaving childishly, that it was wrong for her to air her differences with Sarah in such a public place, but a tiny devil implanted in her jealous mind forced her to proceed upon her disastrous course. If she couldn't have Adam, then she didn't care!

"How dare you!" Sarah protested indignantly, pulling her arm away, then uttering a small gasp of dismay as the sleeve of her blouse tore at the shoulder seam with an accompanying sound. "I refuse to be treated in such a shabby manner!" she stated, her temper rising as Clem merely laughed, her eyes sparkling in devilish amusement.

"It serves you right!" she declared with a triumphant smirk. She was immensely gratified as several of the onlookers also chuckled, though others simply viewed the scene as a shocking display of poor manners. Several of them knew Clem, or at least knew who she was, and they had also heard about Sarah. Although not fully aware of the situation between the two young women, they were certainly able to sense that there was no love lost between these two battling females! Not a one of them would dare to interfere.

"If I weren't a lady . . ." Sarah angrily threatened, forcing herself to try and remain composed. She was afraid of what Clementine might prompt her to do, and she tightly clamped her mouth shut and again turned to leave.

This time, the devil urging Clementine onward caused her to snatch at Sarah's luxuriantly thick curls, which were neatly pinned atop her head, and tug at them quite ruthlessly, causing the thick masses to tumble out of their pins and down about Sarah's shoulders in a shower of disarray.

Now, Sarah could no longer remain either ladylike or dignified, for she had finally reached her limit of endurance with Clem. Forgetting that she was from Philadelphia, that she was a well-educated young woman, that she was a prim schoolteacher, she uttered a tiny shriek as her temper broke and she hurled herself at Clementine, her eyes blazing and her beautiful mouth compressed into a thin, angry line.

"Why, you no-account little tramp!" Clem exclaimed as Sarah's hands grasped a handful of her own hair. She hadn't expected Sarah to have enough gumption to fight back at all, particularly not in such a fierce manner!

The two of them wrestled back and forth, each clutching a portion of the other's long, wildly streaming hair, gasping and muttering as they fought, each intent only on overpowering the other. Although Clem was several inches taller than the more petite Sarah, Sarah possessed a grim determination that would not allow her to surrender.

Most of the women who had been shopping in the store now hurried outside, while the men and several new onlookers crowded about Sarah and Clem, forming a circle as they laughed and shouted encouragement to the two battling females. They loudly protested and vocalized their disappointment when a man suddenly broke through the crowd and proceeded to bodily pull Clementine off of Sarah, where she had pinned her to the floor and was engaged in grappling with her there.

"What do you think you're doing? Let go of me, you dirty coyote!" Clem hollered, her arms and legs flailing as the intruder easily subdued her and pushed her roughly aside. She was surprised to find that it was Frank Mead who had intervened, who had handled her in such a way.

"Frank Mead, you have no right at all poking your fancy nose in where it doesn't belong!" she informed him, still furious, her bosom heaving as she attempted to attack Sarah once more. Frank's hand shot out and mercilessly closed upon her wrist, twisting it behind her back until she cried aloud in pain.

"Get out of here! Don't you ever lay a hand on her again, do you hear?" he demanded in a low, even tone, his eyes narrowed dangerously. Clem's eyes opened wide at his words, and she was suddenly fearful that he would do her bodily harm if she protested further, so she turned upon her heel and flounced from the crowded store, her blond curls streaming about her face, her calico dress dirty and torn in several places.

Frank turned back to Sarah, who was now rising unsteadily to her feet. Her own dark hair was just as tangled and mussed as Clem's, her blouse and riding skirt filthy from the well-tracked wooden floor of the store.

"Sarah, are you all right?" Frank asked, his hands closing upon her waist in order to steady her as she attempted to make herself more presentable. She pushed the hair back from her flushed face and straightened her blouse and skirt.

"I'm all right, Frank," she replied, frowning slightly as she began to extricate the pins from her wildly tumbling hair. She was acutely aware of the crowd still gathered about, and she swayed toward Frank, anxiously whispering, "Frank, please get me out of here at once!"

"Of course, Sarah, my dear." He placed a supporting arm about her shoulders and led her quickly out of the store. The onlookers remained passive and silent until Sarah and Frank stepped through the doorway, at which time Sarah could hear them loudly discussing the humiliating scene.

"What happened?" Frank asked, scowling as he thought of Clementine. He was already feeling vengeful toward the teasing Miss Patterson on his own account, but her treatment of Sarah now added to his vengeance.

"Oh, Frank. It was so humiliating, so very disgraceful! Clem may have begun everything, but I fought back! I forgot myself completely! Oh, how on earth can I ever hold my head up around here again?" she cried in anguish.

"Now, Sarah, I'm sure everyone who was watching would certainly grant you the right to defend yourself! I wouldn't worry about it too much. In a town like this, something as insignificant as your little fight with Miss Patterson will soon be forgotten," he remarked with a grin.

"I pray that you're right. Oh, how could I have behaved in such a manner?" she said, still as furious with herself as with Clementine. She had apparently changed even more than she had believed possible! Brawling in a public place! How very far she had come from being a dignified, proper teacher of young girls! She reflected that she had become as rough and violent as this country, that her lifelong principles and convictions seemed to have disappeared. And yet, she told herself, I'm not so sure that what occurred just now was not for the best. Clementine Patterson had been begging for a setdown ever since she had first treated her so rudely! And now, now,

Clem had been shown that she was no person to be pushed about any longer!

"Why don't you come over to the hotel with me? You can wash up in my room and then have some lunch with me," Frank suggested with a charmingly persuasive smile.

Sarah had almost forgotten Adam's suspicions, but she now recalled them. But Frank seemed so very concerned, she couldn't see the harm in having lunch with her own business partner in a public place. She knew that Adam would probably not approve, but she also knew that it would seem strange to Frank if she refused with a lame excuse.

"Very well. I must confess, I do feel perfectly awful with my hair in such a mess," she responded with a laugh. It occurred to her that she certainly must not appear as attractive to Frank as she knew she must be at that particular moment!

Frank allowed Sarah to use the privacy of his room in order to freshen up while he waited downstairs in the hotel lobby, his attractive face closed and thoughtful as he smoked a cigar. He smiled and rose to his feet when Sarah reappeared, looking much better than when she had climbed the stairs. Her face was fresh and clean, her hair combed and once more neatly secured in its pins, her riding skirt only a trifle smudged, her blouse only torn at the one shoulder seam.

"I'm sorry if I kept you waiting. It's simply that I had to repair the damage done to my blouse as best I could without a needle and thread," she said as she gave him an apologetic smile.

"That's perfectly all right. Now, shall we have lunch, my dear business partner?" He offered her his arm and led her inside the restaurant.

After their lunch together, Frank escorted Sarah back across the busy street to her impatiently pawing horse. As he helped her mount, he suddenly asked, "Sarah, would you mind telling me what happened at the cabin the other morning? One moment, you seemed to respond to me, to return my affection, but you changed quite abruptly and I can't understand why. I've told you that I love you, that I want to marry you."

"Oh, Frank," she answered with a sigh, knowing that she could not possibly reveal her true reasons for treating him that way. "It's simply that I was wrong to behave in such a manner. I am still a married woman, remember? I have no right to become involved with any other man right now, no matter what Adam may or may not have done."

"I see." Then, changing the subject, he said, "I spoke with a friend of mine from Dallas. It seems that he knows of a way you can have that annulment much quicker than if you attempt to get it through that lawyer friend of yours in Philadelphia. Shall I tell him to go ahead and see what he can do?"

"Well . . ." Sarah faltered, uneasy and not knowing exactly what to say. She couldn't simply inform him that she no longer wanted the annulment, that she now never wanted to leave Adam. She sought the answer that would not serve to arouse his suspicions, then settled on a rather vague explanation. "Frank, it's simply that I am not prepared to look into the matter that fully just yet. You see, I still have a business agreement with Adam, no matter what I may think of him personally. I know what I have said, that I want nothing more to do with the man, but, well, it would seem a bit dishonorable to me if I were to break the contract between us now, at least until my part of the bargain has been fulfilled," she finished lamely, hoping he believed her.

If he did not, he gave her no indication of such, simply saying, "All right, I'll tell him to wait a bit. But just the same, I want you to remember that I love you, that I want nothing more than to marry you just as soon as you're free from MacShane." Gazing intently and wordlessly at her once more, he turned and slowly strode back across the street, finally disappearing inside the hotel, leaving a very confused and somewhat distraught Sarah sitting silently upon her prancing, whinnying horse.

How could such a sensitive, warm human being be guilty of the things that Adam suspected? she asked herself as she finally reined the frisky animal about and away from town. Frank Mead was in love with her, and she found that fact most disturbing. If she were not so desperately in love with Adam, perhaps she would be moved by his declarations of love. But as it was, she simply pitied him for loving her. She knew that she could never return his regard, that she could never love anyone but Adam. What was she to do about Frank? she wondered with another heavy sigh.

As Clementine's face suddenly wedged itself into her thoughts, she experienced an increasing anxiety.

If what Adam had told her was true, if there really never had been anything serious between him and Clem, then why did the young woman behave as if the two of them had shared a loving relationship, as if Adam had betrayed that love? If there was nothing there, then why was Clementine so violently jealous?

Musing that it would have been better if she had simply remained at the cabin for the day, Sarah gently kicked the horse into a swifter canter as she rode homeward in the warm afternoon sunshine. Besides her encounter with Clem and the resulting skirmish, Frank had informed her over lunch that there was going to be some difficulty in procuring that new boiler for the steam engine. She had remembered Adam's words about patching the present boiler, but she had remained silent.

She wanted nothing more than to discover the answers to all of her disturbing, plaguing questions. Would she ever know the entire truth about either Clementine or Frank? She knew that she would never have complete peace of mind until she did.

Meanwhile, Frank Mead strode from the hotel, making it obvious to anyone who was watching that he was in somewhat of a hurry. He headed straight for the sheriff's office, opening the door and stepping inside with great haste, taking a last glance around to make certain that no undue notice was taken of his actions.

More than half an hour later, he left the office and marched back across the street. He swung up into the saddle of a horse he had left waiting for him in front of the hotel, then savagely kicked the poor animal's sides with the heel of his pointed boots as he quickly rode from town, turning his mount away from the road he usually traveled.

He had received some most disturbing information after Sarah had ridden away. He had seen Clementine Patterson walking down the boardwalk a short time later, apparently none the worse for her confrontation with Sarah, wearing a fresh calico dress, her brushed and shining blond curls tied back to rest upon her slender neck. He had turned his quickening steps after her, catching up with her as she passed in front of one of the town's busy saloons.

"Miss Patterson," he said, clutching her arm and forcing her to acknowledge his presence as he pulled her to an abrupt halt.

"You!" she spat at him, obviously put out. "I don't have anything to say to you!" she said, her face sullen and angry. She twisted away from him, but he caught her arm once more and refused to relinquish his bruising hold.

"Well, I have plenty to say to you, Miss Patterson," he responded, his face deceptively smiling, the smile not quite reaching to his eyes. "First of all, I want to repeat my warning that you keep away from Sarah. Secondly, I want to know who put you up to coming up to my hotel room?"

"I don't know what you're talking about!" she hotly denied, trying to free her arm from his tightening grasp. "Let go of me, you're hurting my arm!" she demanded, growing a bit frightened when he ignored her command.

"I want the truth. I want to know who told you to

come up to my room, who told you to spy on me!" he spoke through tightly clenched teeth, his eyes suffused with a dull light. He had become increasingly suspicious ever since Clem had run from his hotel room the other night, and the only thing he had been able to come up with was that she had perhaps been doing someone else's bidding. Now he intended to find out if his hunch was right.

"If you don't tell me, Miss Patterson," he said, pulling her closer so that his face was mere inches away from hers, "I'll have to resort to violence. And, I can assure you," he said with a wolfish grin, "that you won't be pleased with what I will do to you."

Clementine opened her mouth to deny once more that she knew what he was talking about when an idea suddenly occurred to her. Well, why not? she asked herself. Why not go ahead and tell him that it was Adam's idea? After all, I certainly don't owe Adam MacShane anything after the way he's been treating me! Maybe this was one way she could get even with him for treating her like a child, for daring to spank her in such a humiliating fashion!

"Well, Mr. Mead," she told him, smiling up at him coquettishly now. "I don't see as how it's going to hurt for me to tell you the truth after all. It was Adam MacShane who put me up to it. It was all his idea that I come see you, that I act friendly to you."

"MacShane?" Mead muttered, half to himself. "Yes, I thought so. What else did he tell you to do?"

"Nothing, nothing at all. He just said to be nice to you and find out anything about you that might prove interesting, that's all."

"And what did you tell him?" Mead demanded sharply, his hand tightening quite painfully on her arm once more, causing her to wince.

"There wasn't much to tell him, was there?" she insisted a bit nervously, regretting her decision to mention Adam's name in the matter at all. "I just told him that there wasn't anything out of the ordinary about you, that you were a man who had to leave here on some private family business, and then had come back because of your oil wells. I can tell you, he was mighty disappointed in the information, too," she lied, suddenly realizing that she would only come to harm if she revealed to him the real information she had passed along to Adam. She decided to pretend that her mission had been completely unsuccessful. "You yourself must know that you didn't tell me anything important the two times we saw each other, and that's what I told Adam, that there wasn't really anything that he should know."

Frank's eyes narrowed until they were mere slits in his face as he intently searched her face and eyes for any evidence that she was lying. Finally telling himself that she was too stupid to have been of much help to MacShane, he released her arm with a contemptuous curse, then turned and stalked away.

Clementine had stood rubbing her arm, knowing that she would be sorry she had told him anything about Adam's involvement. What would happen now? she wondered silently as she watched Frank disappear inside the hotel. Would he tell Adam what she had said? She just couldn't bear to have Adam become so angry with her again, not just now, not after what had happened today. No matter what, she still believed that she loved him, that there might yet be some hope for her with him. But, she asked herself as she stared in the direction of the hotel, had she just destroyed that last little hope?

Chapter Twenty-Two

"I want the job done right away, just as soon as you can arrange it," Frank Mead ordered, his well-bred features appearing cruel in the fading afternoon light. "There's just one thing, something you have to make absolutely sure of," he stipulated. "It's got to look like an accident. No one must be in the least bit suspicious; no one must think that it was anything more than an accident."

"Sure thing, Mead," one of the three men to whom he was speaking readily answered, his own coarse features drawn up into a grin. "We'll get the job done right. You ain't got no call to worry at all, not at all. It ain't as if this was the first time we took care of a job for you, you know."

"That doesn't matter," Mead snapped. "The other jobs were quite different from this one, and I want everything clearly understood. Now, are there any questions?"

"Yeah," one of the other men spoke up, his gruff voice carrying easily on the wind. "What you want done with the girl?" he asked with a meaningful leer.

"I'll take care of her!" Mead snarled. "She's none of your concern!"

"All right, all right, I was just asking. It's just that it would've been mighty enjoyable to have a go at her again, even if it didn't last long enough to suit me!" he remarked with a knowing grin. He glanced downward and grinned even wider as his gaze alighted on a small lizard crawling along in the dirt. Taking careful aim, he pursed his meaty lips and spat a stream of the tobacco he was chewing, striking the dirt a fraction of an inch in front of the scurrying lizard. The wind was slowly increasing in velocity as the evening drew near, and Frank stepped closer to the man who had just spoken.

"It lasted a little too long!" he said. "I told you to frighten her, to shake her up a bit, not to rip the clothes from her back!"

"Well, I guess you could say we just got carried away, Mead," the first fellow retorted with a loud guffaw. "It don't matter, we still got the job done, didn't we? She was mighty glad to see you, wasn't she?"

"You'd better get this job done!" Frank commanded irritably, before reaching into the pocket of his coat and withdrawing his fine leather wallet. "Here," he said, placing several bills into the outstretched hand of the gang's leader. "This is a down payment. Once you've done it, you'll get the rest of the money I promised you."

"Okay, Mead. We'll start working on it right away. You don't have to worry none, though, for it'll sure enough look like an accident, a simple little accident," the man assured Frank with a deep, rumbling chuckle.

Frank, appearing suddenly disgusted with the

sight of the three, turned about and mounted his horse and rode back toward town. If everything went as he had so carefully planned, if those three jackals didn't foul things up, then this would be the last time he would be forced to do business with them. He reflected that things just might work out splendidly after all.

It was two days later before Sarah finally remembered the letter she had hastily stuffed into her bag that day in the general store, when Clementine's actions had made her completely forget the reply she had been awaiting. Her relationship with Adam had also forced a great many things from her mind lately, for she was more in love with him than ever, more than ever preoccupied with her love.

Last night, she thought back with a dreamy smile, had certainly been no exception! Adam had made glorious love to her with great expertise, then had held her lovingly against his warm, broad shoulder and told her a bit about his life in Scotland, before he and his older brother had decided to make the long journey to the United States. Sarah had listened quite intently, wanting to know absolutely everything she could about this handsome, maddening, virile, wonderful man she had married.

"James and I were very close," he had told her, "even though we had other brothers and sisters. There were nine of us in all, five boys and four girls, but James and I were the two eldest. We were barely a year apart in age and were always a pair. When he first told me he was leaving Scotland to come here, I tried to persuade him that it was foolish, that he could never leave Scotland behind. After a while, though, he turned the tables on me and actually convinced me to come along as well! My grandfather was none too pleased with our decision, for we were both very young and very headstrong, but I suppose he always knew that we would eventually have our way. My parents, you see, had both died when James and I were still quite young, as well as two of our brothers and one of our sisters. Being the eldest, the responsibilities for our remaining brother and sisters weighed heavily upon our young shoulders. But my grandfather, who was quite wealthy, decided that he would simply pack us all off to live with him, which he then proceeded to do."

He had paused a moment in order to lightly clear his throat before continuing. "So there we were, James was thirteen and I twelve, while the youngest of the children was barely two. My grandfather had seen very little of us before my parents' death. He had stubbornly declared that he would disinherit my father when he had married my mother, for he had not considered her quite well-heeled enough to wed his only son. But my parents had been so much in love, that they openly defied my grandfather. And even though Grandfather lived only a few miles away, we rarely encountered him. I remember that James and I had been invited to the castle when we were no more than nine and ten, but my father wouldn't grant his permission for the visit. But when my parents both died within a week of each other of the typhoid, my grandfather became our legal guardian."

"Then you lived with him since you were twelve,

and in a genuine castle?" Sarah had prompted, fascinated with his story, her eyes continually straying to his face as he spoke.

"Aye, lass. And believe it or not, even with all the bad blood between my grandfather and my folks, we all grew to love the old devil! He proved to be a harsh taskmaster, but he was always just."

"But what about your other brother and your sisters? Are they all still living at the castle then?"

"No. James and I were the first to leave the castle. The brother and sisters who have since married have moved to various places with their families, all remaining in Scotland. I was very surprised when I received news of my grandfather's death. I thought for certain that he would outlive us all!" Adam had remarked with a soft chuckle, though the deep sadness in his eyes was apparent to Sarah.

"So you never saw him again after leaving Scotland?" she had quietly asked.

"No, I never did. And that was more than ten years ago now. James and I came straight here to Texas and made this our home, though we did do a bit of traveling for a while. We learned about the oil business up in Pennsylvania before coming back here. James married a few years back, but his wife was killed after only a year of marriage."

"And what happened to your brother?" Sarah had questioned, her eyes filling with silent tears as she realized how much Adam had loved his family, his grandfather, his older brother.

"His wife was killed by a pair of cutthroat outlaws while James and I were away from home. That's when we were living on a ranch just south of Fort

Worth. We had gone away to see about buying some cattle. We were only absent for a day and a night, but it was long enough," he had said, his face grim and tight. "We arrived home to find Louisa dead, the house ransacked, our stock gone. They had obviously raped Louisa before killing her, and I thought poor James would go mad with grief and rage. After we buried Louisa, James stayed around for nearly a week, before suddenly disappearing one night. I realized that he must have gone in search of the men who had killed his wife, and I immediately set out to find him, but he had a good day's start on me by the time I picked up his trail. I finally caught up with him four days later."

"What happened?"

"James had been killed, shot in the back. He had apparently found the two men in Abilene, had evidently satisfied himself that they were the ones who had killed his wife and stolen our stock. I don't know exactly how it happened, but James had been dead for no more than a day before I arrived. There were no witnesses, at least none who would talk. I took him back home and buried him beside Louisa. I searched for those cowardly bastards who had killed him for a long time before I finally received word that they had themselves been killed in a shootout down in San Antonio. I guess I'll never know for sure if it was them, for I didn't have much of a description. But I sold the ranch and came out here when news of the boom hit. As I said, James and I had already learned a great deal about drilling for oil in Pennsylvania, so I decided to invest the remainder of my funds here."

"Did you ever pay a visit to Philadelphia?" Sarah had wanted to know, finding it thrilling to think that Adam had actually been so close to her before the two of them had even met.

"Aye, lass, a few times. I must say, though, I certainly never saw anything like you there!" he had remarked with a teasing grin.

"Oh, Adam," Sarah had then sighed, entwining her arms about his neck and pulling him closer for her kiss. She felt so very grateful that he had allowed her a glimpse of his former life, that he had revealed some of his deepest feelings to her.

They had made love again, then had drifted into a peaceful sleep, snuggled closely together. Sarah now reflected that she would never forget last night; she would always cherish the time that Adam had first told her a bit about his mysterious past.

Adam had already dressed and left for work, so she went into her bedroom and searched for her bag. Finally locating it beneath her discarded nightgown, she tore open the envelope and withdrew the rather crumpled letter, then sank down upon the bed to scan its contents.

It was indeed from her uncle's friend in Philadelphia, the attorney. It said that he had received her inquiry, that he had considered her situation most carefully, and that she would apparently not qualify for an annulment. However, he went on to tell her that he would be more than happy to draw up the papers for a divorce, and that she should notify him as soon as possible so that he could begin with the necessary proceedings.

Divorce? Sarah repeated to herself as she allowed

the letter to slip unheeded to the floor below. Heavens! She certainly didn't want a divorce, not now! She silently chided herself for ever having written the man, and she bent down to retrieve the letter, then hurried into the kitchen and threw the offending piece of paper into the fire at the stove. She wanted nothing more than to forget all about the matter, for she knew that she never wanted to be free of Adam!

At that same moment, Adam was busy overseeing the work at one of his wells.

"Well, Mr. MacShane, I know we was planning on doing that today," the foreman of the roughnecks was saying, "but our derrick man's sick. He come down with some kind of fever or something. Anyways, one of his buddies said he won't be able to do any work for a spell, I reckon." The tall, slender man of indeterminate age shaded his eyes with his hand as he gazed upward to the top of the derrick as he spoke, the early-morning sunlight peeking out from beneath the rising cover of clouds.

"Well then," Adam replied, his face thoughtful as he contemplated the situation, "I suppose I'll have to be the derrick man today."

"But you ain't no derrick man no more, Mr. MacShane. Why, you've been a driller for a long time now," his top hand protested.

"I still recall what to do, Thomas," Adam said with a wry grin. "Don't worry, I'll be able to handle it all right. You just get everyone ready to begin work."

A short time later, Adam strode up to the platform and took hold of the ladder that ran from the bottom of the derrick floor to the very top of the majestic wooden structure. He stepped up and carefully climbed the ladder, climbing up to where the small platform referred to as the "monkey board" was located, nearly fifty feet up in the air. He kept a firm grip on the ladder until he had his feet firmly planted on top of the small wooden platform, then released his hold on the ladder and stepped into the length of rope that served as a safety belt.

"All right! Let's get things going!" he called down to the derrick floor where the men watched and waited for his signal.

Adjusting the safety belt to a more comfortable angle, he stood looking downward as the top of the stand of pipe came up from below and approached the monkey board. Grasping hold of the top of the long piece of pipe, he moved it slowly over to the side so that another stand could be brought up out of the well.

They continued in this manner for several minutes before Adam suddenly felt the monkey board beginning to give way beneath him. Uttering a curse as he realized what was going to happen, he felt the monkey board now give way completely. The men below raised startled eyes upward as Adam's body slipped through the restraining safetly belt and the monkey board clattered noisily to the derrick floor below.

Adam had miraculously managed to grasp hold of the safety belt with his hands as he fell, and he now dangled nearly fifty feet up in the air, the rope burning his hands as he literally held on for dear life.

"Hang on, Adam!" the man known as Thomas shouted, frantically searching for some way they could save him. He gazed helplessly upward at Adam, not knowing which action to take.

Adam forced himself to think fast as he began to carefully place one hand over the other on the safety rope. He wouldn't allow himself to look downward, knowing that it could be his doom if he did so. Finally, he managed to reach the ladder on the side of the derrick, and he swung his muscular legs over to the top rung as he let go of the safety belt and grabbed the side of the derrick.

The men below all heaved a loud sigh of relief as they perceived that he was safe, and they watched as Adam slowly descended the ladder, his face taut and grim.

"Damn, Mr. MacShane, we all thought you was a goner for sure," one of the men commented as Adam's feet gratefully touched solid ground once more.

"Aye, so did I," Adam replied, his features beginning to relax a bit as he realized that the ordeal was over with. After receiving several similar comments from the men, he finally drew his foreman aside, out of earshot of the other workers.

"Hell, MacShane, I ain't ever seen a monkey board give way like that!" Thomas remarked, shaking his head in disbelief.

"I know. But Thomas," Adam told him, his gaze returning to the top of the derrick, "it wasn't an accident."

"No accident? What are you talking about?"

"I happened to glance down in time to see that monkey board just before it broke. It had been sawed through enough so that a man's weight would eventually force it to give way."

"But there ain't been no one up there. Ain't no one goes up there at all, excepting for the derrick man. You really think it's been tampered with? Are you certain you didn't just think you saw something different?" Thomas cautiously insisted.

"It's been tampered with all right. But I don't want any of the other men to know, do you understand? I want it kept quiet, at least until I have a chance to do a bit of investigating into the matter. In the meantime, I want you to have the board replaced, but make sure no one suspects it's been sawed. You'll have to remove the remaining piece of it first," Adam instructed.

"All right, Mr. MacShane, whatever you say. But if you're right, if someone's been up there messing with our derrick, then something like this might just happen again," Thomas pointed out. "As a matter of fact, there might be someone out to sabotage this well."

"I don't think it has anything to do with the well. I have my own ideas as to who planned this little 'accident,' and I intend to take care of him. For the time being, though, you take over here while I see to some business of my own."

"Yes, sir. I still can't get over it, though," Thomas remarked, half to himself, as he turned and walked away.

Adam swung up into the saddle and galloped straight back to the cabin, where he found Sarah engaged in the task of sweeping the myriad of dust that had gathered on the floor of the cabin. She looked up as he dismounted and approached the cabin. She had opened the front door in order to sweep the collected dust outside, and she smiled as she saw him approaching.

"Adam! What are you doing home at this hour of the day?" she asked in surprise, then grew uneasy as she viewed the solemn look on his face.

"Sarah, lass, I need to talk to you right away. Let's go inside," he told her, gesturing toward the cabin's interior. Sarah's gaze alighted upon his hands, and she gasped as she viewed the blood on his palms, the reddened, lacerated flesh.

"What's happened to your hands?" she demanded, then drew him inside with her without waiting for an answer as she led him into the kitchen and pushed him down on the bench, hurrying to fetch water and bandages.

"Oh, I just hurt them a bit while working at the well. It's nothing much. What I have to tell you is much more important than my hands," he grimly responded.

"Very well, but you can tell me just as well while I see to these hands." She sat down opposite him and proceeded to gently cleanse the wounds.

"Aye. My derrick man was too ill to work today, so I had to be the derrick man. I climbed up the ladder to a small platform near the top of the derrick, known as the monkey board. It suddenly gave way beneath me as I worked, and I would surely have fallen to my death if I had not managed to grasp hold of the rope we use as a safelty belt. I managed to get over to the side of the derrick and climbed back down the ladder, very much shaken by the incident, I must confess," he admitted with a rueful grin.

"Oh, Adam!" Sarah exclaimed, hating that her beloved had been so near death just a short time earlier. She shivered uncontrollably as she pictured the horrible scene. "Thank God you're all right!"

"Aye, but that isn't the main thing I wished to tell you. You see, that monkey board had been tampered with, had actually been sawed in order to break that way."

"But how can you know that?" Sarah gasped, realizing the terrible implications.

"Because I happened to look down in time to see it before it was went crashing to the derrick floor, that's why. I know that someone must have planned this so-called 'accident' and that it was probably no illness at all that kept my derrick man away from work today. Everyone knew we were going to be doing that job today, and they must also have known that I was the only one capable of taking over for the derrick man. I happen to believe that this whole thing was planned in order to kill me," he said grimly, wincing slightly as Sarah finished with his hands.

"If that is true, if you believe that everything was planned in order to achieve your death, then you must surely have some idea as to who would wish you dead," she remarked a bit breathlessly, still dazed by the terrible fact that someone might have tried to kill Adam. To think that she had come so close to losing him, after only just discovering how much she loved him!

"I have an idea. That's what I wanted to tell you. I think this was Frank Mead's idea, that he arranged it especially for me," Adam admitted, his eyes glowing dangerously as his face became more savage at the thought of Mead.

"Frank? Oh, Adam, no!" Sarah responded, not wanting to believe it.

"Aye, Sarah, lass, I'm afraid I don't know of anyone else who would wish me dead, who would stand to gain so much from my death. You see, Mead must have somehow discovered that I had been asking questions about him. I figured that he'd hear about it eventually. Besides that, he probably thought it would be most convenient for him if you were suddenly widowed!"

"But how can you know all of this? How do you know Frank knows anything about your suspicions? It could just as easily have been someone else, couldn't it?" she insisted anxiously.

"Aye, it could have been, but I don't think it was. I can't prove anything yet, but I certainly intend to. I intend to find out once and for all what Frank Mead is up to, how much he had to do with your uncle's death, why he disappeared so abruptly, why we couldn't find any of his workers after that, why he came back all of a sudden, and particularly why he is keeping your wells out of production."

"What about my wells?" Sarah demanded, not following his entire train of thought.

"Sarah, it's been obvious to me for some time now that Frank Mead doesn't want those wells producing, for reasons still known only to him. It's obvious that he's got some reason for putting you off. I don't for one minute believe that story of his about the boiler, and I certainly don't intend to stand by and let him get away with it!" he sternly informed her.

"Oh, Adam, all of this is so very confusing!"

"I know, lass, I know. But you've got to see now that you cannot have any further contact with Mead. He's even more dangerous than I originally believed he might be. I think he's possibly got a few more little plans up his sleeve, and I damned sure don't want you caught in the middle of all of this! So, from here on out, you're to stay away from him, to avoid him at all costs, is that understood?" he commanded authoritatively.

"I suppose so," Sarah unwillingly agreed after a moment's hesitation. She wanted to help him in some way, to assist him in discovering the truth. "But what am I going to say to him when I see him again? He'll certainly wish to know why I began avoiding him all of a sudden, don't you think? After all, we are supposed to be business partners." She knew that she still couldn't tell Adam that Frank wanted them to be much more, particularly not after what had occurred today!

"I know all of that, but you're to do as I say, is that clear?" he masterfully repeated as Sarah finally nodded in agreement. "Just don't have anything to do with him. It's gone beyond the point where we don't want him to become suspicious. After this failed attempt on my life, he's bound to realize what's going on, that I am indeed on to him."

"But, Adam, you still don't know for sure that Frank is the one who arranged to kill you."

"I intend to get enough proof to satisfy myself right away," he responded tightly, then broke into a crooked smile as he looked across at her and said, "Sarah, love, don't worry. We'll find Frank Mead out soon, and then there'll be the devil for him to pay!"

"It's just that I'm so afraid you'll be hurt," Sarah told him with a worried frown.

"I intend to be very careful, I can assure you. After all, I can't leave you a widow until I get that inheritance, now, can I? I can't be killed until I can leave you a rich widow instead of a penniless one!" he remarked with a laugh at the horrified expression that had appeared upon her beautiful face at his words.

"Don't you dare to joke about such a serious matter, you wretch!" she cried, unable to resist melting against him as he stood and came around the table to lift her high in his arms, the pain in his rope-burnt hands completely forgotten as he carried her swiftly toward the bedroom.

Placing her on the bed, he quickly stripped himself of his own clothing as Sarah hurriedly pulled off the rather worn cotton dress she always wore while doing the housework. Soon, the two of them were both naked and locked in a passionate embrace.

"Adam, I couldn't bear it if anything happened to you!" Sarah fervently whispered as she grasped his head between her hands and gazed deep into his glowing green eyes.

"Aye, so you do care!" he responded mischievously, then instantly sobered as he suddenly demanded, "Sarah, please tell me that you love me. Oh, lass, stop denying what we have together. You know it's much more than physical desire," he entreated, his hands gently caressing her soft curves as he gazed deep into her opal eyes. "Tell me that you love me," he quietly repeated.

Sarah knew that she wanted to tell him, that she could no longer keep the precious secret to herself, that nothing else mattered for the moment except for herself and Adam, together and alone in their own little world. Forgotten for the moment was her jealousy of Clementine, her own doubts as to Adam's love. She wanted nothing more than to shout her love to everyone, to bask in the glory of her love for her husband.

"Yes, Adam," she said softly, "I do love you."

"Oh, my lovely lass!" Adam exclaimed, his face exultant as he planted a kiss on the very tip of her nose. Closely scrutinizing her face to ascertain if she was indeed speaking the truth, he felt himself growing happier than he had ever been in his entire life. "I've been waiting so very long to hear those words from your lips! Now there's nothing in this world that can ever come between us!" he spoke with a triumphant laugh, hugging her closer.

"I hope so, Adam, I truly hope so," Sarah quietly replied, the feeling of dread refusing to remain pushed aside. "I love you so very much! I fought it for so long, Adam, but I can't fight it any longer. I'm no longer confused about my feelings for you, my dearest. You were right, you know," she shyly admitted, "I am certainly capable of loving one man with all my heart, with all my body and soul."

"Yes, lass, yes," Adam huskily whispered against her ear as his hands moved up and down her womanly softness. "We will always be together, loving each other just as we do now." Then, before Sarah could say anything more, he had captured her lips with his and caused her mind to reel with the building fires of desire.

She silently prayed that Adam's words would prove true, that they would never be separated by anything or anyone. Then, as her own passion began to overtake her, she could no longer pray or even think. Adam's lips and hands soon brought her to a tumultuous climax, as she felt the delicious sensations taking hold of her entire being again.

Chapter Twenty-Three

Sarah and Adam shared in a leisurely breakfast the following morning, each preferring to prolong their special closeness for as long as possible before tending to the various problems that were facing them. After the meal, Adam informed her that he was riding directly into town, where he planned to find Frank Mead and question him extensively, and where he also intended to look in on his derrick man and discover precisely what had caused his sudden, unexplained illness.

Sarah begged to accompany him, but he was firm. She watched him go with a heavy feeling of dread, knowing that his encounter with Frank could very easily turn violent. She knew that Frank might prove very dangerous if Adam confronted him with accusations concerning yesterday's "accident" at the well. Dear Lord, she prayed as she waved once more toward the retreating figure of her husband on horseback, please keep him safe for me.

Sarah forced herself to remain occupied throughout the morning, knowing full well that, if she were to allow her mind to dwell upon Adam's trip into town to see Frank, she would certainly have to disobey him and ride after him with great haste! So she busied herself and occupied the greater majority of her thoughts by concentrating her efforts on repairing a few of Adam's torn work shirts. She sat in the large central room of the cabin, her hands nervously shaking just the slightest bit as she sewed.

Suddenly, after Adam had been gone for nearly an hour, she was startled by a loud knock sounding on the front door. Quickly putting aside her sewing, she cautiously approached the front window in order to catch a glimpse of whoever was there. She perceived that it was a rather small, thin man of middle age, and that he was clothed in a very proper dark suit. Although he looked anything but dangerous, Sarah ran into her bedroom and fetched her pistol, tucking it away in her skirt pocket before she returned to open the front door.

"Yes? May I help you?" she politely inquired.

"Yes, ma'am, perhaps you may. I am looking for Mr. Adam MacShane. My name is Harold Spencer," the stranger answered a bit stiffly. He had removed his hat as soon as he observed that it was none other than a beautiful young woman who greeted him, and he was momentarily stunned by the sight of her in such rustic surroundings. She was certainly not the sort of woman he had expected to find here!

"Well, Mr. Spencer, I am Mrs. MacShane," Sarah told him, still puzzled by the fact that this strange man, so obviously not native to that part of the country, was looking for Adam.

"How do you do, Mrs. MacShane? May I please speak with your husband?" the man repeated politely.

"I'm afraid he isn't home right now, Mr. Spencer.

However, I expect him back shortly," she said, adding the word "hopefully" to her own thoughts. She was increasingly curious as to what this gentleman's business with Adam might be, and she hesitated a moment before inviting him inside. "Mr. Spencer, would you perhaps care to come inside and have a cup of coffee? Perhaps you can tell me what it is you need to see my husband about."

"No, thank you. I really must wait until your husband has returned. You see, the matter I have to discuss with him is to be kept strictly confidential."

"Very well," Sarah responded with a slight frown. "Why don't you return this afternoon then? You will most likely be able to catch him then."

"Thank you, Mrs. MacShane. Good day to you," Spencer replied, replacing his hat upon his head as he headed back down the path to the wagon. Sarah watched him drive away, then slowly closed the door.

How strange, she thought as she went back to her sewing. It wasn't often they received any visitors at all, much less ones as proper and polished as Mr. Harold Spencer. She again wondered what such a man could possibly want with Adam, then finally forced her mind back to her task. The time was passing so very slowly for her as she awaited Adam's return, she thought with a heavy sigh.

Adam strode across the street to the hotel, his handsome features frowning as he stepped inside and approached the front desk.

"Is Frank Mead still in Room 202?" he demanded of the clerk, who glanced upward at Adam, then abruptly straightened.

"No, sir, Mr. MacShane. Mr. Mead checked out first thing this morning."

"He's gone?" Adam asked, wanting to make certain before jumping to any more conclusions. Damn! he swore silently. I should have expected this.

"Yes, sir, he's gone all right. Took all his bags with him."

"Did he say where he was heading?"

"No, sir, Mr. MacShane, not a word. Just paid his bill and left bright and early this morning," the clerk assured him.

"All right. Thanks," Adam muttered, a ferocious scowl on his face as he turned and stalked from the hotel.

Now, he told himself, it was definitely all fitting together. He had just come from paying a visit to the derrick man at his boardinghouse, only to learn that the poor fellow had been the victim of food poisoning. Although he would recover, he would be absent from work for a few more days. His mysterious poisoning, coupled with Frank Mead's abrupt departure, was enough to convince Adam that his suspicions were correct. He had acquired all the evidence he needed to satisfy himself that it was Frank Mead who had arranged to have him killed, among other things.

Thinking back now, several other factors contributed to his conclusion. Sarah's being attacked on the road home from town that day, only to have Frank come to her rescue so heroically, so conveniently, after which he had merely ordered her attackers to leave. Frank's vague explanations concerning John Bradford, his leaving so soon after John's death, and his workers disappearing as well. His return, which had coincided with Sarah's coming to Wildcat City. Aye, it fit together too well to be mere chance, he grimly told himself.

He swiftly rode back toward the cabin, anxious to relate to Sarah the news he had discovered. Unsaddling his mount in the barn, he marched inside the cabin and found Sarah still sitting in the central room, still trying to occupy her wandering thoughts with her various tasks.

"Adam! Oh, I'm so glad you're home!" she exclaimed when she saw him, jumping to her feet and throwing herself into his arms. She closed her eyes in silent gratitude as his strong arms closed about her, drawing her tight against him as his hand came up to entangle itself in her thick hair.

"Sarah, lass, I told you not to worry, that nothing would happen to me," Adam chided her with a soft chuckle, actually very pleased with her reaction. It only served to prove to him that she had spoken the truth about her love, that she really did love him as she had declared last night. He reflected that nothing could ever defeat him now that he was sure of her love, for she was the one thing in the world that truly mattered to him.

"What happened?" she inquired anxiously, finally raising her widened blue eyes to his face.

"Well, I paid a visit to the derrick man and found out that he didn't have a mysterious fever at all. It seems that it was nothing more than a bad case of food poisoning, though no one can figure out exactly where he got it. Someone had apparently planned this quite carefully."

"But did you speak with Frank?"

"No. It seems that our friend Frank Mead has disappeared. I went looking for him at the hotel, but the clerk said that he had checked out early this morning and left no word as to his destination. I then realized that by his actions Frank was foolishly exposing himself to me as the culprit. He must have thought things were getting a trifle uncomfortable around here after that attempt on my life failed."

"If he really is gone, then how will you ever know for sure that he was involved? And what will you do?" she asked with a worried frown. So it was true after all, she thought. Frank Mead had apparently arranged to have Adam killed, had possibly even done the same to her Uncle John. It was simply too horrible to think about!

"Well, I certainly don't intend to allow him to escape so easily, I can assure you. I will have to continue to do a bit of investigating, but I intend to locate him eventually and force the truth from him! For now, however, I intend to go on as usual, to go ahead with the work on my wells, to continue loving my irresistible little wife," he remarked with a teasing grin and a mischievous wink.

Sarah initially gazed at him with a bit of exasperation, unable to understand how he could treat everything so lightly after what he had discovered. However, she was finally forced to smile at him in response, wanting nothing more than to forget all about the unpleasant subject of Frank

Mead, at least for now. She realized that she was now solely responsible for her uncle's wells, that she and Adam would once more become business partners. Thank goodness their relationship had developed into much more than that! she told herself.

"Oh, I nearly forgot," she suddenly stated. "There was a gentleman who came calling for you today. His name was Harold Spencer, but he didn't say what it was he wanted to see you about, only that it was a most confidential matter."

"Harold Spencer?" Adam repeated with a pensive air. "No, I don't believe I know anyone by that name. What did he look like?"

"He was rather small, middle-aged, and obviously not the usual sort of person you would expect to find in Wildcat City. He was stiffly polite and very businesslike."

"Did he say if he was going to return?"

"Yes, I told him to come back this afternoon. I must say, I am very curious," she admitted with a slight smile as Adam released her, planting a last little kiss on her cheek.

"We'll find out soon enough. I've shut down operations on the well for today, anyway. I thought it would do the men good to have an unexpected holiday for a change. Now, then, how about fixing your wonderful, adoring husband some lunch, dearest wife?" he demanded in a booming voice, causing Sarah to respond by punching him in the arm with a mock exclamation of indignation.

Later, after the noon hour had come and gone, Mr. Spencer returned to the cabin. Sarah once more greeted him at the door, politely asking him to step inside.

"I take it your husband has returned, Mrs. MacShane?" he said a bit cooly, removing his hat and crossing the threshold, his rather squinty gaze traveling swiftly about the cabin's interior.

"Yes, he has, Mr. Spencer. If you'll please take a seat, I will be more than happy to call him." Sarah turned her back on him, silently musing what a strange man he was, then went to the rear entrance of the cabin and opened the door.

"Adam!" she called, her gaze traveling to where he was involved in gathering wood from the large woodpile several yards away from the cabin. "Mr. Spencer has returned and wishes to speak with you," she told him as he set aside the wood, wiped his hands on the sides of his trousers and strode through the doorway.

"All right, lass," Adam responded, stepping inside to meet the mysterious Mr. Spencer. "How do you do, sir? I'm Adam MacShane," he said, extending his large hand in greeting.

Mr. Spencer rose to his feet and politely took the hand offered to him, wincing almost imperceptively as Adam's firm grip closed on his own hand.

"I am Harold Spencer, Mr. MacShane. I have traveled all the way from Dallas to discuss matters of the utmost importance with you. Now, if I may please speak with you, in private," he requested, casting a sideways glance at Sarah, who stood next to Adam.

"Mr. Spencer," Adam replied rather gruffly as his

face tightened, "anything you have to say to me can certainly be said in front of my wife."

"But I told you, these are extremely confidential matters, and we usually make it our policy to speak only with the client himself," Spencer obstinately insisted.

"Adam," Sarah interjected, sensing that she had better speak up in order to avoid any further unpleasantness, "I don't mind. I was going down to the creek for a while, anyway. Please, continue with your business, Mr. Spencer," she said. She left the cabin with a quickening step. As she strolled toward the quietly rushing water of the glistening creek, she told herself that she would most certainly ask Adam to tell her about everything that transpired after that decidedly secretive little man had gone!

"What is it you wish to speak with me about?" Adam demanded rather curtly as he took a seat opposite the solemn Mr. Spencer.

"Mr. MacShane, I may as well come straight to the point. You see, the solicitors employed by your late grandfather in Scotland contacted my firm concerning your grandfather's will. It seems that everything is finally in order, and that you will indeed receive the inheritance you have already been contacted about. I have a few papers here with me that I need to have you sign, once I have satisfied myself that you have met all the terms of the will, that is."

"I see," Adam thoughtfully remarked. "What you wish to know is whether or not I have met my grandfather's stipulation that I marry before the age of thirty. Well, it's certainly obvious that I have done so."

"Very well. May I then inquire as to how long you and Mrs. MacShane have been married?"

"I don't see that it matters, but it's been little more than a month now."

"I see. Well then, it appears that you perhaps married primarily in order to meet the stipulation of the will, doesn't it?" Spencer pompously inquired.

"Aye, that's right. I went right out and married the first woman I could find to ask," Adam drily retorted, not realizing that the humorless little man opposite him would actually take him seriously.

"You must know that your grandfather naturally assumed that, once wed, you would remain so until the end of your days," Spencer pointed out, rather shocked.

"Actually," Adam continued with subtle sarcasm, "we planned from the very beginning to obtain an annulment just as soon as I received the inheritance. But, of course, an annulment is no longer an option for us, if you know what I mean. Aye," he remarked with a sigh, "I'm afraid it would have to be a divorce now."

"A divorce?" the other man responded, his composure nearly shaken. "Surely you wouldn't want to create such a scandal?"

"Why should that bother you?" Adam replied nonchalantly. "But that's all beside the point. The reason you're here is to have me sign those papers, right? Well, then, let's get on with it."

"Very well, Mr. MacShane," Spencer answered withdrawing the papers from the inside pocket of his coat. His solemn face was very disapproving as he handed the papers across to Adam.

Adam put his signature to all of the necessary documents, then stood and briskly ushered the man outside, saying, "I appreciate your traveling all this distance, Mr. Spencer. Please send my best to my grandfather's solicitors. They already have my instructions concerning the inheritance."

"I shall, Mr. MacShane. Good day to you, sir," the man politely replied, climbing back up onto the wagon seat and driving away at a sedate pace. His expression was one of severe disapproval as he thought of the disgusting situation. Imagine! he fumed to himself. Such a coldhearted, ruthless thing to do, marrying a woman for no other reason than to inherit a sum of money!

Adam smiled to himself as he watched the strange little man drive out of sight, then turned his steps toward the stream. He arrived to find Sarah seated on the bank beside the inviting water, her beautiful hair free from its pins and flowing about her shoulders, her boots and stockings discarded as she trailed her slender feet in the cool stream.

"Well, if it isn't the beautiful and desirable Mrs. MacShane," he remarked in his deep, resonant voice as he took a seat beside his wife.

"Oh!" Sarah exclaimed, then laughed as she grasped his arm. "You startled me! Is that dreadful man gone?"

"Aye. His visit didn't take long at all."

Sarah impatiently waited in silence for a few moments, before turning to Adam with an accusing frown.

"Well, aren't you even going to tell me what happened?"

"I wasn't sure you'd want to know," Adam responded blithely.

"Of course I want to know!" Sarah retorted, sighing at his maddening air.

"All right then, I'll tell you. It seems that the proper Mr. Harold Spencer was here because of my grandfather's solicitors in Scotland. They contacted him to pay a visit to me. I had to sign a few papers pertaining to my inheritance. It seems that I should be receiving a goodly sum of money within the next few weeks."

"Oh, Adam, that's wonderful!" Sarah exclaimed. "I'm so happy for you. I'm also pleased to learn that my part of our original bargain has finally been fulfilled!" she told him with a saucy grin and a toss of her shining black curls.

"What do you mean 'your part of the bargain has been fulfilled?' I've tried to do my best to live up to my part of our agreement!" Adam said with a grin.

"Why, you beast! You have lied to me on more than one occasion, you have behaved quite horribly at times, and you sit there and tell me that you have fulfilled your part of the bargain?" Sarah mockingly demanded, then sobered as a sudden thought occurred to her. "Adam, did you by any chance mention our business arrangement to Mr. Spencer?" She would be so embarrassed if anyone in Adam's family learned of the circumstances of his "marriage of convenience."

"I mentioned it, but he didn't seem too concerned. All he wanted was to get his precious papers signed and be on his way. But it's all taken care of now, Sarah love. It seems that you may have just married a wealthy man after all!"

"Yes, and I suppose I shall now be accused of having married you for your money, is that it?" she laughingly asked.

"There may be some who would say so, but they won't affect us at all. No, my dearest wife, from now on, nothing can harm us!" he said, quite happily. He reached out and drew Sarah against him, bringing his warm lips down on hers before she could protest the fact that he was probably getting grass stains all over the surface of her skirts.

Adam suddenly released her and jumped to his feet, drawing her up beside him.

"Come on, Mrs. MacShane, we're going for a swim!"

"Oh, Adam! Not in the middle of the day, out in the open like this!" she cried, then squealed as his large hands whirled her about and began deftly unfastening the buttons at her back.

"Why not? You've been swimming here once before, remember? I can assure you, madam, I certainly haven't forgotten that delectable sight!" he remarked softly as he bent over and nuzzled her playfully behind her ear.

"You are utterly impossible!" Sarah commented, trying vainly to escape his working fingers. She was soon standing in the warm afternoon light clad only in her chemise and drawers, while Adam drew off all of his clothing and stood naked beside her.

"Come on, off with the rest of those things!" he commanded with a mockingly stern frown.

"Adam, you're being silly! I do not intend to go swimming, particularly wearing nothing at all! I may have done so before, but that was before I realized the possible consequences. Why, what if someone rode by and happened to see the two of us here, frolicking about in the water together, completely naked? she gasped, backing away from him as she viewed the determination on her beloved's face. Squealing once more, she attempted to run from him, then stared downward in surprise and dismay as the chemise and drawers were suddenly torn from her body, leaving her bare to Adam's searching, admiring gaze.

"Now see what you've done!" she threw at him, instinctively trying to cover her nudity.

"You are supposed to obey your husband, remember, Mrs. MacShane?" Adam remarked with a disarming grin, before lifting her squirming body high in his muscular arms and striding purposefully into the gentle current with her.

"Adam, put me down!" she demanded only half in anger, unable to resist his infectious, playful mood.

"Very well," he suddenly capitulated, before lifting her even higher and pitching her unceremoniously into the deeper waters of the creek, where she landed with an indignant shriek and a loud splash.

She came up out of the water with her hair streaming about her face, her mouth spluttering as she cried, "That was very ungallant of you, sir!" She pushed the wet hair from her face and swam until her toes once more touched the sandy bottom of the creek. "I shall make you pay for that, you cad!" she boldly threatened, before launching herself at her husband and pulling him under the cool water with her.

The two of them swam and played for nearly an hour before climbing back up on the bank and lying down upon the grassy earth, partially shaded by the tall, thick trees that swayed gently in the afternoon breeze. The day was comfortably warm and sunny; two mockingbirds were happily chirping and singing as Adam and Sarah stretched lazily out on the ground and proceeded to make passionate, leisurely love together.

After the ecstasy of their rapturous idyll together, they dressed and walked slowly back to the cabin, each totally absorbed with thoughts and dreams of their future together.

It was not until much later in the evening that the earlier events of the day returned to Sarah's mind. She thought back to Mr. Spencer's visit and the things Adam had told her, and a decidedly uncomfortable notion occurred to her.

Now that Adam was indeed receiving the inheritance he had been awaiting, the very reason he had married her, would he no longer want her as his wife? Telling herself that she was being absolutely ridiculous, she tried to shake the persistently nagging thought, only to have it return to her unbidden in the night.

What if Adam did not truly love her, had only been

toying with her, enjoying her sexual favors until such a time finally arrived? Would he now perhaps consider divorcing her, perhaps return to Clementine? Such thoughts continued to plague her dreams that night, and she tossed and turned relentlessly as she attempted to sleep, Adam's own peacefully sleeping body beside her in the bed.

Chapter Twenty-Four

The following two weeks were blissful ones for Adam and Sarah. They had heard no further word concerning Frank Mead, and their lives resumed at least a semblance of normal routine. Adam still left the cabin early every morning in order to oversee the operations on his wells while Sarah either remained at home and occupied her time with more domestic tasks or rode into town. She was exceedingly happy, even though her present life was a far cry from the one she had been accustomed to living back in Philadelphia.

She had put off writing a letter to the school in Philadelphia, but had finally forced herself to cease procrastinating and simply do it. So she wrote and informed the headmistress that she would not be returning to her position as a teacher, that she would most likely not be returning to Philadelphia at all, at least not in the near future. She requested that the last amount of salary owed to her be sent to the post office in Wildcat City. That done, she sat back with a sigh, realizing that she had just made a very important decision, the decision to remain in Texas with Adam.

Of course, she thought, there had really been no other option open to her. She loved Adam more and more each day; she never wanted to leave him. Although she was still occasionally plagued by the nagging doubt that he might no longer want her as his wife now that he was finally receiving his inheritance, that he might no longer need her in order to fulfill that part of their original business arrangement, the very reason he had married her, she attempted to push such unpleasant thoughts aside. At times, she felt almost completely secure in his love, but, at others, when the doubts crept into her mind, she had to reassure herself over and over again that Adam loved her, that he wanted no one but herself.

One evening after dinner, Adam told Sarah, "I think it's about time I saw to those wells of yours again. Mead's been gone long enough to convince me that he's not coming back, so we may as well see to your business again, Mrs. MacShane," he stated with a smile.

"Why, I had almost completely forgotten about those wells," Sarah remarked, rather amazed that she could have forgotten something that used to seem so very important to her. "I must confess, however, that it will be most satisfying to earn money of my own once more. After all," she teased, lifting her pert little nose a trifle higher in the air, "I do not intend to be entirely dependent upon any man!"

"And I had almost completely forgotten that I married a suffragette!" Adam retorted with a mocking glance heavenward and an accompanying sigh.

As was usually the case, their teasing and good-natured banter culminated in their tumbling into bed, where they once more became totally absorbed in pleasuring each other. Sarah wondered on more than one occasion if she would perhaps discover that she was to have Adam's child, but she resolutely decided not to concern herself with that possibility just yet. She would so dearly love to bear Adam a child, and yet she realized that it might perhaps be better if she did not become pregnant until her own doubts, insecurities, and confusion had been resolved.

Sarah rode into town one day and paid a visit to the bank. She contemplated withdrawing a small sum of money in order to purchase one or two more lengths of dress goods, as she wanted to appear attractive for her husband. She found that it gave her a feeling of immense satisfaction that she was able to spend her own money instead of having to ask Adam for funds, though she knew he would certainly not begrudge any amount she wished to spend. She pondered what she would buy, then smiled to herself as she reflected that it would please Adam even more if she were to wear nothing at all!

"Yes, ma'am, what can I do for you today?" the bank clerk asked as Sarah stepped up to the window. She saw that it was still apparently out of the ordinary for a woman to walk inside a bank, as there was only one other woman within the building at the moment.

"I wish to withdraw some money from my account. The name is Mrs. MacShane," she told the polite young man, vaguely wondering what had happened to the other young teller she had encountered on her last visit.

"Yes, ma'am, Mrs. MacShane. I'll be just a

moment," he said, turning about and walking away from the window. He soon returned and shook his head as he told her, "I'm sorry, Mrs. MacShane, but there's no longer any money in that particular account."

"No money? But, that's impossible!" Sarah insisted, bewildered and thinking that there must surely be some mistake. "I haven't withdrawn any funds whatsoever for a few weeks' time now. There was nearly five hundred dollars in the account at that time."

"Yes, ma'am, I see here that there used to be. But, your partner came in about two weeks ago and withdrew the remaining balance," he said, glancing downward at some papers he was holding in his hands.

"My partner?" she repeated in puzzlement, then widened her eyes as she asked, "You mean Mr. Mead, Mr. Frank Mead, was the one who withdrew all of the money?"

"Yes, ma'am. We have his signature right here, along with an affadavit signed by you allowing him to withdraw the money."

"But I never signed such a document!" Sarah protested indignantly.

"Well, this here's the paper he gave us. You're saying that you didn't know anything about this?" the young clerk asked, frowning in confusion now himself.

"I most certainly did not! Why, he had absolutely no right to take all of that money, no right at all! This is absolutely preposterous!" she cried, unable to believe that this could have happened. "That money was not his!"

"I'm real sorry, Mrs. MacShane, but he gave me this paper and said you gave him the okay," the clerk attempted to explain, flushing uncomfortably as he began to realize his error. He knew that he was probably going to be in a lot of trouble!

"Well, I demand that you do something about this! You had no right to allow him to withdraw that money in the first place. The account was arranged for in my name, was it not?" she told him, nearly shaking with the force of her anger.

"But, ma'am, I had the authority to let him have the money once he presented me with this here paper. I'm afraid there isn't much I can do about it now," he attempted to defend himself, yet knowing that he would be unable to placate the angry young woman across from him.

"Then you are saying that there is nothing I can do about this?" Sarah demanded, extremely upset as the poor clerk nodded with an apologetic smile. She turned upon her heel and flounced from the bank.

How dare the bank give Frank Mead the money from her wells! For they most assuredly were her wells now that Frank had seen fit to disappear once more. Oh! she fumed silently. To think that he had played her for a fool and then absconded with her money! She knew that Adam would be just as furious as herself with the disturbing news, and she decided that it might perhaps be best if she herself were to calm down a bit before attempting to explain it to him.

She headed toward the boardinghouse now, then climbed the front steps with a distracted, still preoccupied air. She rapped lightly upon the door, smiling with relief as she saw that it was Emma Patterson, and not her daughter, who opened the door. She had not been to visit her friend for a while, not wishing to encounter Clementine after the way she had tried to cause trouble. But she finally told herself that it was not fair to withhold her friendship from Emma Patterson simply because her daughter was a jealous little vixen!

"Sarah! Oh, I'm so glad you came by. I haven't had a chance to talk to you since what happened with Clem and all. I've been meaning to come on out and apologize for everything Clementine did, but, well, I wasn't so sure you'd ever want to see me again," the kindly older woman said as she motioned for Sarah to enter.

"Of course I wanted to see you again," Sarah assured her with an answering smile, glad that she had stopped by. "I understand that you only did what you thought was for the best concerning your daughter, Mrs. Patterson. There are certainly no hard feelings on my part concerning yourself." She stepped inside and entered the parlor, closely followed by her friend.

"Well, I'm right glad to hear that, honey. I promise you right here and now, there ain't going to be no more trouble from my Clem. I think she's finally learned her lesson this time. At least I sure enough hope so," she remarked with a heavy sigh.

"By the way," Sarah asked, taking a seat, "is Clementine home?"

"Yes, but she's upstairs in her room. She's been moping about for quite a spell, but she'll pull out of it sooner or later, don't you worry. Now, what brings you into town today?" she inquired with a friendly smile. "Ain't it getting to be a pretty sight, this old town of ours? There's more and more good folks coming here every day."

"Yes, I've noticed that. I came into town primarily to visit the bank, where I received some very shocking and disturbing news. It seems that I have been robbed."

"Robbed? You don't mean to tell me there was a holdup at the bank?" Mrs. Patterson gasped.

"No, nothing like that," Sarah hurried to say. "It's simply that my former business partner has withdrawn every cent in my account and left town. There doesn't appear to be any way I can get the money back, either," she told her friend with a bitter expression.

"Oh, I sure am sorry to hear that, Sarah. Maybe Adam can do something about it," suggested her friend helpfully. "You know, I never did like that Frank Mead. I'm awful glad my Clem didn't get any more mixed up with him than she did. It's a downright shame, though, that he took all your money and then lit out like that."

"Yes, it is. However, I do not wish to dwell on that unpleasant thought. I still have a bit of shopping to do in town. Would you perhaps care to join me?" Sarah asked.

"Why, I don't mind if I do! I don't get much of a chance to go shopping, what with running this here boardinghouse and all. Just as soon as someone checks out, someone else is clamoring to move into the empty room," she remarked as she rose to her feet and led Sarah back into the front hallway.

"By the way," Emma Patterson suddenly asked, appearing a bit hesitant as she turned to face Sarah squarely. "I hope you don't mind me asking, but, well, how's things going between you and Adam? I sure do hope Clem's little bit of mischief didn't cause you too much trouble."

"On the contrary, Mrs. Patterson," Sarah admitted with a shy smile, "things couldn't be going better! Adam and I are so very much in love. I fail to see how I could ever have doubted that I loved him. As a matter of fact, I have already written to the school where I was teaching in Philadelphia and informed them that I won't be returning."

"Why, that's wonderful!" the other woman declared with a wide grin. "I can't tell you how happy I am for you, Sarah! I just know you and Adam are going to be happy from now on, and I'm mighty glad to hear that you're going to be staying on here."

With that, the two of them stepped through the doorway and out onto the front porch. As the door softly closed behind them, Clementine stepped out of her room.

Sarah and Mrs. Patterson had both been unaware of the fact that Clem had been standing at the head of the staircase, just within the doorway of her room, listening to every word they had said.

So, Clem thought as she slowly descended the narrow stairway, trailing a hand negligently upon the wooden rail, Sarah and Adam were very happy together. It seemed that everything Adam had told her must have been true, he must really believe that he loved that little schoolteacher. Maybe it was time she stopped dreaming that he would get rid of Sarah and come to her.

Heaving a rather desperate sigh, which had the faintest ring of finality to it, she was finally forced to acknowledge the fact that she had been a fool to try and win him away from his wife. She was feeling guilty about having revealed to Frank Mead that it had been Adam's idea that she spy on him, but thankfully it had come to nothing, since Mead was now gone. Maybe it was about time she started looking around for another man, she told herself with a sad little smile.

She believed that she would probably always love Adam, but that she could perhaps try and find a bit of happiness with another man if she had to. As is usually the case with the young, she did not realize that her broken heart would mend very quickly, that she would once more be happy and fall in love.

Sarah and Emma Patterson shopped together quite companionably for a good part of the afternoon, after which Sarah rode back toward the cabin in order to prepare dinner before Adam returned from the oil fields. She had purchased another split riding skirt, rationalizing it to herself by musing that she would certainly need such attire if she was going to be a frontier wife from now on!

She and Mrs. Patterson had been introduced to several other women while shopping in the general store, and Sarah reflected that it indeed appeared as if Wildcat City would soon resemble a civilized settlement. Construction of a church was due to begin within the next few weeks, as well as a schoolhouse. She thought that it wouldn't be long before her newly adopted town began to lose its reputation as a wild, untamed boomtown.

Acting on a sudden impulse, she slowed her horse to a walk when she neared the bend in the road where her uncle's old cabin was situated. She drew the horse to a halt and looped the reins over the limb of a tree as she dismounted and approached the cabin. She didn't really know why she liked coming here. After all, it had been here that she had last seen Frank Mead alone, but she wasn't thinking of him as she entered the deserted abode. Instead, she thought of her beloved uncle who was buried out there, that the old cabin had once been his home, for at least a brief period of time.

Taking a seat on the wooden bench at the lone table in the one-room cabin, she placed her chin in her hands as she recalled the happy memories of her uncle. She remembered how lonely and frightened she had been upon learning of her parents' death, of the kind and loving way Uncle John had come to her and scooped her up in his strong arms and declared that she was now his little moppet, that she would be his responsibility and his delight. She reflected that she was so very glad that Uncle John had been a friend of Adam's, that the two men she had loved most had known each other.

Her silent, nostalgic reverie was rudely shattered as the door of her cabin was abruptly flung open, revealing two total strangers to her startled gaze. She jumped to her feet and reached for her pistol as she faced the intruders, noticing immediately that they were rather well-dressed men, that they were eyeing her with just as much surprise and curiosity as she was doing to them.

"Pardon me, young lady, but would you mind telling us what you are doing here?" one of the men politely inquired, his dark features drawn into a slight frown as he appraised her silently. His companion was gazing at her with something akin to wonderment.

"You certainly have no right to ask that, sir," Sarah retorted courageously, still fingering the gun within the confines of her skirt pocket. "This cabin happens to be my property, and I must insist that you leave the premises at once!" Who on earth could they be? her mind raced.

"I am afraid that there has been some sort of misunderstanding, young woman," the man insisted. "You see, we have a deed to this property, as well as to those three oil wells out there."

"What on earth are you talking about? This property belonged to my late uncle, and I am his legal heir. I don't know exactly what sort of underhanded deal you are trying to pull, but you had better get out of here and off of my property at once!" Sarah threatened, now withdrawing the pistol from her pocket and pointing it toward the two well-dressed strangers. She could tell from their voices that they were obviously not native Texans, and she wondered to herself if this was yet another attempt by someone to dishonestly gain control of her uncle's wells, as she recalled that Adam had mentioned to her on more than one occasion that such attempts were quite common in the oil fields. Well, she declared silently to herself with determination, I will not allow them to succeed!

"I don't know who you are, or who your late uncle was, but we have a legal document stating that we are the new owners of this property. You see, we purchased this property and those oil wells a few months ago, from a Mr. Frank Mead. It was agreed upon that we would acquire ownership on this particular date," the other stranger attempted to explain, somewhat puzzled as he and his partner instinctively took a step backward as they viewed the weapon in Sarah's hand.

"Frank Mead? You're telling me that Frank Mead sold you this property, sold you those wells? A few months ago?" she repeated, totally flabbergasted by the man's claims. No, it can't be true, she stubbornly told herself.

"Yes, that is correct. Mr. Mead approached us while we were in Dallas, some time ago, and we agreed upon the deal. Now we have simply arrived to take control of our property, legally bought and paid for, legally transferred if you would perhaps care to read the documents for yourself," the first man offered. He had no wish to upset the young woman, since she was obviously dangerous! It appeared that she was laboring under a misconception as to the true ownership of the property, and he suddenly had the sneaking suspicion that Mr. Frank Mead was the cause of her obvious consternation.

Sarah reached out and took the proferred papers and hastily scanned them, then reread them a bit more slowly. She hated to admit it, but she saw that they indeed appeared quite legal, at least from what she was able to ascertain, and that they indeed stated the terms of the sale, the date of the transfer, and the names of the three men involved. She handed the papers back to the gentleman with a sinking feeling in the pit of her stomach as she realized that Frank Mead had done much more than steal her money from the bank.

He had apparently sold the property soon after her uncle's death, according to the date of the sale. He had not even bothered to attempt to contact her, had not even tried to find her. He had surely been planning to cheat her uncle all along, had probably even arranged Uncle John's death in order to achieve his goal. She was now thoroughly convinced that it had been Mead who had arranged to have Adam killed, Mead who had deceived her, lied to her, flattered her with his protestations of devotion in order to cheat her. How could I have been so blind? she furiously berated herself, sinking back down on to the bench as she slowly lowered the pistol to her side.

"I am sorry, young lady, if this is something of a shock for you. May I inquire if it was Mr. Mead who caused this present confusion?"

"Yes, it was Mr. Mead. You see," she explained, raising her face to the two men once more, "Frank Mead and my uncle were partners. My uncle was killed soon after they formed that partnership, and apparently Mr. Mead sold you this property just after my uncle's death. I was under the impression that I was the legal owner of the property, gentlemen," she declared with an air of distraction, still stunned by the news.

"I really am sorry. Perhaps if we spoke with Mr. Mead, we could clear up this matter . . ." the man suggested kindly.

"No, I'm afraid Mr. Mead is no longer here. I don't know where he has gone. I'm afraid he has deceived us all." She quickly averted her face as she tried to think of some way she could fight Mead's latest fraudulence, then decided that she would certainly have to inform Adam of these developments right away. Yes, she told herself, Adam would think of something to do!

Rising to her feet once more, she approached the two men near the doorway and said, "My name is Sarah Bradford MacShane, Mrs. MacShane. My uncle, the former owner of this property, was John Bradford, of Philadelphia. I intend to do everything in my power to see that Frank Mead is brought to justice, which will mean an investigation into his business practices. You see, I am still by rights the legal heir of my late uncle. Mr. Mead has absolutely no right to negotiate a sale without my approval. Therefore, it appears that this will have to be a matter for the law to decide," she declared cooly.

"I understand, Mrs. MacShane. And may I say how sorry we are that this misunderstanding, this unpleasantness had to occur?"

"Thank you. I appreciate your attitude, gentlemen, and I certainly realize that this is not your fault. Good day to you." She swept past them and hurried to her horse, mounting and urging the animal into a gallop as she raced toward the well where Adam was working that day. She must speak with him immediately, must ask him to help her!

If she truly did no longer own the three wells, if she was no longer the rightful owner of the property, she would use the funds she had coming from the school in order to see that Frank Mead was indeed brought to justice!

She silently gave thanks that at least her personal life had not been as disastrous as her financial business. Thank goodness she still had the one thing that was most important to her, her husband. She prayed that she would never lose him as well!

Chapter Twenty-Five

Adam proved to be every bit as furious and astounded by Sarah's news as she had anticipated he would be. However, after his initial outrage had abated somewhat, he consoled his wife with the assurance that he would see to it that something was done about the deceitful Mr. Mead. He informed her that he had a friend who happened to be a member of the Texas Rangers, and that he would contact this friend immediately and request that he locate Frank Mead. Now that they possessed concrete evidence and not mere conjecture, Adam was certain that the Rangers would be interested in opening an investigation into the matter. As for the bank's allowing Mead to withdraw all of the money in Sarah's account, he tightly vowed that he would make them admit their mistake and set it to rights.

For the moment then, Sarah was forced to acknowledge the fact that there was little she and Adam could do to prevent the two gentlemen from taking over the property and the wells. She tried to convince herself that, if she would simply remain patient and bide her time, she would surely regain control. It was important, however, that she realize that it might take quite some time.

Sarah was becoming increasingly secure in Adam's love. He was taking great pleasure in teaching her new delights every time the two of them made love, and she found herself responding with even more fervor and passionate abandon than she had ever believed possible.

Only last night, she now remembered with a fiery blush, Adam had demonstrated to her that there was more than just the conventional manner when it came to making love. They had slowly, tenderly undressed one another after which Adam had gently pulled Sarah back with him toward the bed, pulling her soft, naked body on top of his. Sarah had laughingly protested, "Adam, what are you doing?"

"Why, I'm about to make love to my wife, of course," he had lightly answered, holding her fast atop him.

"But we can't make love this way!" she had told him with a puzzled frown.

"Aye, that we can, my lassie," he had replied with a meaningful grin and a mesmerizing gaze as he had proceeded to show her.

His hands had roamed freely over her soft curves, and she had moaned softly as his lips took hers. Sarah had soon discovered that her husband was right, that there was something deliciously wicked about the unconventional method!

Adam returned home that next evening, his handsome face smiling happily, his whole manner exuberant as he exclaimed, "Sarah! Sarah, lass, the well came in today!"

"Oh, Adam, I'm so happy for you!" she cried, flying into his strong arms as he lifted her high into the air.

"It appears that your husband, Mrs. MacShane, may just become a wealthy man even without that inheritance!" he remarked with a wide grin, twirling her about until she was breathless.

Sarah later reflected that it appeared things were going very well for herself and Adam, that she had much to be thankful for, and she again prayed that nothing would occur to spoil their happiness, to intrude upon their own special little world. She had been almost entirely successful in forgetting about Clem's taunts, and she was striving to put all worry aside.

Riding into town the following afternoon, Sarah saw that there were quite a number of people milling about the dusty streets. She realized that Wildcat City was indeed beginning to fade as a boomtown and beginning to come alive as a real, civilized town. Adam had told her that so many men had completely lost their investments when they had failed to strike oil, and it appeared that the oil boom was beginning to slow down considerably.

As Sarah swung down from her horse and looped the reins across the hitching post in front of the general store, she was suddenly startled to hear a loud, clanging sound in the air. Quickly searching the streets for the source of the resounding noise, she saw that a man down near the hotel was striking a large metal triangle with a matching metal rod. It was apparently some sort of warning bell, and Sarah stood watching curiously for a moment as crowds of people rushed toward the man.

"Fire!" he called loudly, continuing to strike the huge iron triangle. "There's a fire in the oil fields!" he yelled. People gazed at one another in stupefaction before coming to life and scurrying to mount their horses or climb up into their wagons. Women hurried their children out of the path of the wildly galloping horses and wagons, while Sarah dodged several moving obstacles as she made her way across the street to where the man was still sounding the warning.

"Please, what has happened?" she demanded, tugging impatiently at his sleeve.

"There's a fire in the oil fields, ma'am! Them storage tanks are exploding like mad, and if it ain't put out soon, everything, including this here town, could be wiped out!" he informed her excitedly, then turned back to his task.

Dear Lord, Sarah breathed to herself. Adam! Adam could be in danger right at this very moment. She whirled about and ran back across the street to her horse, swung up into the saddle, then kicked the animal into a frenzied gallop. She must reach Adam, she must make certain that he had come to no harm!

Clementine Patterson observed Sarah's frantic departure, and she too mounted up and then followed. The same thing was running through her mind at that very moment, the fact that Adam was in danger! She knew good and well what an oil fire in the fields could do, as she had listened to stories of the destructive blaze from several of her mother's boarders, men who were experienced hands in the oil fields.

As Sarah inexorably urged her horse faster, she realized that she didn't even know which direction to turn, didn't know exactly where the fire had started. But her momentary confusion was quickly rectified as she observed the telltale curls of black smoke rising high in the air, billowing up from behind a large hill a few miles to the southwest of where she rode. She guided her mount off the well-traveled road and set out across the open fields of tall, waving grass, riding toward the ominous clouds of smoke.

Suddenly, without warning, her horse stumbled, catching its hoof in a deep hole in the cracked earth. Sarah cried out sharply as she felt her mount falling, as she felt herself thrown free of the saddle, flying through the air to land safely in the tall, fragrant grass.

She staggered to her feet, much shaken by her fall, and hurried to inspect the damage done to her horse. She noted with dismay that the poor animal was favoring its front leg, that it was obviously in no condition to take her farther. Peering about at the open landscape and the darkening sky, she frantically searched for some way she could reach Adam, for she was certain that he would be helping to fight the fire at its very source. Though she was unlearned in the ways of the oil fields, she knew well enough that a fire of any sort could be quite devastating, that there would possibly be subsequent explosions and that the blaze could sweep uncontrolled across the dry grass.

She glanced up as she saw someone else approaching. There were three men on horseback riding directly toward her now, and she gasped aloud as she perceived their identities. They were the same three ruffians who had attacked her that other day on her way home from town!

She turned about and attempted to run from them, knowing full well that they certainly meant her no good, but she was hopelessly trapped as the three of them formed a ring about her. She pulled the pistol from her skirt pocket and fired, the bullet striking one of the three in the left arm as he yelped loudly in pain. Sarah started to shoot again, but was roughly taken hold of by the other two men. She screamed as a large sack was pulled down over her head, her hands roughly tied behind her back and her ankles bound by a leather thong. She felt herself being lifted, then thrown across a saddle as the very breath was knocked from her lungs. Her captor put a hand out to keep her steady, then cruelly spurred his mount as he and his companions rode away, leaving Sarah's horse standing still and alone in the open meadow.

The unfortunate fellow who had been the recipient of the bullet from Sarah's gun muttered and cursed loudly as they rode, complaining that he'd be damned before he'd let a mere woman get away with shooting him! His partners gruffly ordered him to keep quiet, and the three of them continued on in silence.

Sarah didn't know how long they rode, able only to concentrate on trying to keep from being violently sick as she was bounced uncomfortably across the hard saddle. She was bruised and shaken when she was finally lifted down from the saddle by large, hairy arms. She was carried swiftly inside a building, then set upon her feet and the sack was removed from her upper body. Her hands and ankles were left tied as she swayed and blinked rapidly in order to adjust to the darkness inside the unfamiliar place.

"Who are you? Why did you abduct me and bring me here? Don't you realize that I will soon be missed, that my husband will kill you all when he finds me?" she threatened bravely, actually quaking inside as a lamp was lit and she viewed the leering faces of the three burly men. She could see their coarse features quite well now, and she knew that it was probably hopeless to try and reason with the three mercenary creatures.

One of them shoved her roughly back against the wall of the empty cabin, his hand running freely across her breasts, his lascivious gaze raking her body with an insulting air as his eyes seemed to undress her. She struggled violently against his hand, then cried out as he slapped her savagely across her face.

"Now you ain't got no call to act that way, you little bitch! We're old friends, ain't we? Yes sir, you better be nice to old Ben here, and I might just be nice to you!" the fellow said with an evil grin, laughing loudly.

Sarah's eyes narrowed and she screamed, "How dare you! Let me go at once! You'll never get away with this, you fiend!"

"She ain't taking much of a shine to you, is she, Ben?" one of his partners remarked with an amused cackle.

"She's gonna pay for what she done to my arm!" the injured man threatened viciously as he glared toward Sarah. He was holding the wound with his other hand as he tried to staunch the bleeding.

"Aw now, what she needs is a little taming, that's all. I think we might as well have a little fun out of her before the boss gets here, don't you?" Ben suggested with a leering, toothless smile as he stepped closer to her.

Sarah couldn't move, for her ankles and hands were still tightly bound, and she leaned back against the cabin wall with frightened eyes as she screamed, "Don't you dare touch me! I swear, I shall kill you myself if you ever touch me again!" she threatened, her voice rising shrilly. Dear God, she prayed, what am I going to do? Please, God, please help me!

She knew that it might possibly be hours before anyone missed her, that Adam would be too involved in fighting the fire to notice her absence. He would naturally believe that she was safely back at their cabin. Oh, she thought, struggling against her bonds, I must do something! I must think of some way I can escape!

"What did you say about your boss coming here?" she suddenly asked, feverishly stalling for time.

"That ain't none of your concern, missy!" Ben pronounced with an ugly scowl. He was obviously the leader of the motley gang. "You just got to be nice to us until he comes, if you know what's good for you! Yes sir, we can get to be right good friends in the time we got left," he suggested with a wide grin as he stepped closer and grasped a handful of Sarah's thick hair, tugging on it fiercely and causing her to cry aloud in pain.

"Hey, Ben, why don't we at least get a good look at what's under them duds of hers? That couldn't do no harm, now could it?" one of the other men said.

"I think we ought to do a hell of a lot more than that!" the injured man growled, still grimacing with pain as blood dripped from his arm to the dusty floor below. "I hope he gets here soon. I'm gonna bleed to death if we don't get out of here!" he mumbled to himself.

"I guess our boss surely don't expect that we're just gonna sit around here and twiddle our thumbs while this here fancy piece can be entertaining us!" Ben replied with a loud chortle of laughter. "All right, honey," he spoke to Sarah, his scraggly, bearded face mere inches from hers as he stooped down a bit, "let's start taking off them clothes!"

"You most certainly will not!" Sarah retorted indignantly, refusing to back down, knowing that she was lost if she weakened. Where was this so-called boss of theirs? Why didn't he come?

"I said let's take them things off!" Ben repeated with an ugly frown. As Sarah stood silent and proudly defiant, his hand shot out and took hold of her blouse, then savagely ripped it away from her trembling body as she screamed in angry protest.

"How dare you! I'll see that you are punished for this, you vermin!" she declared with a loud gasp. She screamed again and struggled to escape as he took hold of her fine chemise and followed suit, rendering her almost completely naked from the waist up as her blouse and chemise hung in tatters about her waist. Her beautiful, full breasts were now revealed to their lustful gaze.

"Damn!" one of them whispered, almost reverently, as he admired Sarah's well-formed bosom.

As Ben began to reach out and fondle one of the white globes, the door of the cabin flew open, startling both Sarah and the three men into immobility.

"I told you not to lay a hand on her, you dirty bastards!" a voice that sounded vaguely familiar to Sarah's ears spoke from the direction of the doorway, although Sarah could not see his face, her view completely obstructed by the huge fellow named Ben.

"We didn't mean nothing by it! We was just having a bit of fun, killing time till you got here!" one of the other three defensively insisted.

"Yeah, and besides that, she done went and shot me!" the wounded man exclaimed angrily.

"All right," their boss spoke through tightly clenched teeth, "get out of here! You've all been paid well for your troubles, so I don't ever want to see any of you again!"

"But you still ain't paid us the rest of the money you owe us!"

"I said to get out! Consider yourselves damned fortunate that I didn't kill you!" the mysterious man ground out. The three men hesitated, each obviously weighing their chances in defying him, then apparently decided that they had best do as he commanded. They cast one last, lustful glance at Sarah's exposed breasts, then stomped noisily out of the cabin, affording Sarah a clear view of her "rescuer."

Her eyes opened wider as she observed him step inside the cabin and close the door softly, leaving the two of them completely alone together.

"Frank!" Sarah whispered in fearful surprise.

Chapter Twenty-Six

"Sarah, love," Frank replied with a rather crooked grin as his gaze traveled downward to her heaving white bosom. "I'm sorry about that," he said, frowning as he obviously referred to her torn clothing. "I told them not to harm you in any way," he told her apologetically, still standing near the door, his arms nonchalantly crossed as he stood staring at her.

Sarah took a deep breath before speaking, then slowly said, "Frank, will you please untie me? Please allow me to cover myself." She hated having to ask him for anything, but she felt so very humiliated and at a decided disadvantage standing there half naked before him. She still hadn't decided how she would seek to convince him to let her go, but she knew that she had to try. Her mind was in a tumultuous whirl, for she had certainly never expected to see him again, much less as the boss of that gang of mercenaries!

"Very well. I do so hate to see you looking so uncomfortable," he remarked with a soft chuckle as he now approached her. He stood before her and withdrew a sharp knife from a sheath at his belt as he proceeded to cut the leather thongs from her hands and then her ankles. Sarah instinctively pulled the tattered remains of her blouse and chemise about her breasts, hastily averting her gaze from Frank's. She could feel his own intense gaze upon her, and she told herself to remain calm.

"Sarah, I never wanted anything like this to happen, but it was necessary, don't you see?" he attempted to explain, a faint note of entreaty in his voice. "I love you, Sarah. I would rather you had come with me willingly. I would rather you had gone ahead with that annulment from MacShane!" he muttered viciously, causing Sarah to glance sharply up at him now with no small degree of panic.

"Frank, please, please don't do anything to Adam!" Dear Lord, she thought, what if this insane scoundrel attempted to kill Adam again, what if he were to succeed this time? She could not allow that to happen!

"So it is as I expected then. You're in love with MacShane, aren't you?" Frank suavely demanded, though the dangerous light in his eyes revealed his inner turmoil to Sarah.

"Frank, if you truly love me, then why did you do all of those things?" she countered, endeavoring to steer him away from the subject of her relationship with Adam. "Why did you take all of the money, why did you sell the property and the wells and then disappear like that?"

Her scheme evidently worked, at least for the moment, as Frank answered, "Sarah, I had to. I needed that money; I needed to get away in a hurry. As for selling the wells, that happened long before I had even met you. None of those things had anything to do with you personally, don't you see?" he replied, stepping a bit closer as he gazed intently down into her upturned face.

"Very well, Frank," Sarah said calmly, taking another deep breath as she continued. "Why did you have those three men abduct me and bring me here? And why did you have them accost me that other time as well?"

"Because I wanted you to trust me, to view me as your protector. Oh, Sarah, I've loved you from the first moment I saw you. I had those men frighten you a bit on the way home from town that day in order to allow me to rescue you heroically. As for today, well, I just couldn't see any other way. I've waited so very long for you, waited for you to leave MacShane and allow me to love you. But you didn't leave him!" he spoke tightly, his eyes gleaming brightly.

"You lied to me, didn't you, Sarah? You never had any intention of getting that annulment, did you? After all this time, don't you think I guessed what was really going on between you two? Don't you think I've had my men watching the two of you, reporting back to me? I couldn't wait any longer, I had to have you! You're the only woman I've ever loved, even if you did deceive me, even if you led me on. Well, I have you now. You are mine, Sarah, and I'm going to see to it that MacShane is out of your life forever!"

"Frank," Sarah fearfully whispered, thinking only of Adam now. "Frank, what have you done to him?"

"That oil fire was no mere accident, my dear Sarah. You see, I had it all planned. It was begun at your precious Adam's wells, to insure that he would be quite occupied while I had my men bring you here.

However, MacShane will not survive his heroic firefighting today. No, on the contrary, he will meet with another unfortunate 'accident' during the fire. As a matter of fact, you should be a widow very soon now," he pronounced with a twisted smile and a triumphant gleam in his eyes.

"No!" Sarah cried, grasping hold of the front of his coat with both of her hands as she pleaded with him for Adam's life, completely forgetting about her exposed nakedness. "I'll do anything you say if you won't go through with this! If you'll only let Adam live, I swear that I will do anything you say, go anywhere you wish me to. You say that you love me," she attempted to reason with him, forcing herself to try and remain calm, though her mind was screaming that Adam was in terrible danger. "Very well, then, prove that you love me, Frank."

"It's too late now, Sarah. It's all been taken care of and it's much too late to change my plans now. I'm afraid you'll just have to accept that fact. As for doing anything I say, going anywhere I wish, why, darling, you'll do all of that and much more!" he informed her with a meaningful grin as his eyes once more fastened on her naked breasts, his desire for her growing as he stared. "As a matter of fact," he said, wetting his dry lips with his tongue as his eyes feasted on her beautiful charms, "I don't think I'll wait for our marriage ceremony at all. I think I'll take you right here and now, force you to forget all about Adam MacShane!"

"No, Frank!" Sarah exclaimed, drawing back and snatching up her torn clothing to cover herself once more. "If you truly love me, you will at least have the decency to wait until we are man and wife!" she said, her mind frantically searching for some way to escape and go to Adam! "There must be no secrets between us, Frank, if we are to be married as you plan. I want to know everything about you. You were responsible for trying to kill Adam once before, were you not?" she demanded, still stalling as she glanced toward the doorway and pondered her next move.

"Yes, of course. I couldn't allow him to remain alive," Frank answered simply, no sign of remorse in either his voice or his manner.

"Then you also arranged to have my uncle killed?" Sarah asked, knowing that she was treading on thin ice, but wanting to hear the truth from him, wanting to gain precious time as well.

"Yes, Sarah," he replied with a heavy sigh, finally turning away from her as he walked to the doorway once more. "But I didn't know anything about you then," he said, turning about to face her. "I didn't know that I was going to fall in love with his niece!"

"Why did you kill him, Frank, why? Uncle John was one of the kindest, most generous men who ever lived. Why did you find it necessary to kill such a man?"

"Because I needed to gain ownership of those wells for myself. I had already planned to sell them, don't you see? Your uncle was a very obstinate man, Sarah. He refused to listen to me, he wouldn't heed my advice about anything. So I simply saw the opportunity to make a lot of money. He had never really wanted me as his partner, but I convinced him by promising him a huge sum of money to invest in his wells. When he started to become suspicious, I was forced to arrange an accident for him as well."

"But what about the men who were present when it happened? Why didn't any of them go directly to the law about this, why didn't they expose you?"

"Because the sheriff here was well paid and knew what was going to take place. He conveniently turned his head from what was happening. As for the workers, they were all paid and then warned that if they happened to speak of it to anyone, anyone at all, the sheriff would arrest them for your uncle's murder, would see that they were hanged for it."

"I see," Sarah murmured, the tears rushing to her eyes as she thought of her poor uncle. She realized that it must have been one of those workers who had written that anonymous letter to her in Philadelphia. It didn't matter any more, none of it truly matters, she thought numbly, for Uncle John was dead, and Adam was going to be if she didn't do something about it.

"I only came back here because the sheriff sent me word that you had arrived. Oh, Sarah, why couldn't you have simply gone along with all my plans?"

"Frank," she said, walking slowly toward him. "Frank, please don't kill Adam. I know that you say you love me, that you want me as your wife. Very well, I will be the most devoted wife to you that I could possibly be, but only if you desist with this plan. If you will allow Adam to remain alive and unharmed, I shall divorce him and marry you. I will be a good wife to you, Frank. It is true that you can kill Adam and then force me to go with you, but you cannot ever force me to love you," she told him.

"You're only making these promises to save your precious Adam!" Frank accused her, his face appearing ugly as he faced her.

"If you will only do as I ask, I will prove that I mean what I say," she said. She straightened her shoulders and lifted her head proudly as she prepared to sacrifice herself for the life of her beloved husband. She must think of some way to escape, and this was the only way she could see of possibly getting away. She slowly withdrew her hands from her chest, allowing the tattered clothing to fall once more about her waist, allowing her shapely breasts to be totally revealed to Frank's lustful gaze once again.

"I will give myself to you, Frank, I will love you, but only if you allow Adam to live." She didn't pause to consider how she would escape once he embraced her. She knew only that she had to do something, that she would give her very life to save Adam.

"Do you swear it, Sarah? Do you swear that if MacShane is allowed to go free you will love me, that you will be my loving wife?" he demanded, his eyes still riveted on her breasts.

"Yes, Frank, I swear it," Sarah answered softly, knowing that she was lying. She knew that this was her only chance, and she pressed closer, closer until her naked breasts were barely touching his chest, rubbing against the thin material of his cotton shirt as she raised her eyes to his and silently pleaded with him to take her, to accept her desperate offer.

"All right, Sarah. I promise that MacShane will live, in return for your love. But be forewarned," he cautioned severely, his breathing becoming increasingly ragged as his lust surged upward, "that I will kill him if you ever break your promise."

"Yes, Frank, I understand," she whispered, then lifted her arms and wound them about his neck as she pulled his head down for her kiss. Her mind still searched for a plan, for she knew that she would die if she allowed him to take her!

As she pressed even closer, she suddenly felt the hilt of the knife at his belt, the one he'd earlier used to cut her bonds. She kissed him even more passionately as she slowly drew her arm downward, then made as if to slip her arm about his waist, instead stopping as her hand closed upon the knife. She quickly pulled it from its sheath, then raised her arm to strike.

However, Frank was too quick for her. He pulled away just in time, knocking the knife from her hand with a painful, bruising grip upon her tender wrist as he wrenched her arm up behind her back.

"I knew that you would attempt to do something as foolish as that, my darling Sarah," he ground out, holding her struggling form against him as he tightened his grip on her arm and caused her to cry out sharply with the searing pain. "I suspected that you were only bluffing, that you were stalling for time, that you couldn't mean anything you said. You see, Sarah, I know that as long as MacShane is alive, you'll do anything you can to be with him, to save him. But after he's dead, after he's gone, you will be mine. You'll no longer have him, you'll only have me, and I will make you love me, I'll make you see that I am the only man you have ever needed!" he declared with fierce determination, his other hand closing upon one of her breasts as she uttered a piercing scream.

"I'll never be yours! I'll always hate you for what you did to Uncle John, for what you did to Adam! I'll kill you, Frank Mead, I'll kill myself before you'll ever have me!" she threatened, the hot tears coursing freely down her flushed cheeks now as she attempted to lash out at him with her other fist, her feet kicking frantically at him as she struggled to escape his bruising hold. She had failed so miserably in her attempt to save Adam, and she knew that she would rather die as well than live without him. Oh, Adam! she cried silently. Please, God, please don't let him be killed!

"Be still!" Frank suddenly commanded, his hand closing cruelly upon her open mouth.

Sarah attempted to scream against the pressure of his hand, then grew silent as she heard the sound of hoofbeats approaching the dimly lit cabin. She initially believed it to be the three men hired by Frank returning, then knew that it could not be as she glanced upward at Frank's viciously scowling features. He dragged her roughly across with him to the window, then cautiously peered outside.

"Mead? Mead, this is Adam MacShane!" a deep voice rumbled from behind a large rock a few yards away from the front door of the cabin.

"Damn!" Frank exclaimed, perceiving that it was Adam MacShane who had ridden up, Adam MacShane who had apparently come to save his wife.

Sarah managed to free her upper lip and bit down

as hard as she could upon Frank's hand, then screamed as loud as she possibly could, "Adam! Adam!" The hand was quickly clamped back upon her mouth, and Frank whispered savagely against her ear, "If you make another sound, I swear that you'll regret it!"

It was then that Sarah realized that she might possibly be in as much danger as Adam. She had been deceived into thinking that Frank really believed he felt something for her, no matter how twisted his mind was, but she now realized that he might just be capable of killing her as well if she defied him. She stood in agonized silence as she heard Adam's voice again.

"Mead! Mead, come on out here and face me man to man! Let Sarah go and we'll settle this matter between us!"

Frank's mouth twisted into an evil grin as he dragged Sarah with him to the doorway and flung open the door, holding her squirming body in front of his as a protective shield, knowing full well that Adam would not attempt to shoot him for fear of hitting her.

"Get out of here right now, MacShane," Frank ordered, withdrawing his gun from his holster as he held it up to Sarah's head, "or I'll kill your pretty little wife!"

"Don't hide behind a woman's skirts like a coward, Mead!" Adam shouted, still safely hidden behind the boulder. Sarah vaguely wondered what he must be thinking, seeing Frank holding her there, her breasts embarrassingly exposed, a gun pointed directly at her head. But he was alive! she thought happily. No matter what, Adam was alive! She only prayed that he would remain so as she wondered what he was planning to do. She hated that he had put himself in such danger, and she started to open her mouth to speak as Frank removed his hand in order to clamp an arm about her waist. But she told herself that Adam would prefer that she remain silent and let him handle the tense situation in his own manner.

"And I said to get the hell out of here, MacShane, or I'll kill her!" Frank threatened again, pushing the gun a trifle closer to Sarah's head. "By the way, MacShane," he suddenly asked, "how did you know where to find me?"

"Your three henchmen were seen bringing Sarah here. A friend of mine rode up to where I was fighting the fire and told me. As you can see, your little scheme to have me killed backfired."

"What the hell are you talking about?" Frank demanded, frowning as he narrowed his eyes.

"Let's just say that your plan failed. Your three 'friends' are in jail now, where they'll be lucky to stay if the townspeople don't decide to lynch them!" he loudly declared. "If you'll let her go free, I'll allow you an hour's lead time," Adam offered, his handsome face more brutal and savage than ever before, his eyes glinting with a murderous light as he crouched behind the boulder, wanting nothing more than to kill Mead like the mad dog he was! He would make the bastard pay for treating Sarah that way!

Sarah could hardly breathe as Frank's arm tightened about her waist like a band of steel. Before she had taken the time to contemplate her next action, she suddenly threw her upper body forward, causing Frank to loosen his hold on her and curse aloud. She screamed toward the spot where she knew Adam was watching.

"Now, Adam, now!"

Then, before she realized what had happened, a single shot had rung out and she felt Frank's hold upon her completely relaxing as he slipped slowly to the ground below, shot through the head, a hideous expression upon his dead face as Sarah glanced at him, shuddering violently.

"Sarah!" Adam called, racing to her side as she crumpled to the ground beside Frank, her legs no longer able to support her weight. His strong arms went about her, and she gratefully leaned against him.

"Adam, oh Adam, he's dead! I was so frightened that it would be you who was killed!"

"I know, I know, my lassie," Adam comforted her, removing his coat and placing it lovingly about her shoulders. He lifted her in his powerful arms and carried her back toward his horse, not even sparing a backward glance at the body of Frank Mead. He swung her up into the saddle, mounted behind her, then held her close against him as he reined his horse about and started on the long ride to town.

"Adam, he told me that he had arranged Uncle John's death, that he had planned to have you killed as well. He truly believed that you would be dead by now. I can't understand why his plan failed, but I am so very grateful it did!" she murmured with another involuntary shudder.

Adam gathered her even closer against him as he replied, "Clémentine was the one who saw you being abducted and rode straight to me and warned me that something terrible might have happened to you. When I left my wells, which were all burning by that time, there was a loud explosion at the very spot where I had been standing, engaged in fighting the fire. I assume that's what Mead was talking about when he spoke of arranging to have me killed. Those three henchmen of his probably set everything up when they started the fire. But I guess Clem arrived in time to tell me about you, and therefore I wasn't there to fit in with Mead's devious plan," he explained, and it was the first time Sarah noticed his rather blackened face and equally filthy clothing.

"Oh, Adam, what about the fire? Was everything destroyed?" she asked tearfully, still in shock after her harrowing ordeal, yet wanting to know the truth.

"Aye, lass," Adam replied with a heavy sigh, hugging her closer. "I'm afraid all of my wells were wiped out. But don't you worry, we'll start up again. I'm taking you to Mrs. Patterson's now. Clem is there waiting for us. I'll have to leave you with her while I go back and help fight the fire. I hate to have to leave you after all that's happened, my love, but I really must go. I don't care if I lose everything in the world, as long as I have you, but there are others who will need my help."

"It's all right, Adam, I understand. I'll be fine. Just come back to me safe and sound," she murmured, exhaustion beginning to set in as she leaned against him and closed her eyes.

When they arrived back in town, Adam tenderly lifted Sarah down and carried her inside the boardinghouse, placing her in the care of the anxious Clementine, who felt somewhat responsible for what had happened. Adam brushed Sarah's cheek softly with his lips before striding back out the door.

Chapter Twenty-Seven

"Come on, Sarah, we'll get you straight on up to bed," Clem told her with genuine concern. "I've got to go back outside and help the others get ready in case the fire blows this way," she said, her arm comfortingly hugging Sarah's shoulders as she stood with her at the foot of the staircase.

"Fight the fire? I don't understand," Sarah replied, obviously puzzled. "Adam said the fire was out at the oil fields."

"Yes, but it's heading this way. If that wind keeps on blowing that way, the fire could wipe out the whole town!" she informed Sarah with a worried frown. "Ma's already outside, down at the edge of town, where everyone's taking up buckets and forming a water line and all. I hate to have to leave you, Sarah, knowing what you've just been through and all, but you'll be all right till we get back. That is," she ruefully remarked as she started helping Sarah up the stairs, "if the whole town ain't burnt down!"

"I'm coming with you!" Sarah suddenly insisted, climbing the stairs now in greater haste. "Help me get out of these things, Clem! And have you got something else I can wear?"

"Are you sure you're well enough to go out and help?" Clem asked, following her into the bedroom.

"Of course I'm well enough!" she replied with determination.

Clementine stood staring at her for a few seconds, shaking her blond head with grudging admiration. She had to give that little Yankee schoolteacher Adam had married one thing, she sure enough had gumption when the time came for it!

The women and children and few men who had remained in town were all gathered at the livery stable at one end of the town, just as Clem had told Sarah they would be. When the two of them arrived, the black smoke was beginning to curl up over the rooftops of the buildings in town, causing everyone assembled to view the telltale signs of the advancing fire with increased dread.

"It's heading this way all right!" one of the onlookers cried.

Sarah watched as the ominously dark clouds overhead appeared to grow even darker and more menacing, but she told herself that it was only the thick smoke that made them appear that way. However, she felt herself shiver involuntarily, as if she could actually feel the impending disaster, as a loud clap of thunder suddenly rang out.

"Glory be, it just might make it after all!" Clementine remarked with an excited smile as she led Sarah closer among the group.

"What are you talking about?" Sarah asked, confused by all the bustle of activity as she stood helplessly by for the moment, not certain of what she was supposed to be doing to help. She knew nothing whatsoever about oil fires, and even less about fighting them!

"Before Adam brought you back to town, he said that it looked like the only way we were going to lick this fire was for one of those sudden rainstorms to come through. Well, it sure enough looks like our prayers have been answered!" Clem told her. "I only hope it comes in time!"

They were suddenly joined by Emma Patterson, who had made her way through the noisy crowd toward them when she had spotted Sarah with Clem.

"Sarah! Oh, honey, I heard about what happened to you!" she said, hugging Sarah close. "I am sure sorry, but I just thank the good Lord that it's all over with now."

"Thank you," Sarah replied warmly, the ready tears starting to her eyes once more.

For the next busy half-hour, Sarah helped fill the myriad of buckets with water, as she and the other townspeople anxiously waited, hoping almost beyond hope that the fire would somehow be stopped before it reached the town's limits, that Adam and the other courageous firefighters would be able to bring it under control, most preferably with the aid of the gathering rain.

Sarah worried and fretted about Adam as she worked, waiting for further news of the fire. She nearly fainted with relief when she finally saw Adam riding into town, closely followed by several other men on horseback, their tired faces blackened by the grime and smoke.

"Adam!" Sarah cried frantically, striving to reach him through the crowd that had gathered about him as he dismounted.

"I'm afraid it's no use," he was grimly telling the people. "We'll have to make our stand on the edge of town here and pray that we can stop it. The wind's simply too strong to stop it before then," he admitted with a frown and a weary shake of his head, appearing as if he might drop with exhaustion any moment.

"Adam!" Sarah called once more, finally succeeding in pushing through the crowd to reach her husband's side. She felt herself clasped in strong arms as he held her against his muscular chest, smelling of smoke and sweat. "Oh, Adam, what's going to happen? Isn't there some way we can manage to save the town?" she anxiously inquired.

"I'm afraid I don't know the answer to that just yet, my lass, but we've got to work fast," he said, putting her firmly aside after giving her one last hug and an encouraging smile. "All right, everyone grab a bucket and follow me!" he commanded authoritatively.

Sarah watched with tears in her eyes as the men with Adam rounded up the townspeople and began showing them what to do. She turned about to look for Clementine once more, then abruptly halted when she once more perceived the nearing rumble of thunder. She glanced upward, just in time to feel a single raindrop splash upon her face.

"Rain!" she exclaimed almost breathlessly. "It's starting to rain!" she now shouted, causing the other people near her to peer expectantly up at the sky as well. As they all watched and waited, several other large drops of the cool rain fell, swiftly followed by more and more. In a matter of a few seconds, the full clouds had burst and a drenching downpour came crashing down upon the heads of the grateful, exuberant crowd of people.

"It's a miracle!" one of the women exclaimed, to the accompaniment of several other such comments.

As the rain now poured in steady droves, Adam and his men mounted once again and rode back out to the spot where they had last left the raging fire. They soon perceived that the ordeal was over with, that the devastating blaze had finally diminished, leaving only a trail of smoking ruins in its wake, the sheets of heavy rain covering the blackened countryside.

Sarah later discovered that the fire had destroyed nearly twenty oil wells and storage tanks, among them Adam's own wells. Many men had lost everything they had, and they had sadly shaken their heads as they had vowed that they were giving up, that they had been wiped out one time too many. Adam, however, was not one of these. Even though his wells had been destroyed, he planned to use the inheritance money to begin anew, and his mind was full of future plans for himself and Sarah as they wearily rode homeward in the heavy rain that evening.

It was two days later before Sarah felt that she was fully recovered from her emotional ordeal. It took nearly the same amount of time for Adam to recover from his efforts in fighting the fire.

Adam had ridden out to the wells early this particular morning, leaving Sarah alone to get on with the cleaning she knew the cabin so desperately needed. Adam had been so gentle and kind and loving to her, and she knew that she loved him more than ever for his treatment of her during the past few days. Not once had he mentioned Frank Mead's name.

As she now hummed softly to herself, she entered Adam's room with her cleaning rag. Although he had been sleeping in her bed for the past few weeks, his clothing and other personal articles were still in his own bedroom. She wrinkled her nose a bit in distaste as she tugged the soiled bedclothes from the bed and piled them on the floor. She began to pick up the various shirts, trousers, socks, and anything else she could find that was scattered throughout the room, when her gaze suddenly alighted on some papers lying on the top of the large chest of drawers. She had only been able to see them because she was perched atop the room's lone chair, searching about for a button that was missing from one of Adam's flannel shirts.

Her curiosity overruling her better judgment, she reached for the papers and stepped down from the chair, sinking onto the bed as she scrutinized the unfamiliar writing. The letter on top was addressed to Adam and there were several important-looking documents attached. Sarah read:

"Dear Mr. MacShane, I take great pleasure in informing you that I am enclosing a bank draft for the first payment owed to you as a result of the settlement of the inheritance you received from your late grandfather's will. If you have any further questions concerning this matter, please feel free to contact me at . . ." It went on to state an address, then contained a few more details that seemed of no particular importance to Sarah. She was rather astounded by the large sum of money Adam was receiving, then realized that it was merely the first payment. It was true, she told herself ruefully, I married a wealthy man and didn't even know it!

She started to put the papers aside but saw that there was another letter beneath the first one, and she hastily pulled it from beneath the cover letter and read it as well.

"As for the matter we discussed when I visited your home," (her glance fastened on that particular phrase immediately), "I am also taking the liberty of enclosing the various legal papers you will need in order for you and your wife to obtain the divorce. If you will both simply fill in the necessary information and sign the papers, then return them to me . . ." There was a bit more, but Sarah knew that she had certainly read enough!

So, she thought to herself in a miserable daze as she clutched the papers in her tightened fist, Adam had been planning all along to obtain a divorce! He apparently didn't love her, had never really loved her, had really only used her to ensure that he would get the inheritance, used her for his own sexual gratification while she, like a complete fool, had believed his passionate declarations of love! Oh, Adam! she silently cried in anguish as she sat in stunned desperation upon the bed. Adam!

She rose to her feet and stumbled tearfully back across the floor to her own room, unaware that she still clutched the hateful papers. She closed the door and leaned against it for a few moments while she pondered what she was going to do about the terrible predicament. She glanced down and saw the papers, then viciously crumpled them and hurled them to the floor. She threw herself face down across her bed as she proceeded to sob most bitterly, the tears flowing freely and unheeded as she felt her heart breaking. She cried for over an hour, until the tears simply would come no more, then drew herself shakily upright and tried to form a plan.

She knew that she should confront Adam with the issue first, but she also knew that she could not bear to do so, could not bear to hear him tell her the awful truth! No, she must not force the man she loved so dearly to cast her aside. She knew that she could no longer remain here with him. She realized that she could not force herself on a man who did not return her love, no matter how much she loved him, no matter that she felt she would die if she were separated from him!

But, her mind reasoned, didn't he risk his life to save her? Why would he do such a thing if he didn't care? Because, she told herself firmly, her mouth twisted bitterly, because he had his own reasons. He wanted to make Frank Mead pay for his crimes and was only rescuing her while achieving his own selfish means at the same time! She knew that she was being irrational, but she could not seem to help herself, her old insecurities surfacing once more.

If he did not love her, if he no longer wanted her as his wife, then she simply could not stay. She loved him so much that she was actually willing to leave him if she thought he would be happier without her. So she squared her shoulders and dried her eyes as she set about her task.

For the next half-hour, her beautiful features appeared stony and emotionless as she did what she believed she must do. She gathered up all of her belongings and packed them in her valise, then opened the door of her room and walked out into the large central room of the cabin, setting her bag and valise down upon the bare wooden floor as she took one last glance about the cabin.

It crushed her to be leaving this cabin, for it had been the first real home she had ever possessed, for even a brief period of time. She had begun to consider it as hers, had thought ahead to the future she would share with Adam within its walls, the children who would happily play outside. Now, as she slowly peered about one last time, she knew that her heart was truly breaking, that she was leaving the one man who would ever mean anything to her, the one man she could ever love, the man who did not love her.

Sniffing with determination, she miserably clutched her bag and valise and marched from the cabin out toward the barn, where she quickly saddled the horse and tied her things behind the saddle. She firmly urged the animal on toward town, back down the dirt road she believed she would never travel again.

As she cantered toward town, she admitted to herself that she still hoped Adam wanted her, that he really loved her as he had so often declared. She wanted to believe that he had arranged for those papers to be drawn up before he had realized how much he loved her, before he had known how much she was in love with him. But no, she sternly told herself as she endeavored not to shed any more tears, the evidence was right there before her. Adam wanted a divorce, and she was now left to return to Philadelphia in abject misery, her heart and soul broken.

She had hastily penned him a note before leaving, a note that revealed nothing of her inner torment. It had simply informed him that she was returning to Philadelphia, that she had discovered the divorce papers that were now in her room, that she would not cause any difficulty for him concerning the divorce. She had left the brief note lying on the kitchen table, for that was always the first place Adam looked for her when he returned home from a day's work in the oil fields.

As she rode into town, she considered stopping by Mrs. Patterson's to say good-bye but knew that she could not bear to say good-bye to her good friend, the first real friend she had ever possessed, had ever been able to confide in. She left the horse at the livery stable, then proceeded on to the railroad station.

She approached the man inside the small wooden building as she went to purchase her ticket with the small amount of money she carried in her bag, and she was relieved to find that it was enough to see her home. She took one last glance at Wildcat City as the conductor assisted her in boarding, handing her baggage up to where she stood upon the platform as the train pulled away from the station, the smoke curling about her head as she began to weep once more.

If Adam decided that he didn't want the divorce, that he loved her, then he would surely come after her, would at least send for her to return. She told herself that she was being ridiculous in considering such a desperate hope, but she still could not help holding on to that one small glimmer as she silently waved good-bye to the town of Wildcat City, to the man who meant more to her than life itself. She hung her head and began to cry in earnest once more as she turned and slowly walked inside the car of the moving train.

Chapter Twenty-Eight

Sarah picked absentmindedly at her dinner that evening at Miss Warren's, then hastily excused herself as she climbed the stairs to the privacy and seclusion of her small room near the head of the stairs. She had been very fortunate that Miss Warren had been able to let her have the room, and she now closed the door and threw herself upon the bed, the tears welling up in her eyes for the hundredth time since she had arrived back in Philadelphia two days before.

She told herself again and again that she had been foolish, that she should never have left Adam, that she should have stayed and at least confronted him with her discovery about the divorce, at least given him the opportunity to explain. But no, she furiously chided herself now, she had been too hurt and humiliated to remain, to face the consequences like a mature woman. Instead, she had childishly run away, back home to Philadelphia, back to Miss Warren's Rooming House for Single Ladies, back to the security of the so-called "civilized world." Now, she waited in agonizing impatience for some word from Adam, knowing that it could be weeks, even months, before she received any sort of correspondence from him.

Once more, her mind turned to the thought that he might just love her after all, that he surely wouldn't have risked his life to save her from Frank Mead if he didn't care a great deal. But no, she would reason with herself again, he would have done the same for any defenseless woman, and he had more than one reason to hate Mead himself. She sighed unhappily as she placed her head between her arms upon the bed, as she closed her eyes and thought back to the happier times she had shared with Adam.

Why couldn't he have loved her? she asked herself repeatedly. Why did things have to turn out so miserably for her? Perhaps something such as this had happened to Uncle John in his younger days, perhaps that was the true reason he had never married. Oh, Uncle John, she entreated silently, why can't you be here with me now, to advise me, to tell me what I should do, to tell me whether or not I did the right thing in coming back here?

Suppose Adam really loved Clementine? she wondered again and again as she dejectedly contemplated the situation. Suppose Clem's words had been true, suppose she and Adam were making plans for their future together right at this very moment? No! she told herself, rising abruptly to her feet and crossing the room to the front window. Don't think about Adam and Clementine, don't think of him at all!

If he truly loved her, if he truly cared, he would have come after her immediately upon finding that note; he would have been there by now. So she must simply assume that he really wanted the divorce, that he no longer wanted to remain married to a woman he did not love.

She strolled across to her dressing table, then sank down on to the cushioned bench as she stared unseeingly at her reflection in the mirror. She was so very deep in thought, it was several moments before she became fully aware of the commotion downstairs. She rose to her feet and swung open the door to her room, then walked out to the head of the stairs in order to discover what all the shouting was about.

"Miss Warren?" she called down in puzzlement, then gasped, her hand flying to her open mouth as she viewed the tall, muscular, handsome intruder who had so upset the ladies still at dinner when he had burst in without ceremony.

"Adam!" she uttered, not trusting her voice to say anything further, simply standing upstairs gazing downward at him, as if she could not get enough of the sight of him.

"Sarah! I've been telling this woman here that you are my wife, that I have come to take you home with me where you belong!" Adam declared in a booming voice, causing Miss Warren to shake an admonishing finger at him.

"Young man, I do not know who you are, but I intend to see to it that you are forcibly removed from these premises if you do not leave at once!" the small gray-haired woman threatened bravely, glaring upward at the tall young stranger.

"I'm sorry, ma'am, but Sarah is my wife, and I'm not about to leave without her," Adam repeated commandingly, finally turning his full attention to Sarah with a stern frown upon his face. Sarah felt herself melting as she met his gaze, and she finally recovered her voice, and her composure, enough to speak.

"What are you doing here?"

"What the hell do you think I'm doing here?" Adam thundered angrily. "What do you mean by running out on me that way? Blast it, woman, I've been searching all over this blasted city for the past two days now!"

"I left you a note explaining," Sarah quietly murmured, still unable to believe that her dreams had come true, that he was actually here, that he had actually followed her all the way to Philadelphia. However, she cautioned herself to discover why he had come, as it could perhaps have something to do with the divorce. "Are you by any chance here to discuss the matter of the divorce with me?"

"Divorce?" he shouted, then scowled fiercely as several more of the curious ladies crowded about the sternly disapproving Miss Warren. "Well, it appears that this is going to be a rather public affair, Mrs. MacShane, but if that's the way it has to be . . ." his voice trailed off, then continued, "Sarah, love, I never wanted any divorce! You must know that! Those papers were sent to me by mistake, because that damned fool Mr. Spencer misunderstood when I was talking to him that day. I never for one moment believed he was taking any of my jesting seriously, but he apparently did. Anyway, I left those papers lying there in my room, never thinking you'd come across them, with the intention of returning them to Mr. Spencer, along with a decidedly firm 'no thank you and mind your own business!' I love you, Sarah, lass, I've always loved you, and I can't for the life of me understand why you left me without at least giving me the chance to explain!"

"I'm sorry, Adam," Sarah responded in a tremulous voice. "I thought you didn't love me anymore, didn't want me as your wife any longer. I could not stay with you, I could not wait until you asked me to leave, don't you see? I came back here, believing that you no longer wanted me, but that, if you did, you would surely come after me. And you came, didn't you, Adam? You came, my darling, and I'm so very glad you did!" she cried happily, running down the stairs now to fly into his outstretched arms.

"I swear, if you ever leave me again . . ." Adam started to threaten, then was silenced by the pressure of Sarah's loving lips on his.

Miss Warren gasped as she viewed the passionate embrace her young ward was participating in at that moment, then slowly smiled to herself as she realized that her Sarah must really be in love, was indeed apparently married to this forceful young man. She turned away from them, impatiently ushering the other ladies back through the parlor to the dining room, wanting to give the two young people a chance to be alone. She brushed a single tear from her eye as her thoughts traveled back to another day and time, a time when she, too, had been young and in love as Sarah now was.

When Adam finally released his wife, she beamed upward at him as she said, "Oh, Adam! I promise that I shall never leave you again!"

"You had better not! I don't intend to let you out of my sight long enough ever again. I intend to take you home with me right now, back to where we belong, back to where we're going to begin a new life together. Aye, lass, we're going to take my money from the inheritance and start all over again. Only this time, we'll start together," he declared solemnly, gazing down at her with a possessive intensity in his green eyes.

"Yes, Adam. We have each other, and we'll start that new life together," Sarah agreed with a happy sigh, giving herself up to his kiss once more.

ENTRANCING ROMANCES BY SYLVIE F. SOMMERFIELD

REBEL PRIDE (1084, $3.25)
The Jemmisons and the Forresters were happy to wed their children—and by doing so, unite their plantations. But Holly Jemmison's heart cries out for the roguish Adam Gilcrest. She dare not defy her family; does she dare defy her heart?

TAMARA'S ECSTASY (998, $3.50)
Tamara knew it was foolish to give her heart to a sailor; he'd promise her the stars, but be gone with the tide. But she was a victim of her own desire. Lost in a sea of passion, she ached for his magic touch—and would do anything for it!

DEANNA'S DESIRE (906, $3.50)
Amidst the storm of the American Revolution, Matt and Deanna meet—and fall in love. In the name of freedom, they discover war's intrigues and horrors. Bound by passion, they risk everything to keep their love alive!

ERIN'S ECSTASY (861, $2.50)
Englishman Gregg Cannon rescues Erin from lecherous Charles Duggan—and at once realizes he must wed and protect this beautiful child-woman. But when a dangerous voyage calls Gregg away, their love must be put to the test . . .

TAZIA'S TORMENT (882, $2.95)
When tempestuous Fantasia de Montega danced, men were hypnotized. And this was part of her secret revenge—until cruel fate tricked her into loving the man she'd vowed to kill!

RAPTURE'S ANGEL (750, $2.75)
When Angelique boarded the *Wayfarer*, she felt like a frightened child. Then Devon—with his gentle voice and captivating touch—reminded her that she was a woman, with a heart that longed to be won!

Available wherever paperbacks are sold, or order direct from the Publisher. Send cover price plus 50¢ per copy for mailing and handling to Zebra Books, 475 Park Avenue South, New York, N.Y. 10016. DO NOT SEND CASH.

WHITEWATER DYNASTY BY HELEN LEE POOLE

WHITEWATER DYNASTY: HUDSON! (607, $2.50)
Amidst America's vast wilderness of forests and waterways, Indians and trappers, a beautiful New England girl and a handsome French adventurer meet. And the romance that follows is just the beginning, the foundation... of the great WHITEWATER DYNASTY.

WHITEWATER DYNASTY: OHIO! (733, $2.75)
As Edward and Abby watched the beautiful Ohio River flow into the Spanish lands hundreds of miles away they felt their destiny flow with it. For Edward would be the first merchant of the river— and Abby, part of the legendary empire yet to be created!

WHITEWATER DYNASTY #3: (979, $2.95)
THE CUMBERLAND!
From the horrors of Indian attacks to the passion of new-found love—the second generation of the Forny family journey beyond the Cumberland Gap to continue the creation of an empire and live up to the American dream.

Available wherever paperbacks are sold, or order direct from the Publisher. Send cover price plus 50¢ per copy for mailing and handling to Zebra Books, 475 Park Avenue South, New York, N.Y. 10016. DO NOT SEND CASH.